Rachel

Phoenix Rising

I hope you like it.

Love

[illegible]

This is a work of fiction. The characters, incidents, and dialogue are drawn from the author's imagination and are not construed as real. Any resemblance to actual events or persons, living or dead, is entirely coincidental.

Cover Design Caedus Design Co.

Published in 2017 by Laci Maskell through Createspace

ISBN-13: 978-1979536240

ISBN-10: 1979536244

Phoenix Rising

Laci Maskell

Also By Laci Maskell

Still Life Moving
So . . . That Happened

Phoenix series:
Phoenix Born
Phoenix Burn

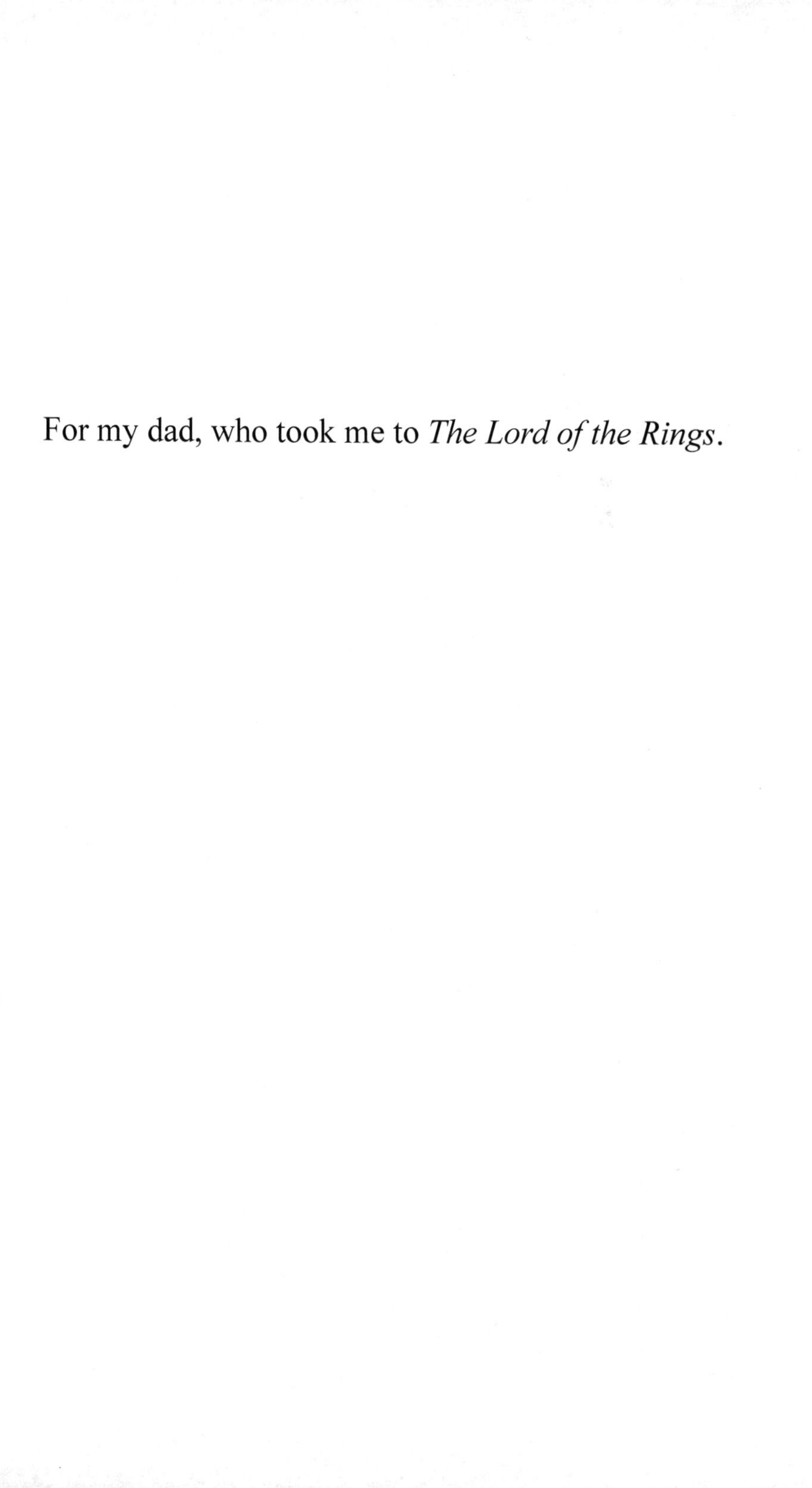

For my dad, who took me to *The Lord of the Rings*.

One

I don't feel the rain as it hits my skin. I don't feel the chill in the air as it whips my hair. I feel the deep seated ache of loss.

Tucker was my best friend. And I have lost him.

Logan was right. He told me not to bring Tucker into this world, my world. Logan was right. And I lost him too.

It's been three days and it still doesn't seem real. Three days and I still can't convince myself I will never again speak to Tucker. Never again kiss Logan or feel the warmth of his skin. Never laugh with Tucker until our sides hurt. Never spar with Logan until we are both sweaty and our chests heave from exhaustion.

Tears stream down my face, but I can't feel them leak from my eyes. I can't feel the dampness on my cheeks as the salty tears mix with the fresh rain.

My heart exploded when I woke up to the news that the two most important people in my life were no more. Screams tore from my throat until I'd broken something I needed fire to repair. Sobs racked my body until I could no longer breathe.

Now I am empty.

The priest talks on about how Tucker was an amazing person who was taken too early. He says things about Tucker's spirit and drive and kindness. He talks about Tucker like he would any other person he was burying. He didn't know Tucker. He didn't know Tucker would do anything anyone ever asked of him. He didn't know Tucker would sacrifice his own happiness if it meant someone he cared for could be happy. He didn't know Tucker could make peace in the toughest of times. He didn't know Tucker gave his whole heart but never asked for more than you could give him. He didn't know Tucker was the best human being I have ever known. And he never will.

Cool fingers lace with mine. It is several moments before I register this and turn toward Xander. The look on his face says he's not sure if this is allowed. He's not sure how I feel about him right now. Really, I'm not sure how I feel about him.

But he's all I've got left in this world. I'm not about to let him slip away like Nash. Like Logan. Like Tucker.

I squeeze his fingers with my hand then rest my head on his shoulder. His suit jacket is soaked from the rain, but I can't find it in me to care. His warm breath washes over my skin before he presses a kiss to my forehead.

My free hand is taken by someone on the other side of me. I lift my head from Xander's shoulder to find Gray pulling himself closer to me. His signature white mohawk lies flat to his head. His normally eyeliner ringed eyes are naked. He has forsaken his purple colored contacts for his true eye color, a blue so clear they might as well be white. The whites of his eyes are now a dark pink. I bring our clasped hands up to my lips to kiss the back of his hand. The polish on his nails is chipped, the ends cracked as if he's chewed on his nails with fangs. Tucker always did get on Gray for biting his nails. He said Gray would get an ulcer from all the nail polish he was ingesting. After a while it became a game. Gray would bite his nails just to get Tucker to chastise him. Tucker knew it too. But he went along with it because he knew it made Gray happy. Putting a smile on Gray's face quickly became Tucker's obsession.

Watching the two of them together was fascinating. It gave me hope. Even in the midst of all the chaos and destruction and hatred that surrounded us, that was beginning to take over our lives, there was still love. The love between Gray and Tucker was pure and magical and intoxicating. Spend a minute in the company of Gray and Tucker and you were happy, even if seconds ago you were mad about something. I only wish they would have gotten to spend more time together.

Tucker knew what he wanted in life and he went after

it. He wanted his best friends to always be together and to be happy. He wanted to spend all the time with Gray he possibly could. He wanted his parents to be happy and healthy. He knew what college he wanted to attend. He knew exactly who he was. He knew what he wanted to do with his life. But he will never get the chance.

And it's all my fault.

Tucker thanked me for bringing him into my world. Not because it enabled him to meet Gray. Although that is part of it. But bringing him into my world allowed him to know me on a deeper level. I am thankful he learned my secret before he died. But knowing that secret is why he died.

Living with that guilt is crippling. To the point where I can no longer tell where I begin and the guilt takes over.

I can't even come to terms with the fact that I've lost Logan too. Phoenixes have healing tears right? Wrong. I cried on Logan's ashes. I wept on Logan's ashes. Logan healed me countless times. And the one time it mattered I couldn't heal him. What good am I as a phoenix if I couldn't heal him? What good am I as the future leader of the phoenixes if I am their downfall?

The cool rain pelts my skin, only to simmer and evaporate. The fire under my skin rages, begging for me to unleash it. I could ignite myself right now. Take everybody with me. Burn us all. I can't deny I've thought about it as we stand here. Only trouble is, a phoenix cannot be burned by the fire of her own kind. So not only would I not be rid of the guilt of the deaths of Logan and Tucker, but I would still be riddled with the pain of their loss, and I would be charged with the deaths of all the people around me. And I would still be here.

There are times in the last three days I wish Cohen's ice knife would have hit home. Times where I am so angry with Nash for making me heal myself. For him convincing me to come back. Why would he do that to me? Why would he make me face this?

The priest was talking about Tucker's parents when he said God doesn't give us more than we can handle. I'm not sure I believe him. I am dealing with more than I can handle. And I am not handling it. The absence of feeling inside me is proof of that. The unwillingness to wake up in the morning and put one foot in front of the other is proof of that. I don't want to live in a world without Logan. Without Tucker. The year without Nash was hard enough.

I don't know what I'm going to do. There is no future I can see in which I want to live without the three of them.

Beyond the staggering guilt weighing me down, I can't grasp any other emotion. Tucker's parents cry. Gray cries. Xander is angry. Sad. Angry. Those are emotions. I would take those. If only I could feel something.

I watch as the casket is lowered into the ground. I watch as those closest to Tucker throw roses into the hole, Xander, Gray, and I throwing our own. I watch as Tucker's father shovels mud onto the casket, the wet earth slapping against the wood. My heart shreds with every scoop. Small pieces of me are chipped away as the hole fills.

Our lives are made up of the seconds, minutes, hours

we spend making friends, loving, finding ourselves. Tucker deserved more time than he got.

The priest finishes his sermon and clasps hands with Tucker's weeping parents. The rain soaked crowd disperses to join again at the reception. My parents linger until it becomes apparent I'm not about to leave. Xander and Gray continue to hold my hands, the three of us refusing to abandon our post. But eventually they too get tired. Tired of being sad. Tired of being soaked through to their aching bones. And yet I remain. Because I am not ready to say goodbye. I didn't get to tell Nash goodbye the first time. I didn't get to tell Logan goodbye. I didn't get to tell any of them how I felt about them or how much they meant to me. So that's what I'm going to do. I'm going to sit here and tell Tucker how much he means to me. I'm going to stand in the rain and bare my soul to my best friend.

I tell Tucker how much I loved him. I tell him I am thankful for everything he's ever done for me. I thank him for accepting me for who I am, for every part of me. I thank him for doing his level best to keep Xander and I together. I tell him all my hopes and dreams for us as friends, for him and Gray, for him as a person. I apologize for the part I played in the destruction of those dreams.

I'm not sure how long I stay, but it's dark when I return to the world around me. My skin is dry from the fire within. My clothes steam from the damp heat of them. Tears have dried on my face. My eyes burn from the salt. But I am still empty. Empty as the moment I watched Nash disappear in front of my eyes. Empty as the moment my heart exploded.

There is one thing I feel. I don't even have to search deep within me to find it. And that is hatred. I hate the griffins more than I have ever hated anything. The hatred for them doesn't eat away at me. It doesn't consume me. The hatred inside fills me. It grows every day. It festers and burns and crawls under my skin. My hatred for the griffins drives me forward. It is the reason I get up in the morning.

My hatred leaves me one option.

I will get revenge for Nash. And my parent's divorce. And for Kristina. And for Logan. But mostly Tucker. Tucker was innocent. And he was punished even so.

I am going to take down the griffins. I am going to destroy them. I will kill every one of them if I have to.

The fire within me is about to explode and I'm going to let it. I am going to light their world on fire and burn it to the ground.

It's about time I became the monster they think I am.

Two

Xander waits by my car. I haven't returned from Tucker's fresh grave with feelings, but I have returned with a new resolve.

Xander drives us back to my house. I'm not sure I'd be able to get us there in one piece. Tears still burn the corners of my eyes and the back of my throat.

We ride in silence. We enter my house in silence. We move to our respective rooms in silence. Xander mourns Tucker as much as I do. We both need our space. I'm willing to give it to Xander. For now.

The night after the attack. The night Tucker and Logan were taken from me, was also the night Xander decided to forsake his upbringing, his race, his birthright, and move in with me, to join the fight against his people. I'm going to use him in any way I have to. Although it's been three days, Xander has not spoken a word to his parents. They have not yet contacted my mom to get Xander to come home, though I'm sure it is only a matter of time. My mom thinks Xander is staying here because he and I need each other right now. We do. But what she doesn't know, is that when she was at work the other night, Xander moved all of his things into the spare bedroom.

It is hard to have him this close. To know that he's been the enemy for so long. To know the people who raised him are the sole reason I am without Nash and Tucker and Logan. But I also know that he wanted out. He made the right choice. I know he needed out. And I needed to help him.

I strip myself of the black dress I wore to Tucker's funeral. Like the loss of Tucker, the dress strangles me. I trade it for a pair of sweats and a t-shirt. My bed sags a few inches as I take a seat, not knowing what to do with myself.

My mom should be getting ready for work. I need to wait long enough for her to leave. I don't want to face her. She's got a lot of questions. As she should. She's given me space merely because she knows I'm mourning Tucker. But I can feel her need to press in on me. I don't want to have a run in with Xander. As much as I love him, as much as we need each other right now, I'm not ready to go back to our friendship as it was before everything happened, or as it has been lately. But even my room is a place I can't stand to be. And that is a result of the silver urn sitting on my desk on top of the last thing I ever gave Logan, a DVD of cartoons.

The urn in which my father placed Logan's ashes. I thought they should belong to Aspen, Logan's sister. I wish they belonged to Aspen. But as much as it pains me to see the urn every time I enter or exit my bedroom, I wouldn't want them anywhere else.

I shouldn't be walking on egg shells in my own house, but I don't have anywhere else to go. Tucker's parents fawn over me when I'm there. They take one look at me and weep. They talk to me about Tucker until they are blue in the face and fresh tears leak out of their eyes. And then they feed me, continuously, so I leave them alone. It's so sad. But I can't take the pain they feel. It's overwhelming to the point of suffocation. I can't go to my dad's house. Like my mom, he's suspicious. He's curious. He has questions. Questions I'm not ready to answer. If Tucker's death is any indication of letting nonmembers into this world, I'm in no hurry to bring my parents in. As welcoming as Logan's house once was, I no longer feel welcome. Not one of the phoenixes has outright told me they blame me, but I can feel it covering me like a wool blanket. These are my people. We should have each other's backs. We should be there for each other. We are supposed to love and forgive each other, no matter what.

But I messed up.

They are right. It is my fault there are deaths in our ranks. I am to blame for our losses. I brought the wolf into our straw house and he blew it over.

I trusted Cohen. I believed him when he told me he wanted nothing to do with the griffins' war against us. I believed him when he said he wanted out. I believed him when he said he didn't want to even discuss our races while we were together. I believed him. And I was wrong. I was duped. I paid the price.

I'm going to get back at him. He's going to pay. He and his entire family. His entire race. They will fear me before I am through with them.

I know exactly who my first victim is going to be. He is the person who started this. The person who turned my world on its axis. The person who took away from me the one person who meant the world to me. And then the second. Ashley's boyfriend, Colt, will be the first griffin on my hit list. In trying to kill us both, he failed. He failed to kill me alongside Nash. He is going to pay for his mistake. I should have killed him the night my father came into town. I should have killed him when I had the chance. Yet I hesitated. And it cost me Tucker. I will not hesitate again. I will make the griffins pay for everything they've taken from me.

And it starts tonight.

Searching through my drawers and closet, I pull out every black piece of clothing I own. It may be cliché, and I may want the griffins to know I'm coming, but I'm not about to out myself to the rest of the town. It is already in an uproar after my house was attacked and Tucker killed. An investigation has been launched. I've talked to police officers. But what was I supposed to tell them? That I am part of a race of creatures descended from ancient fire birds that just happens to be in an ageless war against another race of people descended from a creature who is half eagle and half lion? They would drug me and lock me up in prison or a mental hospital. No thank you. I can't take down the griffins if I'm locked up. So I lied. It's becoming a habit of mine. One I'm getting very good at.

The door to my mom's bedroom opens then closes seconds later. Her room was the only room in the house that wasn't trashed the night of the attack. I'm not entirely sure why. Maybe the griffins didn't figure they'd find anything in there. My mom didn't want to leave me that night, not after I'd lost Tucker. Not after I died and then came back. Even though she didn't know that. She didn't want to leave me alone after I'd been through such trauma. But I couldn't have her that close to me that night. I couldn't have the griffins come back for someone else I loved. So after a lot of convincing, and promising her I wouldn't be alone, my mom went to spend the night with my dad. Though their relationship is on rocky soil, they are back together. It's what I've wanted since they got a divorce, but I can't find it in me to be happy for them, or myself. Does it mean my family is back together? No. Because without Nash that will never happen. Without Nash, there is a black hole that can never be filled. And I don't want to fill it. What I want will never be possible so there's no point in even trying.

I listen for my mom working her way around the house. With my advanced hearing, thanks to my phoenix powers, I can tell exactly what she is doing in exactly what part of the house. I'm aware of the coffee percolating in the pot. Her tennis shoes barely register to my ears as she grabs her mug from the dishwasher. Her intake of breath as she inhales the coffee while pouring it into her mug almost brings a smile to my face. Then she finds her purse and rummages through it until she finds her keys. She places her mug, keys, and purse on the counter. Just as I'm expecting her to finish up her pre-work routine, she does something off book. She takes one step, two steps, more steps, until she's standing at the foot of the stairs, and she stops. I don't want to talk to her. I don't have the energy to talk to her. Not after Tucker's funeral. Not after everything that's happened. I don't have the energy to lie to her, or to not yell at her.

"Casslyn, can you come down here for a minute, please?" my mom calls from the bottom of the stairs.

I could pretend I've got head phones in and can't hear her. But then she might come up the stairs and I'd have to actually put the headphones in and blast some music. I could just flat out ignore her. I could pull the grieving card and say I can't right now. But that would be me being an asshole, and my mom deserves more than that. Especially after everything I've put her through. Everything I'm about to put her through. So I get up from my bed, and I march my sorry ass down the stairs, my head down, until I reach her at the bottom step.

I walk past her into the kitchen. I know Xander will still be able to hear our conversation. But maybe more distance from his room will muffle our words a bit. I can only hope. Not that I don't want him to hear what we are saying, but I'm not sure how this conversation is going to go. So it's best to be safe.

My mom follows me into the kitchen. Her steps are slow and a bit draggy. These past three days have taken just as much out of her as they have the rest of us. If she knew the truth, she wouldn't be able to walk.

My mom stays at least five steps away from me. The tension in her stance tells me she's not sure how to approach me. She watches me for several moments before speaking. And when she does it's cautious. "Casslyn, I know you are grieving right now. And I know you've gone through something very traumatic, but there are some things I need to know."

I watch her. She opens her mouth then closes it, several times. It's as if she is afraid to talk to me, though I'm not sure why or in what way. I don't answer her. I'm not going to give anything away if she's not asking for it.

The large sheets of plastic covering the holes in the front of our house shift and slap back into place when the wind moves across them. If there wasn't already to be no sleep in this house, those plastic tarps would do the trick. They were crudely taped, stapled, and nailed into place. Random boards cover smaller holes in the walls. It's a patchwork repair job. Hasty, haphazard, and done in a desperately sad manner. My father said he and the phoenixes would come help me restore my house to its former glory. There was no former glory to this house, so they'd be doing it a favor.

The wind whips the plastic bulbously into the house and

then sucks it back out again. My mom flinches every time it whaps against the house. Her eyebrows furrow, straighten, then furrow again. She swallows hard before speaking.

"I know you don't want to talk about it, but I need to know what happened that night. Casslyn, someone needs to know what happened that night. My house has human sized holes in it. The door is hanging off its hinges. There are scorch marks in every room of this house. You say a gang attacked. There are no known gangs in Cedars. Were there other victims? Is someone hurt and won't come forward? If so, they need help. I'm a doctor. I can help. Why would you and your friends be targets?"

My mom stops at this question, but only because her throat has constricted. It's one thing to see my mother in pain, to see her struggling to talk to me, struggling to get through a conversation. But it's a whole other thing to actually hear her body fight itself. The liquid flowing through her tear ducts reminds me of water running through a faucet. Her throat tightens and pulls down as she swallows hard. Her lungs collapse and expand deeply but rapidly as her emotions get the better of her.

I've told her what I'm willing to tell her. I fed her the fabricated story my father and the rest of us came up with. As far as my mom is concerned Logan and I were still broken up and hadn't spent any time together lately. The party was a going back to school party. Logan's disappearance is not suspicious. Tucker is the only victim whose body lingered. There were only a few of us and we were outnumbered. The gang came with sledge hammers and torches. I don't know why we were targeted. We were taken by surprise, trapped, and outnumbered.

"I don't want to talk about it."

"At some point, you need to talk about it," my mom says, holding onto the top of a chair sitting in front of the island. "Would it help if you saw a specialist? Someone you don't know?"

"I'm not going to a shrink," I tell her, though not harshly.

"Casslyn, I can't imagine what you are going through right now. I want to help you. But I can't help but feel like you're hiding something from me."

"Mom, I really don't want to talk about it. Aren't you going to be late for work?"

My mom opens her mouth as if to say something, then closes it. She fills her lungs with air, holds it for one, two, three counts then blows it out through her mouth. "We'll talk later. I should be home around eight."

"Okay," I say.

"I love you," she tells me, taking a step closer to me.

My heart jumps into my throat. I've been fighting these past few days on whether to keep my mom as close to me as possible, or to keep her at arm's length. Neither side has won that war. So it rages on. Pacing the few steps from where I stand to my mom and pull her into my arms. She's tense, but then relaxes into me.

"I love you, mom," I tell her.

It's only moments before she is shaking in my arms. The

smell of salt water wafts into my nostrils.

"Why are you crying?" I ask her, not knowing how stern to be with her.

"I thought I'd lost you. When the call came into the hospital, you have no idea how scared I was," she says through wracking sobs.

My eyebrows knit together. The thought had never occurred to me. I was dealing with the destruction of my house. The fact that I'd just been betrayed. And the loss of Logan and Tucker. I never imagined what my mom was going through. It never occurred to me that my mom was so close to being in the shoes of Tucker's parents.

"I'm sorry," I tell her.

"Oh, honey," she says, pulling away enough to cup my face in her hands. I lean one cheek into the warmth of her hand and close my eyes, savoring the touch of her skin.

A lump in my throat thickens to the point it's difficult to swallow. Caught in a moment of awkwardness and emotion I say, "You're going to be late for work."

She smiles, pats me on the cheek, and says, "You're right. I'll see you in the morning."

I watch her as she grabs her purse from the table, along with her keys and mug of coffee. I watch her walk across the kitchen floor and to the front door. I watch as she looks back at me then leaves the house. Then I continue to stare down the door, wondering if I'm going to see my mom again. Tonight is going to be dangerous. I may not make it out alive. But I'm not about to turn back now.

Like hours before, Xander's fingers slide through mine and squeeze in an act of comfort. It does little, but I'll take what I can get. I haven't told Xander what I'm going to do tonight. There is a huge part of me that wants to ask him to join me. But that would be asking him to not only leave his people, but to betray them in the worst form. I would also be asking him to put his life in danger merely for my revenge, and I'm not that selfish. Even though he knows nothing of what I'm about to do, he seems to sense it.

I allow myself to take comfort in him for a minute longer before I let go and return to my room. I need to plan tonight. I need to focus. I wish I could go to Logan's and work off some of this built up tension, but I'm afraid of what I might run into there. Or rather who I might run into.

I'm caught in my thoughts when I notice Xander standing in my doorway.

"How long have you been standing there?" I ask him, weighing the hard look on his face.

"Long enough to know you're up to something," he says, crossing his arms over his chest.

"I'm not up to anything. We just buried Tucker. I'm just sad," I tell him, lying through my teeth.

"I've knows you our whole lives, don't think I don't know when you're lying to me. Just tell me if I need to join you or stop you."

I don't want to tell him. I shouldn't tell him. But I don't think there's any getting around the stern look on his face or his firm stance. I don't know how he will feel about me killing the people he grew up with, the people he believed in. If he's still on their side, he will try to stop me. I can't have that. But after everything we have been through, I think he deserves the truth.

"I'm going after the griffins," I tell him straight up.

Xander takes a deep breath, pulling it in through his nose and pushing it out through his mouth. He takes another. And one more. Finally he says, "Who is first on your list?"

"Colt."

"I'll get dressed," he says and walks out the room.

But before he can get back to his room, before we can strategize, there is a banging from down stairs. Instead of rushing down the stairs to investigate, or start anything on fire, I listen. I listen to feet shuffling on the porch. I listen to boards being put in place, hammers striking hot against nails being forced through wood. My father and the phoenixes are here.

Not exactly the best timing in the world. But if there are enough of them and we all work hard, we can get it done quickly and they can leave. At least that's my hope. Because whether or not we get it finished, I am going after Colt tonight.

Xander and I share a look between us and then head down the stairs to join the phoenixes working on my house. When we reach the bottom of the stairs they all turn to look at us. More like stare at us.

Lydia is the first to speak. "What is he doing here?" There is pure hatred in her voice.

Not in the mood to take her shit Xander and I move further into the kitchen where most of the phoenixes are stationed. I say, "Xander left the griffins. He's staying here with me. If anyone has a problem with that, they can take it up with me."

There is a moment of silence before Thomas says, "There is no leaving the griffins. They will come for you. And they will bring you back."

The tone of his voice is ominous but not threatening. I sense he's got some experience in this area, but I'm not about to ask him about it. If he wants us to know, he'll come to us.

Thomas, Lydia, and the rest of the group go back to work, choosing to ignore Xander and I. My father pulls away from the group to walk up to me.

"Hi, Dad," I say to him once he's a foot away.

I could see the look on his face. The I'm-going-to-ask-her-if-she's-okay look even though he knows I'm nowhere in the realm of okay. I needed to distract him. And this is the perfect way. Although I also feel like it's time to start calling him dad. Calling him Aris was getting a little weird.

He stops and stares at me, his mouth agape. "What did you just call me?" he asks.

"Don't make a big thing of it," I tell him.

"Oh, Casslyn," he says, a tear or two springing to his eyes. "It is a big deal. I've wanted to hear you say that since the day I learned I had a child."

He takes a step closer to me and wraps me tight in a hug.

I'm rigid for a moment, like my mom was a little while ago. But then I relax in the hug, letting my father hold me up. We've still got a long way to go with our relationship. It may never be as solid as my relationship with my dad, because I was raised by him, but I'd like it to be somewhere in the range of that.

My father holds on for moments longer than is necessary, but I don't pull away. We both lost Logan, something I'm still not ready to think about, and we both need comfort. My father practically raised Logan and Aspen when their parents were killed. Logan was like a son to my father. It wasn't until recently I learned my father cared for Logan as more than just his best soldier. It wasn't until recently I learned a lot of things about my father. All because I was too stubborn to let him into my life. But the bridges have been burned. Now all I can do is build new ones to take their place. Something I'm willing to work on.

When my father finally pulls away, he looks at me as my mom did, and says, "I love you, kid."

"You too, Dad," I tell him, not quite able to say the actual words.

He continues to look at me, like my mom did, like for a moment they thought they'd lost me and would never see me again. That look is more than I can handle twice in one day, so I pull away from him and ask, "What can we do? Put Xander and I to work."

My father frowns for a second then says, "Grab a hammer and join a group. Let's put your house back together. I can't imagine your mom was too happy to come home to it like this."

"You have no idea," I tell him, reaching for a hammer on the kitchen table.

He chuckles but it feels strained. There was a time my mom and my father loved each other. There are parts of me that think my father may still love my mom. But my mom and my dad are working on getting back together. My father's presence here hinders that. He has assured them he is only here for me, to get to know me. But still tensions are high, emotions strained. My father and my parents have only spent a few occasions in the same room since my father returned to town. I know he's got the phoenixes, and he's got me, but I can't imagine he doesn't get lonely. I certainly would. My hope is that when this griffin war mess is all sorted out all three of my parents can sit down together and work out their problems, with themselves and with each other. I want them all to get along. I want us to be as much of a family as we can be. Missing parts, spare parts, and all.

I nudge my father in the side, silently telling him it will all work out. He nods to me and joins a group of people working on fixing the front door. I scan the room and do a mental count. Not everyone is here. I'm sure by now some of my race hates me so much they can't stand to be in the same room as me. Lydia's presence here shocks me. I would have expected her to be on the first flight out of Cedars the moment Logan died. Lydia has never liked me. I know it's because of Logan. I also know I didn't even try to be friends with her. I don't have any time in my life to try to befriend a bitch. I don't think there is any hope of us ever being anything more than part of the same race. And that's fine with me. It's just hard not to look at her, and myself, and compare us. Even now that Logan's gone. I don't understand what he ever saw in me, but at the same time, how could he have been with such a nasty person, and for so long? Maybe there is a different side to her she is unwilling to show me. Maybe not. But that's still where my stray thoughts go.

Gray and Anna work together to replace the broken bay window in the living room. I move to help them. Anna and I hold the window in place while Gray pounds in the nails. Xander starts to hammer in his own nail when Gray and Anna both give him glaring looks. It's enough to make him back off and join another group. I can't imagine he'll get a better welcome anywhere else, but he's trying, and it's not like the phoenixes will be able to get over the prejudices like flipping a switch. I know I can't. I want my people to welcome Xander. He's been my best friend for as long as I can remember. But Anna and Gray both lost someone very dear to them recently, and Xander's people were the cause. I can't blame them for their anger. I can't scold them for their treatment of him. It will take time.

Once the window is in the three of us move into the kitchen. I reach into the fridge and grab us each a bottle of water. We sit at the island quietly, drinking our water. Anna recently cut off most of her hair. Her braid is now about three inches long, instead of three feet. I miss seeing it swish against her back like it did when we ran long miles together. Like her, Gray's grief has manifested in a change to his hair. His Mohawk lies flat to one side of his head. He seems stronger now than he did hours ago at Tucker's funeral. Maybe having a job to do, a purpose, if only for a little while, is enough to distract him from what he lost. It doesn't work for me, but I hope it works for him. And Anna, and Aspen. Aspen, who is not among my people helping to repair my home.

Lydia walks into the kitchen, her flawless chestnut ponytail swishing the top of her shoulders. Even with the loss of Logan, she doesn't sport a wrinkle in her appearance. She still cares. She pushes past me to get into the fridge. I'm not about to call her out on not asking for anything. She is here, helping, and I'm not about to start anything. But once she openly sighs disgustedly, slams the fridge without taking anything, then knocks into my shoulder with hers, I nearly lose my shit.

"Excuse me," I tell her, attitude ringing out.

She turns on her heel, her ponytail whipping back, she says, "Maybe you should get out of the way."

"I wasn't aware I was in the way, in my own house," I tell her.

"And maybe that's your problem. You don't know you're in the way. Because you don't care. It's all about Casslyn, all the time."

"Are you kidding me? We just lost two people very dear to us and you've got the nerve to call me out on it?"

"Are you trying to tell me it wasn't your fault?" Lydia says, crossing her arms over her chest.

The kitchen has filled with the remains of our group. They watch our exchange, not willing to get involved. Likely because they haven't chosen a side.

My father parts the crowd and steps into the kitchen. "That's enough, Lydia."

"I don't think it is," she says, without pulling her death glare from me. "She may be your daughter, but it's time to stop making excuses for her. She didn't even know the person closest to her was the enemy. She constantly thwarted commands from Logan. She brought the enemy into her home, into our circle, and we paid the price for it. Logan paid the price. Her so called best friend paid the price for her stupidity."

As soon as she brought Tucker into this, I lost it. Anger was building in me, raging the fire under my skin, pulling it to the surface. It breaks loose as soon as she mentions Tucker. Fire balls ignite in my hands. One by one I throw them at Lydia. If only they could light her up. I'd love to teach this bitch a lesson on proper etiquette. I run at her before anyone can stop me, my whole body going up in flames. Grabbing her wrists, I yank her to me, spreading the fire from my own hands to hers. She lights up. I know it won't harm her, but at this point I don't care.

"How dare you," I scream into her face. "You have no right to bring him into this."

"I'm just saying what we're all thinking," she says

calmly. "You killed him," she spats at me. "He would have followed you anywhere. And he followed you to the grave."

I look around the circle. Everyone's eyes are on me. I see the judgement reflected back at me. I see their blame laid bare. Since arriving at Cedars they have lost five of their own. It all circles back to me. They are here because of me. I am Xander's friend and it lead the griffins to me. Raphe wants me dead but will take others as sacrifices. They were at my home when we were attacked.

I extinguish my fire and release Lydia.

They don't want me. Less so today than they did when they came. And they came for my father, not because of me. I will never be a part of them. I guess I always knew that, but I held out hope.

"You can all leave now," I tell them.

My father chimes in and says, "We will go back to Logan's for the evening."

"No," I tell them. "Leave Cedars. You all hate me. You all hate it here. Just go. I don't need any of you."

There is stunned silence. Lydia is the first to walk out of the newly fixed front door. She leaves it wide open, knowing others will follow her. Let them. They can't help me if they don't want to. One by one they trickle out. Last to leave are Gray, Anna, and my father. Xander stands beside me all the while. His stance says he's willing to defend me if it comes to it. Gray and Anna stand on the other side of the island from me. They watch me. When I do nothing but stare back at them, they too, leave.

My father comes up to stand in front of me. The disappointed look on his face is hard to deal with, but this time it's not aimed at me.

"I'll talk to them," he says.

"Don't bother," I tell him. "Don't make them hate you too."

"I love you, Casslyn. It will be okay. This will all work out."

I stare at him, waiting for him to leave. I have things I need to do. But when he walks for the door something spurs in me.

"Why don't we fight them? Why don't we attack them?"

"It is not our way. We defend only. We are symbols of hope. We represent better versions of ourselves and of others. How can we honor that when we are viewed as vicious murderers?"

"Fine," I tell him, not willing to fight the matter.

If he is not willing to change our ways, I'll change them for him. If the phoenixes are leaving town, I'll be a different kind of phoenix, a new kind of phoenix. I was never truly a part of them anyway. I'll do things my own way.

"Casslyn," he starts, unsure of where to go next with the conversation.

"Just go home, Dad."

He closes his eyes and sighs. It's clear he feels like we just took a step back in our relationship. I don't feel that way. He's just trying to please everyone. He's trying to choose between his people and his daughter but make us all cohere together. He's trying to keep the unit together. And sometimes that's just not possible. Especially when their unit was fully formed and functional. Adding me was like throwing a screw in with a bunch of nails. I just didn't fit.

He takes one last look at me then follows his people out into the night.

"Cass, are you-," Xander starts but I cut him off.

"Get ready. We're leaving in twenty minutes," I tell him, storming up the stairs to my room.

"Do you have a plan?" he asks.

"Of course I have a plan," I tell him like he's thick. "I've been planning this for two days."

"Mind filling me in?"

"Get dressed," I say, slamming my bedroom door behind me.

I fling through the black clothes on my bed. It's the dead of summer so I won't need a sweatshirt. But I'll need to conceal myself. Since I don't feel shifts in temperature I'll be able to wear a long sleeve shirt without burning alive. I stop rummaging through my clothes when I come upon a black, long sleeved Under Armor shirt and black full length tights. I never wear anything besides black socks, so I don't have to go looking far for them. What might take me a while is to find a black ski cap. I don't necessarily need to cover my face, but my stark white blonde hair might give me away. I've got a few black beanies from my hipster phase I could wear. Searching through the back of my closet I find one that will work and pull it on over my messy bun. With my wardrobe complete I sit on my bed, face Logan's urn, and run through my plan.

Xander moved in with me the night they attacked us. But he knew their plan was to lie low after the attack, to avoid suspicion. If that is still the case, Colt will be easy to find. I'm going to his house, finding the most likely place for a house to start fire, and then I'm going to trap him inside while his house burns down around him. Having Xander with me will actually make my plan go more smoothly. Unbeknownst to him, I'm going to have Xander distract Colt while I light the house on fire. Then I'm going to join them, beat the shit out of Colt, then let him burn to death.

My cold calculating doesn't even get to me like I know it should. But that's what being numb has done to me. That's what the griffins have done to me, and it's time they paid for it. I almost hope Ashley is with Colt. It would be a two for one special. And it would be special. If not though, that's okay. Ashley will get her time to shine. Cohen too, and their dad. I'm going to wipe out their whole family, and not feel a thing for it.

"What's the plan?" Xander asks from my door frame. I didn't hear him open my door. But I'm not about to let that bother me. We've got work to do.

I run through the plan with him. Telling him the ins and outs. The things I need to do and the things I need him to do. We go through everything that could go wrong. Things that I'm hoping will go right.

"Xander, if you want to back out, do it now," I tell him.

I can't have him getting soft and feeling guilty in the middle of this. It would break down the whole plan. "I'm asking you to not only forsake your people, but to murder them. I'm not asking lightly. But I am telling you, if you can't go through with it, you're not coming."

Xander crosses his arms and folds in his eyebrows. He cocks his head to the side, smirks, and says, "Can I at least mess up his pretty face before we light him on fire?"

"Be my guest," I tell him, moving for the door.

I follow Xander through my house, paying close attention to his attire. Like me, he's wearing all black clothes. I went for ballet flats to give me a little more stealth, but Xander wears huge black army boots. His part of the plan is to be detected, so they can stay. Otherwise he's wearing dark jeans and a black t-shirt. Like me, he's got a beanie on his head.

I grab my keys off the counter, walk to the door, look around wondering if this will be the last time I see my house, then click off the lights and walk out the door, shutting it behind me. Xander and I walk silently to my car and get in. We've lined the inside of the car in plastic so the smell of the fire won't infiltrate the cloth of my seats. There is a bottle of fabric freshener, all-purpose cleaner, and paper towels in the back. I've seen enough movies to know how to prepare for this. I drive with clear vision all the way to Colt's house, drive past it and park two blocks away.

I look down at the clock which reads 12:27. I look around outside. Half of Cedars' population is comprised of people over fifty years old who go to bed at eight o'clock every night so there is no one in the neighborhood wandering around after that. I take a few deep breaths, which elicits a nervous look from Xander, then open my car door. It's now or never. And I've never been more ready.

Xander, knowing his job, heads for the front door of Colt's house. I walk all the way around two blocks down and cut back over to the back of Colt's house. It's a dark night. Very few stars shine above me, the new moon barely visible through a cover of clouds. I move quickly to his back door. I peer through the window in the door. Xander, having been inside Colt's house twice before gave me a vague outlay of his house. I can see the front door from the back door. I can see Colt pushing himself up from his recliner to answer the door. I open the back door just as Colt opens the front. I slip in through the door while Xander greets Colt. I glide through the back room, move to the kitchen and find the stairs leading to the basement right where Xander said I would.

I take each step quickly but as quietly as I can. Like myself and Xander, Colt has superhuman hearing. If I make one wrong step, he'll know this is a set up.

My heart hammers in my chest with every step. My brain beats out a rhythm against my skull, causing my vision to blur. Sweat beads at my temple. I've never been this nervous in my entire life. I'm not sure I can pull this off. Why did I think I could pull this off? I'm going to do something dumb, tip off Colt, who's going to kill Xander, alert the rest of the griffins, who will come find me and finish me off like they've been trying to do for over a year.

No.

Stop panicking.

You can do this.

This is for Tucker.

And Kristina.

And Nash.

And Logan.

Get your fucking head in the game, Casslyn.

My mental pep talk over, I move through the basement and look for the furnace. It's the middle of August so there is no reason for it to be running. That won't work. It wouldn't light on fire if it's not even running. Okay. Think. Do breaker boxes light on fire? I look around the basement for anything I think the fire department would deem worthy of engulfing an entire house. I thought lighting the house on fire would be enough, but Xander assured me it would be suspicious if the fire originated from nothing. Yet another reason I'm glad I have him.

I listen closely for electrical outlets down here. The water heater. Anything. I can faintly hear Xander and Colt arguing upstairs. I've got to move quickly. That's when I hear the washer and dryer running from a different room. Dryers cause house fires all the time, right? And it's not like a twenty year old guy is going to properly take care of a dryer.

I practically prance through the basement and into the room where the dryer is running. I make sure to turn the dryer's heat all the way up. I find some lint Colt's thrown away in the trash and shove it into the outgoing vent of the dryer.

Calling upon my fire to light my right hand, I place it against the vent and wait until it ignites. It does so quickly, the lint burning quickly. With a little help from myself I spread the fire. The fuse box is screwed to the wall above the dryer. The flames lick up the wall and spark the fuse box. The metal of the box heats as the fire spreads, melting the box. It snaps and pops until the breakers blow.

All the power to the house shuts down. I'm left in the dark basement, lit only by the spreading flames. They've moved along the wall. The clothes in a bin sitting next to the dryer have caught fire as well. A smile spreads across my face. This is working. My revenge starts tonight.

I wait until the whole room is engulfed, until the flames kiss the ceiling and feast upon the wiring that lines it, knowing it will spread to the rest of the house.

That's when I ascend the stair case and head for Colt. What I find in the living room is quite the scene. Xander and Colt have got each other in a head lock, their asses jutting out in opposite directions.

They scream at each other, throwing punches as they do so. Colt calls Xander a traitor. Xander calls Colt a psycho. Colt calls Xander a phoenix lover. Xander calls Colt a monster. It goes back and forth until I clear my throat. Surprised they let each other go and sprawl to the floor. I get their attention and breathe in deeply, smelling the fire progressing through the house I can feel the flames from underneath me burning through. I've got to distract Colt long enough so he doesn't have time to escape. Either that or incapacitate him.

I stare at him, filled with hatred. Xander, good to his word, has gotten some good shots at Colt's pretty face. Blood runs from him nose and out his mouth.

Now that they are no longer tangled together the two can get control of their senses. Xander smells the fire traveling through the house and smiles. Colt smells the fire and says, "You bitch."

"Payback is a bitch isn't it, Colt," I say to him, moving one step closer to him.

Colt lunges for me while saying, "I'm going to kill you."

Xander grabs for him while I throw a fire ball right at his chest. His shirt ignites and moves across his chest.

"You came after me not once, not twice, but four different times," I tell him. "You killed my best friend. Did you really think I was going to let you get away with that?"

Colt snarls at me. He has managed to pat out the fire lighting his shirt. But I throw another ball at him. It hits his pants and spreads. He hits at it with his big hands. I take his momentary distraction to charge him, landing a solid punch to his face. Xander holds his arms behind his back so I can have my way with him. Placing my hands on his chest I let my fire spread out from under my skin to caress his. As the heat and flames spread he clenches his teeth, unwilling to give me the satisfaction of seeing him hurt. I hold him tighter, make the flames burn hotter, move in close to his face and whisper, "It's nice to see you again, angel."

Colt sucks in a deep breath. I move my hands to his throat and let the fire eat away at him. This time he screams and I'm hit with a wave of satisfaction. A gratified sigh rushes past my lips. The power does feel good. I pull away from Colt far enough to knee him in the balls. It's a cheap shot, but one I had to get in.

"Cass," Xander says from behind Colt.

I look up and notice the walls around me have caught fire, the flames half way up.

It's time to go.

"You're not going to get away with this," Colt says.

I glare down and him, pull back my arm, and slam a flaming fist into his face. I feel his jaw crack as my hand connects with it. "Watch me," I tell him, before striking him again.

I hit him three more times before he's unconscious. He falls limp from Xander's arms.

"Let's put him in bed," I tell Xander.

If he's in bed, the fire fighters will think he slept through the fire and died because of it.

Xander grabs Colt around the chest while I take his feet. We haul him through the living room and into his bedroom. I drop his feet then pull back the covers on his bed. We place him in it, pull the covers back up, and I stare down on him. Knowing full well what I've done and accepting it completely.

The flames have reached the ceiling now. Sweat glistens on Xander's face, runs down his neck, and coats his arms. The heat is too much for him. I find comfort in it. I embrace it.

I watch the shallow rise and fall of Colt's chest, knowing his life is about to be over. But Nash's life was over more than a year ago. Tucker's life was over the moment Colt shoved his knife into his heart. Colt's life ended the moment he ended those of the people I care most about. The griffins call us monsters, but it's only because they drive us to the point of monstrosity.

I watch him, wanting to just get it over with, to lay a hand on him and light him up. I hate him. I hate him with every fiber of my being. I hate staring at his wretched face. I hate the power he's held over me for over a year. I hate that he could so easily take away the people most important to me. I hate him so thoroughly I can't see straight. But as the flames spread down and around me, I know I'm ridding myself of him. I'm ridding myself of a little bit of that hate. And oh does it feel good.

I look at him one last time, not committing his face to memory, because that would be too good for him. But I look at him, knowing Nash and Tucker can rest in peace.

"Let's get out of here," I tell Xander, turning towards the door.

Colt's bed has already caught fire.

"Good idea," Xander says next to me, looping his fingers through mine as we exit the back door of the now fully engulfed house.

I kiss the back of Xander's hand, release it, and take off in a different direction than him. I move through houses, fences, close to threes and large bushes, trying to conceal myself. By now someone has got to have noticed his house on fire and called for the fire department. As I think this, sirens wail in the distance. I watch Colt's burning house from a distance. The roof collapses in on itself from the heat of the flames. There is no way Colt will survive this. The fire department won't arrive in time.

Knowing this, I move through town until I feel safe enough to return to my car. I find Xander there, already inside, his skin still slick with sweat.

We grimly grin at each other. We both breathe heavily.

"Let's go home," I tell him as I turn the key in the ignition.

Xander holds my hand as I drive us back to my house. We travel in silence, the both of us needing to process what we did tonight.

When we're back at my house, and I've turned off the car and am about ready to get out, Xander says, "We killed someone tonight." His voice isn't in shock, it isn't in awe, it's matter-of-fact.

I turn to him, and say, "This is a war, Xander. And I intend to win it."

That is answer enough for him. He opens his door, gets out, opens the back door and pulls the cleaning supplies from the back seat. He hands me the all-purpose cleaner keeping the fabric spray for himself. I get to work on wiping down the dash, face of the radio, and any other surface that could hold the smell of fire. Xander rips the plastic from the fabric seats and gets to work spraying them down. When we've finished, we move to the back yard and throw the plastic into the burn barrel. I throw a couple fire balls into it and watch as the plastic burns away to nothing.

We march into the house, one by one and go upstairs.

"Give me your clothes," Xander says, stripping out of his.

When I give him a puzzled look he says, "I'm going to throw them in the washer. You get in the shower. I'll take one when you're done."

I duck into the bathroom and following his lead, I strip out of my clothes and through the door hand them to him, panties, bra, and all.

I turn the water in the shower on as hot as it will go. Waiting for the room to warm up and steam over, I stare at myself in the mirror. My face is covered in soot and burn marks. In the past few days I've lost a few pounds and it shows. My cheeks pull in under my cheek bones. My collar bones stick out more than they did. Dark circles under my eyes make is look like I've taken a severe beating. Grief tripled over the past year has made me look haggard and drawn. My skin has lost all color it once had. I'd rival a ghost pretty well. The girl I was the morning I turned sixteen would not recognize the girl before the mirror today. Newly sixteen-year-old me had it all. A happy family. The best brother a girl could ever ask for. Friends so amazing you'd think they were made up. A life anyone would want. I'm not sure anyone would want my life now. I'm not sure I want it.

Flashes of this evenings events play out in my head. Images of a burning house and a beaten body. I did what I had to. I'll do it again.

But something about it has me turning around and burying my head in the toilet. Everything within me retching and burning up and out my throat. I heave and vomit until there is nothing left. And still I keep going. My shoulders shake with the force of being sick. When I've finally finished I return to the sink and brush my teeth, trying to rid the foul taste in my mouth.

I step into the shower and let the hot water cascade down around me. My shoulders continue to shake. Goosebumps erupt on my flesh, though hot water beats down on it. When standing becomes too much, my knees wobbly and knocking into each other, I sit down on the slick porcelain. I wash my hair and body from a seated position. When I'm clean and no longer find refuge in the shower, its waters now cold, I turn it off and step out. I wrap myself in a towel and move slowly into my bedroom, where I find a t-shirt and shorts to wear to bed. The clock on my nightstand reads 2:58. I pull back the blanket that covers my bed and lie down. When I close my eyes I'm hit with images of flames and Colt's face. My eyes snap open and stare at the ceiling.

I hear Xander move from his room to the bathroom. I hear the water of the shower turn on and the rings of the curtain move as he steps into it. He doesn't even swear when all he's left with is cold water. Shortly after stepping in, Xander steps out of the shower. He moves from the shower back to his room. Then his light footsteps move toward my room. He knocks and opens the door without me giving permission.

"How are you holding up?" he asks, coming to sit next to me.

Without realizing it, my bed vibrates under me.

"Cass?"

Lurching up from my bed I run for the bathroom and only just make it over the toilet before gagging into it. Nothing comes up, but that doesn't mean my body stops heaving. Strong hands pull my hair back away from my face. Xander kneels down beside me and rubs my back. I heave and hurl until my throat is raw, until my eyes bulge, and my brain hurts. I brush my teeth again when the attack is over. I stand on unsteady legs, not yet able to walk myself back to my room.

Xander pulls me back and lifts me into his arms. I loop shaky arms around his neck. Goosebumps form an army all over my body. A cold sweat has broken out my fire can't defend. Xander walks with me through the hallway and into my room. He lays me down, covers me up, then takes a step away from me.

"Stay with me," I say. "Please."

He turns back and crawls into bed with me. Placing the blanket over the both of us, he settles in and pulls me to him. Shakes wrack my body. I can't stop them. Xander's hand moves over my hair and down my face. His other arm is tucked under my head and holds me firmly to him. He murmurs shushing sounds to me and my body loses control to the tremors. I close my eyes, try my best to block out the horrifying images that run across my mind's eye, and slowly fall asleep, the quakes following me into my dreams.

Three

If there was anything normal about my life recently, I have returned to it. School started a week ago. As much as I wanted to drop out, my parents, all three of them, put their foot down. So Xander and I returned. As did Ashley. The tension and hatred is palpable. She tried cornering me in the bathroom the first day but as soon as I held a fireball in my hand and reminded her I killed her boyfriend, she backed down and practically ran out.

The fire department has an open investigation going into Colt's house fire. So far they believe the cause is lint build up in the dryer, as they should. The griffins weren't convinced. They sent the police to my house to question us. Raphe and Ashley told them Xander and I believed Colt to be part of the gang that attacked us and killed Tucker. My father happened to be at the house finishing up the repairs to my house when the police showed up. He assured them he was with us all night fixing up the house. Xander and I were dropped as suspects on the spot. Nice try Ashley. When the police left my father questioned us, but I told him I was so distraught from my fight with Lydia I sat on the couch for hours, Xander force fed me popcorn while we watched *The Fault In Our Stars*. I was worried he'd see right through my lie, but he bought it, didn't even question our lie.

Before Ashley departed the bathroom I noticed her eyes were blotchy and ringed with red. Her hand shook as she reached for the doorknob. She looked heart broken. And I put that look on her face. A smile spread across my face with that realization. She was instrumental in taking Logan from me, as well as Nash and Tucker. Her payment has only just begun. I'm not sure if I'll save Ashley or her father for the last griffins I kill. Maybe I'll make them face each other and slowly kill them together.

After the night I disposed of Colt I wanted to get back out there right away and rid Cedars of more evil people. But Xander said killing another griffin so quickly would be more than suspicious. I hated him for it but I agreed. I can't continue to fight the war if I'm constantly being watched. The fire under my skin is itching to get out. I've lit my bed on fire on more than one occasion. Every time I woke up to my sheets on fire around me I could only be thankful that Xander wasn't in the bed next to me. But the burning of my bed didn't start until the first night Xander left my bed. I would like to think I'm strong. I would like to think I can hold myself together. But after Nash died I had Tucker and Xander to hold on to. And then Logan came and I had him to hold me together. For a week after we got rid of Colt, Xander stayed in my bed. I am not strong. I'm as weak as they come. But as long as I've got someone to hold me together, I'm going to allow it. Because I am weak, and I'm afraid of the strength it would take to keep myself intact.

After the summer I spent training, running, fighting, loving and losing Logan, meeting the new phoenixes, being attacked by the griffins, after all that, being in school learning biology, statistics, and reading classic novels seems mundane. I float through classes, staring at the seat next to me that should host one of my best friends. My teachers yelled at me on multiple occasions to get me to pay attention, but they quickly gave up. I'm not sure if it's because they feel bad for me, or if they've just given up on me. No one has noticed Logan's absence because he graduated last year. It hits me deep in the gut. Logan was so focused on keeping me safe he didn't get to share his specialness with my town. I wish more people could have known Logan. I wish more people missed him as much as I do. I wished more people loved him as much as I do.

I haven't dissolved since the night they died. I'm afraid once I do, I won't be able to survive it. I can't face the loss of Logan. Not now. Not when I have a mission to complete.

Today is already as hard as it could possibly be. Not breaking down in the middle of class has taken all my strength and more. The same goes for Xander. I've seen his tear ducts water more than once today, and it's only third period. Today isn't only hard. Today is impossible.

Today is Tucker's birthday.

When Xander, Tucker, Nash, and I entered our freshman year we talked about our senior year. We talked about the fun we would have. We talked about the things we wanted to accomplish before we left high school. We talked about how relaxing but exciting the year would be. We would be on the downhill slide. Coasting into the end. We would all be together and we would all make every moment count. Missing two of our group is not how I pictured my senior year. Being miserable and incapable of feeling is not how I imagined I would feel entering into this year. I had expectations for this year, none of them any longer possible to accomplish. I am sick and tired of losing people closest to me. I'm not about to let it happen again.

Since we became friends Xander, Tucker, and I have never spent a birthday apart. That list used to include Nash, but my birthday a few months ago marked the first one of those without him. Now Nash and Tucker have their own list. Xander and I have ours.

"I need to get out of here," Xander says from his locker beside mine.

He throws his bio book into his locker, grabs his worn copy of *To Kill A Mockingbird* and slams his locker shut. Then he slams his head into his locker door. I reach out to grasp his hand. He squeezes it harder than he would normally. I feel my bones pop, the pain is intense, but if this is what Xander needs to get his pain out, I'll let him. I'll go to the bathroom and heal myself if I have to. He lets go before he breaks my hand. I close my eyes on the tears that have sprung.

"Let's just go," I tell him.

"We'll get in trouble," Xander says.

"Are you really worried about that? Let's go. Let's get Gray and do something Tucker would love."

He looks unsure of this plan. Normally I would be too. But today is Tucker's day and I'm not going to spend it in school surrounded by people who don't give a shit that he's gone.

"Xander, Tucker is gone. He is proof life is short. Especially for us. Would you rather stay here and be a good little boy, or would you like to leave and spend the day in honor of our best friend?"

This time he doesn't even take a second to think about it.

"Let's go," he says. He slings his bag over his shoulder, grabs my hand, and pulls me down the hall and out the front doors.

The moment we burst through the front doors I feel liberated. The shuddered breath that escapes from Xander's mouth indicates he feels the same.

High school used to be fun. Our freshman year was the time of our lives. The first half of our sophomore year was even better. The four musketeers loved going to football games. We loved getting popcorn and nacho cheese to dip it in. Mt. Dew was a must. We would scream at the top of our lungs to cheer on our team. We got so into it we would slam our hands on the top of the fence and shout at the referees when we thought they'd made a bad call. We went to volleyball games and basketball games and thought we were hot shit sitting on the bottom bleacher with the upper classmen. We were nowhere near at all popular, but the four of us liked to walk the halls like we owned the place. It's easy to do when everyone ignores you. I was never happier than I was the first year and a half of high school. Isn't that how it's supposed to be? Isn't high school supposed to be the best time of our lives? As of right now I certainly hope high school isn't the best time of my life. If that's the case I'm looking at a pretty shitty life.

Xander and I walk briskly to my car, so as to not get caught escaping school in the middle of the day. I get behind the wheel and turn the key, throwing my backpack into the back seat. There isn't a time I drive my car I don't think about how I still wouldn't be able to drive if it weren't for Logan. He pushed me into driving, into getting over my loss and pain. He pushed me into being stronger. I never got the chance to thank him for it. Now I never will. Like some of the things he's told me about living my life after Nash, I'm sure the act of me driving would be thanks enough.

I pull out of the student parking lot and head for Logan's house. The phoenixes are now staying there. With most of the phoenixes gone my father felt it important to stick together, not to have anyone displaced or spread out. That is, the phoenixes who decided to stick around. There aren't many of them, but I didn't expect much. As much as I wanted to be a part of them, I knew from the beginning they weren't going to accept me, and I was too different to fit in to their well-oiled group.

Some of the phoenixes still in town do not like me. I'm not sure if it's because of my father, or because they have nowhere else to go, or if they want to see me continuously fall on my face in failure, but nevertheless, they have remained. One such individual is Lydia. I'm about eighty seven percent sure she stayed because her brother, Nathan stayed. Nathan happens to be one of the rare members of my father's group of phoenixes who likes me. Nathan, Thomas, Aspen, Lydia, and Anna have stayed in Cedars. I'm not sure how any of them feel about me right now. Thomas and Gray are best friends. It's my fault the love of Gray's life is gone, so who knows if Thomas holds that against me. I'm the reason Kristina is dead. Kristina is Anna's best friend. So there's that. Lydia has always hated me. More for the fact that Logan loved me. But there's still that. And I got Aspen's brother killed. The fault circle revolves around me, the jury members standing outside, leering in at me. Besides them, Gray and my father stuck around.

I desperately miss working out. I don't have any exercise equipment at my house and working out as hard as I do would get suspicious to anyone who would happen to be at the gym at school or in town. So that leaves Logan's. And working out in a house filled with people who either hate you or harbor extreme emotions toward you is more than slightly difficult. I have stopped wearing headphones in fear of Lydia taking a surprise stab at me. It wouldn't be out of character for her. And I wouldn't hold it against her. There are days I'd like to take a stab at me.

It's been nearly a month and the passing of Tucker has not gotten any easier. It's so quiet. In my house, in school, in my head, and in my heart. Missing Tucker is like forgetting to breathe. All of a sudden you're about to pass out but your brain kicks in, forces your body to function, and saves your life even when you didn't ask it to. I want to forget he's gone, want to live life like he's still here. I can even picture him in everything I do, imagine what he would say or how he would act, but then my brain reminds me he died, and I'm forced to relive the pain over and over.

"Cass," Xander says sternly from beside me. "Eyes on the road."

I jerk back into reality, into my car, driving down the road, Xander at my side. My car straddles the center line. I ease it back into my lane and take a deep breath. Honestly, being over the center line is better than being in the ditch. I'm not sure what Xander is so worried about.

"Sorry," I mumble at him.

"It's fine," he says, resting his head back on the seat. "What did you have in mind for today?"

"I don't really know," I tell him. "I just had to get out of there. If Ashley would have said anything to me, even looked at me today, I would have burned that school to the ground."

"You don't say," Xander says, side eyeing me. One side of his face turns up in a grin when he says, "You looked pretty murderous in Bio this morning."

I stick out my tongue at him and focus on the road. I turn off the highway onto the gravel road and make my way towards Logan's. I didn't text Gray to let him know we're kidnapping him for the day in honor of his late boyfriend, but since that night, he hasn't done much more than wake up in the morning and get out of bed. He won't be busy. He may even be glad to get out of the house. At least I'm hoping.

I pull up to Logan's and cut the engine. Xander reaches for the door handle but I turn to him and say, "Some of the phoenixes are still on the fence about you. Maybe stay in the car and I'll get Gray by myself."

Owing to the fact that Cohen is a griffin and betrayed me in a big way, the phoenixes are a tad jumpy when it comes to my association with Xander, even though he has proven himself to be on my side time and again. The severely drooped eyebrows on his face make me feel horrible for suggesting he stay in the car. Moreover, they practically speak to me, asking when or even if he will ever be accepted by anyone. I feel for him.

"You know what," I tell him opening my car door. "Forget I said that. You're with me and if they have a problem with that, they can take it up with me. They are bound to anyway. Let's go."

Xander looks hesitant for a moment then gets out of the car. He follows me to the front door. For a split second I bring my hand up to knock, but lower it and walk into the house. Every occupant of the house has super human hearing, they know we pulled up, they know we're here, and they know we both got out of the car. Knocking on the door would be redundant to them all.

When we walk in, the living room is quiet. Like too quiet. I'm sure Lydia is off painting her nails, or shopping, or doing her hair. It would suit her. I haven't seen much of Aspen lately, so I have no idea what she does to occupy her time. I see her and Anna together more often than not. I'm glad they have each other to lean on. Nathan is usually playing video games so it's odd not to find him parked in front of the TV. I'm not sure where my father is. Hopefully he's off doing something to help in the fight against the griffins. I love my father. I respect him as a leader. But at the same time, this passive aggressive shit isn't getting him anywhere. It's ridding him of his people, and fast. If he doesn't take a stand against them, they will overrun him. It's just a matter of time. I know nothing about war, but the small bit I've been a part of has taught me that much.

We move through the house in search of Gray. I can hear bodies moving throughout the house, so I know there are people here. Apparently they don't want to see me.

I make my way straight to Gray's room, if he's not in there, he's in the kitchen, eating his sorrows away. But I find him in his room, lying on his bead, headphones in blaring classic rock music. His eyes are closed but dark circles have deeply shadowed the skin under them. His hair is a mess. He's wearing loose fitting pajamas and only loose fitting pajamas. I rap my knuckles against the door knowing even with the blasting music shooting into his ears he'll hear me. He opens his eyes but doesn't make a move to acknowledge my presence.

"Mind removing those so we can talk?" I say, indicating his headphones.

"School over already?" he asks, as he pulls the ear buds from their place. "What time is it?"

"We left," Xander tells him from beside me.

Xander and I move into the room, and stand in front of Gray's bed. If Gray is bothered by Xander's presence he doesn't show it. In the short time Tucker and Gray were together I know for a fact Tucker told Gray how much Xander meant to him and how much he wished we could all be friends. I also know Gray loved Tucker so much he was willing to set aside his prejudice in order to make that happen.

"Good for you," Gray says, though his tone says he could care less.

"It's a special day," I tell him. "We thought we should be out celebrating instead of stuck in those walls."

"Celebrating what exactly?" Gray asks.

"It's Tucker's birthday," Xander tells him.

"I'm well aware of what day it is," Gray says, anger building in his throat.

"Xander and I are going to do something that Tucker

loved, in honor of his birthday. We thought you might like to join us."

"Cass thought you might like to join us. I didn't object."

"How kind of you," Gray says. "You can leave now."

"Fine," Xander says.

Having about as much of their attitude as I can on this day I shout at them. "That's enough. Both of you. Tucker spent the last year trying to keep our friendship alive. He loved all three of us. He supported all three of us. And while we were all on opposing sides, he tried to bring us together. I will not have you two rip it apart. Do you understand me?"

The both of them are silent, still, and then nod as if they've been scolded.

"Good. Now. Gray. Take a shower, get dressed, and meet us down stairs. We are going out. And try on a new attitude. Today is Tucker's. Not ours."

"Whatever you say, fireball," Gray says. Grabbing a towel and handful of clothes from his closet he moves past me to head to the bathroom.

The fact that Gray used my nickname to address me gives me hope. For a month now, if he's addressed me at all, it's been my name. Using my nickname means the Gray I knew and loved, the Gray Tucker knew and loved, is still in there. He's just hurting. Hurting I can work with. Broken, not so much.

Xander and I head back downstairs and wait in the living room for Gray. I spend the first five minutes flipping through the channels. When nothing looks appealing I stop on a random channel and leave it there. From what I gather it's a documentary on the ongoing war between lions and hyenas.

"Seems fitting," Xander says on the couch next to me.

He's sprawled out, his arms on the top of the sofa, one leg resting on the coffee table.

Sitting here, watching TV, reminds me of when it was just Logan and I watching cartoons on Saturday mornings. I clear my head of all thoughts of Logan before it becomes too painful to bear.

Ten minutes after we arrived Gray walks into the living room showered and presentable. His eyes are ringed with his usual black eye liner but his mohawk still lies flat to his head. I hope to one day again see it standing strong and proud. Unlike the first time I met him, when he was wearing acid wash jeans, a concert t-shirt, and a leather jacket, Gray wears plain dark blue jeans, and a grey fitted long sleeve shirt. Xander gives him a raised eyebrow look at the long sleeve shirt because it's ninety four degrees outside. But, because our bodies don't register the outside temperature we are never hot or cold. From the look on Xander's face this must not have been in the griffins' handbook on us. Though that makes me wonder what is. I might have to question him on it sometime.

Gray follows Xander and I out to my car. When we're all in, I start it and take off back towards town and then continue on. I'm not entirely sure what we are doing yet, but it feels good to leave Cedars behind, if only for the afternoon.

As though he's still not one hundred percent sold on today, Gray says, "So what is your plan?"

"I don't know," I tell him honestly. "We just wanted to do something for Tucker."

"We could go to the zoo," Xander says from the seat beside me.

The air is taut inside the car. Gray hasn't fully accepted Xander into his world, into this life, into his heart. I haven't fully forgiven Xander for being so willing to give up on sixteen years of friendship for this war, for any part he may have played, or didn't, in Nash's and Tucker's and Kristina's and Logan's deaths, and for not trusting me enough to put our friendship first. And of course it's hard for Xander to be in a car with two members of a race of people he has been brainwashed his entire life to hate. There are so many unresolved issues in this car we could script a teenage drama film and sell millions. But, today is Tucker's birthday and one of Tucker's life wishes would be for the love of his life and his best friends to all get along and find peace with each other. So that is what we are doing. We are coming together, despite our plights, for our shared love of Tucker.

"That's my thing, remember," I say to him, remembering the time Xander and Tucker took me to the zoo to cheer me up on the six month anniversary of Nash's death. That was a hard day. I thought that would have been about as hard as my life was going to get. Joke's on me, right?

"Right," Xander says as though he feels embarrassed that he couldn't remember that.

"We could go shopping. Tucker loved shopping," I say, though I'm not sure it's the best idea ever.

"As much as that would definitely be something Tucker would do, I don't exactly have a lot of money to shell out right now," Xander says, though, again, he sounds embarrassed.

"Yeah, me either," I say.

"We could just go talk to him," Gray says from the back seat.

My heart plummets in my chest. Xander and I look at each other. A secret look passes between us. We are both ashamed the newest member of the group is the one to know exactly what Tucker would want. Xander and I may have loved Tucker longer than Gray did but Gray knew Tucker on a different level.

"Yeah, alright," Xander says for the both of us. I can't seem to find my voice.

I haven't been to Tucker's grave since we buried him. I never did visit Nash's grave site. He was still in my head. I didn't need to visit him when he was still with me. Plus, visiting him at his resting place would mean that he really is gone forever, and I wasn't ready to face that.

I drive until I find a road to turn off onto. I pull in and make a U turn, heading back to Cedars. Escape was in sight but only to be short lived. I drive through town, the inside of the car silent, and pull up to the cemetery. When I cut the engine, the silence is eerie, but holds so much pain. The three of us slowly get out of the car. The slamming of the doors permeates the stillness and makes us all jump. Gray strides purposefully to the freshly packed earth that marks Tucker's grave. Xander and I follow him, our heads bowed.

Gray stands at the foot of the grave, Xander on one side, me on the other, the headstone taking the fourth side. Thin blades of grass sporadically stick out of the cracked dirt covering Tucker's casket. It was only a month ago we were here, filling in the hole that was to be his place of rest.

I feel exactly as I felt a month ago; cold and empty. I watch Gray and Xander for their reactions, their emotional state. They both stare at Tucker's head stone, their faces alike, hard like the polished rock in front of them. The dry grass rustles against my sandaled foot as I move it nervously. The headstones making their permanent homes in the cemetery line up in neat rows. As messy as death is I wouldn't expect its' results to be so uniform. The sky above is cloudy and threatens rain. We haven't had so much as a drop of rain since Tucker's funeral. It would be fitting for it to start pouring on his birthday, on the day we decide to visit him.

We are all silent for several outstretched moments. I can't bring myself to face Tucker's head stone. I don't want it to be the last image I have of him. I don't want Tucker's smiling face to fade from my memory. As long as the griffins don't find a way to bring me down I will live forever, as long as forever is for a phoenix. At some point down the road, though it may be several years, Tucker's face will fade from my mind. I fear that day more than I fear the next hit from the griffins.

Gray is the first of us to speak. "Happy birthday, Tucker," he says then pauses. I watch as the Adam's apple in his throat bobs up and down. "You didn't know this, but I had today all planned out. You have no idea how excited I was to celebrate your birthday. I had dinner reservations at your favorite Italian place in the city. I was going to take you to the river so we could sit on the shore and make out to the sound of the water crashing and lapping onto the beach. I had your gift bought and wrapped. The things I was going to do to you once we got back to my bedroom." Gray stops. I wonder if he's embarrassed by what he's just said, but then I see tears shining in his eyes and know that's not the reason. "I love you, Tucker. I miss you so much. It hurts every morning to wake up and know I'll never again get to wake up next to you. It hurts to breathe without you. It hurts too much sometimes and I think about finding a griffin with an ice knife and just being done hurting. But then I know you would hate me for it, and I'm not about to find you in the afterlife knowing you hate me. So I will stay here. I will protect Casslyn like you asked me. And I will go on loving you for eternity. Until I see you again."

My head snaps in the direction of Gray as he said he would continue to protect me like Tucker asked. I had no idea Tucker asked him that. It melts my heart a little. It also makes me mad. What if Tucker died because Gray was trying to protect me and neglected Tucker? That would mean Tucker's death is triple times my fault than I originally thought. It angers me to think that no matter what, Tucker was always putting me first. I may have hooked him up with Gray, but I feel like that's not enough payback for everything Tucker has ever done for me. I will never be able to repay him.

Gray stares at me, knowing he revealed what he did. He's trying to assess me reaction to it. I'm not about to give him one. Not now. Maybe not ever. If he wanted me to know he was protecting me, he would have told me before deciding to drop it like a bomb at Tucker's grave.

It does make me wonder if Gray and I were ever really friends or if he was just acting like my friend because Tucker asked him too. But then I push my doubts aside because Gray and I were friends before he and Tucker became a couple.

"You're finally eighteen," Xander begins "How does it feel? Did you know I was always jealous you were older than me? It may only be by two weeks, but it still bugged me. You never threw it in my face, you were far too big a person to do that. I'm not sure if being older than Nash, Cass, and I made you feel like you had to protect the three of us, but that's always what you did. And we can't thank you enough for it. You always put everyone before yourself. I wish you wouldn't have. You deserved to be happy. In the end I think you achieved that, and I can't tell you what that means to me. But I wish you could have gotten there a little sooner. I guess I can blame that on myself. I always put myself first. I thought being a griffin was the be-all and end-all. I loved being one of them. I thought we were doing something more than ourselves. And in a way I thought I was protecting you. Turns out I was wrong in a big way. And for that I am sorry."

Xander takes a short pause, righting himself and getting his emotions in check. Like Gray, Xander has tears in his eyes. Then he continues on, this time his tone and his words a little lighter. "Cass and I started senior year. Let me tell you, it is everything we thought it would be. Just kidding. Ashley is still a bitch, but who's to blame her now that she's boyfriendless. The teachers can't decide whether to pile on the homework or be lacks about it since we're seniors and they're not actually convinced we'll do it. The new set of freshman are pretty skittish. I'm not sure if they got wind of what a badass Cass is or if high school just frightens them. But man, look at them the wrong way and they run to the bathroom to hide. You would rule that school. I'm telling you. You would most certainly be Homecoming king. Guaranteed. And you'd be the best looking too. Have you seen our classmates recently? Summer was not kind to them. Of course, Ashley is bound to get queen and I'm not sure you'd want to dance with her so it's probably for the best. But anyway, it's not the same without you. But because of you, Cass and I have each other. I will miss hanging out on the couch with you and playing video games. You always pretended to be bad because video games are my thing, but I know you could have kicked my ass every time. So thanks. I hope wherever you are that you are happy. I'll see you again someday. You know I'm looking forward to it. Happy birthday, Tucker."

It's my turn. I don't know what to say. Gray and Xander did better than I'll ever do. What do you say to the person you got killed? Somehow I just don't think sorry is going to cut it.

"You were always looking out for me, weren't you? Even when I didn't know it. What did I ever do to deserve you? I've been thinking about it. Over and over, every day, I think about our friendship and I can't figure out what I did to deserve you. I have to be honest. I have no idea. You are the perfect best friend. I am so sorry, Tucker. I love you so much. I am so sorry."

"Cass," Xander says, taking a step around the grave toward me.

"I'm sorry," I tell Gray and Xander. "I can't do this. I can't have these be the first words I say to Tucker after what happened."

I eye them both, but skim over Tucker's head stone, and walk off, not before saying, "I'll meet you two at the car."

I walk away from Gray and Xander needing space from them and from Tucker's grave. I thought this was a good idea when Gray brought it up, but now I'm not so sure. I didn't realize how hard this would be. Cedars is a small town but it's been around a while. There are only two cemeteries in town so more than half the people who have died in town are buried here. I walk on, crest a small hill, and lose sight of my friends.

When we were kids, the four of us would come to the cemetery at night and bring a Ouija board. One of us would always push the planchette, pretending we didn't, and imagine we could speak to the residents of the cemetery. Now that

I think about that, I really hope children don't come here and pretend they can talk to Nash or Tucker.

I walk through the rows of graves, careful not to step on any of them. That proves to be tricky because I'm not sure where they end or begin. I trip on the rough ground and catch myself on the headstone nearest me. I look down and read the name on the headstone. It's Nash's.

I was in the hospital recovering from the accident when they buried him. And I never visited his gravesite after that. I never had to, Nash was always in my head. But now he's gone.

I look down at the headstone. It's small, smaller than those that surround it, and a rough black, unlike the polished light gray stones that border it. It's so Nash I find it funny. But I'm glad that the place he's buried reflects who he is.

I feel far too formal standing in front of Nash's headstone, like I'm his doctor not his twin sister. I sit down next to his headstone and cross my legs under each other. I stare at his name etched into the rock. I stare at his birthdate and the date that follows it. It's sad that Tucker died before his next birthday. But Nash was killed on his birthday. I'm not sure what's worse than that. Possibly having your twin die on your birthday. Either way, dying before you're at least eighty years old has got to be the worst. Not making it to certain milestones. Not being legal to gamble, or drink. Not graduating high school or getting the chance to experiment in college. Never getting married or having children. Never having grandchildren.

"Hey, Nash," I say. "It's been a while. I've got to admit, not having you with me all the time is weird. Even after you died I still had you with me. Now you're really gone. It's really quiet in my head now."

Tucker may have been my best friend. But besides being my best friend, Nash was my twin, my equal. Talking to him is just easier, natural, effortless.

"Wherever you are I'm sure by now you know what's happened to Tucker. Your knowledge is no longer first hand, but you did always seem to know a little more than I did so I'm sure you've heard. Whether through the great vine or divine intervention or what have you. I really hope the two of you are together. I'm sure he's rocking the afterlife, but I hope he's got you just in case he's having a hard time. If you could give me some sign that the two of you are together and that you're both okay, that would be great."

I look around me for a sign from Nash but find nothing. Maybe it takes a while for messages to travel to Nash's new home.

"I've got to be honest, Nash. I'm drowning down here. I don't know what I'm doing. I'm losing everyone I care about and I don't know how to stop it. I don't know how to keep anyone safe, let alone myself. I'm trying to get revenge for you and Tucker and everyone else, but I'm not even sure that is the right thing. When I look in the mirror I don't even see myself anymore. I've lost Logan and I'm lost without him. I'm trying to hold it together but I'm barely doing that. Mom and dad are getting more suspicious every day. When the police questioned me about Colt's death I really thought mom was going to have it out with me. I'm trying to keep her out of this, to keep her safe, but she's bound to find out eventually. I'm starting to think I should tell her sooner rather than later, so she doesn't start asking questions and putting herself in danger. It's only a matter of time before Raphe and Ashley use mom and dad against me."

"I could really use some good old fashioned Nash advice right about now. Even when you were trapped in my head you always knew what to say. But that's me being needy and selfish, two things I really need to work on. And I'm trying. I really hope you are okay. If this gets to you, maybe send that sign my way. And if you see Tucker could you tell him that I love him, that I'm sorry, that I hope he's okay, and that I'll take care of Gray for him. As for you, Nash. I love you. I will miss you forever. And I'll try to visit here more often."

I close my eyes and try to feel his presence around me or in my head. I receive silence, pure and simple. I know Nash is still with me, but it's different than before. When I know nothing is going to change I stand up, dust myself off, and head back to the car. That's when the first rain drop lands on the tip of my nose. It is quickly followed by several others until I'm drenched. One side of my mouth curls up, the other joining is soon after. This is the sign I asked for. It's got to be. I quickly say thank you then walk to the car.

Xander and Gray sit in the car. As I walk toward them I see the warry weathered looks on their faces. I'm sure they wondered where I'd gone to. Maybe if I was even coming back. But when I smile at them through the windshield and the pouring rain, their faces along with their shoulders, relax.

Sliding into the car, water drops slipping off the end of my nose, I smile at them and say, “Shall we get a pizza, head back to my house, and watch Tucker’s favorite movie?”

As their way of answer, Gray and Xander both say, “*Sweet Home Alabama*?”

I start the car and head to Casey’s while Xander calls the pizza in.

Tonight is going to be good. It’s going to be better than it started off. Tonight is going be a start to setting things right.

Four

Xander and Gray are seated on the couch, each with one leg propped up on the coffee table. I sit on the floor, leaning against the couch, in between their legs. If feels as close to the old times with Tucker and Nash as it possibly could.

The three of us stuff our faces on two large pepperoni pizzas, staring attentively at the part in *Sweet Home Alabama* where Reese Witherspoon and Josh Lucas scream at each other through a screen door, one calling the other a dumb, stubborn, redneck hick, and the other calling the first a hoity toity Yankee bitch. Besides their make out session at the end, this is my favorite part. It was always Tucker's favorite part.

My mom popped into the living room to steal a slice of pizza before hopping in the shower. I could tell that she came in to talk to me, but upon seeing Xander and Gray, she decided now wasn't the time. I'm hoping when she's ready to leave for work she will still feel uncomfortable talking in front of them.

Watching this movie makes me feel connected to Tucker. I know exactly what he would say at every part of the movie. Both times in the movie when the line *so I can kiss you anytime I want* is said, Tucker would dramatically reenact it. It never got old. I glance at Xander to see if he's waiting for it to come. I'm taking the fact that he's biting his lip to mean yes, he's waiting for it. Like Xander, Gray wrings his hands over and over. He's waiting for it too. I thought today would be healing, that it would honor Tucker and his birthday. I wasn't expecting today to make us feel so bad. I guess it's too soon after his death to remember him without being depressed by his absence. I'll be waiting for that time on baited breath.

My mom walks into the living room in her scrubs. She'll be leaving for work soon. She's been working the night shift a lot recently. It's not her favorite because she and I don't get to spend a lot of time together. However, now that she works the night shift and my dad works the night shift, when they aren't sleeping they can spend time together. It's a lose, lose, win situation. Kind of. I'm not really sure but it gives me a lot more freedom, and right now, going after the griffins, freedom is something I need.

My mom's gaze travels from me, to Xander, to Gray, and then back to me. I watch her from the corner of my eye, keeping my focus on the TV so she might decide not to talk to me. I'm still sitting in the middle of Gray and Xander so getting out would be more of a hindrance to her being casual about wanting to talk to me.

"Casslyn," she says from the kitchen.

No such luck.

I look at her over the top of the sofa, knowing if I don't, I'll be in bigger trouble than if I just talk to her.

"May I speak with you?" she asks, very cordial. This can't be good.

Gray and Xander turn to look at me. I raise an eyebrow at them, one at a time, indicating they are allowed to listen in, and hop up from the floor. I step over Xander's legs and walk from the living room, past the front door, and into the kitchen. My mom has turned to the coffee pot to start her wake up brew. I walk up to the island, on the other side of it as her, and wait for her to speak. I may have fire balls on my side, but there is always something scary about moms.

"I got a call from the school today," she says without turning to look at me. She knows this is more intimidating than actually looking at me when she yells at me. When we were younger she would employ this tactic and Nash would cave immediately. Of course she would forgive him quicker than me. I'm not sure if that was because he was her favorite or because he caved so easily she couldn't stay mad at his weakness. She could always stay mad at me.

When I don't answer her, she continues, "Mind telling me what was so important you and Xander thought it necessary to skip school?"

"It's Tucker's birthday," I say simply. It should be answer enough.

But to moms nothing is ever enough of an answer. She raises an eyebrow at me to get me to continue.

"We went to talk to him," I tell her.

"You left school to talk to a headstone?"

I stare at her, willing to slap her if I have to.

But it is clear she realizes she sounded uncaring and says, "I'm sorry. That was insensitive. I know you are hurting. I know you need to heal. But I cannot have you skipping school. I cannot have you disappearing. I need to know where you are. I can't lose you too." She breaks down at that sentence. She's been doing that a lot lately. Clearly she was far more affected by the attack in August than she first let on. I walk around the island moving toward her, in case I need to comfort her, or hold her up, maybe both.

"Mom, I'm fine. I just couldn't be stuck in school today. I'm sorry. I didn't mean to upset you."

"Just don't do it again," she says, wiping tears from her eyes.

"Got it," I say to her.

She pulls her mug from the dishwasher and pours steaming coffee into it. She caps it and turns back to me, a strained smile on her face.

"Hey, mom," I say. When I've got her full attention I say, "I talked to Nash today."

"Oh, honey," she says, fresh tears stinging her eyes. "I'm so glad. I was afraid you would never visit him."

That's not at all what I was expecting from her, so words I didn't plan slip from my mouth. "Why would you think that?"

"The two of you were so close I was afraid you would never . . . get past what happened to him."

"I haven't," I admit. "I'm not sure I ever will."

I'm well aware Xander and Gray are still listening. There is a part of me that wishes they weren't. But the rest of me is glad they are. It may help explain some part of me to them.

"I don't think any of us will, Casslyn. It will forever be a part of us. But the time we had with him should be more important than the time we don't." The way she says this, so quote like, makes it sound like she's been to talk to a counselor or a psychiatrist. I wouldn't judge her if she did. I would commend her for it. In a way, it's braver to talk about it than to keep it bottled up. If it helps her, I'm happy for her.

"You're right," I tell her.

"Casslyn," my mom says, her tone returning to one of scolding.

"Yeah?" I ask.

"Would you mind telling me why Xander is still living in my house and eating my food?"

"Look, mom, Xander and his parents had a fall out. He needs someplace to stay while they sort it out. He can't stay there right now. Please just let him stay."

"His parents have been in contact with your dad and I. They are worried."

"He is here, under your roof, he couldn't possibly be any safer." I say this hoping flattery will distract her from any further questioning.

"He can stay for now. But I don't like the fact that he's left home. And so soon after we all lost Tucker. Xander's parents were as worried about losing him as I was of losing you."

I highly doubt that, but whatever they need to tell my mom to get her on their side, right?

"I'll talk to him," I say, though I won't be talking to him about it.

"Good girl," she says, placing one hand on my cheek. I'm really not sure why she keeps doing that to me. "Oh, look at the time, I'm going to be late for work. I'll see you tomorrow. I better not get another call that you skipped school."

"Got it," I tell her, vaguely aware I said it a little while ago.

"That's my girl. Now have a good evening."

"You too, mom."

The minute she walks out the door Xander walks in the kitchen and leans his elbows on the island opposite me, his I'm-going-to-question-you look prevalent on his face.

I cut in before he can speak, "I'm going after another one tonight." I make sure to keep my voice low enough so Gray won't hear. I'm not about to have him run to my father and blab. My father would more than likely do what he can to shut it down. And I'm not having that.

"But it's Tucker's birthday," Xander says. I'm not sure

what he's trying to get at. His tone is vague and noncommittal. He could be trying to talk me out of it to keep me safe. He could not want to do it tonight because we are supposed to be honoring Tucker. He could also not be ready to be getting rid of another member of his race. I can definitely understand that. But he also doesn't need to come with me.

"Revenge is a dish best served with birthday cake," I tell him, the look in my eyes turning sinister. "You don't need to come."

"You know I'm not letting you do this alone," Xander says, leaning closer to me, his voice hushed.

I get right up in his face and say, "Then get on board, Xander, because it's happening."

"I got it," he tells me, nodding his head.

"Do you know who we're going after?" he asks.

I remember every face of every griffin that played a part in any of the last two years of my life. Every griffin who abducted me from my car, every griffin who helped torture me, every griffin who entered Logan's house and stabbed Kristina, every griffin who broke into my house and helped Cohen betray me. I stalked every social media account on the internet to find the names and locations of these people. Their names I will forget, but it's where they reside that matters to me. I got lucky enough to have two of them in one place.

Tonight I'm getting two for the price of one. The two griffins I'm going after each held an ice knife they plunged into Kristina's body. I've got two of my dad's hunting knives

I plan on working them over with.

"I have a list. Next up is two of the guys who stabbed Kristina with Ashley. You know who I mean?"

"Yeah. They were talking about it, more like bragging about it, at the warehouse after the attack. You know where they live?"

"Yeah. I told you. This is happening."

I'm not sure Xander is ready for it. I'm not sure if he'll be able to do it. They are still the people he grew up with. When the time comes, if he can't do it, I'll take care of it, but I'll be thankful just to have him there with me.

Xander and I return to the living room to finish the movie with Gray. I decided to make some popcorn so that our absence would be a little more plausible. I hand Gray a bowl and sit next to him on the couch. He nods his thanks without taking his eye off the screen.

When we get to the second time a character says they want to kiss the other character any time they want I mouth the words alongside them, not as over the top as Tucker would, but the sentiment is there. And then the couple ends up happily together and the movie ends.

Now I have to send Gray away so that I can avenge his boyfriend and one of his friends.

So I fake a large yawn, stretch myself out next to him, and check the time on my phone. Turning to Gray I say, "It's been a long day, I think I might call it a night."

"You know, I was wondering if I could stay a little longer. I've just spent so much time alone since I lost Tucker and I feel like I really need to be with you guys right now."

"Oh, um, okay. A little longer is okay. I guess."

I get up from the couch, take his popcorn bowl from him, and take it to the kitchen.

I turn to Xander and widen my eyes at him. He gives me the same look. It's the what-can-I-do look. I guess neither of us knows what to do. Gray and Xander follow me to the kitchen. Xander rummages through the fridge until he emerges with three bottles of water. He hands one to each of us then again leans his elbows on the island.

"Thanks," Gray says, a tremor in his voice. "Do you maybe want to watch another movie?"

"Well," I start.

Xander jumps in and says, "Cass and I have school tomorrow. We probably shouldn't stay up too late."

"Oh, right," Gray says. "I forget you are still in school."

"We could hang out more tomorrow night," I say.

"Look," Gray says, taking a step full of purpose towards me. "I know you two are trying to get rid of me so you can go take down another griffin. That is not going to happen."

It shouldn't come as a surprise to me that Gray thinks it was me and Xander that killed Colt. It doesn't really, but the fact that he just knows, not suspects, is what gets to me. It makes me wonder what the other phoenixes think of me. At this point I don't really care. They can think of me as they like. They have as long as they've known me.

What I really want to know, is how they found out. It's not like griffins would just drop like flies, without someone coming after them, but surely I'm not the only one who would go after them.

Quickly realizing I'm not going to get far by trying to outwit, or argue with Gray I simply say, "You can't spend every moment with us."

"I can't let you do it, Casslyn," Gray says, crossing his arms over his muscled chest. He's trying to intimidate me. It works, because I've seen him spar with Logan, and the two are on par, but it only works so far.

"This isn't for Cass, Gray. It's for every one they've ever taken from us. Do you think we like this?" Without giving Gray time to answer, Xander says, "We don't, but it's time someone stood up to them."

"And what gives you the right to bring them down? They've taken two people away from you? Until two months ago you were one of them? How can I believe you've fully turned against them? How can I believe you're not just another Cohen and you're playing us only to betray us? How can you have turned against them so easily?"

"Because I was questioning them for a lot longer than this. Because Nash and Tucker were two of the three most important people in my life. Because they are evil and it took me too long to see it. Shall I go on?"

Gray watches Xander speak then turns to me. I know he trusts Xander because Tucker did. I know he believes the truth in Xander's words and in the sincerity in his voice. But he looks at me for confirmation, or an answer, not only to trusting Xander, but to why we are going after the griffins.

I give him my most steely gaze, then say, "I trust Xander. I know I trusted Cohen. I made a mistake. But I would trust Xander with my life. I have. And he hasn't let me down. As for who this is for and why we are doing this. I can't lose anyone else. I won't survive it. Living without Tucker and my brother is nearly impossible. I'm doing what I can to survive it."

"It's too dangerous, Casslyn," Gray says, slapping his hand down on the granite countertop. The popping noise is harsh and reverberates around the three of us. "You can't lose anyone else? Well we can't lose you."

"I know what I'm doing," I say, looking to Xander for some assistance in the argument. He shrugs his shoulders and gives me the I've-got-nothing look.

"Do you? Going in halfcocked. Angry. Seeking revenge. That's not knowing what you're doing. That's looking to get yourself killed."

"I'm not going to in alone," I snipe back at Gray.

"No. You are taking Xander, who is openly betraying his own people. Do you think they are going to take that lightly? Do you think they're going to come after you and not him? Because I guarantee they hate him more than they hate you right now. I thought you couldn't lose anyone else?"

"Leave her alone, man," Xander says walking between the two of us.

"She needs to hear it," Gray says like we are both children.

"They're gone, Gray," I shout at him, angry that he

doesn't understand I'm about ready to bust if I don't go after the griffins. "I lost them."

"Grow up, Casslyn. You don't think we haven't all lost someone? I've been around a lot longer than you have and I've lost a lot more people than you have. But I moved on. I got past it. Which is what you're going to have to do."

I thought Gray would be on my side. I thought that losing Tucker would spur him to let me go, knowing I was doing it for the love of his life. Never did I think he would try to stop me.

I can't let him stop me. I'm going after the griffins. I have to go after the griffins. They have to pay for what they've done.

"Gray, there are two of us and one of you. Please don't make me hurt you. They killed Kristina, and Nash, and Logan, and Tucker. I'm killing them. Do you understand me?"

"I do. And that's why I'm going with you. I want in."

"Uh. What?" I ask, dumbfounded. There is no way he just said that. Did he?

I turn to Xander to make sure I heard right. He stands to the side of us, his mouth agape. So apparently Gray is agreeing not only to let us go, but to join us. After all that arguing.

"I had to make sure you were doing it for the right reasons," he says like it's obvious.

"Am I?" I ask slowly, not sure how he came to that conclusion.

"Cass, we all thought you were on a death mission. Your own. You may take down some griffins but you may take yourself out in the process. If that was the case, we were prepared to stop you at all cost."

"Why would you think I wanted to die?"

"Don't you?" Gray asks.

"Some days. But no. That would mean they win. I'm not going to let them win. Plus I kind of like living. Even if it has sucked the last year and a half."

"Look," Gray says, taking a step towards me. He places a hand on each of my arms and makes me look at him. "Despite what you may think and how some of us have treated you, you are one of us, fireball. And I meant it. We can't lose you."

Something near my heart tugs at the use of his nickname for me. But he could just be using it as a tactic. If so, I can't let him.

"Did my father tell you to say that?" I ask, snark in my voice.

"Aspen did," Gray says holding my gaze.

I pull out of his grasp and turn away from him. I feel insecure when he's holding me so close.

"I thought she might hate me," I tell him from over my shoulder.

"She just misses her brother."

"I know the feeling." I do know the feeling. I know the feeling of missing a brother. And I know the feeling of missing her brother.

"Then maybe you should be spending time with her instead of avoiding her." Gray crosses his arms over his chest again. He raises an accusing eyebrow at me.

"I thought she was avoiding me."

"Misconceptions."

"I'm sorry to cut in," Xander says. I'd almost forgotten he was in the room with us. Gray and I were having a real moment there, or a break through. Whatever it was I forgot about Xander for a moment. "But I have two questions. One. Have we all made up? And two. Are we going to kill some griffins tonight?"

"Yes," I say.

"Yes," Gray answers.

"I'll find you a knife," I tell him.

"What do you mean a knife?" Gray asks.

"We used fire last time," Xander explains. "We're changing tactics so no one suspects foul play. And if they do they won't know it's the same people."

"Plus," I say, "The two we are going after stabbed Kristina in the chest. We are going to return the favor."

"And the two of you planned this while making popcorn?" Gray asks, a stunned look on his face.

"No. We planned it after our last attack. We just weren't sure when we were going to put it into motion. We needed to keep away suspicion."

Gray looks off balance. Like my words have made him sick. Or like he's not sure he can go through with this after all. Or like he's not sure he really knows me. It's amazing what grief can do to a person. Mine has turned me into a weapon. A deadly, broken weapon.

"It's okay if you can't do this. Just go back to Logan's and convince everyone you forced us to stay home. I won't blame you."

"No," Gray says, resolving himself to the mission ahead of us. "I can do this. They killed Tucker in front of my eyes. That image will never leave my head. They are going to pay for that."

"Good. Let's get ready." I say to Gray and Xander both.

I head for my room and find a new set of black clothes. Xander and I washed our last set of black clothes. But for some reason paranoia set in for the both of us so we took them out to the burn barrel and I set them on fire. After that we headed into the city for new black clothes. After tonight I will burn these and the knives we use. If they burn. I'm not sure if my fire is hot enough to burn metal. If not, we have a second option for getting rid of the knives.

When all three of us are ready, Gray borrowing some of Xander's clothes, Gray heads over to Logan's to get his SUV. We thought it would be a good change from my car. There aren't many Dodge Chargers in Cedars but there are about a billion and one SUVs.

Gray pulls up in front of my house, Xander and I climb in, and we head into town and to our next victims house.

Xander hasn't actually been to this house so we're going to have to wing it on the floor plan side of things.

I sit in the back of the SUV, having given Xander the front, and try not to think too hard about what we are about to do. I want payback. I want justice. I do. I want this war to end. And I'm ready to play my part. I am. That doesn't mean I want to think about the part I have to play. The part where I end a living breathing person's life. But I remind myself they deserve it. That they've taken innocent lives without a second thought.

Xander watches me from the rear view mirror. Last time we did this, I got home and threw up, massively. Like breaking blood vessels in my eyes power throwing up. Then after that I got the shakes. Xander and I chalked it up to me coming down from so much adrenaline. We both convinced each other that's what it was. I don't think either of us convinced ourselves. So he watches me. Checking my temperament. Trying to get a read on my vitals, though that's not possible from where he's sitting. He's worried about me. I know he is.

I talk big about killing the griffins. I guilt Xander and Gray for being nervous and being too weak to kill the griffins. But if my little episode after the first killing was any indication, I think we know I'm the weak link. I pulled it off, I killed the griffin, but I also had nightmares about it afterward. But this is not about me, it's about getting revenge for all the lost souls taken away at the hands of the griffins.

Before we left the house I made Xander promise not to tell Gray about the affects killing the griffin had on me. If Gray knew how I reacted to killing someone the first time, even someone I hate, there is no way he'd let me go this time, and I am not being left out of this. Especially when it was my idea in the first place.

We're in town and parked three blocks away from the house before I know it. We planned while in the car. Adjusted the plan Xander and I already had worked out. We get out of Gray's car, tuck our knives into our pants, and head in three separate directions. Like a month ago, it's around midnight and not many people are out and about. And because it's so dark out it's easy to dart in and out of shadows if need be. From cover of darkness I head for the front door while Xander and Gray head around the house. We know enough about the outside of the house from a scouting mission we did after the first killing. There is a front door, a back door, and a door that leads into the basement. Xander and I had just planned on going for the front and back doors. But with Gray taking the basement, they won't have any way to get away.

I listen to movement around the house checking to see if Xander and Gray have made it to their positions. Once I know they have, I knock on the front door. There is movement from inside. Two voices that cut off as I knock again. One set of footsteps moves toward the door. Another set moves away from it.

When one of the griffins opens the door, I smile as sweetly as I can force myself to and say, "Hello."

"You," the griffin says, nearly spitting it at me.

"Yeah, me," I tell him, dropping the sugar tone. "Are you going to invite me in?"

"Why would I do that?" he asks.

"So I can kill you," I tell him.

The griffin laughs right in my face. The other griffin

is nowhere to be seen, but I know where he is. I also know Gray is waiting at the bottom of the basement stairs, and that Xander is standing just inside the back door.

"Come right in, I'd love to see you try."

The griffin thinks I'm outnumbered. He thinks I think it is just the two of us and that he has the element of surprise. I'm going to cherish the look of surprise on his face when he realizes he and his friend are in big trouble.

The griffin opens his door wider and steps aside to allow me entrance. I step in the door and move to the middle of his living room. I turn to face him, giving my back to the second griffin. I know if he tries to attack Xander will have my back. I want the griffin standing in front of me to think he's got the upper hand.

"Lovely place you've got here," I tell him, pulling the knife from the back of my pants and indicating around the room with it.

Again the griffin laughs at me.

"That's cute. You brought a knife. Wouldn't think you'd need it, what with you having magical powers and what not."

"Magical powers? What, like this?" I ask and form a fire ball in my free hand.

The griffin's eyes narrow the slightest. He schools his expression quickly, but I saw the fear in his eyes. I also see them dart, for a millisecond, to the griffin standing behind me. They think I couldn't hear his footsteps cross from the linoleum onto the carpet. I would think, with their enhanced hearing, that they could hear Xander and Gray moving about the house, but their focus is on me, and that's where I want it.

"What's with all the talking? I thought you were here to kill me?" the griffin asks.

"Oh I am," I tell him, extinguishing the fireball against my thigh. "But first I wanted to ask you about something,"

"And that would be?"

"My friend, Kristina."

The griffin looks at me blankly and says, "And that would be?"

"The phoenix you helped stab to death. Remember her? You baited her into following you into a corn field and then you and three of your friends stabbed her in the chest. You remember?"

The griffin raises a cocky eyebrow at me, grins, and says, "It must have slipped my mind."

"Then let me remind you," I say, and charge for him.

He darts to the side away from the hand that holds the knife. I anticipated this and moved the blade to the other hand mid strike. He's quick so as I bring the knife down at him it only nicks his arm. He hisses through his teeth as we face each other again. As I turn around both he and the second griffin stand in the living room ready to take me on. Behind them Xander and Gray appear.

"You're outnumbered," the second griffin says.

"Not quite," Xander says.

The griffins nearly break their necks as they turn towards my accomplices. They uniformly take a step back. And another, until I am able to jab the point of my knife into one of their backs. He jerks forward but stops as Gray and Xander converge on them. The griffin I met at the door turns to face me while his brother challenges my friends. By the look in the griffin's eyes they are not about to go down easily.

The five of us stand in the living room facing each other. None of us moving towards the others. It's like in movies when wrestlers dance around the ring and act like they are going to lunge against their opponent but never do. So I take the initiative and thrust my knife at the griffin who invited me into his home to kill him.

He grabs my wrist in both his hands and twists my arms around behind my back. I should have seen that coming. The pain in my arm as he pulls it up and back is intense and sharp, causing my grip on the knife to loosen. The griffin takes this advantage and grabs for the knife. With his focus on the knife I pull my body weight around and swing at his face with my free hand. I land a solid punch to the side of his face. He stumbles backwards which gives me a second to glance towards Gray and Xander who have their hands full with the griffin's brother.

Xander attacks the griffin's face while Gray aims lower on his body. They haven't worked together before so they don't know each other's moves. This causes them to pause in their attack, to second guess each other, to trip each other up. The griffin uses this advantage to strike Gray in the face. The punch is hard and hits Gray right on his sharp cheekbone. The skin breaks open, but before it can start to bleed, Gray's fire ignites and heals his wound, then goes out.

My attention returns to my opponent when he yells out, readying to charge me. I grip my knife firmly and brace myself for his assault. He's too close to me to avoid his attack, so I lean into it and swing my knife at him. I didn't do much training with knives, so I'm not really good at it, not sure how exactly to hold the knife or how to strike. I know where I need to strike, but getting a clean shot at it is proving to be difficult. Air escapes my lungs in a harsh grunt as the griffin lowers his shoulders and hits me in the center of my chest, driving me back into the wall. I try to react to the blow, try to stab my knife into his heart through his back, but his hit is hard and throws me off balance. The hunting knife in my hand swings down and buries into the griffins back, but it isn't deep, not a fatal blow. He jerks back from being stabbed but recovers. Swinging his arm out he connects with my arm and makes me lose my grip on the knife. It stays embedded in his back, but now he's got me pinned against the wall. I swing my arms at him, I reach around him to get my knife, but he parries my blows and keeps me trapped between him and the wall. I hit at him, but it's no use. He anticipates my hit. He spreads his body out so it covers mine, dwarfs my attack. I do the only thing a girl could in this situation. I wrench my knee up as hard as I can and nail him in the balls. The sound that escapes him makes me think his heart has jumped into his throat and cut off his oxygen. I take his incapacitation to my advantage and kick him while he's down. Metaphorically, of course. I twist the knife in his back and then pull it out. He gasps and lets out a strangled scream. I place my foot onto his back and push him onto the floor.

I look up to see Xander and Gray have their griffin lying unconscious at their feet. They look at me, awaiting my instructions. This is my mission after all.

Gray looks unscathed, of course he could have a myriad of injuries his powers have healed already. Xander has a black eye and a busted lip. He may not heal as rapidly as Gray and I do, but by the time we get home tonight he will be healed. My arm still aches from being yanked behind my back, but the pain fades as the minutes tick by.

The griffin under me stirs and tries to rise from the floor. I use my foot to step on the cut in his back and drive him back into the carpet. He moans in pain as his blood coats the bottom of my shoe. That will definitely need to be burned, before I get in Gray's SUV. But, like Xander, and every other griffin, the one under my foot will heal quickly. The three of us need to end this. Before the griffins have time to recuperate and lead a second wave attack.

With Xander and Gray watching over the unconscious griffin I roll over my enemy and make him face me. I sit him up against the wall and jab my knife into his chest. I lean into it so it digs through his shirt and into his skin, but only slightly.

He snarls up at me and growls, "Do it." He spits in my face and laughs despite the predicament he's in. I press the knife further into his skin, breaking one layer after another.

"Kristina. You killed her. Do you remember now?"

"Please," the griffin says, turning to pleading. "I only did it on orders. You don't understand. He makes us kill you." His voice sounds sincere. He stares at me like the words he's saying could save his life.

"You disgust me," I tell him. That's what griffins are good at, lying and making others believe their lies, especially their own people. That's what led Xander to try to kill Logan. That's what led other griffins to kill countless phoenixes. I don't believe him for a second.

"Back at you, bitch," he says, realizing his lie is getting him nowhere.

I dig the knife further into his chest until I hit his rib cage. His hearts beat against his ribs, which vibrates against my knife, runs up my hand, and pulses through me. It's an eerie feeling. But it doesn't give me pause. I'm killing this griffin in front of me. And his brother.

The griffin hisses as the knife advances through his chest.

"I remember her," he says through his teeth. His voice is full of hate. I knew his pleading was a lie. "I led her to her death. I stabbed her in the chest. And I was rewarded for it. Is that what you wanted to know? I'd do it again too."

Searing hate fills my heart and spreads through every vein in my body. I hate this griffin. I hate his brother. I hate all his people and their leader.

My heart slams into my chest, begging me to plunge this knife all the way in, into his two hearts, pleading with me to end his life.

I place both my hands on the handle of the knife and

lean, hard, into it, forcing it past his rib cage and into meaty, beating flesh. His heart pulses around the knife, attacking it, trying to force it out. Blood pools around the knife and flows down the griffin's chest. The griffin stares at me, his eyes wide, as I push deeper, into his second heart. I stare right back at him, watching as his life leaves him. Inches from him I see the light leave his eyes. I feel both his hearts stop beating. Taste his last breath moving past his lips.

I don't even bother closing his eyes as I get up from his body.

Xander and Gray stare at me as I face them. Shock paints their faces but neither says a word, neither judges me, neither thinks worse of me.

The other griffin's body jerks and he wakes up. He becomes aware enough to know he's in trouble. Then he sees his brother and screams and thrashes. He tries to attack me but Xander and Gray hold him back.

"Kill him," I tell them, feeling gone from my cold body.

I walk past them as the two of them converge on the griffin. Like his brother, he pleads, then turns to insults when he knows it won't work. I search for the door that leads to the garage and enter it once I've found it. I open the car door and get in, searching for the keys. They rest in the ignition.

From where I sit in the car I can hear as my friends kill my enemy. Returning to the living room I find Xander wiping blood from his knife onto his pants. We're burning them so I don't see a point in fussing about it.

"Grab the bodies," I tell them.

Gray takes the feet of the griffin lying under them while Xander takes his head. They lift him up, without questioning me, and follow me into the garage. They lift the body into the trunk of the car then turn back for the second griffin.

Once they are both in the trunk I tell Xander and Gray my plan. They both look at me like I'm crazy, but then Gray says, "It's so crazy it may actually work."

"They are going to be so pissed," Xander says.

"That's my plan," I say.

We clean up the house as much as we can, until it looks as it did when we entered it. Gray and I go about burning our fingerprints off of anything we have or might have touched. Then Xander gets in the griffin's car and pulls out of the garage. Gray and I split off in different directions once again and head for his SUV. Once inside we follow Xander.

He leads the way to the griffins' warehouse. The same warehouse they took me to when they abducted me. The one they tortured me in. The warehouse where we are dumping the bodies. Being nearly two in the morning he didn't think any griffins would be in the warehouse. Gray and I watch from over a block away as Xander punches in a code to the garage door of the warehouse and then drives the car in, closing and locking the door behind him. Then he runs away from the warehouse to where we are parked, circles the block and jumps in the car, telling Gray to gun it as he does.

We drive home in silence, none of us sure what to say. We can't really tell each other good job. High fiving would be highly inappropriate. So we stay quiet.

When we get to my house we run through the normal routine, scrub down the car, burn the clothes and weapons. Only, as I feared, when we try to burn the knives, the combined fire of Gray and I barely takes the shine off the metal of them.

"What do we do?" Gray asks.

"We bury them," I tell him.

"Won't freshly dug soil be a bit suspicious?" he asks.

"Not where I'm burying them."

"And that would be?"

"In Colt's grave."

"You've got to be kidding me."

"Have you got a better idea?"

He has no answer for me. So the three of us find shovels in our garage, get in my car, and drive to the cemetery. We find Colt's grave, and alternately start shoveling scoops of dirt and earth until we reach his empty casket, open it, and place the knives inside. Then reverse the process, until the hole is once again filled.

When we get back to my house we have a second set of clothes to burn. Once that's done Gray returns to Logan's, leaving Xander and I to ourselves.

"I'll be back," I tell him.

"Where are you going?" Xander asks me.

"I need to do something. Do you trust me?"

"Yeah."

"I'll be back."

I walk in the direction of Logan's house. When I get

almost all the way there, I turn and walk into the cornfield next to the road. I walk through tight rows of corn, the leaves cutting my cheeks, and find the exact spot I held Kristina as she burned and disintegrated in my arms. I kneel down in the dirt, corn growing from her ashes, and am still. And when I can no longer stand it, I lie down in the dirt and wait for something to happen. Anything. I wait for Nash to come back. I wait for Tucker to come back. For Logan to regenerate. For Kristina's body to regenerate in my arms, in this spot, where she disappeared.

"Kristina?" I ask the silence. "Are you there?"

"Is anybody there?"

"I avenged you. Please come back."

"Come back," I plead into the night.

"Kristina?"

"I still need you. I don't know what I'm doing."

I lie in the dirt, amongst the corn, Kristina's ashes kissing my skin. The earth against my skin tingles, and that's my sign. That's all I need to know I'm doing the right thing. Kristina, in her own way, answered my plea.

I walk back to my house, without brushing the dirt and ashes from my skin and clothes, and see that Xander has waited for me outside of my house.

On heavy sighs we walk into my house. Once I cross the threshold of my front door I am instantly exhausted. I need a shower and my bed.

"Do you want to shower first?" I ask Xander. It's only fair since he let me shower first last time.

"Go ahead," he says.

This isn't the time for fairness arguments so I find a towel and new clothes in my room and head for the bathroom. I face myself in the mirror while the water heats up. The face that stares back at me is further from the girl I once knew than ever before. I can't believe my parents still recognize me. I can't believe Xander and Gray and the other phoenixes recognize me. My hallow face scares me. The black circles under my eyes scare me. The blank stare in my eyes scares me. Gray asked if I wanted to die. I'm not so sure I don't. But I can't. I have to see this through. And I will, without losing anyone else.

I stand in the shower, the hot water cascading over me, and wash the filth of the griffins from my skin. I wait for the shakes to settle in. I wait for the nausea to take over. I wait. And nothing happens. A smile spreads over my face. Maybe it was adrenaline last time. Feeling it necessary to leave Xander some hot water, I turn off the shower, dry off, dress, and head for my room.

I pass Xander on the way to my room and smile at him. He smiles back, and closes the bathroom door behind him.

I comb through my hair and crawl into bed. With the light off and my eyes closed, the dead eyes of the griffin stare back at me. My eyes pop open, my heart beating fast. My right hand starts to vibrate. The pulse of the griffin's two hearts pulse and beat through my hand. The veins in my hand bulge and throb. Sweat breaks out over my whole body. My head throbs to the two pulsing beats in my right arm. Every time I close my eyes, every time I blink, I see his dead eyes, I see the blood leaving his chest, I see the life leaving him.

This isn't what was supposed to happen. I am doing what is right. I am getting justice for my fallen loved ones. I'm not supposed to feel guilty. I'm not supposed to feel wrong.

Once the shower shuts off, once Xander has dried off, he enters my room. Without questioning my need for him, he knows. He senses my weakness. And he's here for me. I wish I didn't need him. I wish I was stronger. But knowing I am not, accepting I am weak, I move over in my bed and let him slide in next to me.

Xander opens his arm to me so I can crawl into his embrace. I rest my head on his chest, and listen to his hearts beat. Xander, my best friend, the enemy I didn't know I had, the ally I didn't know I needed, the friend that came back. With his other hand he takes my pulsating hand in his and presses on my pressure point. The pulsating, the beating, the throbbing, the heart attack I thought I might be having, eases to my single heartbeat. I breathe calm, deep breaths, and fall asleep to the beating of Xander's two hearts.

Five

Ashley hasn't been in school since Xander, Gray, and I killed the griffin brothers. The other three griffins still show up to classes. They are either unafraid or are unimportant. The latter seems more likely. It would seem Ashley and her father are more concerned about their well-being than that of their people. It shouldn't surprise me.

Xander hasn't told me everything he endured while he was with the griffins. Mostly because until recently it was all good. Or at least he didn't think it was bad. But he has told me some of the worst bits towards the end of his time with them. The beatings he endured. The lies they fed him. The secrets they kept from him.

So it shouldn't surprise me that Ashley and her father care more about themselves than their people. And yet there is a nagging in my subconscious that would have me feel bad for the griffins. And that makes me feel even worse. It makes me feel guilty. It makes me hate myself. It makes me feel like I'm betraying everyone I have lost.

So I put it behind me and focus on my hatred of the griffins. I focus on our next kill and ridding my life of every single one of the griffins.

In the past few weeks my obsession with taking out the griffins became so all-consuming that Gray and Xander had to hold an intervention. That is, after my parents became suspicious.

I watched them. I stalked their homes. I followed them in my car. I planned different ways to torture and kill them. I knew in which way I was going to kill each of them. I was dedicated. And a bit too addicted to the power it gave me. That's when Xander and Gray stepped in. I'm glad they did.

Recently I've spent less time on my revenge plot and more time rebuilding the bond I had with my fellow phoenixes. My relationship with Gray is thick and cemented. Everything we've been through in the past few months, everything we've done together, I'm not sure there is anything that could break or even crack our connection. Aspen and I connected instantly and powerfully. But then I was responsible for the death of her brother. That attachment bent and then broke. After Kristina's death, Anna needed space from me. After Logan's, Aspen took her cue from Anna. They were then both poisoned by the deadly words Lydia had for me. They were grasped by her hatred for me. Her jealousy. Her unwillingness to accept me as one of them. Anna and Aspen took it to heart, if only a little, it took hold and spread. I have spent the last two weeks trying to repair the damage Lydia and her toxins inflicted.

The first encounter was rocky. Lydia and I tolerated each other, but that's about as far as it went. I didn't know what to say. I could tell she didn't know what to say. We didn't know how to act around each other without yelling or attacking each other. I didn't know if she still hated me. Who am I kidding? Of course she still hates me. I'm pretty sure she always will. I wasn't sure how I felt about her abandonment after the attack. I wasn't sure I felt anything to be honest. And the more I didn't know, the harder it was to be together.

I tried again the next day. It was about the same. We were polite. We didn't know how to act around each other. I left.

I tried again. This time with Anna and Aspen. There was a lot of awkward silence. The room was filled with silence. But I had an idea. So we moved to the basement and beat the shit out of each other. We yelled at each other. We hit each other. And we got out everything that was keeping us from being friends. It's something Logan would have done. Like the time he forced me into driving my car. It was the little push we needed to get through our issues with each other. Neither Anna nor Aspen once said they blamed me for the deaths of their loved ones. It did a lot to chip away at the ten ton blame boulder sitting on my chest.

The first week was about fixing our friendship. The second week was about growing and learning and loving. We spent an hour every day working out together. We spar but there is no need to nearly kill each other like the first time. Now we work together, make each other stronger, build each other up. Working out together before we hang out gets the edge off, lessens the tension. Spending time together is easy after that. It's effortless and comfortable. It's fun like it was in the beginning. It has also done a lot to make Lydia hate me even more. The rest of the phoenixes skipped town. Lydia stayed. It was okay in the beginning because she had Aspen and Anna to hang out with. Now they hang out with me. Lydia is alone once again. And she hates me for it. This time I don't care. I don't care that she hates me. I don't care that she's trying to take my friends away from me. I don't care that she is using Xander against me. I don't care that she will never accept me. She never would have and that's finally okay with me.

The last few days Anna, Aspen, Gray, as well as Thomas and Nathan have worked out with us. We work with and around each other. Trading machines and benches. Sparing in pairs and groups. These sessions with my fellow people have helped a lot. Not only my friendship with the other phoenixes, but it has also helped me. Some color has returned to my sallow skin. My face is no longer so thin and drawn. The circles under my eyes still remain, but are far less black.

I fear my heart was broken beyond repair after Cohen's betrayal. And while my body healed, and my friendships are repairing, I'm afraid my heart will never again be whole. I will never again be what I was before Logan died, before Nash died. The new me is going to have to be enough.

Intense pain in my face brings me out of my thoughts and into Logan's basement. I guess I should probably stop calling it Logan's basement. My father bought the house for Logan to live in and watch over me. So it's technically his house. Not to mention the fact that Logan is gone and will never again be living in this house. It's about time I get used to that. But I'm not ready. I'm not sure I'll ever be ready. Aspen and I haven't talked about him. I don't want to talk about him. I don't want to put him in the past. I'm not ready to accept the fact that I will never see him again. I'm not ready for him to be gone forever.

My face stings as momentum from the hit to my face sends me sprawling to the ground.

"Oh, Casslyn. I'm so sorry," Anna says, standing over me. She thrusts her hand out to help me back to my feet.

I grasp her hand with one of mine while rubbing at my jaw with the other.

"I didn't mean to hit you," Anna says.

"It's okay," I tell her. "I wasn't paying attention."

"Yeah. What was that about?"

"Just got lost in thought, I guess."

"Are you okay?" Aspen asks from the treadmill next to the sparing mat.

"Yeah. Fine."

Neither Aspen nor Anna look terribly convinced, but they don't pester me about it.

"You want to call it quits for the day?" Anna asks.

"No. I'm fine. I'm just going to run on the treadmill for a little while."

"Sure," Aspen says, moving off the treadmill to face off with Anna on the mat.

I start up the treadmill and start walking, then jogging, cranking the treadmill up until I'm running at a clipping pace, my heart rate rising. I focus on my running, my feet slapping against the belt of the treadmill, my arms shuffling at my sides, blood pumping through my veins. Getting punched in the face by a friend is one thing. I'm not about to fall off a spinning treadmill and kiss the wall behind me. I've seen enough of those videos to know it's not too pleasant. I close my eyes but focus on running, on not falling off and bending my body in all manner of unnatural positions. I wish I had my head phones. Music puts me in a place of freedom. The songs I listen to speak to me. It's like the singers know who I am and are telling me everything is going to be okay. And I believe it. I need music to survive. Having head phones in while working out with other people isn't the most considerate thing in the world so I leave them at home. But I wish I had them now. I could use a little saving grace right now.

Since I can't listen to music, I sing to myself. There's a new song by the X Ambassadors called *Unsteady*. It is my new favorite song. It is my religion. It is saving my soul. It's a song about a breaking family and the child desperately clinging to hope and love. The theme is close to my heart. But even if I couldn't relate to a broken family, I can relate to feeling unsteady and needing a loved one to hold onto me and save me. Feeling unsteady, unstable, broken, has taken over my life. I'm no longer sure what it's like to not feel broken. So I sing to myself. I sing to myself about wavering and needing someone who loves me to hold on to me. And I think I'm singing to myself in my head, that is, until Anna and Aspen have stopped sparing. I open my eyes to see them both staring at me as the last words of the song pass my lips. Tears fall from both of their eyes while I gasp for breath. Running and singing at the same time is not the most breathing friendly.

"Casslyn, you," Anna says.

"Don't," I tell them both.

"Did Logan know you can sing?" Aspen asks.

"I don't sing," I tell her.

"Why not?" Anna asks. "If I had that voice I'd be making millions right now."

"I don't sing," I tell them. "And you do have that voice. You all sang karaoke. You all have great voices.

"Not like you."

"I don't sing," I repeat.

They both hold up their hands in surrender. Anna shakes her head and gives me a look that says you-might-be-more-difficult-than-you're-worth. Aspen watches me. I can tell she's studying me, trying to learn something about me, trying to figure me out. Good luck, Aspen.

I continue to run for a few more miles then move on to jumping rope. I jump the rope a thousand times, pushing myself until my legs are jelly. Again I notice Anna and Aspen have stopped their workout and are focused on me. It's beginning to creep me out. So I stop, hang the rope back onto the wall, and face them.

"What is it?" I ask them. It's better to just get conversations over with than to prolong the inevitable.

They both take measured steps toward me until they are right up in my face.

Aspen leans close to me, as if she doesn't want anyone to hear, and says, "We know what you and Gray and Xander are doing."

I take a deep breath in and out. And several more. If they know, that means the rest of the phoenixes have to know. Right? I mean they had to figure it out eventually. Griffins are pretty healthy creatures until facing a phoenix. Three of them dying in the span of two months is a bit unusual. They had to figure it out. But what do I do now? What is my father going to do with this information? Are Anna and Aspen going to yell at me? Are they going to try to stop me like Gray did?

Before I can say anything in response to them, Aspen says, "We want to join you. We want to hunt them down."

"We want revenge too," Anna says.

"If we have too many people, this could get out of hand," I tell them.

"Out of hand?"

"Too many?"

"You mean like they attacked us?"

"With so many of them?"

"You think they were out of hand?"

They both berate me with words and accusations.

"I'm not doing this just for me," I tell them.

"And we would?" Anna asks.

Aspen turns on me and asks, "What about the loved ones we've lost?"

"Xander and Gray and I know what we signed on to. We know what we stand to lose. We know the risks. We aren't bringing you two into it."

"We've been fighting a lot longer than you and Xander have," Anna snarls at me.

"You think we don't know the risks?" Aspen retorts.

"What would my father say? How would he feel if all of a sudden his people, whom he loves and would do anything to protect, decided to go against his wishes, against his ways, turned their backs on him?"

"Casslyn, we love your father. We would do anything for him," Aspen says. Then her face shifts from adoration to determination. "But we've lost too many people just defending ourselves. It's time we fought back."

She pauses and stares at me a moment before adding, "It's what Logan would have wanted."

"Fine," I tell her. Because who am I to turn against what Logan would have wanted, even though I'm not so sure it is what he would have wanted. "But we plan meticulously. We know what we are getting in to. And we are not going to lose any one of us. Do you understand me?"

"Cass," Anna starts.

"Do you understand me?" I demand.

"Got it," they both agree.

"Good. Now you have to get Xander and Gray to agree."

"But."

"Thems the rules girls," I tell them.

"Fine."

"Alright. Now let's go eat. I'm starving," I say and head for the stairs only to run into Lydia.

I don't even bother saying sorry. She would have some snide remark that would negate the apology anyway. So I move past her and make for the stairs.

Before I can place my foot on the bottom step Lydia says, "Looking to get more of us killed are you?"

"Leave her alone, Lydia," Aspen says from behind me.

"Why should I? So she can convince the rest of you to run head on into your deaths?"

"None of that was her fault?"

"Wasn't it?" Lydia asks. "Logan came here on orders from her father to protect her and he lost his life. We all came to this forsaken town for her and no fewer than four of our people were killed. She got her best friend killed. So explain to me how any of this isn't her fault."

"You're a bitch," Aspen tells Lydia stepping straight into her personal space.

"At least I tell it like it is. At least I'm trying to keep some of us safe."

"And I'm not. Is that what you're saying?" I ask her.

"That's exactly what I'm saying," Lydia says, crossing her arms over her chest.

By now the four of us have moved away from the stairs and further into the basement. Anger rises in my chest and gets stuck in my throat. I've never tried to be nice to Lydia because I knew I would never be treated equally. But I always left it at that. I never sought out more and I never held it against her. I'm holding it against her. I'm not perfect. I've never claimed to be perfect. But I've never given her a true reason to hate me, and still that feeling has persisted. Well now, the feeling is mutual. I hate Lydia in this moment almost as much as I hate the griffins. And that's saying something. The griffins have earned my hate. And now, after all these months of horrible treatment, I hate Lydia as much as she hates me. I'm not sure if that is what she was looking for, but it's what she's gotten.

"You know what?" I say moving swiftly, intently in her direction. Anna and Aspen step back, away from us. They aren't going to stop whatever is about to happen and they aren't about to get caught in the cross fire. "Fuck you, Lydia. You have been a bitch since the moment you met me. I'm sorry you had to come here. I'm sorry you hate it here. I'm sorry Logan chose me over you. And I'm sorry that you lost him too. But I will not let you treat me like shit any more. I don't deserve it and I'm not about to take it any longer. Do you understand me?"

I'm right in her face now, staring her down, breathing hard. She stares right back at me. "I will treat you however

I like to," Lydia says. She places her hands on my chest and shoves me. The force of her push sends me flying back several feet. My foot catches on the sparing mat sending me sprawling on the floor in a tangled mess. "Do you understand me?"

"Casslyn," Anna says, making her way over to help me up.

I get to my feet without her help and face Lydia once again. Fire burns under my skin, begging me to unleash it, to punish her. It pools in my hands and pulses in my fingertips. I pull my arms back, form a fire ball in each hand, and throw them at her. But what is released is not a fire ball. Streams of blazing fire shoot from my hands and attack the bitch standing in front of me. Endless streams. Connected bands of fire make my hands look like a flame thrower. The power feels good. The release is ecstasy.

Lydia shrieks and bats at the flames, then pats herself down, trying to extinguish the flames coating her clothes. I know the fire won't harm her. I would never intend for it to. Unless I would. So I keep the flames ignited and trained on her until she's learned a lesson. The don't-piss-off-someone-more-powerful-than-you lesson. Only then do I let the power go. Only then do I stop the flow of fire and let the flames rest under my skin.

Lydia stands before me, her clothes almost all burned off of her. Her hair and her skin remain unmarred. But the expression on her face is that of murder, but also like it's finally clicked that I'm no longer going to be taking her shit.

I continue to stare at her, willing her to say something, anything. Just so I can hit her again. But she doesn't. She just stands there.

Silence permeates the basement. I can hear footsteps from above but I don't pay them any attention. This is not over between Lydia and I. I'm not about to break the silence. I know Lydia won't. I can feel the tension radiating off of Anna and Aspen. I know they want to say something. I know they will too.

They wait another good ten seconds before they both burst at the same time.

"Holy shit," they both say in unison.

A small smirk juts out on one side of my mouth, but I'm quick to hide it from Lydia.

"How can you do that? Did you know you could do that?" Aspen asks both questions quickly.

I want to answer her. I want to tell her I had no idea. I want to comment on how fucking awesome what I just did was. But I'm not about to break the stare down I've got going with Lydia. She will be the first to break.

I can see the anger building behind her eyes. She knows what I'm doing and she wants to win as badly as I do. But then her expression changes. Something akin to a softness, but not really, spreads across her face.

"That was incredible," Lydia says, deciding to lose the battle. I mentally give her bonus points for it. "In all my years I've never seen anything like it."

"Thank you," I tell her.

"What the hell was that?" Anna shouts at me.

"I honestly don't know," I tell them all, because they are all wondering.

"You don't know? You've never done that before?" Aspen asks.

"No. I just got so angry a fireball wasn't enough, I guess.

"You're my hero," Aspen says, awe colored on her face.

"Shut up," I tell her and playfully shove her away from me.

"We have to tell your father about this," Anna says, wheels spinning behind her wide eyes. "We are totally winning this war with that kind of power."

"Guys. It was nothing. It was probably a onetime thing. There's a possibility I won't even be able to do it again."

"Try it again," Anna says, bouncing on the ball of her feet.

"No," I say, taking a step away from them. "I'm not a lab rat."

"We have to know," Aspen says. "This could be a game changer. This could be what wins this war, Casslyn. You are the one getting revenge for Tucker and Logan and everyone else you've lost. What if this is the weapon that could have saved them? What if this could save someone else in the future? Don't you want to know?"

Lydia watches me, waiting for my reaction. Her jaw twitches. She wants to say something. But after what went down, I know she won't. I'm thankful. I might end up burning the house down if she did.

"Don't put that on me," I tell Aspen and Anna. "I thought we decided this wasn't my fault? Up until recently I couldn't even use my powers properly. I couldn't even heal myself until two months ago. You can't expect me to win this war single handedly, as much as I want to. I'll try it again. I'll be a fucking flame thrower if you want me to be. But if I can't. If I can't make that happen again, you are going to have to accept it."

They both look dejected. Disappointed even. But there is nothing I can do about it. I don't believe in myself half the time. Having others putting all their beliefs in me is too much. It would devastate me to let them down. More than I have already. And so soon after getting them back in my life.

"Can we please go eat?" I ask, the tone of my voice somber. "I'm still starving."

"Yeah, let's go," Aspen says, trying to sound more upbeat than she is. It only works so well. The effort is what counts.

"Have fun," Lydia says from the bottom of the stairs. Somehow I missed her shuffling away from us.

It occurs to me then she may not like me because most everyone else does. Gray, Anna, Kristina, Aspen, and even Lydia's brother Nathan became friends with me soon after they arrived. Perhaps it's hard for Lydia to make friends and that's part of the reason she hates me. I can easily see why it would be hard for her to make friends. But maybe there is something I'm missing. Maybe she's shy. Maybe she doesn't know how to be nice. Maybe something holds her back from being the person that easily makes friends. I haven't spent that much time with her, and the time I've spent with her has not been pleasant, but I don't know her life. Maybe I've judged too harshly too soon. And that could be my fault. But it's also hers.

She will never like me. And that is okay. But we seem to have some sort of acceptance, or rather, truce. And that's all I could ask for.

"Let's go eat," Anna says.

"Would you like to join us?" I ask Lydia, using every ounce of kindness I have stored up.

She considers it. She looks between us girls and truly considers it. I can see when she makes her mind up. I can see that it is too soon. Maybe it will always be too soon. "No, thank you," she answers.

I tried. In her way she tried too. And that's all I can ask for. So Lydia goes upstairs for new, unburnt clothes for her workout, while Anna, Aspen, and I head out the front door. It is not soon enough. My stomach rumbles from hunger. Xander and Gray, who have agreed to join us, are already waiting in Gray's SUV.

"What took you guys so long?" Xander asks. "I'm starving."

"You are never going to believe what happened," Anna says, nearly bouncing in her seat.

"Did you have an eye liner debacle?" Gray asks, sarcasm in his tone.

"Says the one who wears more of it than we do," I shoot

back at him.

"Touché," he says.

Aspen claps her hands together and excitedly says, "Casslyn can shoot fire from her hands like a flame thrower."

Xander and Gray turn in their seats to stare at me, their eyes giant saucers in their heads.

"Can we talk about it when I've got some food in my stomach? Please?" I ask the other four occupants in the car.

They all grumble their agreement and Gray heads for the road.

I'm not even sure how I feel about my new power. Or my advance in power. I know I want to talk to Logan about it. But that isn't an option. My options are talking about it with my friends, the people who care about me, the people I hunt down our enemies with. Or I could talk about it with my father. Really I could talk about it with all of them. The ones in the car with me are excited and want to see what I can do with my new power. I'm hoping my father will have advice for me. I hope he can assure me I'm really not as different from the other phoenixes as I seem to be. The fire balls were one thing. When that happened every one of the phoenixes was surprised, in awe, said no other phoenix could do that. But flame throwing puts me on a whole new level. I don't want to be any more different from the other phoenixes. I want to be one of them, a part of the whole. I don't want to stand out from them. And I certainly don't want to be put on an island all by myself. I honestly hope I'm unable to throw flames the next time they want me to. It would be almost a relief.

When we get back to Logan's, Xander and I head back to my house. It's a little after six so I'm surprised to see my mom's car in the driveway. I'm even more surprised to see my dad's truck beside it. I'd really rather not walk into them going at it on the couch, or anywhere in the house for that matter, so I'm warry to go inside. I shut off my expanded hearing and turn to Xander to see what he thinks. I can tell he's listening in.

"It's clear," he tells me and takes a step towards the house.

I follow his lead and step onto the porch. I open up my hearing to anything strange that could be going on, but the house is silent. Maybe they're both asleep.

Xander follows me in as I open the door and step into my house. I head for the kitchen and a bottle of water when I hear my mom clear her throat. It startles me so badly I scream and jump off the ground. Clutching my chest, my heart hammering away, I turn to see my parents seated on the couch.

This cannot be good.

"Are you trying to kill me?" I ask, then turn to see Xander in as warried a stance as me.

Ignoring my comment and my distress my mom looks at my dad, then looks back at me. "We need to talk to you, Casslyn," she says, her eyebrows low over her eyes.

"Are you pregnant?" I ask in all seriousness. It's the only thing that pops into my mind.

"This isn't about us," my dad says.

This really can't be good.

"Okay," I say, still standing in the kitchen.

I look to Xander and to the door. If we both stay close enough to it, we can make a quick getaway. I never thought I'd need a getaway from my parents, but desperate times.

"Would you come sit down?" my mom asks.

So much for staying close to the door.

Xander moves with me into the living room. I turn my gaze on him, silently thanking him. His return look is one that says we're-in-this-together.

"Xander, we'd like to talk to our daughter," my dad tells him.

Xander looks at him like, duh.

But my dad says, "Alone."

"He's not leaving," I tell them.

"This is a delicate issue, Casslyn," my mom says.

"I assure you, he can handle it," I say to her.

"We're not exactly sure how to bring this up, sweetheart," my dad states.

My mom jumps in and says, "We just want the truth."

"What are you guys talking about?" I ask, suddenly nervous.

My parents look at each other and back at me. They've planned this, they've rehearsed it, and still it's not going as well as they'd like. I can't wait until we get to the end of their script. It should be a good time for all of us.

"I found burned clothes in the barrel," my mom says.

Oh no. I try my damnedest not to turn to Xander, it would give us away. But my head, my neck, my eyes itch to look at him, to see just how screwed we are.

What do I do? How do I lie myself out of this one? Think, Casslyn, think.

Burned clothes, how do I explain that?

"They were ripped. Some had stains on them. I just didn't want them anymore. And I didn't want to bother you with it. So I burned them myself," I say on a sigh. That was good. That was better than I could have expected.

"Honey, I've heard you crying out in your sleep. I've seen the blood on the bathroom floor. What is going on with you? Are you hurting yourself?" my mom asks, tears leaking from her eyes. I can hear the sob building in her throat.

"No, mom. I'm not hurting myself."

"Are you being honest? We can get you some help. It's nothing to be ashamed of," my mom says, clearly trying to hold it together. They really have practiced this.

"I'm telling you the truth."

"Then what is going on with you?" My dad asks. "You haven't been yourself lately. We know you're hiding something from us."

"Oh do you?" I ask, directing the questioning at him. "You know I'm keeping something from you? Based on what? All the time you've spent with me lately?"

"Don't you turn this on me. We are here about you. If you have a problem with me we can discuss it at a later time, but right now, we are trying to figure out what is going on with you."

"What is it, Cass? Are you in trouble? Are you into drugs? Did you do something you can't tell us?" my mom asks, guessing anything troublesome. She is way off the mark. She couldn't even hit the mark is she had a machine gun and started shooting in circles.

"No. It's not any of that," I tell them.

But shit. I've outed myself.

"But it is something?" my dad asks.

"You don't want to know," I tell him, turning the depth of my gaze on him. I always got away with everything with this when I was younger. I can tell it's working now. "I'm not sure you could handle it. Mom won't handle it well."

"Nothing could turn us away from you. Don't you know that? Whatever you've done, if you've done something, we can get past it. We will find a way to deal with it."

"I'm not sure you can," I say. Tucker took the news exceptionally well. But Tucker is my best friend, Tucker knew something was going on. And Tucker was exceptional. My parents are a different story. They have never encountered anything like this.

After I learned about being a phoenix. After I'd met my father and learned of his affair with my mom, I wondered if he'd ever told her about being the creature that he is. I wondered if he'd ever showed her his powers. But he told me he never did. He knew she loved him, but he knew she was also torn between him and my dad. My father was afraid showing her his powers would drive her right into the hands of my dad. She ended up in his arms regardless, but it was my father's decision. He's lived seventeen years wondering what could have been, wondering if she would have accepted him for who he really was, wondering if she could have loved him as he is.

This time I do turn to Xander. This is part of his secret. I won't out him. I would never do that. But he and I both know, bringing Tucker into this world got him killed. My parents are safer not knowing what I am. They are safer being kept as far away from me as possible. I jabbed at my dad for not spending much time with me, but right now that's safer for him. People close to me end up dead. And that's not an option for my parents. I won't lose them.

But at the same time, keeping such a monumental secret from them is increasingly difficult. Not to mention the fact that I feel like my parents don't even know who I am. I have my father, who knows I'm a phoenix, merely because he is too. But my parents raised me, they love me, they know me, the me before Nash died. I'd like them to know the me now. Tucker knowing my secret was freeing. When I told him about me being a phoenix and he accepted me, with open arms, it was like feeling alive again. It made me feel whole again. There was nothing left unsaid between us. I want that with my parents. I'm prepared this time. I can keep them safe. I could tell them.

Xander shrugs his shoulders, leaving the decision entirely up to me. I'm not sure how I'm going to keep his secret out of it if I do tell my parents. They will wonder if he knows. They will know he knows if I light up right in front of him. They will wonder if he is like me. They will flip if they find out he was supposed to kill me and Logan. I surmise they will have a lot of questions. They will be shocked. They might even try to stop me, maybe keep me locked up in the house. What if they try to stop me? I can't let that happen.

I'm not sure I can tell them. But the more I think about it, the more I want to tell them. It feels right. I need them to know. I can't keep this secret from them any longer.

"I'll tell you," I tell them. "But it's not in the realm of things you can comprehend. I need you to promise me you'll still love me."

"Casslyn, you know your mom and I will love you no matter what," my dad says, scooting further to the edge of the couch.

"I need you to promise me," I say, feeling strong emotions filling my chest. I didn't expect this. I haven't felt much of anything since Tucker and Logan died. I'd begun to think I'd never feel again. And yet I feel too much. Need for acceptance. Yearning for love. Wanting them safe beyond all else. Freedom, release, anxiety. It all bubbles up. Every emotion knocks against another, forces the other aside, fights for power over the others. It's overwhelming, and more than I can deal with right now. So I clamp a lid over it all and face my parents head on.

Xander runs his hands over the tops of his knees, over and over. I can smell the sweat coating his palms and rubbing off onto his jeans. He swallows hard, his Adam's apple bobbing up and down. His heart ticks quickly in his chest. He's as nervous as I am. He too has as much to lose right now as I do. I try not to think about it too much. If my parents don't accept me as I am, if they can't find it in their hearts to love me, if they kick me out, I know I'll have a place at Logan's. But this house has slowly become my home. I'm not ready to leave it.

"I love you, honey. I will always love you. There is nothing that will change that. I promise you."

I stand up from the couch next to Xander. My mom won't like me very much if I light her couch on fire. I walk several steps away from them and from anything flammable. I haven't yet decided if I'm going to light my whole body of fire or just form a fire ball in my hand. I don't necessarily want to lose another set of clothes, and when it's all said and done I don't want to be naked in front of my parents.

I take a deep breath, pull strength from my center, and let my hands burst into flames.

Chaos erupts. My mom screams. My dad jumps up from the couch. And Xander, in true best friend fashion, laughs at it all.

My dad frantically searches around him, his eyes landing on a blanket. With the blanket in hand he rushes for me.

"Dad, wait," I say, holding up my hands in front of me and extinguishing the flames coating my palms.

My dad's eyes widen. Xander has to catch him when his body goes still and teeters. Xander places him on the couch next to my hysterical mom.

"Mom, Dad, I need you to stay calm," I tell them.

My mom stares at me, her eyes dancing with the flames that engulfed my hands. She says, "What was that?"

"What are you?" my dad asks. He asks it in a way that doesn't have me running from the room, my hands covering my face as I sob. He isn't curious, but he isn't disgusted. It's more awe or wonder. I can deal with wonder. It's disgust I can't.

It takes me several moments to answer. It's not that the sentence is hard. It's three words. But getting them to understand. Hoping they will accept me. That's hard. Finally I answer, "I'm a phoenix."

Neither of my parents immediately reacts. I honestly think they are both in shock. The dazed look on my mom's face shows she's still seeing her daughter's hands spontaneously light on fire. I mean, that's got to be a shock. I was in shock when I saw Logan's thumb light on fire for the first time.

Like usual, my dad is the first to gather himself. "You're a phoenix," he says. "What does that mean? Are you in a gang?"

"I'm not in a gang, Dad. It's not like that."

I side eye Xander and see him smiling. The notion of me in a gang is really laughable. The griffins I would consider a gang, they're crazy, they are strict, they won't let anyone out without trying to kill them. But the phoenixes are about as far away from a gang as you could get. They are like a preschool group compared to the griffins as far as gangs go. But I can't laugh about that right now, not while my parents are reeling from what I just revealed to them.

"Then what is it like, Casslyn, because I am freaking out right now," he says.

"Do you know what a phoenix is?"

There is silence for several heart beats. They are thinking. Shock dulls their brains, makes it hard for them to think. I give them the time, needing them to come to some conclusion on their own. Finally some recognition hits home.

"Like the bird in Harry Potter?" my mom asks.

I have to do a double take. I thought my mom hated Harry Potter. My mom dislikes anything that isn't as close to real life as you can get. This is part of the reason revealing myself to her is so difficult.

"Yeah, mom, like the bird in Harry Potter."

But seriously, is there no other phoenixes to make the connection to?

"So you're a bird?" my dad asks.

"No. I'm not a bird. But I'm descended from that bird."

"I have a headache," my mom says.

"I'm sorry, mom," I tell her, sudden remorse filling me. I knew this would be a shock to them, but I didn't know how hard it would be. Learning the supernatural is real isn't easy. It takes everything you've ever believed in and turns it on its head. This has got to be killing my mom.

"Oh, honey. I just . . . ," she stops because she's not sure what to say. I'm not sure how to comfort her. I'm not sure what to say to her.

"So what are you?" my dad asks again.

"I'm a phoenix. Centuries ago the phoenix, the bird, shed its bird form and became human. I have all the powers of the phoenix, fire, regeneration, healing tears, I'm just in a human body."

"How did you become a phoenix? Did you choose this?" my dad asks.

My mom's eyes widen with realization. She looks up at me. There is an apology in her expression. "Your father," is all she says.

I nod, not needing to say any more to her.

That's not enough for my dad.

"What do you mean, 'your father'?" he asks.

"My biological father is a phoenix. The phoenix is a patriarchal race. My father is a phoenix. Nash and I got the gene."

"Oh my God," my mom says, her whole body sagging in on itself. "Nash."

I forgot they would figure that out. But there is more they are still figuring out. My mom, though with no previous information, seems to be catching on faster than my dad.

"How did we not know you kids had fire under your skin?" my dad asks.

"We don't mature until we are seventeen. I've only had my powers for six months," I tell him, but inform them both.

"And Logan?" my mom asks.

"He's a phoenix. He was sent here by my father to protect me."

"And where is he now?" my dad asks.

"It's a long story. Which I will get to. But not right now."

"And you, Xander?" my mom asks.

Xander lets out a strangled laugh and says, "That's an even longer story."

"And Tucker?"

"Another time, mom."

"Does this have anything to do with why you are living in my house, Xander?" my mom directs her question at Xander.

"Yes," he says, without elaborating.

She doesn't ask for more. I think she is taking in the information she needs. I think she is getting what she can but retaining what she needs.

"You said Logan was here to protect you," my dad says, swinging back to that bit of information. "Are you in some kind of danger?"

"I am," I say. I'm not sure at this point what to tell them. I don't want to info dump on them. It would be too much at one time. Plus we would be here all night. Not to mention the fact that they probably would lock me up in my room and throw away the key. Also there are some things I can't tell them. I feel like they should both have a chat with my father.

"And Logan isn't here to protect you?"

"My father is here. Plus about five other highly trained phoenixes."

"So all the new kids who moved in next door?" my

mom asks.

"Yup," I say.

"I'm going to need a drink," my dad says.

"Do you still love me?" I ask them.

"Of course we do," my mom answers for them both. "Why would you think we wouldn't?"

"Did you miss the fire that came out of my skin? Because I can do that with my whole body," I say, using my hands to motion all over my body.

"We certainly did not miss it," my dad says.

"It's just going to take some time to get used to the idea of you . . . ," my mom says.

"Being a freak," I say, filling in the blank for her.

"Do not say that about yourself," my mom reprimands.

"Sorry," I say.

"Casslyn?" my mom says. "I need to ask you something."

"Shoot," I tell her.

"How did Nash die?"

I swallow hard. I knew she would get there eventually. I wasn't ready for it. I'm not ready for it. But she needs to know. "The people who are after me. They killed Nash."

My mom's chest rises heavily. I hear her lungs pump an extra time. I hear her heart pump harder. I hear the cry in her throat. I see her trying to hold it together. But then she and my dad reach for each other and begin to collectively sob. It's hard to watch. So hard my chin starts to quiver until tears form in my eyes and spill over.

"And you've lived with that knowledge?" she asks, tears streaming down her cheeks.

"It's not like I could tell you," I say to her. She has to know it was for her own protection. I was trying to keep her safe. And my dad.

"Oh, honey," she says for about the fourth time. I'm not sure what to do with her. Emotions have flooded my system, but I'm not ready to break down yet. I'm not ready to face my pain. I'm not ready for it to destroy me. So I can't comfort her in the way she needs me to. I let my dad do it.

They collapse into each other. They both sob into each other, their sorrow and tears mixing together. It hurts to watch them. I have to look away. It's when I do that I notice Xander has disappeared. It's probably for the better. I have always considered Xander to be part of my family, but right now I think it just needs to be my parents and I. Xander realized that and is giving us that space, that time together. When you've been as close for as long as Xander and I have you get to a point where you can read the other so easily it's almost as though we can read each other's minds. Almost. There are still a few mysteries about each other we are both still unsure of.

I feel awkward watching my parents mourn with each other, but I'm not sure what to do with myself. Going to the kitchen for food would appear too insensitive, not to mention the fact I just got back from eating. Sitting on the couch and watching them would seem creepy. Going to my room would be leaving my parents up to their own imaginations about Xander, myself, and my people. I don't feel comfortable sitting here with them at this moment, but I also can't leave them alone.

After several minutes of sobbing, cajoling, hand holding, back rubbing, and murmurings, my parents pull themselves together and face me. They both open their mouths as if to say something to me, but close them back up when words fail them. They will find them in time. So I wait.

I stare at my hands while I wait for my parents to find the words to confront me. I'm sure that's what they're going to do, not because they are angry with me, but because they are overwhelmed. And that's what my parents do when they are overwhelmed, they over react. As I stare at my hands I think about the fire underneath my skin. I think about how I pull it from my body. I think about how it feels when the flames pass through my skin and dance atop it. I snap my thumb and forefinger together and flames ignite on top of my thumb. The thrill that runs through my body as my flames come to me at will, as they answer my command, is powerful. The knowledge that I am powerful and can inflict untold damage has me thirsting for more.

I snap my fingers together once more and the flames go out. Just like that. It reminds me of Chris Evans' character in The Fantastic Four. That's probably where I got the idea. Like me, he can light his whole body on fire and do some damage. But unlike me, and here's where I'm more than slightly jealous, he can fly. What I wouldn't give to be able to fly.

I continue to snap my fingers. Flame on. Flame off. A small smile plays on my face. When I realize I've been at it for minutes, my parents silent in the same room as me, I look up to see them staring at me. There is fear etched on their faces. Fear, and yet awe. I was worried they would fear me. I was worried they could never find it in themselves to love me. Not when I'm no longer the daughter they raised. Not when flames burst from under my skin. But the fear on their faces is not fear of me, it is fear for me. The awe in their eyes is enough to show me they accept me and can still find it in their hearts to love me.

"I still have a lot of questions," my dad says.

"I'll try to answer them to the best of my knowledge," I tell him.

"How did you find out about . . . this whole . . . you being a . . . ," my dad pauses, not sure he can say the word.

"In a roundabout way, Xander stabbed me in the chest and I didn't die," I say.

"He did what?" my mother shrieks.

"Way to out me, asshole," Xander says from his room upstairs. It's not loud enough for my parents to hear, but I can, and I can't help but smile.

"It's a long story, mom. But I promise we are on good terms now."

"Had I known he stabbed you, he would not be living here, let alone breathing," my mom says.

"Thanks mom. But it was all just a misunderstanding."

I can tell she would like to say something about that too,

but I raise my eyebrow at her and she remains silent.

"Okay, so," my dad says, trying to puzzle something out. "When you were in the hospital after the accident and the blood transfusions weren't taking. And your mom had to call your father in to donate blood. This is why, isn't it? Because you're a phoenix. And your father is a phoenix."

"Right," I say.

"He saved your life," he says.

"Technically," I say, "I saved my own life. Even before my powers came in, I healed myself. That's why I didn't have any cuts or anything. But without my father's blood, yes I probably wouldn't have lasted long."

"You kids were never sick," my mom says. "Not even a cold. It's because of your magic, isn't it?"

"I wouldn't necessarily call it magic. But yes."

"Why didn't you tell us?" my dad asks. There is sorrow and so much hurt in his eyes. Like I've somehow betrayed him. I get it. I kept a huge secret from them. I purposely put distance between us by not telling them. But I did it to keep them safe. I also did it because humans aren't supposed to know about us. Sure Tucker took it well. Sure my parents are taking this far better than I anticipated. But if the whole world knew there were super humans living among them, people who could light not only themselves on fire but others around them, I can't say that it would go well. In fact, I know it wouldn't go well. When I learned Logan was a phoenix I freaked out. I freaked out on him and threw him out of my house. And I loved him. I can't imagine how people, perfect strangers would react to knowing there are beings out in the world who could easily destroy them.

I mean honestly, I am aware there are phoenixes and griffins in the world. But if you told me that vampires, werewolves, dragons, unicorns, or fairies were real, I wouldn't believe you. And if I happened to come across one of them in my day to day life, I would freak out. The supernatural is there to be aware of, to give us an escape from reality, to make children desperately want to go to Hogwarts. But it is not supposed to be real. But there is that saying that all fiction is based on some sort of reality. So who knows? Maybe there is a vampire running around Cedars I'm unaware of. Maybe the howling in my backyard I thought was coyotes is really a werewolf. I'm not ready to find out.

"I couldn't, Dad. There were too many reasons why I couldn't tell you. I still shouldn't be telling you. Your protection being one of them."

"Casslyn," my mom says, "We are your parents. We should be the ones protecting you."

"But you can't, mom," I tell her. "Not from this."

"Who is trying to hurt you?" my dad asks.

I answer quickly, stamping down his need to be my hero. "I can't tell you, dad. Just know that I am taking care of it."

"Oh, that worries me," my mom says, shaking her head from side to side.

"I'm being careful," I tell them. "I promise."

My parents sit on the couch in a moment's silence, gathering themselves. This can't be easy for them. I'm trying to ease them into it. But they are asking a lot of questions. They want to know the hard stuff.

"Are you guys okay?" I ask them. "You're not going to pass out on me are you?"

"The jury is still out on that," my dad answers.

"Are you okay?" my mom asks me.

"I'm . . .," I begin to tell her that yes I am okay. I should be convincing her that I'm okay. I'm not sure it would ease her worrying, but it would at least reassure her that I don't need to see a therapist. But I've been lying to them for a long time now. If I'm going to be honest with them about being a phoenix, I should at least be honest with them about my feelings, my state of mind, my broken heart. "No. I'm not okay."

I swear my mom is going to say 'oh, honey' again, but she bites her tongue. Instead of saying anything, instead of using words, she leaves my dad's side, walks the few steps from the love seat where they sit, and sits down next to me, folding me into her arms, and hugging me tight. I breathe deeply out my mouth. Tears sting my eyes threatening to spill over. I can't break down right now. I'm not strong enough to hold myself together. I need to keep myself in check. If I break down right now, in front of my parents, after I've told them everything, they might admit me into a mental hospital. I can't have that. I've got griffins to kill. And a best friend's birthday to celebrate. So I pull away from my mom and smile at her in the most assuring way I can.

"I hate to cut this short, as I'm sure you guys have many more questions, but it's Xander's birthday, and Gray is going to be here soon to celebrate with us."

"Oh," my mom says, almost sounding dejected.

"I'm sorry," I tell her.

"We are not done with this conversation, young lady," my dad says.

"I understand."

"I took the night off," my mom says. "We weren't sure how this talk was going to go. I can't say I anticipated how it went, but you aren't in a gang, and you aren't in any immediate danger, as far as I can tell. As long as you are okay, your dad and I might go out to eat. Is that okay? Or would you like us to stay home with you?"

"No, go out. Have a good time. I will be fine," I tell her, waving my hand to indicate all is well.

Xander walks down the stairs to greet us, having heard the whole conversation, he knows it's about over.

"We're just going to stay here, make some grilled cheese, and watch movies," Xander says, walking towards me. "Who knows, I may even make them play video games. It is my birthday after all."

My mom glares at Xander. I forgot I told her he stabbed me. I can imagine the tension will be strongly felt between my mom and Xander for at least the next several weeks, but she hasn't come at him with a butchering knife yet so I feel like he is safe. He smiles at her weakly, he too realizing she's mad at him for stabbing me.

But after she's gathered her purse and keys from the counter, she walks towards him. He stills in his spot, not sure whether to run or fight. When my mom gets to him, she kisses him on the cheek, and says, “Happy birthday, Xander. Your cake is on the counter.”

Xander’s eyebrows knit together with clear emotion, a smile spreads his mouth. “Thank you,” he says.

“Hurt her again and I’m coming after you,” she says, lightly slapping him on the cheek.

“Understood,” he says, nodding.

My dad comes up to me before he and my mom leave the house. He surprises me by pulling me in for a strong hug. And I mean strong. He nearly suffocates me. When he pulls back he kisses me on the forehead and says, “I love you, kid. Don’t you ever forget that.”

“Got it, Dad,” I say, a lump forming in my throat.

It’s only minutes after they leave that Gray shows up in my living room, not even bothering to knock on the front door. Xander and I are in the kitchen frying up some grilled cheese and bacon sandwiches. My mouth waters when the scent of melted cheese and bacon hits my nose. There is something special about buttery, crispy bread, melted cheese, and bacon that makes the perfect combination. When I was little I could have lived off grilled cheese. Then one day my mom decided to add ham to the mix and I was in love. But one day while watching *Diners, Drive-Ins, and Dives* a sandwich shop was making grilled cheese with bacon. I found my new addiction that day. I haven’t turned back since.

Xander plates them up while I grab chips from the cupboard. Gray helps Xander with the plates, grabbing the bags of chips as he goes. I grab pop and bottles of water from the fridge and meet them in the living room. Gray and I asked Xander what he wanted to do for his birthday. I thought maybe he'd want to go out to eat, or to a movie, maybe go bowling. But all he wanted to do was spend the night in, watching movies. It was an easy enough request to fulfill.

Xander puts the third X-Men movie into the DVD player and starts it up. Again, the two guys sit on each side of the couch while I sit in between them on the floor. I feel protected. Like nothing can get to me.

When we get to the part early on in the movie where Angel is trying to cut his wings off so his dad doesn't find out he's a mutant Xander pauses the movie. I turn to him, curious as to why he would pause it, only to find him deep in thought.

"What's that look for?" I ask him.

"I've been thinking about something," he says.

"Oh, no," I joke.

"No I'm serious," Xander says.

"What is it?" Gray asks, more to get Xander to get to his point.

Xander sits up on the couch and sets his plate next to him, readying himself for full Xander conversation mode. Gathering that he really has something to say, I turn fully around to face him head on.

"Okay," he says. "So I've been thinking about this. We're both in some way descended from birds, right?"

"Yes," I say, wondering where he's going with this.

"So. . . ," he says, trying to pique our interest. "Where are our wings? Birds have wings. I want some damn wings."

"You know," I say, "I was thinking earlier that I really want to fly. So I get the wings thing."

"Trust me," Gray says. "As long as I've been around, I have on more than one occasion wished I had wings. Can you imagine us with wings? Like, they would have to be giant. Just to hold us up or for us to fly. Like, they would have to be able to support our body weight."

"And we'd have to have special muscles in our backs, wouldn't we?" Xander asks.

"Can you imagine how shredded our abs would have to be having wings in our backs?"

"And would they have feathers? Phoenixes have feathers. And eagles," Gray says.

We continue to talk about our nonexistent wings. Whether we would be able to properly rotate our arms if the wings came out behind our shoulder blades. Or would they come out behind our shoulder blades? Would they have bones in them like bats? Or no bones like ducks? Would they fold into our backs? Or stick out all the time? How would we sleep with wings? Would we be able to wrap ourselves in our wings? Would we be able to retract them into our backs? Or would they just be visible to the public at all times? Would the phoenixes and griffins have the same wings? What color would they be? How fast could we fly?

Clearly we've all had time to think about this. Clearly we all wish we had wings. Clearly that was an evolutionary flaw.

Once we've finished our extensive wing conversation, Xander resumes the movie. We don't talk much more after that, but it is nice to just sit together and not have to worry for the time being. There is an unspoken wish for Tucker to be with us. I feel like he is with us in spirit. I know he would love that we are all together and having a good time. But I know he's not selfless enough to not wish he was here with us, his best friends and the love of his life. He was taken away from us far too soon. Something none of us will soon forget.

When we've finished the movie and the movie after that, and had ice cream and cake, Gray heads back to Logan's house. Xander and I take turns showering for school tomorrow. Neither of us likes to wake up early in the morning to shower. Once we've finished, I wish Xander a happy birthday and head to my room.

"Cass," Xander says from the doorway of his room.

I turn back to him to see an odd look on his face. I can't quite place it. He's not sad, or hurt. It almost looks like longing, or loneliness.

"Yeah?" I ask him.

"Would you spend the night with me?" he asks.

For a moment I'm taken back to the night he told me he was in love with me. It makes me wonder in what way he would like me to spend the night with him. But then I remember that he did discover that he was not truly in love with me. Then he fell in love with a fellow griffin named

Greer. That didn't work out. So again, I wonder if he is lonely. I know I am. Maybe he just needs someone beside him. Like the nights I need him beside me.

So, without asking him in what way he wants me in his bed, I agree to it. Loneliness can drive you to do crazy things. Like fall in love with your enemy.

Without a word I follow him into his bedroom. Most nights we spend in my room. But this is his birthday, not to mention the fact that he does live here now. He should get to spend his birthday in his room. He waits for me to curl up under the sheets and shuts the lights off then joins me under the covers.

The joined heat of our bodies soon warms the entire room. We both lie on our sides facing each other. With enhanced eyesight we can both see each other, even in the dark. Neither of us speaks. We stare at each other. Memorizing the other's face. As dangerous as our lives have become, any day could be the last we see each other on this earth. At seventeen years old we are the remaining two of a group of four. Cutting our group in half at such a young age is scary. Xander and I need to spend every second we have appreciating each other, loving the other as much as we can. As Nash and Tucker can attest, we may not get a tomorrow.

"Cass?" Xander whispers to me.

"Yeah?"

His voice shakes as he asks, "Can I have a birthday kiss?"

Instead of answering him with words I lean into him and

plant my lips on his. He places his hand on the back of my head and pulls me into him, kissing me back like I am the air he needs to breathe. He doesn't indicate he wants me to open up to him, he doesn't deepen the kiss. There is nothing romantic about it. This kiss is pure need. Need of physical contact. Need for companionship. Need to know he is still alive. That there is something to keep fighting for. I fill that need, and take what I can get in return.

We break the kiss, I curl into the crook of his arm, and together we fall asleep, content for the moment.

Six

Another month has passed. As smoothly as the night I told my parents I'm a phoenix went, I can't say the same has gone for the past few weeks. Sometimes my mom is my best friend, wants to take me shopping, spend time with me. Sometimes all she wants to do is ask me questions about the griffins and the phoenixes. She and my dad broke Xander down and made him tell them about his race. They didn't have to wear him down too much. My mom threatened to throw him out and he came quietly. They both had even more questions after that. Sometimes my mom asks me questions I don't have answers for, either because I can't answer them, or because I don't know the answer. And there are times my mom can't even look at me. Whether that be because she is afraid of me, afraid for me, or grieving the loss of Nash and

Tucker. We had to tell her what happened to Tucker. She figured at least half of it out. What with all the holes in the house the night he died. And the scorch marks all over everything. There were some details we had to fill in, but I was impressed with how much she put together.

Now that they know the truth, the whole truth, about me, Nash, our father, all of it, my parents have found a way to get past everything that was hanging them up from completely getting back together. I'm not entirely sure how it's going to work with them each owning a house, but I'm sure they will figure it out. Half the time my dad sleeps over at my mom's and the other half, reversed. When we first moved here, I hated it. I hated everything about it. Living so far away from town, from my friends, from school. Having no one close to me. Living close to the creepy haunted house next door. I hated not living with my dad. But now that I've been here for as long as I have, now that I've had Logan as a neighbor, now that I have my people as my neighbors, I can't imagine living anywhere else. Plus, when we first moved out here, all I wanted was to be close to Nash's room. I wanted to go in it, I wanted to feel him, even if it was just from his clothes. Now, I'm not even sure I'd like to step foot in his bedroom. I don't think either of my parents have gone in there. At least if they have, they haven't told me.

While my mom plays three different people with me, my dad is a different story. It took him a little longer than my mom to come to terms with what I am, but he did. And now, it's like nothing has changed. My dad treats me like he did before everything happened, like before Nash died. When he made this decision, he told me it was because I am still the same person, still the daughter he has always loved. He doesn't ask me questions about being a phoenix or fighting the griffins, although I'm sure he gets enough information from my mom. He doesn't look at me differently. He doesn't appear to be frightened when he pulls me in for a hug. I went so long after the accident craving his love. And now I've got it back. I've got both my parents back in my life, nearly stronger than ever. Plus I've got my father. I've got three loving parents, for the price of a brother. I'm not sure that balances out, but it's what I've got. Since there is no trading, I'll live with what is handed to me.

My lot in life isn't the best. It certainly isn't what a girl would ask for. I would never ask for it. But it's what I'm living with, and I have the griffins to thank for that. The griffins I've got a list of and am working to cross names off.

Another month has passed, another griffin was killed. Gray, Xander, and I with the help of Anna and Aspen dispatched her easily. Stupidly, the girl was holed up in her house, just waiting for us to come for her. When you've barricaded yourself into your house, it's difficult to get out when a gas leak slowly kills you. I wondered if we would think of enough of a number of different ways to kill the griffins. It is becoming far easier than I would have thought.

Falling asleep that night went more smoothly than I would have anticipated. Playing a smaller, less active part in the death of this griffin had a smaller effect on me than the previous griffins. I was thankful. It wasn't only the night after we killed the griffins I struggled to fall asleep. But nights and nights after. My hands shook, my head hurt, my heart throbbed, my body rocked with uncontrolled shakes. I looked like a zombie for days after each killing.

Killing the griffins does a lot to ease my anger. It helps me feel like I truly am getting justice for my people, revenge for my loved ones. But the griffins, while playing a large role in the deaths of those loved ones, are not the ones I truly want to destroy. The griffins we've gone after are not Raphe, not Ashley, not Cohen. They are the ones I want gone from this town, from this world forever. I will not feel accomplished, I will not feel satisfied until I've killed them. And I will kill them.

I'm going to start with Cohen.

I'm so angry with him for betraying me. I'm so angry with myself for trusting him. I've spent the past few months thinking back on the months I spent with Cohen, trying to figure out where I went wrong. Trying to figure out how he could have so easily duped me. And it wasn't only me. Xander had no idea Cohen would betray me. Logan would have done more to keep me away from Cohen had he thought Cohen would betray me. Cohen had Tucker fooled. And that's not easy, especially when it comes to being in the lives of those closest to him. So how did he have us all convinced of his innocence?

I cannot figure it out. I was warry of him on the night I met him. I should have remained that way. And yet he was able to pull me into his web of lies and deceit. He talked a pretty game. Telling me he wanted nothing to do with the griffins' war against us phoenixes. He even went so far as to refuse to talk about being more than human when we were together. I wonder now if that was just because he was afraid talking about our respective races would somehow make him slip up and give away his plan for betrayal. But as convincing as his ruse was, I'm sure there is no way he would have given himself away unless he planned it.

Every time I let my mind be filled by thoughts of Cohen's betrayal I am overcome by fierce anger and yet such sorrow. For the time we were together, a time I learned was all a lie, Cohen helped me to find a release from the burden that had become my race. Cohen gave me an excuse to have fun, he gave me a reason to enjoy life. He taught me I could be a part of my race, but also have a life outside of it. He showed me it didn't have to be all or nothing.

So while I am angry he pulled me into his lie, while I hate him for making me believe him. I mourn his loss. I mourn what he gave me. I mourn how he treated me. How he doted on me, but also pushed me. How he was kind and yet tough. He made me laugh when I had no reason to. He teased me but knew when to be serious.

There is a small part of me that believes that not everything he did could have been a lie. Some of the looks he gave me. When I'd catch him staring at me, but then quickly turn away. There was no lie in the way he kissed me. There was no sense of betrayal when he touched me. The thing that nags at me most, is the moment before he tried to kill me, right before he plunged the knife into my chest. Those words he spoke haunt me. They are the sole reason I didn't go after him first. They are the reason I haven't yet gone after him. He stared deep into my eyes, there was truth when he spoke, "I could have loved you. I'm so sorry." Can you betray someone you truly love? Would someone apologize to that person for betraying them if you don't mean it?

That is what holds me back from inflicting the largest dose of revenge I have to offer up. Cohen didn't just wage war against me. He infiltrated the system and tried to bring it down from the inside. He betrayed me in the worst way possible.

He made me fall for his ruse. He made me fall for him and then stabbed me, literally. I did fall for him. For all the reasons that keep me from killing him.

But the further away I get from the good side of him, from the Cohen that made me fall for him, the angrier I get. It is time to go after Cohen. I'm hoping waiting this long to go after him will have him in a state of paranoia. I'm hoping he will be over cautious like the girl we just killed. But Cohen is cocky, he's daring, he knows how to play people. I'm hoping it will be his downfall.

Gray, Anna, Aspen, Xander, and I have planned it. We know his whereabouts. We know he's alone. We know he's only seen his father and sister once since he betrayed me and Tucker and my people.

We have planned, and planned, changed our plans, solidified our plans, and changed them again. We know what we are doing. We also know I am the one who will deliver the killing blow. Cohen is mine. I brought him into this, and I will be the one to take him out. My four friends and fellow killers will be there for back up. For moral support.

I sit it silence in the darkened SUV as we drive to Cohen's loft. I've thought this over. I've gone over everything that could go wrong. I've worried over the ways he could try to manipulate me into trying to let him live. I've been over everything, and am ready. Cohen will not survive the night.

Gray cuts the engine as we pull up a few blocks away from Cohen's loft. Twice while we were together, Cohen brought me here. We didn't do much more than watch movies and play video games, sharing the rare kiss I was willing to give him. But it was nice to have a place to get away from my world, to escape to a place that wasn't marked with Logan.

Trepidation fills me as memories of being here flash against my eyes. I force them back and sneak around buildings until I come upon Cohen's loft. I'm not even going to go through the back door. If I'm going to do this, I'm going through the front door.

Xander, Aspen, Anna, and Gray will stay outside unless I call out in distress. I won't need them. The anger burning inside my belly fuels the fire under my veins. I want him dead. I need him dead. It won't bring Tucker or Logan back. I know that. In my head I know that. But I can't let Cohen live in a world he took a hand in washing Tucker and Logan from.

I stride up the steps to his loft, not even bothering to silence my steps. He'll know I'm coming anyway. Cohen always had a way of knowing when something was amiss, he could always hear things two beats before I could. It was like his senses were slightly more tuned in than mine. Like they were what kept him alive as long as he'd managed. My four partners go with the stealthy approach. Maybe if I make enough noise it will drown out the sounds of their steps.

I don't knock. That would be redundant. I grab for the door handle, expecting it to be locked, but am surprised to find it unlocked. Xander and Gray stand on either side of the door frame. I give them both a look before turning the knob and opening the door. The room is dark when I enter, lit only by a silent TV.

Cohen sits on his couch, his face turned toward the TV, his back to me. He doesn't move, doesn't acknowledge my presence, just continues to stare at the TV. If it's a ploy to throw me off, I'm not going to let it.

"I knew you'd come for me," he says, his voice even, steady. "I thought it might be sooner. But I knew you'd come."

"You deserve it," I tell his back.

"I know," he says.

He says it with complete honesty. It unnerves me. The person who betrayed me isn't supposed to be repentant. The person who betrayed me is supposed to be spiteful, he's supposed to try to finish the job, not sit on a couch without even facing me. I wasn't prepared for this. I wasn't prepared for him to do nothing.

Silence permeates between us. Cohen continues to watch the muted TV. I stare at the back of his head, trying to glean something from him, anything.

"Cohen," I say, my whisper ringing out like I've yelled.

"Don't play with your food, Casslyn. Just kill me and get it over with. That's why you're here. I'll sit here and you can cut my throat," Cohen says. Still he doesn't move. His inaction boils the blood running through my veins, angering the fire blazing under my skin.

"Why?" I ask him.

There is silence before he answers. He knows what I'm asking him.

"He told me I could get out," Cohen says, a subtle shift in the pitch of his voice.

Knowing he's not about to spring on me, I round the couch, stand in front of the TV, and face him. Cohen looks horrible. There are black circles under and around his eyes, like he hasn't been getting any sleep, but also like he's gotten the shit beat out of him. His hair is dirty and sticks together with grease. Facial hair grows long and unkempt on his cheeks and chin. His clothes hang loosely off him as though he hasn't eaten since I last saw him. He isn't wearing any socks and his feet look like they've been coated in mud and dried.

This is not the Cohen I knew. This is not the Cohen I fell for. This isn't the Cohen with fight in his eyes. This is a defeated Cohen, one I'm apprehensive to even touch. He's dying, without my help.

Cohen continues his answer, "He told me if I got close enough to you, if I could enable them to attack you in your own home, I could get out. If I killed you he would never again ask me to do anything griffin related for him, he'd never even speak to me again."

Cohen finally breaks his stare on the TV behind me, looking up at me, tears welling in his eyes. "I wanted out, Casslyn. I just wanted out."

Hatred fills my heart. But not hatred for Cohen. Hatred for his father. It is evident Raphe doesn't care about the fate of his people. He refuses to protect them in their time of need. He beats them when they refuse him. If this is how he treats his own son, I can see why Cohen would want out. It heavies my heart and makes it difficult to find the desire to kill the filthy creature before me. And that fills me with hate. I am beyond sick and tired of feeling so much hatred. I am repulsed by the state of my own heart these days. This isn't what Nash, or Tucker, or Logan would have wanted for me. And yet they aren't here to replace that hate with love, and for that reason alone, I continue to detest the life I'm living.

Tears spill over Cohen's eye lids and streak down his dirty face. I'm disgusted by him. I want to fight him. That's what I came here for. I want to finish him off, kill him, rid my life of the man who is responsible for taking the two most important people from me. And yet I can't.

The finishing blow is when he stares right into my eyes,

tears coating his voice as he says, "I'm so sorry."

Fury fills me, shades my face an angry red, radiates from my toes and into my fingers. "Get up," I tell him, speaking through clenched teeth.

Cohen stands up and faces me. He looks pathetic. He can't even stand up straight. I strike him across the face with the back of my hand. His head whips to the side, a small noise escaping his mouth. Blood wells from a cut in his cheek as he faces me again. Tears spring to my eyes when I punch him, hard, in the same cheek, forcing the cut to spread wider across his face. The blow knocks him back into the couch.

"Get up," I say to him.

He stays seated on the couch. He tries to rise, but struggles.

"Get up," I scream at him.

He gets to his feet only to fall back to the couch when I punch him again.

"Get up," I say through my teeth.

Tears stream down my cheeks, mirroring Cohen's face.

"Get up," I say to him.

Again he struggles to his feet.

I land blow after blow into his abdomen, his ribs, his stomach. He struggles to stay standing, taking every blow as I deliver them.

He's taking the punishment as I dole it out. And I hate him for it. I hate him for betraying me. I hate him for not wanting to.

I scream as I hit him, tears falling down my face and

running into my mouth. The salt of them leave a bad taste on my tongue.

Cohen has fallen to his knees, his legs no longer able to keep him upright.

I can't imagine what Gray and the rest of my friends are thinking right now. I haven't called out to them. I'm not going to. They would be disappointed in me. But I can't stop. I can't stop until Cohen has paid.

I kick my foot up into his ribs over and over, howling and crying as I do so. It wasn't supposed to be like this. I was supposed to come in here, make him sorry he betrayed me, then kill him and be done with it. This wasn't supposed to happen.

Cohen collapses onto the floor. I stop kicking him. The room is still but for my heavy breathing. If it weren't for the slow rise and fall of Cohen's back I would think he wasn't breathing.

"I'm sorry," he says.

I can barely hear it from his lips pressed into the floor.

I look down on him, trying to decide what to do now. The longer I stare at him the harder it is to hate him. With every second my eyes lay on him, a little piece of my hate for him chips away. All I can hear are his words, *I just wanted out*. That's when I snap.

I walk away from him, open the door, and walk out. Four sets of eyes stare at me, looking for orders, waiting for the go ahead.

Without looking at them, without acknowledging any of

them individually I say, "Don't let him die," and jog down the stairs, leaving them behind me.

I kick off hard from the bottom step and run. I'm not sure where I'm going, I just know I need to go. I need to run. I need the air to pierce my lungs, to make them hurt. The rusty scent of Cohen's blood sticks to me and permeates my nostrils. It churns my stomach and gags me, but I swallow it down and continue to run.

It doesn't take long before I can hear languid footfalls behind me.

"Cass, stop," Xander says, coming up behind me.

I come to a slow stop, unable to stop on a dime. Not now. I'm breathing heavy. From knocking Cohen around. From running. From emotions. Xander stands in front of me, his chest rising easily, like catching up with me did nothing to him.

"What happened back there?" he asks me. His eyebrows cross low over his eyes. It's his I'm-concerned-about-you look.

"I couldn't do it. You heard it. You guys were listening, right?"

Xander nods his head, yes they were listening. "But we weren't in that room with you. What happened? You can talk to me," he says, resting his hands heavily on my arms.

"He was messed up. It was like what he did, betraying me, broke him. Or maybe the Cohen I spent months with wasn't the real Cohen. I don't know. But what I saw in that room . . . I just couldn't do it. He kept saying he was sorry for betraying me. He kept saying he just wanted out. I couldn't do it, Xander."

"It's okay, Cass."

"It's not okay," I shout at him and pull away from his hold. "He needs to pay for what he did. It's his fault. If he wouldn't have betrayed me, Tucker and Logan would still be here."

"I think he did pay. You inflicted a lot of damage. And like you said, it looked like he was broken. Cass, it's not your fault, it's not even really his fault. The griffins, Raphe, they would have found a way to get at us. That's what they do. I didn't want to tell you, but they've come after me a few times since I left."

"What?" I ask.

How could I not have known this?

"They've cornered me a couple times. After school. On my way to your house. Once when I went to the cemetery."

"Why didn't you tell me?" I ask him, unable to reason out why he would keep this a secret from me.

"You have enough on your plate," he says. But when I raise an accusing eyebrow at him he continues. "I wasn't sure how you would react. You keep saying you're not going to lose anyone else. I thought knowing that they've been after me would send you in a tailspin."

"How have you gotten away?" I ask, refusing to acknowledge what he's said.

"I got lucky mostly. There were witnesses at school. I was lucky enough to drive a little faster than them. I got enough punches in at the cemetery to get away."

"I'm so sorry. Were you hurt?"

"It's not your fault. You heard Colt, it wasn't like they were just going to let me walk away. They got a few hits in a couple of times, but I healed. I'm getting good at that."

"Okay, here's what we're going to do," I tell him, like I know what we're going to do. I stopped knowing what we were going to when I lost my twin brother. "We are never going to be apart. Where you go, I go. Got it? We be extra vigilant. We bring Gray with us if we have to. Logan went back to high school to protect me. Gray can too."

Xander smiles and nods like I'm crazy but it's his brand of crazy. Whatever keeps him safe. I'm starting to think I'm going about this all the wrong way. I'm not sure I've got all the facts. I'm no longer sure I know the true enemy.

"Can I ask you a question?" I ask Xander.

He nods.

"What was it like being with them?"

"When I was growing up, good. Great even. They trained me to be the perfect soldier. They taught me that phoenixes were a danger to the humans. And that we were the saviors of the humans. Do you know how good it feels to be told you're a hero? Honestly, until Logan came into town, until I learned you were a phoenix, I ate every word they served to me and asked for seconds. I didn't question them for a second."

"Were there others that wanted out? Like Cohen?" I ask him.

"I didn't hear about them. None of us were told anything about people trying to leave. But once I started questioning the lies they fed us, I started to wonder if there were others who tried to leave. Turns out, there were a lot of people. Raphe just got rid of them. If you weren't a perfect griffin, if you poisoned the system, you were eliminated."

"Oh my," I say, unable to finish the sentiment. "But they treated you well? I mean, until they beat you up?"

"Not always," Xander says. His eyes lose focus, like he's no longer here talking to me, but like he's remembering something he doesn't want to. "When you did something they asked of you, and you did it right, they acted as if you were a prince. But if you made a mistake, did even the slightest thing wrong, you were punished, so that you might learn and do better next time. Before I aged they would always hit me where it wouldn't show. Ribs and stomach mostly, sometimes legs in the winter. I could heal quickly, but not fast enough for it not to show."

"How did I never notice this?" I ask, feeling like a terrible friend.

"You did," Xander says. "I tried to act normal, walk like nothing was wrong with me. But you always knew. I just tried to play it off as a sports injury or something like that. I think I once told you I fell down the stairs. You would always consent to my lies, but you would side eye me for days until I healed."

"I should have done more," I tell him.

Xander shrugs his shoulders. It's in the past. There is

nothing I could have done about it. There's nothing I can do about it. These are the things his shoulders say in the one shrug.

"What do we do about Cohen?" Xander asks, indicating behind us with his head.

"I can't kill him," I tell Xander.

"Do you want us to?" he asks me. He knows Gray, Anna, and Aspen will have no problem doing it.

"No," I tell him. "I need to talk to my father. I need to figure some things out. And then we will decide what to do with him."

"Okay," he says slowly, like I've lost my mind.

"Do you trust me?" I ask him.

"With my life," he answers.

"Okay. Look, you don't have to treat him like royalty. Just don't let him die," I say.

"Okay," he says, this time more assured. "Are you okay?"

"I'm fine. I'm going to run home. I need a shower. And I need to talk to my father."

"You're going to run twelve miles back to your house?" he asks me, astonished, by the look on his face.

"Yeah. I'll be fine," I tell him.

We nod at each other, silent permission to depart. Xander heads back to Cohen's loft. I have somewhere else I need to go.

I take off at a jog but soon pick up the pace. The air is warm for late October Nebraska weather. But I'll take it. I'm not the biggest fan of snow. I didn't like sledding, I didn't like the wet coldness of the snow, or the way it chapped my skin when it got stuck between my gloves and coat. But Nash loved the snow. We used to take a sled onto the roof and slide off it. I didn't like it. I didn't like making snow men, or snow angels, or rolling down the hills in the snow. But I did it, because Nash loved it. But he's gone, so I no longer have to pretend to like the snow.

My lungs burn a little more with each mile I run. But it's a good burn. It's a burn that lets me focus on the pain radiating from my lungs to my legs to my stomach, and not on the thoughts in my head. I'm not sure I'll be able to stand up in the shower, but that's okay. The further I run, the clearer my thoughts become. Everything Cohen said to me. The way he looked. The way he acted. Things other griffins have said before we killed them.

By the time I reach Logan's I'm sweating so much Cohen's blood coating my skin and clothes has turned to a pink color and pools in my shoes. Yet another item of clothing I'll have to throw away. I wonder what the average yearly clothing budget of a phoenix is. It can't be low. I've nearly run out of money replacing my clothes in the last few months. And that's only a few months. Once I finally settle this whole war with the griffins ordeal, I'm going to have to get a job to supplement my clothing habit.

There are lights on in the house when I walk up to Logan's door. I'm sure Nathan and Thomas are up playing video games. I realize they don't have school, or jobs, or responsibilities, but as often as I don't see them during the day, I'm convinced the two of them are nocturnal. And sure enough, when I walk into the house and head for the living room, the TV is blaring with animated gun fire. Thomas is on his feet, standing about a foot from the TV, his shoulders hunched over while he clutches the game controller. Nathan sits at the edge of the couch, bearing nearly the same posture as his friend. What surprises me is finding my father seated in the recliner, his feet hanging off one of the arm rests. He's reading a book, but eyes the boys playing their game. I'm sure Lydia is somewhere in the house, but I'm not about to listen for her.

I step further into the living room and clear my throat. Neither Thomas nor Nathan look my way. My father moves his eyes, and only his eyes, to face me. His head still pointed into the book. When he gets a better look at me, his head moves to me, giving me his full attention.

"Perhaps you'd like a shower?" he asks, slight sarcasm laced into his voice.

"I need to talk to you," I tell him.

I can tell he's not about to give in, not about to give me what I want unless I comply to his wishes. He does swing his legs so they now hang over the front of the chair, but he does not otherwise move. "Can it not wait until you've washed the blood from yourself?" he asks.

"Yeah," Nathan says, "You stink."

"Can I use the shower here? Or would you prefer I went to my house?"

"Whatever you prefer," he says. "I do believe you keep a spare set of clothes here."

I incline my head and nod at him before turning away and heading upstairs for the shower. I should have just gone to my house, showered, and then came here. It's not like I like standing around soaked in blood and sweat, but I wanted to talk to my dad while the thoughts were fresh in my head. Then again, what is fifteen minutes going to change? I can just think about everything while I'm in the shower so my thoughts are organized and concise. Not that they will remain that way when I try to express them.

As I stand in the shower, the water washing the blood from my skin, my arms begin to shake. They shake as I try to run shampoo through my hair. They shake as I pull conditioner through the long strands. They become weak to the point where I have to rest them at my sides.

I didn't kill Cohen. I shouldn't be racked with this aching quilt. He deserved what I did to him. If I were in his situation I would have died before I betrayed him. At least I'd like to think I would. I'm almost certain I would.

Before the fatigue of the night can wear me down too much, I finish my shower and go in search of my father. It's not too much of a search. He's where I left him. Though as soon as I make it to the living room, he leads me into the kitchen.

"Would you like some hot chocolate, Casslyn?" he asks me.

"That's a stupid question," I tell him.

When he gives me a questioning look, I have to remind myself that he hasn't been here all my life, he doesn't know my every habit, my likes and dislikes.

"The answer to that is yes," I tell him. "It's always a yes when it comes to hot chocolate."

"I will keep that in mind," he tells me. He gives me a thankful nod, a thank-you-for-sharing-a-part-of-your-life-with-me nod.

I give him a half smile and sit at the island as he makes us both a cup of hot chocolate. I watch him work, trying to learn what I can from his movements. My father has been in Cedars almost a year now, and still I don't know much about him. I spent the first few months hating him to the point of trying to run him out of town. Then I spent more time angry he had abandoned us. Then even more time was spent in indifference. It is only now, that I'm beginning to have an actual relationship with him, letting him into my life, that I wish I'd acted different in the beginning. I can't change the past, but I can spend the present trying to make up for it.

When he is finished, my father sets a steaming cup of rich hot chocolate in front of me and keeps one for himself. He stands on the other side of the island from me. We face off, studying each other, watching each other for moments before either one of us says a word. You can learn a lot about a person by just watching them. No words need to be spoken. It is often people say too much when they should remain silent, if only for a moment.

My father is the first to break the silence. He asks, "What

would you like to discuss with me?"

"I know you know what we've been doing," I say, then take a long drink from my cup, giving my father time to interject if he wishes. The hot liquid burns down the back of my throat but I welcome the heat. When he doesn't say a word I continue, "We went after Cohen tonight." Again I take a drink of hot chocolate, giving him time to interlude. Again, silence. "I couldn't kill him, Dad."

My father perks up. I'm not sure if it's because I couldn't kill Cohen, or because I called him dad. I know what he is going to say before he says it, but I still need him to ask it, perhaps so I can defend myself, if nothing else. "Why were you unable to kill him?"

"I'm not really sure," I say, although we both know that is a lie. "I know you know I had feelings for him, and I know you know most of our people blame me for bringing him into our lives. But I want you to know that I didn't keep him alive because of my feelings for him. I guess I did it because . . . he just looked so pathetic. He told me that the reason he betrayed me was because his father told him he would let Cohen out, he would free him, if he betrayed me."

"And you believed him?" my father asks. I expect to hear belligerence in his voice. I expect him to act like I'm an idiot for believing Cohen. But what I get is merely curiosity.

"I did," I say cautiously. "He sounded so desperate. So broken. There was sincerity in his voice. He looked broken, Dad. How could I kill him? If I killed him, it would be like I was as bad as them. I can't be as bad as the griffins. I won't."

"What are you looking for me to tell you?" my father asks.

"I want to know if I made the right choice."

"I think you already know the answer to that," he says, resting his hands around his cup, between the two of us.

"Then why do I feel so terrible?"

"I can't answer that for you," my father says.

"So much for your help," I say, more to myself than to him.

"Casslyn," my father starts.

"It's okay. I think I just wanted to talk it out."

My father rests his weight on his elbows and faces me head on. He's got the look on his face my parents get when they are about to have a deep conversation with me, a conversation they want me to really pay attention to. "Have I even told you what the meaning of the phoenix is?"

"That we're descended from the mythological birds?"

"No. Not what we are. The meaning behind a phoenix. What we represent."

"No. I don't know," I answer.

"It's obvious the phoenix represents immortality, longevity, regeneration." My father pauses, as if needing to know I'm paying attention. I make eye contact with him, letting him know I'm with him, and nod. He continues, saying, "You know all that. Everyone knows that. But what most people don't know, is that a phoenix represents hope. We rise from the flames, from the ashes to become a newer, better version of ourselves. To me, that is what is most important."

"So, you're saying, that . . . what are you saying?" I ask.

"Exactly what I just told you," my father says, like it's obvious.

"Okay, so we are giving hope to our people."

"Not just our people, Casslyn, everyone. We represent hope. We can give hope to anyone who might need it. That may even include someone you might not want it to."

"You mean Cohen."

"I do."

"What hope am I supposed to give him?" I ask, standing up from the chair in front of the island. "What am I supposed to do? Kill his father? I already plan to do that."

"Do you think killing Raphe will give hope to only Cohen?"

I think back to the griffins we've killed. I think about the ones who begged for mercy. The ones who told me they didn't want to attack us, that they were forced. I think about Xander telling me how he and his people were treated by Raphe. I think about Cohen's words *I just wanted out*.

But not all the griffins want out. I mean, there have got to be some who like killing us. I know there are. Colt couldn't wait to get his hands on me. On any one of us. Just because there are a select few who don't agree with Raphe, doesn't mean there aren't even more who do.

"Okay, so I give hope to some of them, Cohen, a few others who hate Raphe. There is just going to be someone who replaces him. It could be someone worse. Did you think about that?"

"So you are willing to sacrifice those few who do want out? I thought you didn't want to be like them? Did you miss the part where I said we rise from the flames to become better versions of ourselves?"

"Oh, it's that easy is it?" I ask, slapping my hand down on the counter. The force of it makes my mug jump and rattle against the granite.

"I never said it would be easy," my father says, remaining calm.

"What do I do?" I ask, my shoulders sagging. I have no idea how we got to the place in this conversation that we have. I have no idea how to bring it around to where I wanted it to go, to the reason I came to my father. I wonder if I've gotten more than I bargained for. But something I didn't know I needed.

Hope. A better version of ourselves. And maybe others.

"What do you want to do?"

"I want our races to change. I don't want to fear the griffins coming after us. But I don't want them to suffer. Is that bad? Am I betraying my own people?"

"Why don't you ask your people?" my father says, looking behind me.

I turn to see Nathan and Thomas behind me. I'd forgotten they were only a room away. I'm sure they've heard every word. They look at me with wary expressions, but also like they are willing to listen.

My father told me to ask them, but first they need to know why. So I tell them. I tell them about my time with Cohen, the words he spoke to me, the words I now know were true, even if he would eventually betray me. I tell them about how he wanted out, how his father treats him and his fellow people. I tell them about my lifelong friendship with Xander, and how after everything we've been through he chose me over the people who raised him. I tell them about how his own people treated him, how his people were treated and are still treated. I tell them about the griffins I killed and how half of them said they hadn't wanted to attack us, how they just want to live their lives. I tell them everything I know and every reason I have for what I want to accomplish.

"I want to free the griffins," I tell them.

Seven

They don't look surprised. They look apprehensive. They look guarded. They look like people who represent hope. And that's all I need.

When they don't say anything right away I feel the need to say something, anything. "I'm not asking you to help me. I can do it alone if I have to. I would never ask you to do something you don't believe in. But I feel like this is the right thing to do. There will be griffins who are just like Raphe, who believe every word he says, who believe we are evil and should be destroyed. And that is fine. But I don't believe the ones who want out should have to suffer."

Nathan and Thomas study me. The two of them might be my hardest sells. Nathan, Lydia's brother will say no, merely because Lydia hates the griffins as much as they hate us. And despite quickly becoming friends with me, and constantly giving his sister a hard time, Nathan loves his sister. He would do anything for her. And then there is Thomas, Gray's best friend. Thomas will say no, for Gray's sake, because Gray lost Tucker to the griffins.

I know the outcome. I know I will be doing this alone. I know that that's alright. Gray, Lydia, Aspen, Anna, Nathan, Thomas, my father. They have all spent years beyond my knowledge fighting the griffins. They have lost countless more people to them. They have seen the atrocities the griffins bring to their doorsteps, not just in Cedars, but everywhere they have ever lived. I shouldn't even have the right to discuss this with them.

"I'm in," Thomas says.

I remain silent, fearful that if I say something he will change his mind.

"Me too," Nathan says.

"I'm behind you all the way, kiddo," my father says.

I didn't expect that. As against going after the griffins as my father ways, I didn't see him willing to fight alongside us. But he was the one preaching to me about hope and bettering oneself.

"I'm in," comes a voice from behind Nathan and Thomas.

Lydia steps around her brother and fellow phoenix. She crosses her arms and stares me down. It's a challenge. It's a quiet acceptance. I'll take it.

"I don't know what I'm doing," I admit to them.

"That's why you have us," my father says.

I want to know why. Why would they help me? Why would they help the people they have fought against for so long? But there are other questions. Will they want my help? Will they fight against their own people? Am I doing the right thing? Am I leading my people to their deaths?

I know I can't just liberate the griffins without actually talking to them, without finding out if that's what they want. It's going to be slightly difficult to get in touch with them, especially after I've spent the last three months killing members of their race. It might also be difficult with Raphe pulling in the ranks. After the last griffin we killed, the rest of them went into hiding. Raphe finally decided we weren't going to be satisfied with the few of them we'd gotten rid of. He finally decided he should protect his people. Or maybe he's getting ready to retaliate. That is always an option. It should be a given. It's certainly something Xander, Gray, and I have been anticipating. But so far all is quiet on the griffin front.

So I'll start with Cohen, if he is willing to talk to me. I can't imagine he would be after I beat the shit out of him. But maybe he's so desperate to get away from his father he'll give me a chance.

"Thank you," I tell the four people who face me. "Thank you for listening, and giving me a chance. And not shutting me out as I make mistake after mistake."

"It's not for lack of trying," Lydia says, but there is an undercurrent of teasing in her voice.

"We will discuss this more when the rest of our group has returned," my father says.

"Yeah," I say, feeling dismissed.

I glance at each member in the kitchen, then step towards the door.

Before I can get too far, my father says, "Casslyn, I was wondering if we could speak about something else."

"Oh," I say, turning back to him. I'm not sure what else there is left to say, or what he could want to talk about, but I spent so long shutting him out, it's time I heard what he has to say. "Sure. No problem."

My father eyes Lydia, Nathan, and Thomas. I guess I wasn't the one being dismissed. It takes a bit longer than I would have thought before the three of them get the hint and disband, leaving my father and I alone in the kitchen. I stand a few feet away from my father and wait for him to say something. He points his hand in the direction of the island. I once again take a seat behind the island and face my father. His silence is eerie, like he's uncomfortable. He looks uncomfortable. It's not a look I've seen on him before.

My father stands on the other side of the island, like we were when we started this night. He places his hands on the countertop. He removes them. He rests his elbows on it then his chin on his hands. Realizing that's not right, he rights himself. Hands behind back, hands at side, hands on hips. He just can't decide.

"Dad, what is it?" I ask, no longer able to stand his prancing.

"Casslyn, I wanted to ask you a favor," he says on a deep breath.

"Okay," I say slowly. "I'll do whatever you need me to."

"No, don't just agree so quickly," my father says. This scares me. "What I'm asking is selfish. It's not something that's going to be easy. If you need to say no, please do."

I don't say anything to him. I'm scared. I'm worried about what he's going to ask me. I'm worried about not being able to fulfill his favor. For the first time, I'm afraid of letting him down.

I'm holding my breath when he opens his mouth and asks, "Will you tell me about your brother?"

My breath escapes on a shaky wave. That is not at all what I thought he was going to ask. I had no idea what he was going to ask. But that is not even in the realm of what I thought he was going to ask.

He wants me to tell him about Nash. Do I want to tell him about Nash? Will I be able to tell him about Nash?

Tears well in my eyes. It's been a long year and a half without him. But it's been so filled with the crazy that has become my life that I haven't been able to sit down and think about him. Even worse is the last three months without him in my head. I miss him now more than I missed him before. I feel empty, hollow, like an essential part of me is missing. I can't imagine how my father feels, never having met him.

But again, how could I not tell him about Nash? Nash was my best friend in the entire world. He was the best person I knew. Isn't it my duty as his sister to tell everyone I can about what a wonderful person he was?

"I'll tell you," I say to my father.

My father doesn't say thank you. He doesn't ask me to proceed. He just watches me. Patiently waiting to learn about the child he had, but never knew. I wonder where to begin. Should I explain Nash as a person? Should I tell him of the events of our lives starting from my earliest memories? How much does he want to know? If I tell him everything, we will be here all night.

I'm not sure where to start, so I dive in head first, hoping I'll learn to swim along the way.

"Nash was my best friend in the whole world," I tell my father. I can't look at him. If I look at him I'll lose my nerve. Plus, it's easier to focus on my memories if I stare at the countertop. "We did everything together. I'm not sure we were ever separated. We went to birthday parties together. We played together. We hung out together. Our parents never separated us. We had separate bedrooms, but they were next to each other. We would sit in our closets like you see in the movies and talk to each other through the walls until we fell asleep. I'm sure our parents knew about it, but they never punished us."

I can feel my father's eyes on me, bearing down on me, pulling information from me. I can smell the salt from his tears, or maybe they're my own, but I don't say anything, don't look at him. I'm not about to judge him for wanting to know about the son he could have had.

I'm who he's got. I know he loves me. Just like I know

my parents love me. But I also know that they wish Nash was still alive. Who wouldn't? But sometimes it feels more like I'm not enough for them. And as a child, feeling that way, feeling inadequate, is worse than them being angry at you. When they are angry at you, they can forgive you, it can always get better. But when you're just not enough for them, as their child, it's debilitating. None of my parents would make me feel this way on purpose. I'm not even sure they know they are doing it. But I can see it in their eyes when they look at me. When they look through me and wait to see their other child and he's not there.

"I was born three minutes and fifteen seconds before Nash. I was the older sibling, but somehow Nash felt it his duty to be my protector. He was always looking out for me. Always doing what he thought was best for me. But he never made me feel like I needed it. He was always very sly, and very cunning when it came to watching over me. Beyond that, Nash and I were equal in every sense of the word. We had all the same classes, got all the same stuff, and shared almost everything we had with each other. We liked the same music, same movies and TV shows. Nash was my mom's favorite, while I was my dad's. I'm not sure how that works, but that's the way it was."

"Everybody loved Nash. He was nice to everyone, even if they weren't nice to him. The teacher's loved him. The girls loved him, though I wouldn't let them near him."

I tell my father about growing up. I tell him about our birthday parties. I tell him about our mutual love for the zoo, how we would spend hours there, watching the animals, entranced by their grace and power. I explain the near ten year friendship we shared with Xander and Tucker and how much Nash meant to them, and in return how much they meant to Nash. I tell him about my parents' relationship with Nash. I don't want to hurt his feelings, but my parents' relationship with Nash is part of what made him, him. So I feel like my father needs to know.

I'm not sure how long we've been at the island talking about Nash. I know I've downed two bottles of water. I know my right butt cheek is cramping and has fallen asleep. I've told my father about the games Nash like to play, which sports were his favorite, which school subjects he excelled in. I tell him the detailed plan Nash and I had set for our future. I've never told anyone this before, not even Tucker or Xander.

Nash and I were going to go to college together. Nash would major in something practical, while I majored in something whimsical. Like Accounting and Art, or Education and Theater. That way, when we were out of college and living on our own, we would always have a steady income but also get to have shit tons of fun with our lives. On occasion we would add a significant other into the mix, but Nash and I were always together, no matter where life took us. If he got a job somewhere different than where we currently were located, I would move with him, and vice versa. We were more important to each other than the outside factors that ran our lives. As long as we had each other, we could conquer whatever life threw our way.

Just thinking about that has tears streaming down my face. It's hard to speak around the lump in my throat. I have to stop for several minutes before I can speak again. My father sits next to me, tears pouring from his eyes. We sit, facing each other, but neither of us brave enough to look into the other's eyes. I haven't finished telling him about Nash, but I'm not sure how much more I can divulge without losing it.

But there is one last thing I think he needs to know. One last thing I only told Logan.

"After Nash died, I could still see him, like actually see him. Whenever I'd pass out, or even sometimes when I'd dream, I would see him. It was him. Not just a figment of my imagination. We would have full conversations. He knew about things that only occurred after he died. He helped me work through issues I was having with the griffins and the phoenixes."

I stop. I haven't looked up yet. I'm not prepared to see my father looking at me like I'm crazy. Logan told me he didn't know of anyone else who could still converse with people once they were dead.

"Has it stopped?" my father asks.

"The night of the attack, when Cohen stabbed me," I say, telling him the story as I know it. "I'm pretty sure I died, or was close to death. I saw Nash. He told me I needed to heal myself, but in order to do that, I had to let him go. So I let him go. I healed myself. And I haven't seen him since."

"So he was just in your head."

"Yeah. I guess. I don't know. But I know I couldn't heal myself when I could still see him. And I can heal myself just fine now."

"So you needed to let him move on, to accept that he was no longer here, in order to heal."

"You believe me?" I ask him.

"Why wouldn't I?"

"Because it sounds kind of crazy. Like I'm not mentally stable."

"It sounds to me like you missed your brother, a brother who was a part of you in a way no other person could be. I was afraid that when your brother died it would somehow affect your powers. I was right. I just wasn't sure in what way."

I look at my father, thankful he understands and doesn't think I'm crazy. I'm thankful he let me talk and didn't interrupt or ask questions. I'm also thankful for the sad look on his face, as mean as that may sound. But he is truly sad he didn't get to know Nash, and that's more than I could ask for. More than anything, I'm thankful I got to talk about Nash. It's something I haven't been able to do since he died. Early on, it was too painful to talk about him. Then Tucker and Xander didn't talk about him because they were afraid it would set me off. My mom would cry every time someone would mention his name. My dad would change the subject. It was like Nash was gone, but also never there. I needed him to be there. I needed to still have him in my corner.

"It also sounds like I've got a lot of issues," I tell him, trying to lighten the mood.

We both break out in laughter. It feels good to laugh. It feels good to talk through something that was once a near forbidden subject.

"Casslyn," my father starts, then swallows hard. "Thank you," he tells me.

I shrug my shoulders like it's no big deal I've just bore my soul to him. But it is a big deal. It's a big deal for him as a father who lost a child. It's a big deal for him as my father. And it's a big deal in our relationship. I would not have felt comfortable telling him everything I just did months ago. But that's how far we have come. It hasn't been easy. It's been more like mountain climbing without any gear or instruction. But we seem to be conquering it nonetheless. And if that's not growth, if that's not representing hope and a better version of myself, I'm not sure what is. Maybe I really am a true phoenix after all.

Eight

To say that Aspen, Anna, and Gray weren't too thrilled with my idea to free the griffins, would be an understatement. To say they were pissed and wouldn't speak to me for two solid days, would be more accurate. But I spoke with them, I got Xander to speak to them, my father even gave it a shot. Eventually they came around. And now, instead of defending ourselves from the griffins, we have a new mission. One I feel far more comfortable with.

I set out to get vengeance for my loved ones. I still want revenge. But I also want to do some good with the powers I've been given. And if that is liberating those I once saw as the enemy, then so be it. If getting freedom for those who are oppressed by a psycho leader is my life's mission, then so be it. Xander was once imprisoned by those people, even if neither of us knew it. The griffins may have tried to take down my people, may have tried to destroy everything I hold dear, but they didn't and now I'm stronger and willing to do what I think is right. I hope Nash, and Kristina, and Tucker, and Logan would be proud of me. I think they would.

As far as freeing the griffins goes, I'm not sure how I'm to go about that, other than killing their crazed leader and his evil daughter. I talked to Xander about it. He nearly cried when I told him what I wanted to do. As much of a macho man as he is, as strong as he likes to portray himself as, I know he misses his parents. I honestly believe they want out too, they are just afraid of what Raphe will do to them. Xander wants to talk to them about being free and how to go about it. But he is also afraid Raphe will go after them if he thinks they have been in contact with Xander. The more distance he puts between them, the safer they are.

I can't say the same for Cohen. We have had phoenixes guarding over Cohen since the night I planned to kill him. Xander, Gray, Thomas, and Nathan have done most of the guarding. I've taken my fair share of turns since this was all my idea. But school tends to get in the way of that. Surprisingly so, Aspen, Anna, and Lydia have even taken their turns at watching over Cohen. And luckily so. Raphe sent some attack dogs to his loft. I'm not sure what they were going to do to him, but I can't imagine it involved having a tea party. I wasn't there, but Xander told me Cohen was inside his loft shaking until Gray and Thomas were able to get rid of them.

I may have been there to guard him, but I haven't yet

talked to him. I'm afraid I won't know what to say. Every time I see him I feel the need to apologize, but then I see Tucker's face in my head and I want to punch him all over again. I need to talk to him. He's instrumental in our plan to free the griffins. Plus, I miss him. I'm going to do it today. But first I have to get through school.

Xander and I have seriously considered dropping out of school. Our grades aren't the best, and while we make it to every class, per my mom's demands, our minds aren't there, so our butts in the seats don't account for much. But again, my mom will not let either of us drop out. So we go to school. We sit through class. A lot of the time the other phoenixes, who haven't been in school in years, end up doing our homework, merely for something to do. Being in school without Tucker and Nash is boring, it's uneventful, it's dreadful. Xander and I do what we can to make the time pass more quickly, but without Ashley here to antagonize, or vice versa, it's just not worth the eight hours we spend in the building. I have to remind myself we've only got a few more months until we graduate and can be free of it all. I can't say I will miss it, or any of my classmates.

Xander and I ride out the rest of the day together then head to Cohen's. Gray meets us there where we relieve Thomas and Lydia. Gray and Xander stay outside. I previously explained to them that I need to talk to Cohen. About many things. They understood and agreed to give me some time with him.

When I walk into his loft, I'm surprised to see Cohen

with a bottle of all-purpose cleaner and a rag in his hands. He is bent over the counter scrubbing away.

"Hey," he says to me when I walk in. He says it like it's nothing. Like we're friends. Like he didn't try to stab me to death and I didn't beat the shit out of him.

"Hey," I say back. What else am I supposed to do?

I'm not sure how to begin. I'm not sure what to talk to him about first. So instead of breaking into what I came to talk to him about, I say, "Do you want help?"

"You can vacuum. I'm going to sweep the floor."

I don't say anything, just plug in the vacuum and press the power button with my foot. I watch Cohen, trying to gauge his mood. He works away, determination furrowing his brow. He looks a lot better than the last time I saw him. The dark circles and bruises ringing his eyes are now a pale yellow. He's gotten a haircut, shaved his beard, dressed in clean clothes. There is a new light in his eyes. He's not out of the woods as far as I can tell, he still fears his father, but he's hopeful.

I'm almost afraid to tell him I want to free the griffins. I'm afraid to give him hope. What if I can't free them? What if I fail him? I'm not sure I can deal with that. I'd not only be letting Cohen and Xander down. Not only myself. I'd be letting two whole races down, maybe three.

Cohen and I work in companionable silence, cleaning his loft. There aren't too many rooms so it doesn't take us long. Surprisingly, the bathroom is the cleanest room in the apartment. Cohen and I work well together. We acknowledge each other when we pass, trading head nods and cleaning supplies.

It's not until we are both in his bedroom throwing dirty clothes into the hamper to transfer to the washer that I can finally face my fear of talking to him. We started out trying to fold clean clothes, but soon realized there weren't any of those.

"Cohen," I start, throwing a pair of rank jeans into the hamper.

"Yeah," he says, not turning to me.

"Cohen," I say again. I couldn't face my father while I was telling him about Nash. But I need Cohen to face me, to know that I truly mean what I'm saying to him.

He holds on to the pile of clothes in his hands but faces me. The worried expression on his face spurs me into action.

"I want to help you," I tell him.

"Keeping me alive is helping me," he says.

"I mean, I want to help you. The griffins. Griffins like you and Xander. The ones that want out. Who don't like the way your father is leading you. I want to free you. Not just keep you alive. Could you imagine not having to worry? Not having to look over your shoulder every moment of your life?"

"Why?" he asks.

"Why what?"

"Why would you help us? Why would you risk your life for people who tried to end it?"

"Because it's the right thing to do," I tell him, like it's

the most obvious thing, because it is.

"This world does not deserve you," he tells me.

"I haven't freed you yet," I tell him.

"The fact that you are willing to is more than enough for me."

Cohen clutches the clothes to him. They are so dirty I'm afraid the sweat and crust coating them will glue them into a filthy ball.

The emotion passing between us is too much. Cohen stares at me like I'm a glowing angel from heaven. His hope in me is constricting.

The material of the shirt in my hands chafes my skin. I throw it at Cohen's face to diffuse the moment. It hits his face and he bats it away, smiling at me. I smile back and get back to work.

"I'm going to need your help," I tell him. "It's not going to be easy."

"I will do anything you ask me," he says, pure conviction in his voice.

"Okay."

"Cass," he says after I've bent over to gather more clothes. Honestly the number of dirty clothes on his floor rivals the number of clothes I've owned in my entire life.

I turn back to him. There is a note in his voice that indicates impending tears.

"I know I've said it before. And I also know there will not be a number of times I could say it that will ever make it okay. But I am so sorry. I will never deserve your forgiveness. I will never ask for it. But I want you to know how sorry I am. If I could go back, I would let Raphe kill me just so I wouldn't betray you."

I swallow hard around the tears in my throat. I'm not sure I ever will be able to forgive Cohen. Whether he deserves it or not, he is responsible for the absence of Tucker and Logan in my life. I can't forgive or forget, but I can get past it. And that is what I'm going to have to do.

My vision clouds. Tears spill over my eyelids when I try to blink them back. My heart beats slowly but with a force that's overwhelming. I know Cohen is aware of my emotional struggles. He lets me work through them without interrupting. He waits for me to say something. Whether I condemn him or not.

"I'm going to need time," I tell him, realizing that's true. I'm not sure I knew it until now.

"Okay," he says.

We continue to clean, piling his clothes into the hamper until it's so overflowing it takes the both of us to move it to the bathroom. I throw a load into the washer then make my way back through the loft, making sure it's all clean. When I'm satisfied that it's livable enough for Cohen, I head out. I've had a long day. I'm worn out to the point I could pass out the minute my head hits my pillow. I didn't realize how late it is until I walk out of his loft to the pitch black. I'm not even hungry, having missed a meal. I just want sleep. I feel like I could sleep for a week. But I have school tomorrow. And a war to fight the day after that.

So I get up the next day and face it head on. Xander and I go to school. We make it through school, then we head home. My father calls me to come over to the house shortly after I've made it home. I walk to his house, taking my time, gathering my thoughts from the day. My father didn't sound too urgent, so I don't feel the need to rush over. I feel like my life has turned into rushing. I don't get a second to catch my breath. It's exhausting. I want a moment to sit and be still. But apparently this is not that moment.

I enter the house to near chaos. The TV is on and loud. Members of our group are moving pieces around the living room and through to the kitchen. Gray and Thomas dart from the kitchen, through the living room and up the stairs, talking rapidly. Lydia and Nathan are guarding Cohen's so they aren't a part of the commotion. Anna and Aspen sit in the living room yelling at each other over the TV. I want to suggest turning the TV off or at least down, but I'm afraid of bothering them. My father sits at the island in the kitchen. Apparently that's our new conversation spot. I do my best to ignore the chaos moving around me and focus on my father. It's odd to see him so at peace with the pandemonium around him. I guess he's got to be used to it, being their leader for as long as he has. I have no idea how long that's been. I'll have to find out at some point.

I sit at a chair next to my father and wait for him to speak. Saying 'what's up' seems too cavalier for some reason.

"I wanted to bring you here today for a few different

reasons," my father says.

"Okay," I say, not sure where this is going.

"It's my birthday," he says, like it's just any other day. "It's also the end of my life cycle. After I regenerate tonight I will wake up as a seventeen year old."

I stand up from my chair with my mouth thrown open. "Why didn't you tell me? I would have done something for you. Or gotten you something."

"Your brother and Logan were both killed on their birthdays. I wasn't about to take that risk."

My mouth remains open. I can't fathom the fact that he neglected to tell me we will be the same age tomorrow. Also what he said about Nash and Logan. It makes me angry. But he has a point. And that makes me angry.

"So why tell me now?" I ask.

"I wanted you to be prepared. Also, I would like you to stay here at the house for tonight while I regenerate. Partly just to have you here. But partly as extra security. I've been alive for a long time. Raphe has been my enemy for a long time. I'm not sure if he's learned the date of my birth in that time or not. Being on our guard is best. Will you stay here tonight?"

"Of course I will," I say.

"Thank you."

I sit beside my dad and listen to the chaos. I'm trying and failing to work through my thoughts and feelings. Another birthday. Another person who's getting a year older, when others don't get the same opportunity. Something that should be theirs by right.

"Could I ask you to do something for me?" I ask him.

"Of course," he says.

"When you're seventeen again, would you talk to my parents? I know you know I've told them about me. And in a way, you. But I'm not sure they grasp everything about who, what we are. I think if they get to talk to you, it might help them on the road to truly knowing me, and accepting me."

"I think I can do that," he says.

"Will it be too hard? With my mom?"

My father smiles at me, one of those smiles you give to someone when you are happy they are worried about their feelings, even if your feelings are hurt. "I will always love your mom, Casslyn. But your mom and dad belong together. I would never regret my time with your mom, even if it put a wrench between your parents, because it gave me you. But I will never again come between your parents. To answer your question, no, it will not be difficult because I believe we are in the places in our lives we should be. And that will make it easy."

"Thanks, dad."

"My pleasure."

I get up from the stool at the island and head for the living room. If I'm going to be here all night, I'm going to get in some good TV time.

Before I can move a step from the stool my father calls after me.

I turn back to him, wondering what else he needs to tell

me.

"You may hate me, and I will accept it. But I wanted you to know that I shouldn't have come between you and Logan. I regret it with my whole heart."

I have nothing to say to him. The anger I held every second Logan and I were apart rises in my throat. The sorrow I feel every second he's been away from me catches my breath. All of the kisses we could have had play across my lonely lips. I do hate my father for taking Logan away from me. But Logan chose to listen to him. And I can't fault my father for that.

We've all made mistakes. We all have things we regret. This is one my father carries around with him. Whether I chose to let him continue to carry it around is another story. He has aired his confession. What I decide to do will show my character.

"It's forgotten," I say, shrugging one shoulder.

My father nods at me, clear gratitude in his eyes. I nod back, not sure what else to say. But when I look to Aspen and Anna in the living room, listen to the guys in the house rummaging around, see my father calmly sitting among the chaos, there's things I wonder about.

"Can I ask you something?" I ask my father.

"You know you can," he tells me.

"I know you know I started going after the griffins. I know you know some of the others have joined me. I also know you were against us attacking them, that you would rather we defended ourselves. So, why do you allow us to do it?"

My father raises an eyebrow at me. I'm not sure if he's thinking I asked a stupid question, or if he's wondering just how crazy I am.

I feel the need to clarify. "I just mean," I say, "As our leader. We are all defying your wishes. Why wouldn't you stop us?"

"Could I have?" he asks. "You seemed quite determined."

"Yeah, but I'm your kid, I'm supposed to disobey you. But the others. I wouldn't exactly be happy if the people under me were openly disregarding my authority."

"I'm not exactly happy about it," he says, a small grin on his face. "But, if the majority of my people want something different than I do, then I have to take that into consideration. Being a good leader isn't about pushing your will onto others, it isn't about asserting your dominance. Being a good leader is listening to your people and doing what is best for them."

"I am not going to be a good leader. Please don't ever leave us."

"I'll try my best. However, you will get the hang of it. I have faith in you, my daughter. I wasn't this good when my father was killed."

"You know, I never thought about it, but we don't ever get old and die. We are all killed. That's like, the most depressing thing."

"Don't think about it too hard."

My father puts a hand on my shoulder and squeezes. I think it's his way of reassuring me. Of what, I'm not sure.

"Would you look at the time," he says, not actually looking at the clock. "I'm about to age backwards. If you will excuse me."

"Yeah, sure," I say. Thoughts of my seventeen year old father run behind my eyes. I wonder if he will look the same, just half as old. The first time I saw him I thought he looked familiar. It was only after I spent some time with him that I was able to put my finger on it. He looks like Nash, or Nash looked like my father.

It will be odd thinking of him as my father when we are the same age. I barely listened to Logan when he was here. I do what I can to undermine Xander. Will I be able to hold my tongue if he gives me an order?

I guess I will find out in a matter of hours.

When my father gets up from his stool and finally walks away from the island I am able to make my way into the living room and to Anna and Aspen.

The two of them sit on opposite couches watching an episode of Gilmore Girls. It happens to be one of my very favorite episodes. The one where Jess comes to Rory and shows her the book he wrote. He tells her he couldn't have done it without her. He faces off with her because she isn't in school and isn't doing what she is supposed to be doing. He opens her eyes and gets through to her when no one else could because he knows her more than anyone else. As a prominent member of Team Jess, it is one of my favorite episodes.

I sit next to Aspen and hunker down to finish the episode. Without taking her eyes off the screen, Aspen reaches out her hand and pats the top of my knee. I'm not sure what kind of gesture she's trying to make, but I let it go and keep my eyes on Jess and Rory.

"Hey, are you guys hungry?" Anna asks.

"Starving," Aspen says. "But we can't leave until Aris has aged."

"I could make us something," I say. I haven't really gotten to stretch my cooking wings since learning about being a phoenix. I miss it.

Aspen perks up at this, and says, "Logan told me you are an amazing cook."

"Really?" I ask, surprised he would have told his sister that.

"Yeah," she says, "He told me all kinds of things about you."

"Really," I say again.

"Why are you so surprised?"

"I don't know. I guess as well as I thought I knew your brother, I didn't know him all that well."

"You spent hours the other night telling your father about your brother. I could tell you some things about Logan. If you wanted me to."

"I would love that," I tell her, sudden and unsuspected tears welling in my eyes.

When the episode is over, Anna starts a new one but

Aspen and I head to the kitchen. I'm not sure what there is for groceries in the house besides frozen pizzas, and I'm not sure what I'm in the mood to cook, so I rummage around while Aspen talks. The house is full tonight, since my father is regenerating, so I will need to make extra of whatever I'm cooking, but the further into the process I get, the more excited I become, my fingers itching to stir and chop and dice.

I find some elbow macaroni and cans of whole kernel and cream corn. If I can find some Velveeta cheese and butter I can throw it all together and bake it into a delicious corn mac and cheese confection. It's a good thing I run so much, as much as I eat. Otherwise I'd be about three hundred pounds by now.

I set about measuring the macaroni, pour in both cans of corn and dice up the Velveeta. I mix it all together then place it in the oven. Once that is all set to cook, I open the fridge and begin my search. On the top shelf sits a few pounds of hamburger, two packages of thick cut bacon, and a pack of sliced swish cheese. Bacon cheeseburgers. Perfect. My favorite dish.

"So," I say to Aspen. "Your brother."

"My brother," she says. "My brother is the greatest."

I flinch at her use of the word is. I think about correcting her, but I'm not about to upset her. They say misery loves company, but why would I make her miserable just so I'm not alone in it?

"Logan used to look out for me like it was his mission in life. Even when I started kicking his ass on the sparing mat."

"You beat him?" I ask, my mouth hanging wide open.

"Oh, yeah. He'd never tell you, but I beat him. On more than one occasion."

We both laugh together while I form the hamburger into patties.

"I have to be honest," I tell her. "When your brother first came into town, he terrified me. Like, legit. I was scared."

A laugh bursts from Aspen's chest. "He told me about that. He also said it was so amusing he played it up more than he should have."

"Ugh. I knew it," I say, though at the time I had no idea.

"Do you have any idea how much he loved you?" she ask, her voice suddenly solemn.

"About as much as I loved him."

"He used to call me and gush about what the two of you had done that day, or how you would frustrate him but it only made him love you more. It was rather annoying, really."

I smile, though inside my heart is squeezing itself to death.

"I can't imagine Logan gushing," I say, hoping we can turn the conversation to more of a lighter tone.

Aspen smiles a knowing smile and says, "Only about you."

I pivot around to face the stove and turn on the front two burners. Once they are warm I fill one with burger patties and the other with bacon slices. Both pans sizzle and crack as the meat hits the heat.

"What about when you guys were younger? What was

he like?"

"I guess it wasn't what you would call a normal childhood. We were groomed for this life. Training as early as was developmentally safe. We got to have fun. I remember when Logan and I would go to the park and play, or sit on the couch and watch Saturday morning cartoons. But otherwise we were training. After our parents died, it was like Logan was the parent. All he cared about was being the best phoenix he could be and protecting me at all costs. He loved me, but it wasn't as a partner, it was more as a ward. I missed my big brother.

"Then he came here. Being with you, seeing how losing your brother, your partner, best friend, affected you, Logan realized what he'd given up. He became my brother again, not so much my guardian. So thank you."

"No problem," I tell her. I had no idea how much I influenced Logan and the way he lived his life. I had no idea the impact I had on him. You really don't know how much you love someone until you lose them.

I flip the burgers and turn the bacon. I hate crispy bacon so I pull it out of the pan before it can overcook. Once the cheese is melting on the burgers and the macaroni casserole is done, I set it all out and call everyone into the kitchen. The boys, Anna and Aspen fill their plates. I do the same once everyone else is dished up, and congregate with them in the living room. Anna plays the next episode of Gilmore Girls. The boys don't even say a word when the show starts to play. I guess being with the same people for so long, you learn what they like, what they don't like, what they will tolerate, and you learn to give and take. The more time I spend with each and every one of these people, the more I want to be a part of them. Sure, there are those who left because they blamed me, there are those who will never accept me. But the ones who stuck around, the ones who agreed to free the griffins with me, the ones sitting beside me, eating the food I have prepared, watching a girly TV show with me, are the ones I can see myself spending the rest of my life with. And for that I am thankful.

When the food is consumed, the dishes washed, and put away. Once the Cohen guarding shift has changed. Once, everyone is settled in for the night, staring at their respective devices, reading a book, playing a video game, watching a movie, talking with a friend. Once the house is quiet, I carefully tread up each and every step to the bedroom where my father currently resides. Where my father's ashes currently reside.

When I regenerated for the first time, when I aged, Logan sat in my room through the whole process. I can't imagine what he was feeling, what thoughts were going through his head. I'm sure he was fine, he knew what was happening. But I've never seen anyone come to the end of their life cycle and regenerate before. I haven't been a part of this world for very long. I learn new things every day. I am overwhelmed with new information at every turn.

The door is shut when I get to it, but I find it unlocked. I open it and step through, not sure what I might be walking into. Will the ashes look like a human body? Will it be hot in the room? Will I be grossed out?

I take a deep breath and walk further into the room. I'm not sure if this is supposed to be a private thing. I'm not sure if I'm overstepping my bounds. I'm not even sure if he knows I'm in here, but it feels right. It feels like I need to be in this room. I walk around the bed and sit in the chair next to the dresser. I've got a chair in my room, Logan has a chair in his room, but I've never actually understood why people put chairs in their rooms. Chairs next to a desk, sure, but just random chairs? I don't know.

The sun has long since set, darkness in full bloom outside, but there is a light in the room that has nothing to do with the bulb overhead. It's a natural light, a glow rather. A calming haze resting over the room. It's peaceful. Tranquil even. So I sit in the chair and stare at my father's ashes.

I'm not sure what I was expecting. Maybe light gray pieces of burnt flesh. But my father is not a log in a fire. Maybe black soot lying on top of the bed. But again, my father is not a fire place. But they are ashes. You would know them as ashes. And they do form the length of what would be his body. But it's not like an exact outline of it. It's not like the police would draw a chalk outline around them.

Really, I should have expected what I've found. I saw Logan's body as ashes on the ground. I've merely forced that memory from my mind. Along with most thoughts of Logan. It's been several months now that I've lost him, and yet I still can't bring myself to face that fact. Now is not the time.

I stare at my father's ashes and think. I think about the times I've had with him since he's been in Cedars. I think about how I hated him and how I've grown to love him. I think about the fact that I have three parents and how they all fit into my life. I think about how I'd love to put an end to this war and try to live some semblance of a normal life. I eventually think myself to sleep.

I'm not sure how long I sleep. I do know that it is a peaceful sleep. One that is for once not plagued by nightmares and bad memories. It is a restful sleep.

I wake to someone calling my name. The voice is a familiar one. When I open my eyes and they focus on the form in front of me I stare unabashedly, open mouthed, at the person kneeling in front of me. A scream nearly rips from my throat. I hold it back and just stare.

"I let you go," I tell him.

"Casslyn, I came back," Nash tells me.

"But I let you go. I watched you disappear. How can you be here?" I ask, reaching out to touch his face.

"I regenerated. That's how it works."

"But you died. You couldn't regenerate," I insist.

"I didn't die. I regenerated. That's how it works. It's me. Your father."

My head snaps back away from the guy in front of me. My father. That can't be. Nash is the person kneeling before me. But when I really look at him, listen to his voice, there are subtle changes, minute details in his face and the cadence of his voice that aren't Nash's.

"Oh my goodness," I say, the words slowly coming forth. "You look almost exactly like Nash."

"Really?" my father asks. There is a proud note in his voice.

"Yeah. I thought I was dreaming again. I can't believe how much you look like him."

I stare at him and honest to goodness think I'm staring at my twin.

"I'm going to need a minute," I tell him.

My father steps back away from me and sits at the foot of the bed. The bed, which happens to be ash free. This really is my father. My mom is going to freak. She has to see this. I can't say that my dad will be happy. Knowing that he isn't our father eats away at him. I know it does. But having the concrete truth shoved in his face is going to make it that much worse on him. It may even drive him away again.

I wonder what it will be like for my mom to watch my father grow into the man Nash would have been. I hope it's not too hard on her. I would want her to be happy. But maybe it will only start the mourning process over again. Thinking back on my father only hours ago, I now know what Nash would look like as an adult. That's crazy to think about. It's not like I'll be able to hide my father from her forever. She knows he's in town. Plus I asked my father to talk to my parents about me being a phoenix. I also told my parents. Which they've already agreed to.

"Take all the time you need," my father says.

Oh, it's so weird to think of him as my father. It was

weird enough think about having a seventeen year old father, but the fact that he's seventeen, my father, and looks exactly like my dead, twin brother is nearly too much to take in.

I look back at my father and watch his face take on the wonderment that his son looked just like him. That's got to be something to be proud about. At least I would think so. I've seen parents who fight over who their child looks more like. I've seen parents concede to the fact that their child looks like their spouse but still claim that at least the child has their nose, or their eyes. Something small, something that makes them feel like the child really is theirs. I guess I never really thought it was that important. I guess I was wrong.

I can't imagine how my father is feeling right now, knowing that if his son had lived, there would be years, cycles of their lives, their whole lives even, that they would look like the same person.

"This is trippy," I say to no one.

My father chooses to remain silent at my comment. I wonder if his thoughts have wondered in the same direction as mine. Looking at my father, with my brother's face, it's almost like I get Nash back. But at the same time, I am well aware of the fact that just because he's got Nash's face, doesn't mean he is Nash. My father will never be able to replace the brother I lost.

"Are you okay?" my father asks after some time. Apparently the silence is getting to him.

"Yeah. This is just weird."

"I understand," he says. "Is there anything I can do that might make it less weird?"

"Have a different face, maybe," I say, only mildly joking.

A nervous giggle escapes my father. I return with an apologetic shrug.

"Can we go talk to my parents?" I ask.

"Now?" he asks. "It's four in the morning."

"Well, my mom gets off work at six. We could be there when she gets home."

"Won't that freak her out a bit?"

"Maybe your right. Okay. I'll text her and my dad and have them meet us for breakfast. Will that work?"

"It's fine with me," my father says, though his tone suggests it might not be as fine as he's letting on. "Text your parents, then get some sleep."

"You don't need any more security?" I ask.

"I think if something were to happen tonight, it would have already happened. I've regenerated. The time for an attack is past. Get some sleep. You can use Logan's room if you'd like. It is available."

"Oh. Ok," I say.

I leave my father's room without another word. I move one foot in front of the other towards Logan's bedroom. The house is nearly completely dark, and quiet, unlike hours before. It's eerie almost. My footfalls are slow and deliberate, yet filled with trepidation. I haven't been in Logan's room since he died. I'm not sure I want to go in there now. I pause when I reach his room, without going in. I stare at the door and contemplate heading down the stairs and spending the night on the couch. But that would be the coward's move, and I'm not about to be a coward. So I open the door and step in.

The room is exactly as Logan left it. I'm not sure anyone has been in here in the months since he died. I'm glad. I don't want anyone messing with his things. I was afraid Lydia might try to take some of his things as hers. I'm not sure I have any right to his things, but as his most recent love, I feel like I do. Honestly the only two people with any right to Logan's things are my father and Logan's sister Aspen.

I stand in his room, alone in what was his private space, and take it all in. Memories of the two of us in here together flash past my eyes. The first time I spent the night in Logan's house, I woke up to find him standing at the window, wearing low cut pajama bottoms. I'd never seen anything so beautiful before. The rising sun splashing his golden skin. It was the morning after I'd found out Logan was a phoenix. I was still nervous about what that meant. I was reeling from the world I knew being completely rocked. And yet in that moment all that mattered was the man standing across the room from me.

My heart aches from missing Logan. My chest heaves as my lungs try to take in enough air to sustain the hurt inside of me. My nostrils flare as broken breaths leave my body only to be replaced by air that hasn't tasted my pain.

I am hit with a barrage of memories, but I suppress

them, not ready to live in a world without Logan. Because how could I ever love again when that love isn't Logan?

Unwilling to think much more about my lost love, I shut out the light and climb into Logan's bed. After months it still smells like him. I lie there and fall asleep slowly breathing in the scent of clean, refreshing rain, a scent I've only known as Logan's.

When I wake a few hours later it isn't to a groggy, sleep deprived mind, when I wake I am ready to go. I check my phone to make sure my parents will be at my house ready to talk with my father, take a quick shower, and head down stairs to meet my father.

He's sitting at the island drinking a cup of coffee, waiting for me. I stop abruptly when I turn the corner in the kitchen, for a moment forgetting that I will find the reflection of my brother sitting at the island, not the thirty four year old version of my father. This is going to take a lot of getting used to.

I smile at him, once I've reined myself in, and stop opposite him in the kitchen.

He returns my smile and says, "Ready to go?"

"I am," I say, more excited than I have been in a long while. I'm not even sure why, but I'm going with it. "Are you sure you're up for this?"

"I am."

"Alright. Let's do this," I say, leading the way to the door.

We climb in the car my father has been using since he

arrived in Cedars. I'm sure the car rental place in the city is happy with all the business the phoenixes have been giving them. I'm not sure why we aren't just walking to my house, it being a mile away, but somehow driving feels right, more formal. My knee bounces up and down as the tires pop over the gravel. I'm nervous and excited at the same time. I hope my mom doesn't freak out too badly. I might get in trouble.

When we pull up my knee has hit a whole new speed. I press down on it with my hands but it does no good. I turn to my father who looks at me expectantly.

"Um, maybe I should go in first and maybe prepare them," I say, though I have no idea if that's what we should do.

"Whatever you think is best," my father says.

"Okay," I say and get out of the car. I walk quickly to my house feeling the need to get this over with.

When I walk into the house I expect to find my parents sitting on the couch ready to ambush me like they did the night I told them I'm a phoenix. But they are not sitting in the living room on the couch. They are both sitting at the kitchen table, a cup of coffee in front of each of them, talking with a smile on their faces. I clear my throat to get their attention. Their smiles don't fade when they see me. It is nice. For a moment I feel like we are back years ago, when we were a family. But I'm distracted for only a moment when I hear my father standing outside of his car, kicking gravel with his boots.

"Good morning, sweet heart," my mom says.

"Good morning," I say.

"Where's your father?" my dad asks me.

"Outside," I say.

"For goodness sake, Casslyn, don't leave him standing out in the cold," my mom says, standing from her chair.

"Wait," I say, holding up both my hands. "There's something I need to tell you first."

"Are you a dragon?" my dad asks.

A laugh bursts from my chest. That's actually really funny.

"No. It's not that. It's just, you know how I told you we have life spans and when we reach those life spans we go back to being seventeen," I say, speaking very rapidly.

"Yes," my parents say together.

"Okay, well, my father has done that."

"We were prepared for that," my mom says. "You told us once he regenerated, or whatever, that you wanted us to talk to him."

"Yeah, I did," I say, nodding along. "I did do that, however, I wasn't exactly prepared for what I saw once he regenerated."

"And what was that? Wings?" my father asks, again with the jokes.

"No. No. That wasn't it. It is more that, um, well, you see, my father looks a bit like Nash," I say.

Suddenly my mother lets out a scream as I have never heard come out of my mother.

"Yeah, that," I say as I feel my father's presence in the

doorway behind me.

My mom continues to scream, her hands plastered to her face, covering her mouth, but not the sound coming from it.

"Shit," my dad says, all the air escaping his lungs.

"Way to wait," I say out of the corner of my mouth.

"I did," my father says, stepping up beside me. "You were taking far too long."

"I was trying to be delicate," I argue, feeling like I'm really arguing with Nash.

"A bit like your brother, Casslyn?" my dad says, crossing his arms and raising an eyebrow.

I shrug my shoulders and say, "What's a bit, really? Breakfast?"

My mom stares openly and in wide shock at my brother. Crap. I mean my father. I walk past her and into the kitchen. My dad follows me. I find breakfast foods sitting on the counter, waiting to be cooked. I take over, not anticipating my mom being ready to cook anything any time soon. I chuckle when I sense my father rooted in his spot, allowing my mom to stare at him, but being completely uncomfortable with it.

I start cooking breakfast potatoes and bacon and sausage and eggs, pancakes and French toast. I love breakfast. Really, I just love food. It's really good I run as much as I do.

The only sound in the house is that of the sizzling food in the various pans. I feel the need to fill the silence, but I tend to put my foot in my mouth when I do that. So I remain silent and wait for the grownups to speak. My mom and father have made it back to the kitchen table. I poured my father a cup of coffee and make a show of setting it in front of him, hoping it would stir my mom into action, into speaking. No such luck. She's having a harder time with my father looking like Nash than I did. Of course, I got to see Nash in my head for nearly a year after I lost him. I never did tell my parents that. I don't think I ever will. I'm not sure how I could explain that without her thinking I'm crazy. Or at least crazier than she already thinks I am.

My dad helps me cook. It's something he and I used to do on the weekends. My mom was always in a hurry when we were younger. I'm not sure why. Maybe she felt like she always had to be running twice as fast since she had twins. I'm not sure, but my dad and I got tired of toaster waffles and pop tarts real fast. That's when we started cooking.

When the cooking is finished my dad and I plate it all up and transition it to the table. The table was already set when I got here, so everyone can dig in when it's on the table. Which I do. I'm nervous hungry, which is nearly the worst hungry. Because until you're no longer nervous, you'll keep eating. It's worse than being hangry.

I dig in. Both of my dads dig in. My mom continues to stare at my father.

"Mom," I say, nearly snapping at her. I'm able to stop myself and it comes out exasperatedly.

"Sorry," she says, using her fork to stab at a slice of French toast.

I grab a strip of bacon and rip it apart with my teeth. I

groan because it tastes so good and because this situation is so absurd.

"I get it, it's weird, he looks like Nash. Can we move past it?" I ask.

"Have you moved past it?" my dad asks.

"No. But I'm working on it."

"It's not just weird," my mom says. "It's like Nash is in this room. Like he's here with us, even if he's not here. Like I have my son back."

"I know, mom. That's how I felt when I first saw him, but then I realized that he's my father, not my brother."

"And you realized it that easily?" my dad says.

"What is with you today?" I ask. "What's with all the jokes? You've never been funny before."

"Sorry," my dad says, though he chuckles as he says it.

"They really are yours," my mom says.

"You were questioning it all this time?" I ask, incredulous.

My mom places her elbow on the table and squeezes her forehead between her fingers. My dad sits in his chair with a goofy grin on his face. My father sits in his chair looking more uncomfortable than I've ever seen him, like he's being studied under a microscope. As long as he's lived his face has never been the subject of scrutiny. For a time he shared it with someone else, that time is gone, and the three people around him would give anything for that time back.

"No, I just, I've never seen anyone look so much like their parents. Nash wasn't just a spitting image of you," my mom says, speaking to my father. "It is literally like you have the same face."

"I'm not sure what to say," my father says.

"You don't have to," I tell him.

It's not like he's here to be stared at. He is here for to speak with my parents, so that they may get a better understanding of who I am, who I'll be, and what it means to be a phoenix.

"Right," my mom says. "Wow, I can't believe how rude I'm being. I just, seeing you, looking as much like Nash as you do, it's a blessing really, to see his face again." She's got tears in her eyes as she says this. I knew she would freak out. I feared that it might start the mourning process anew. But it didn't occur to me that seeing Nash's face might be a blessing. I'm glad that this could be a good thing for my family instead of setting us back. And my dad seems to be taking it well.

"Eat up," my dad says.

The four of us fill our plates then eat in silence. Only satisfied sounds of an enjoyed meal occupy the space surrounding us. When we finish, we set the plates in the sink and worry about the dishes later, something we don't do in my house. But right now, the conversation is more important that a pile of dirty dishes.

We file into the living room and sit, my mom and dad on the couch, and my father and I on the love seat. It's almost like we're taking sides, or are part of a team. I guess in a way my father and I are part of the same team. The explaining-ourselves-to-my-parents team.

There are things I've told my parents about being a phoenix. Things they understood, and things they were unable to grasp. My father is here today to help them take a hold of some of the more tenuous concepts.

We sit on our respective sides of the living room in silence. None of us are quite sure where to start. It would be easier if my parents would just start asking questions. But instead they look at us like we can read their minds, like we should already know what to say to them.

"Is there something specific you would like us to discuss with you?" I ask my parents.

Again my mom is staring at my father, the replica of Nash, but now she tries to hide it. I can't really blame her, it's a lot to take in. She is jolted from her staring at my question.

The first question to come out of her mouth is not one I would have anticipated. "Does it hurt?" my mom asks.

I stare at her, my mouth agape, wondering where she came up with that. But my father answers her. "Not at all. The fire that burns under our skin feels like always being covered in the most comfortable blanket ever. Regenerating feels like going to sleep next to a fire and waking up after the best nap."

"Oh," my mom says.

I sit on the couch next to my father and think about what he's said. Would I describe being a phoenix the same way? Not quite, but I'm sure my mom would prefer his answer to any I would give her. She doesn't need to know about the numerous times I've been stabbed, sliced, diced, and stitched back together, not how any of it felt. She'd only worry more about me. She'd only want me closer. It would only put her in more danger.

My dad poses the next question, or more of an accusation. "You never did tell us who is after you. You never told us about Xander. And you never told us what happened to Logan."

I open my mouth to respond in the way of a petulant teenager would but my father senses it and beats me to the punch. He says, "The people who are after Casslyn and I, our whole race, are called griffins. Like us, they are descended from the ancient mythological being. The griffins of old didn't have any real powers beyond super human abilities, but being that, they are very powerful. We have been wrong to underestimate them for far too long now. We have taken a more passive approach and paid the price for it."

It's my turn to take over. I look to my mom and dad and say, "Xander is a griffin. Both his parents are griffins. Xander has known his whole life about what he is. The griffins have always been trained to hate us, it's ingrained in them. Xander suspected Logan of being a phoenix and went after him. He thought he was protecting me. When I jumped in between them, that's when I found out I'm a phoenix. Long story even longer, Xander hated being with the griffins. They were doing things he thought were shady. He didn't believe in their cause. He also didn't agree with killing me. So he saved my life and left the only one he's ever known. He hasn't seen his parents since and he's been helping me take down his own people."

My mom and dad shift uncomfortably on the couch.

"As far as Logan goes," I start, not fully prepared for this part of the conversation.

So unprepared that I can't even speak. What do I say about Logan? What do I tell them?

I try again, "The thing about Logan."

The thing about Logan. The thing I haven't yet been able to face. I lost Logan over three months ago and yet I still can't believe it. I can't face it. Can't bear it. I've talked to Aspen about him, like he's gone, but in the back of my mind, I never could accept the fact that he's gone. It's been three months, I should really come to terms with it.

My father waits for me to go on. I'm glad he isn't stepping in. I'm glad he is letting me tell Logan's story. Logan may have been my father's soldier, and somewhat foster son, but he was the love of my life.

Logan is the love of my life. When he first came here Logan scared me. He scared me out of my endless self-pity party of grief. Then I got to know him and he no longer scared me, but he pushed me. He pushed me into not just surviving the death of my brother but into coming to terms with it. Accepting that Nash was gone and I needed to live for the life I had without him, not grieve the life I had with him. Then, after I learned my life was not what I thought and more over that it was in severe danger, Logan trained me to defend myself. He taught me how to push my body and make myself stronger. Only after he knew I was looked after, did he take the time to consider a relationship with me, and look after his needs. Because we needed each other. Our relationship, however brief, was passionate and fun and so full of love I wouldn't trade it for anything in the world.

But how do I translate that into words for my parents?

I turn to my mom, know she's the most likely to understand how I feel and to look under the surface for anything I might not have the courage to say.

"My father sent Logan here to protect me," I say, indicating to my father beside me. I've already told my parents this but for the sake of the story I include it in the telling. "He moved in next door and we got to know each other. We loved each other. We were attacked here on Logan's birthday. Like Tucker, Logan was killed in the attack. His body burned and turned to ash. I've told you phoenixes have healing tears, and I tried. I cried on his ashes. I cried on Tucker's body. Gray cried on Tucker's body. But we were too late. I was too late. I couldn't save them. Logan's ashes are in an urn in my bedroom."

My parents are quiet. Quieter than I've ever seen them. They can see the grief on my face, hear it in my voice. And they're not sure how to confront it, not sure how to combat the loss I've been through. Not only of Logan, but that of Logan, Nash, Tucker, and my other phoenix friends. They are not sure how their daughter is still standing yet alone functioning on a level befitting a sane person.

Maybe I am insane and just haven't yet realized it. Does anyone actually realize they are insane?

My parents, all three of them, continue to watch me. It's uncomfortable and causes me to fidget. My eyes move to the tops of my knees when their stares become too much. My thumb presses deep strokes into the palm of my other hand.

It's not like they can say they are sorry, empty words they've all been told themselves. Empty words that bring no comfort. But what can they say? Honestly I wish they'd say nothing.

So I change the subject.

"Anything else you guys would like to know?" I ask them.

"Where to begin," my dad says.

"That's what we're here for," I tell them. "I want you to understand who I am."

"We know exactly who you are, Casslyn," my mom says.

"You know half of me. You know the me from before Nash died. I've changed. A lot," I tell them.

I've killed people.

I don't tell them that. They would never look at me the same way. Even if those I killed had it coming. Even if those I've killed have taken everything I've loved away from me. There is no changing the fact that I am now a killer. There is no coming back from it. The tremors that still overtake my hands and wake me from fitful sleep are a constant reminder of what I've become. But I'm not going to ask forgiveness.

I'm not going to apologize for it. I did what I had to do and that is that.

"You are still our daughter," my dad says. "You've been changing your whole life. But you are still our Casslyn and that will never change."

I want to say something corny like *aw, Dad*, but that would ruin the moment. So instead, I stare at him, like he did to me before, until he has to gaze at his knees and rub his thumb into his palm. I smile at him, at the situation, at the love I feel in this room.

My parents continue to ask questions about what it is to be a phoenix. I try my best to explain everything I have experienced since discovering that I am a phoenix and since aging into one. When I don't have answers for them my father steps in. It's moments like these I understand how he is such a good leader. I understand why our people follow him, why they love him. Because I feel it too. But watching him with my parents, being patient with them, explaining things to them in ways they will understand and won't lead to other questions. I'm far more short tempered and quickly lose my patience with them. But watching my father, listening to him, makes me want to be more patient with them, anyone really. How will I ever be able to lead my people if I can't explain who I am to my own parents? I'm definitely banking on my father living forever, that way, I'll never have to take over for him.

Occasionally I catch either one or both of my parents staring at my father. I must admit, I can't help but stare at him as well. If anyone who knows us, knows my family, were to walk into the room, they would think they've gone back in time, back to when Nash was alive. Because that is what it looks like. In my living room it appears as though my mom and dad are sitting on the couch, Nash and I on the love seat. My heart wrings itself into a tight knot at the thought. I hold my breath and wait for it to pass. Hope it will pass. When it finally does, I can focus on the conversation. My brother is gone, I've come to terms with that, I've faced it head on and come through on the other side. Now is not the time to regress. So I move past the moment and concentrate on being here, in the moment with my family.

I'm no longer sure of what we've explained to my parents and what we haven't. I know they have asked questions I originally answered for them when I told them about me being a phoenix. But I'll admit that was a bit of a stressful afternoon and they might not have absorbed everything I told them.

I can tell the conversation is coming to somewhat of an end when my parents do a recap of everything they've learned.

"Okay," my mom says. "When you turn seventeen you age into being a phoenix."

"Yes," I say.

My dad says, "And you can heal yourself with your regenerating powers, and heal others with your tears. And you can start pretty much anything on fire."

"Yes," I repeat, almost, but not mentioning the fact that

I cannot light hunting knives on fire. I'll have to test the heat of my fire on other materials I may need to dispose of in the future. It's always good to know what one is capable of. Or not capable of in this case.

My parents continue their run down. How old we can be, how we can be killed, who our enemies are, our history, how the bloodlines are passed on, and so it goes. Until we actually come to the end of the conversation.

Fatigue wears on all three of my parents faces, my mom because she's only gotten off a long ass shift at the hospital, my dad from an overload of information, and my father from dispensing a lot of information on himself and his people. I could use a nap myself.

"Thank you both for confiding in us," my mom says.

"Yes," my dad says, "we really appreciate you letting us into your world. We may not understand it but we want to."

"Yes," my mom says. "We love you so much, Casslyn. We want to be part of your world. We want you to feel like you can come to us for anything. We would also love to meet the other phoenixes you have been spending time with."

"Of course we would. Is there a time that would work for all of you?" my dad asks.

"That is so kind of you," my father says.

I'm trying to think of how the other phoenixes will take this. I've never thought about any of them having families, living their own lives, meeting people outside of their core group of people. I wonder what they will think of my parents. They have all already spent time in my home, it's not like I'm afraid they will think less of me. But they aren't the most welcoming people in the world, and I want them to like my parents. They are two of the most important people in my life. And while they may be a small aspect of my life right now, compared to what I am facing with the griffins, they are a huge part of my life. They deserve all the respect in the world. If the phoenixes don't give it to them, they are going to have to deal with me. Of course, I could be making a huger deal of this than it is. I tend to do that. Plus, it may just have been me they had a problem with.

"I will talk with them and find a time that works," my father says.

My mom gasps suddenly, which has me ducking and searching all possible entries into the house for intruders. It would be like the griffins to attack now, when everything is going smoothly, when I've got nearly every one I have left in this world in the same room. But my search comes up empty. There are no griffins attacking. My mom has given me a heart attack for no reason.

"No, I've got it," she says, though at this heart hammering moment, I'm not sure what she's got.

She continues when we eye her. "Thanksgiving is next week. We would love it if you could all join us. It would be like one big family dinner."

She glances at my dad to make sure he agrees with her, even if he doesn't want to. But the wide eyed flashy grin thing going on all over his face says it really is the perfect idea. I must agree with them. It would be like one big family dinner. Something I haven't had in an amount of time I could not calculate if I wanted to. My heart squeezes in my chest again, but this time it's not as painful and not as debilitating. I am honestly looking forward to it, possibly more than my parents.

"That sounds fantastic," my father says. "But that sounds like a lot of cooking, and a lot of mess, and just a lot all around. Are you sure you want to go to all that work?"

"Yes," my parents and I practically shout at my father.

"It's settled then," my father says. "I will let our people know. We will be here for Thanksgiving dinner. Please be sure to let me or Casslyn know of anything we can do or bring. We will be sure to provide anything you need."

"It is our pleasure. We will see you all then," my mom says.

"Thanks, mom," I tell her.

She smiles and nods at me, her eyes shining, like she could cry at any moment. I hug her, tightening my arms around her until I'm sure she can feel my appreciation for her generosity.

When we pull away from each other she holds on to me and says, "Be sure to invite Xander. You know that boy is part of the family."

"He lives here and it's a home cooked meal. He's not about to miss it."

"All the same," my mom says.

"I will let him know," I tell her.

When I think about it, I would love it if I could invite

Cohen. His family would more likely kill him than spend Thanksgiving with him. And he's so alone already, besides his body guards, I don't want him to be alone on the holiday. I will have to talk to my father about it, talk to the rest of the phoenixes, and then see if I can invite him. As much as I would love to hate him, to make sure he spent every holiday from now to eternity alone, I've gotten past that part of my black soul and now I just want everyone I care about to be safe and happy, and apparently have a belly full of turkey and mashed potatoes. One way or another I'm getting him Thanksgiving dinner. It's decided.

My mom and I finally pull all the way apart. I hug my dad good bye, let them know I'll see them later, and leave through the front door with my father. So far this has been a good day and it's not even noon. I'm feeling good about today. It's been a long time since I've had an all around good day. It's about damn time.

Nine

"Blast away," Aspen yells from across the room.

I pull my fire into life on the outsides of my palms and build it then push it out in a continuous stream directly at her. A wicked grin splays across my face as my blast hits her square in the chest. I'm getting good at this. It's about damn time. All those months I spent with my powers out of whack were really getting to me. I honestly believed I was defective and that I wasn't actually meant to be a phoenix.

I release the pull on my power, pulling it back under my skin. Aspen stands across the room from me, not moving, smoke billowing off the fire proof racing jacket we got for just this purpose. It's not like my fire can hurt her, but it got old going through so many clothes.

"That was awesome," Aspen says, pulling off the fire

proof jacket.

"My turn," Anna says, taking Aspen's place.

Lydia, Nathan, and Thomas stand in line.

Gray stands next to me, teaching me technique. Where to aim, how to control the flame, how to make the fire hotter. It's been fun to learn about my new ability. I'm not the only one excited about it. But it's also been exhausting. My friends don't have this capability so they want me down here in Logan's basement with them at all times training, showing them how it works, if I can do other things with it.

It was fun at first, well really it still is, because I can do something they can't. And after they didn't accept me at first for not being phoenix enough, it was nice to show them up. But it's gotten tedious.

I know I need to train as much as I can, especially since I haven't been at this as long as the rest of them, but sometimes I need some free time.

Once Anna has gotten the fire proof jacket on, she takes a defensive stance and waits for me to blast her with my fire. Gray winks at me and grins, ready for the excitement. It's nice to see an expression on his face different from the permanent sorrow etched there these past few months. Everyone close to me lost someone that day, but no one more than Gray and I. There is something deeper to loss when it's someone who owns your heart.

And that is why I have to defeat Raphe, why I have to free the griffins suppressed by such a psychotic leader. I can't lose another person so close to me. I might not survive it.

When I'm not pulling on my power it's buried somewhere between under the surface of my skin and deep within my body. Like now, that I've been using it all afternoon, it blazes right under my skin, causing goosebumps to bubble my flesh, making the hair stand on my arms. It's right where I need it. There the instant I call on it.

The feel of the fire passing through my skin to blaze in the open air is like nothing I've ever felt and yet so familiar. Like when you open the oven door and the heat passes through you. I pull on my power, reveling in the strength I feel, and push it out of my body in a stream just like a flame thrower you'd see in a movie. It streams towards Anna and like Aspen, it hits her in the chest. The force of my flame makes Anna take a step back before she can brace herself. A wide smile covers her face. I'm glad she's getting a kick out of this.

Gray clears his throat, bringing me back to the task at hand. Oh, yeah, we're supposed to be actually training, not messing around. Nathan and Thomas jump out of line and rush me. Without taking my eyes off of Anna, I pull one hand away from her and aim it at my attackers. We could only get our hands on one fire proof jacket so the boys are going to have to replace some clothes.

The flames hit Thomas in the shoulder, glance off and strike Nathan on the side of his face. He jerks his face away from the flame and clutches his cheek with his hands. I know my flames won't hurt him, but I can't imagine what it feels like to get struck by them so close to his eye.

I cut my flames off mid-stream and rush to his side to make sure he's ok. Nathan still clutches his cheek with his hands, his long fingers covering his eyes. I pull them away so I can get a good look. He blinks rapidly and can't seem to focus his eyes. His eye is red and shiny with tears.

Gray is now at my side, peering into Nathan's eye.

"How is it? Are you okay?" Gray asks.

"Yeah, I'm fine," Nathan says. "There's just one thing."

"What is it?" I ask, fear swelling in my chest.

Nathan takes a deep breath then swallows, his Adam's apple bobbing in his throat.

"I . . .," he says, drawing out his response. His voice is thick as he says. "I can't see out of my one eye."

My heart hitches a ride on a fighter jet for a quick trip to my throat. I can't believe I've blinded him. Is that possible? I didn't think our flames could hurt each other. I certainly didn't do any damage to Lydia when I blasted her in the kitchen however long ago that was.

"Are you sure?" Gray asks. "Close your good eye and tell me how many fingers I'm holding up."

Nathan closes his good eye while Gray holds up two fingers. It's a tense moment before Nathan answers, "Four?"

My chest starts convulsing. I've blinded my friend. I've blinded one of the few soldiers we have left.

"Should I get Aris?" Aspen asks Gray.

"You probably should," Gray says.

I sit back on my feet, feeling the world crash around me.

"I'm so sorry, Nathan. I'm so sorry," I tell him.

What else can I say?

Nathan covers his injured eye with his hand and looks at me with the other. It's full of judgement, blame, sorrow, but no anger. If it were me, there would be anger.

I guess he won't be thankful for having me as a friend this Thanksgiving.

"It's not your fault," Nathan says.

"It is my fault," I tell him. "I should have aimed better. I shouldn't have gotten cocky. I'm so sorry."

"Don't be so hard on yourself," Anna says. "It could have happened to anyone."

Lydia snorts from behind Anna. "Not likely," she says. I thought we'd gotten closer. I thought we'd become somewhat friends. I guess I was wrong. I make one mistake and she's back to hating me. "Shit like this only happens to her. She'll be the death of us all."

"What's going on?" my father asks.

Tears well in my eyes. I've shamed him. I've blinded my friend. I've got to be the worst phoenix ever. I hold my breath and will my tears not to spill over.

Lydia crosses her arms and says, "Your *daughter* decided it was a good idea to hit Nathan in the eye and now he can't see out of it." Nathan is Lydia's brother. I can see why she's so angry. But it's not like I did it on purpose.

"Has anyone tried healing him? Why haven't you healed yourself?" my father asks the room and then Nathan.

I hadn't thought about that. We are phoenixes. Everyone in this room has the ability to heal themselves or others.

Surely we can heal him.

"I've tried. I can't," Nathan says. His voice sounds dejected, like he's ashamed of himself because he can't heal himself.

My throat thickens. I can't believe I did this. Lydia is right. Shit like this only happens to me.

"I'm so sorry," I tell him.

"Someone cry into his eye please," my father says.

"I'll do it," I say. The least I can do is heal him. Not to mention I've got tears at the ready.

"You've done enough," Lydia says.

I recoil away from her words, from the acid in her voice. I want to say I'm sorry again but it would be an empty and meaningless gesture.

I want to walk away. I want to escape and never have to face their blame. When they blamed me for Kristina, for Logan, for everyone else. I couldn't take it. But I can't walk away every time a situation gets tough. I'm going to have to face things sooner or later. So I don't walk away. I face their blame. I face their hate. I face it because it really is always me who puts them in the tough situations. It is always my fault.

I let my breath out in short bursts then hold it again, still trying to hold back the tears threatening to spill over. It's working, but it won't work forever.

I close my eyes and wait for Lydia to cry into her brother's eye and heal him, if it is possible. Instead of watching, I listen. I can hear every movement in the room. I hear every breath, everybody shift, every everything. I can even hear as someone snickers.

What?

Yes, a snicker.

I open my eyes and see every single person in the room looking at me. With a smile on their faces. Even Nathan and Lydia. Even my father.

"Don't worry, Cass," Nathan says. "I can see perfectly fine. Maybe even better than when you hit me in the face with your flames."

"What?" I ask, because that's all I can manage.

"It was a joke," Thomas says.

Relief floods my body, but that doesn't stop the tears from rolling down my cheeks.

"Obviously a bad one," Gray says.

"I hate you guys," I say, though don't really mean it.

"Oh, jeez. We're really sorry," Nathan says. "We just wanted you to get out of your head."

"Don't think that happened," Aspen says.

"If anything," Lydia says, "we drove her farther into it."

"Ha ha," I say, not feeling to amused.

"We're sorry, Casslyn," my father says.

"I can't believe you were in on it."

"What is a leader if they can't help their people play jokes on each other?" my father says.

I suck in a deep breath and release it slowly, trying to reign in the harsh rhythm of my chest. I'm glad he's okay, but I felt so terribly about it. Coming off the guilt and adrenaline is nauseating.

Everyone in the room now wears warried expressions. Good. Serves them right. But I'm not mad. I'm glad they felt like they could play a joke on me. It makes me feel like I might actually be one of them. Like they've finally completely accepted me as one of them.

But just to keep them on their guard I ball fire in my hand and throw it at Nathan's face. It hits him where the original flames struck him, and burns out. He dramatically paws at his cheek but smiles at me, clearly glad I don't hate him for the joke he played on me.

I turn away from my people and walk away from them, saying over my shoulder, "I'll see you all at supper. I'm not thankful for any one of you."

They all laugh as I exit the basement.

***

Half an hour later I sit on Cohen's bed as he tosses shirts and jeans out of his closet searching for the perfect outfit to wear to my house tonight for Thanksgiving. My mom was down with the idea of adding another person from my no-longer-secret-life to the party. More than likely because she doesn't know the part of my life Cohen played and I plan on keeping that a secret from her. That is, if I can get every phoenix in Cedars on board. They, on the other hand, took a little more convincing on the idea of inviting Cohen to Thanksgiving. In the end I told them that if it wasn't for me, none of them would be invited. I may have added something like it's my family, my house, and my rules. So Cohen got invited to Thanksgiving.

The person I didn't think would need convincing was Cohen.

"Are you sure I should go?" Cohen asks for about the sixth time. "I don't want anyone to be uncomfortable."

"Yes, I'm sure. Can you just pick something out? I told my mom I'd help her cook."

Cohen throws another pair of jeans out of his closet. They come flying out at me and nearly smack me in the face before I block them with an arm. A disgruntled sigh comes from somewhere deep in the closet.

"How does your mom not hate me? I did try to kill you."

"I haven't exactly mentioned it. So as long as she doesn't find out, you're good to go."

"And if she finds out?" he asks, leaning himself against the door frame of the closet. There's a crease between his eyebrows I'm afraid might become permanent.

"Well, Xander stabbed me too, and he's still invited."

Cohen gives me a look that says, not-quite-the-same and continues to rummage through his closet.

"What are you wearing?" he asks me.

"Currently, sweats and a work out shirt."

"Funny," he says deadpan, his back to me.

"Jeans and a nice sweater," I tell him. "Would you calm down? Why are you so worried about this?"

Cohen turns around and stares at me, his eyebrows furrowed, again with the crease between his eyes. There's a discomfort on his face I've never seen before. It's different than I've seen before. I've seen him scared, I've seen him guilty. I've seen him worried. I've never seen him openly vulnerable.

"It doesn't matter," he says, turning away from me.

"Cohen, what is going on?" I ask, standing up from his bed to move to him.

I corner him in the closet and stare him down.

"I've never had a Thanksgiving. My mom left when I was four and I can't remember anything before that. I can't remember if we ever had Thanksgiving dinner. After she left, my father said there was nothing to be thankful for."

Cohen stops talking. I'm not sure if he has nothing left to say or if he's afraid to go on.

I knew his mom left. I throw it in Ashely's face every time she gives me shit about my parents splitting up. It struck the exact nerve I was hoping for. Every time. But I never wondered how it affected Cohen. It still baffles me to think of Cohen and Ashley as siblings. They are so different. Polar opposites.

My parents split up when I was sixteen. I knew it wasn't exactly my fault that they split up, that my dad left. Though when he was ignoring me I thought maybe it was me. But when your parent abandons you when you are so young, like they didn't want you, didn't love you enough to stick around. Is that how Ashley and Cohen feel? Is that how they've always felt?

But besides the fact that his mom left him, his dad made it worse. Not giving them a Thanksgiving because they had nothing to be thankful for when their mother left. What else did he take away from them? Did they have birthday parties? I know Ashely did. When I was little I was jealous I was never invited. Then when I was older, Nash, Tucker, Xander and I would hang out and act out what we thought was going on at the party. We'd do our nails, talk about boys, watch *Spice World* and listen to the BackStreet Boys on repeat.

Did they get to celebrate Christmas? My parents, Nash, and I had Christmas traditions. Did Cohen and Ashley get presents? Again, I know Ashley did, she flaunted them at school when break was over.

"I was sent off when I was ten," Cohen answers for me. "He thought I was too weak. He thought if I went away for a few years I would appreciate him more. Appreciate the life he provided for me. What he didn't think was that I would embrace the freedom he was giving me and live it to the fullest. Of course there were the occasional visits to see how I was coming along. He would send griffins to check up on me. He even went so far as to have one of them attend the school I was going to. That's when I got caught. That's when I came home, so he could turn me into the griffin he always wanted me to be." Cohen smiles, but it is a dark smile, one full of contempt.

He continues, "The thing is, he still wanted me to lead the griffins once he was gone. He chose me over Ashley, his perfect student. That made her mad. You better believe it. I tried telling him I wanted out. After he beat me and locked me in a closet for a week he told me that if I got close enough to you and killed you, he'd let me out. I was so desperate I believed him. You know how that turned out."

Tears sting the back of my eyes. My father wanted me to be a phoenix, but I know if I told him I wanted nothing to do with them, he would have accepted it, and me. I can't imagine having one parent abandon you and the other not love you for who you are and what you want with your life. I feel bad for Cohen. I know he didn't tell me this story for my sympathy, but I feel sorry for him. I know he didn't tell me his story to get me to forgive him faster, but it did the trick. I will never fully forgive him, but pieces of my anger chip away all the time. Especially moments like these.

"Well," I say, swallowing back the tears. "I hope today can make up for all those missed Thanksgivings."

"So," Cohen says, like he didn't just tell me a sorrowful story, "Which shirt? The blue or the black?"

"You know I have a thing for black," I tell him.

He smiles and says, "I know you do."

Without any indication or asking me to leave or turn around, Cohen strips down to his boxers, and pulls on a new pair of jeans and the black fitted long sleeve shirt I picked out. He runs a hand through his hair, artfully tousling it, winks at me.

"A little warning might be nice," I say to him, my cheeks reddening.

"It's not like I got naked," he says, pauses, then says,

"Would you have liked it if I did?"

"I think you shot that chance in the foot the moment you stabbed me in the heart," I tell him, taking a pillow off his bed to throw at him.

"I'm pretty sure I'd have lost you the second Logan wanted you back and we both know it."

"I'm sorry. I loved him. I wanted to love you, I did, but my heart belonged to Logan."

"Yeah I know. I didn't want to play second fiddle anyway," Cohen says, again running his hand through his hair. A serious look passes over his face before he says, "Can I ask you a question?"

"Sure," I say, though I say it slowly, wondering where he's going with this. It's not exactly a topic I'd have thought we'd discuss after he tried to kill me, but then I never thought we'd be friends again after he tried to kill me.

"Do you think we could ever try again? Like actually try to be a couple? Without an ex-boyfriend in the way and me you know, playing you so my father could kill your people."

I take a deep breath and blow it out slowly.

"I'm not going to lie to you, or give you false hope. I care about you, Cohen, I really do. And I did enjoy being with you. But I will never love anyone again the way I loved Logan. I'm still in love with him. I don't ever see that going away."

Cohen's shoulders and the expression on his face sag.

My heart tugs in my chest. I hate hurting him like this. It wouldn't be fair to lead him on and then it not work between us. I couldn't do that to him, or myself. I will always be in love with Logan. I may try to love again, but I don't see it being with Cohen. I do care about him, but our past is too sordid to make a romantic relationship work between us.

"I had to ask," he says, shrugging his shoulders.

Cohen walks towards me and swings an arm around my shoulders. He gives me a one sided smile and nods towards the door like he's ready to head to my parents' house.

I pull out of his grasp and open the door and check for any signs we might be ambushed. Xander and Anna are posted near the door and as a lookout. I whistle to them, our signal, to see if the coast is clear. When I get the answering all clear whistle Cohen and I head for my car. Once we're in the car, have started the engine and locked the doors, Xander and Anna head for Xander's car. With the go ahead, we head out of town and to my house. It is a bit risky to leave Cohen's loft unattended while we are all at my parents' house, but Raphe wants Cohen, and ransacking his apartment when he's not there isn't going to result in getting Cohen.

I can't say I'm not worried about the griffins staging an attack at my parent's today. With all of their enemies in one place, it would be so easy. I'm sure they think we are prepared, which we are, but I still wouldn't put it past them. I'm worried they are going to do something, whether it be today, or sometime soon. They have been too quiet. Too low key. I know they are reeling from their losses, but I can't see Raphe taking it all lying down. He is planning something. I just wish I knew what, and when it is coming.

But, if I spend my entire life looking over my shoulder and around every corner, that is no life to live. I'm going to be on my guard, but I'm also going to enjoy today with my family and friends.

When I pull up to my house my dad's car is in the driveway, but his is the only one. It's okay. I need a shower, and to help my mom cook. It's hours until dinner, but I'm sure my mom has a list for me a mile long. And trust me, items on her list are many and take a lot of time. You might not think peeling potatoes takes a long time, but when you have to peel ten pounds of potatoes, that shit takes time.

As we walk up to the house my ears tune into the noise coming from inside. A lot of noise. My mom likes to play music when she cooks, but this is far more noise than just a radio. It worries me. I hustle into the house, my heart beating heavy in my chest. But when I swing open the door, ready for a fight, I find all three of my parents and all of my friends huddled in the kitchen, all participating in some task I'm sure was on my list.

It takes me a moment to calm down, but when I do, I notice Aspen in front of the sink peeling the ten pounds of potatoes I mentioned. Lydia has a can opener in her hand opening several cans of green beans and cream of mushroom soup, a large canister of fried onions sitting next to the baking dish. Gray and Thomas are stuffing and basting the turkey. My mom flits around the kitchen passing out instructions. My dad and my father lean against the counter and watch over the proceedings. It takes my brain several moments to come to the terms that it's not my dad and Nash leaning against the counter. It is going to take far more getting used to my father looking exactly like my dead twin brother than I have had. I may not ever get used to it.

Not one of the phoenixes has a disgusted look on their faces. Not even Lydia. If I had to put an emotion to the looks on their faces, I'd say they are all enjoying themselves.

A smile creeps across my face. I worried how all sides of my life would come together. How easy the transition would be. As long as everyone can accept Cohen without crossed arms, I will get off easy. I can hear Cohen swallow hard next to me. His pulse races. He's nervous. I would be too. But I told everyone to be nice to him. I hope they listen. I should have asked them all before I went to pick Cohen up not to out him to my parents today. The last thing I need today is for my parents to learn one of their Thanksgiving guests tried to kill me once upon a time.

I find his hand with mine and give it a tight squeeze. Trying to reassure him that today is going to be okay. He is going to make it through this. I hope he might even enjoy himself. Baby steps. He squeezes my hand back but it's not as firm, not as sure. He hasn't bolted for the door yet so that's a good sign.

I turn to him, smile at him, and pull him further into the house, towards the kitchen full of my family.

"Happy Thanksgiving," I call to them as we near.

"Happy Thanksgiving," my mom says to me, a broad smile on her face. It might be the most earnest and genuine smile I've seen on my mom's face since Nash died.

She moves towards me, her arms held out for a hug. It's strong and filled with love. The perfect hug for the holiday. When she pulls back, my dad is there to replace her. My mom moves on to hug Cohen. I wonder if she would embrace him if she knew his secrets. I wonder if she hugged everyone in the kitchen. If I had to guess, I'd say she did.

I hear the front door open and close and turn to see Xander and Anna walking towards us.

"Happy Thanksgiving," my mom says, rushing them to give them hugs.

Guess that answers that question. Xander hugs her back like it's old hat. Which for him, it is. Anna looks slightly taken aback, but quickly settles into the hug, like it's something missing from her life. I know she's had a hard time dealing with Kristina's death. I know we have all had a hard time dealing with the death of a loved one or more. I really hope tonight can be healing for some of us. If not all.

When my mom is finished embracing the population of the house, I ask her what we can do to help.

"Desserts, of course," she says.

Of course. I can't believe I didn't think of that.

When we were little, Thanksgiving was the only time Nash and I ever fought. Why, you ask? Because he wanted chocolate pie, and I wanted peach pie. So how did we settle this, you ask? My mom broke down and made both. My mom puts Xander and Anna in charge of the chocolate pie, and Cohen and I in charge of the peach pie. It's only fair that because I fight for the pie, that I make the pie. Though, as many people as there are attending this year, my mom has both of my fathers making two other pies. Apple, because who doesn't like apple pie. And pumpkin, because what is Thanksgiving without pumpkin pie.

When everyone has a task to work on, we get down to it. It's not long before the house is filled with foody smells and nearly everyone's stomachs rumble. I love food. I love eating. Ask anyone who knows me. They will tell you, Casslyn loves food. I love meat. I love potatoes and corn and beans and peas. I love desserts. I love chips. I love pasta. I love pizza. I love food. So the more the house smells like food, the hungrier I get.

But, as the years have taught me, my mom won't let us eat until all the food is prepared and everyone is seated at the table. And only after we have said our meal prayer.

Before all that happens, and while the turkey cooks for hours, and once I've showered and changed, we play games. My family has always liked board games. There is a six foot stack of board games in our hallway closet. I tried to play Monopoly with my parents on Christmas last year, but they still hated each other then, so we didn't get past GO before my dad walked out of the house and my mom went to work at the hospital. Today is going to be better. I can feel it. Gray and I head for the hall closet to hunt down some games while the others prep the table to eat. It will be a while before we can eat but it's best to be prepared when the food is finally ready.

For the first time since Tucker died, Gray's mohawk is actually upright. His eyes are ringed in black. He is wearing a black button up shirt but under the top button a Nirvana t-shirt peeks out. It's nice to have the real Gray back. He looked nice without the eye liner, without the piercings, without the standing mohawk, but it just wasn't Gray. I'm happy to see him like this. Losing Tucker devastated him, but if he can power through losing him, maybe I can finally face the fact that I lost Logan, and maybe wade through that too.

"Holy shit," Gray says when I open the closet. "I've never seen so many board games outside of a store before."

"We like board games," I tell him.

"Couldn't guess," he says.

"Shut up," I tell him, then playfully punch him in the arm.

He feigns pain and then reaches for a game. He runs his hand over the stack lingering on certain games. After perusing the games for a time he pulls out Balderdash from the stack. Xander, Tucker, Nash and I loved playing this game. It's a game where you get a category, whether that be entertainment, law, vocabulary, and so on. So like, you get a movie title and you have to write what you think the plot is, or you get part of a law and you have to finish it, or you get a word and you have to write the definition. One time we had to finish the law "you are not allowed to pass a firetruck . . ." I finished the law by saying "you are not allowed to pass a firetruck while in pursuit of a rogue bear." Thinking about it now, it's not that funny, but at the time we thought it was hilarious. The point of the game is to try to have the most plausible answer and to get the card reader to choose your answer and to move up the board until you win.

While Gray reads the back of the game box I tell him, "Tucker never tried to win. He always tried to write the most outlandish answer he could. We never ended a game without our sides screaming from laughing so hard."

Gray laughs along with me as I tell him about playing the game with my friends. I know he can imagine Tucker writing out crazy answers.

I smile remembering one specific crazy answer Tucker gave. "One time he had to write the plot of the movie *Lethal Weapon*. He even knew the plot of the movie, but he decided to describe the plot as two men who go to the zoo, break into the enclosures and see who can ride the most animals. It was ridiculous."

Gray throws his head back and laughs, his Adam's apple bobbing up and down.

"If you knew he was never trying to win, who ever tried to win? How was it ever any fun?" he asks me.

"Xander, Nash, and I tried to win. But besides that, the fun was seeing what Tucker's brain could come up with."

Gray shakes his head and says, "He surprised me every day we were together. He really was special."

"He was," I say.

A silence falls over us. The noise from the rest of the house thickly coats us. The cheer bleeds from Gray's face.

Loss is clear where moments ago love held tight. It's crazy how quickly grief can grip you tight and strangle you.

I am fully aware that I do all I can to hold my grief inside, to not talk about it with others. I like to keep it to myself. I wallow in my own grief. But I am also aware that that's not how everyone likes to grieve. Gray is an open type of person. He likes to let people in. He likes to share his world with people. I feel bad for forgetting that. I feel bad for keeping myself away from him. I think it's time I rectify that.

"How are you holding up?" I ask him knowing full well he will know to what I'm referring.

"About as well as you, I imagine," he says, now staring back at the stack of games.

"I hurt every day without him," I tell him, then remember I've lost more than one person. "Both of them. All of them."

"Me too."

"How do we ever move on? How can we ever get over them?"

"I don't want to get over Tucker. I know that I didn't get to spend that much time with him, but he changed my life. He was the true love of my life."

"I feel the same way about Logan. We may have been apart for a little while, and I may have started something with Cohen, but I never stopped loving him. I was just biding my time until we got back together, because I knew we would."

"Tucker did too. Honestly we all did. Even Lydia. She wanted so badly to be with Logan, but she knew his heart belonged to you."

"I know you know this. But I want to tell you how much Tucker loved you. You would be embarrassed if you heard the way he talked about you. I had never seen him happier than when he was with you. And I want to thank you. He was my best friend and he deserved being happy with you."

We are now seated on the floor on opposite ends of the hallway, our legs spread out and intertwined.

I watch Gray. Watch a storm of emotions play on his face. The longer we sit here, the darker he becomes. I wonder at what could possibly be plaguing him. It's a shadow of something I've seen haunt him since Tucker's death. But I always assumed it was grief. Staring at him now, I know it's something more.

He looks up to see me watching him. I think he'll put a guard up, act as though I saw nothing. But then he opens his mouth. "Do you hate me, Casslyn? I hate myself every day. It's my fault Tucker is dead." Tears slip over Gray's painted eyelashes and run down his cheeks. He doesn't even wipe them away. "I was in the basement with him. I was protecting him. But I could hear what was happening upstairs. I couldn't bear the fact that my people were being attacked and I was hiding away. Tucker knew it. I didn't want to leave him. But then I heard you and Cohen. We must have been right under you. I heard him tell you he was sorry. And then I heard your body hit the floor. Tucker did too. Though he didn't know it was you, it was like he had this feeling. He made me come upstairs. He made me, Casslyn. I left him alone and now he's dead."

Black streaks mar Gray's beautiful face. A war has taken its toll on his emotions and found him wanting. His head is bowed, like he can't bear to see me hate him. But I don't. I don't hate him. I crawl around Gray's legs and sit next to him.

Placing my hands on either side of his face I make him look at me, really look at me. "I don't hate you, Gray. Mostly because Tucker would hate me if I did. But I don't hate you. And I don't blame you. What happened, happened. We can't go back. And we can't change it. But we can face Raphe and take him down and make sure nothing like this happens again. You need to stop beating yourself up about this. I bet you Tucker is looking down on us right now upset because you blame yourself. He would want you to be living life for yourself and for him. Can you do that?"

I'm hoping Gray will say that he can. That he will move on and stop beating himself up over this. But instead, he turns the tide on me and asks, "Can you take your own advice?"

"No. Because I am the real reason he's dead. Logan told me not to bring him into this. And I didn't listen. Raphe has been after me this whole time and I thought I could protect Tucker. But I didn't."

Gray stares back at me and says, "If you can't forgive yourself, how do you expect me to forgive myself? We are more alike than you might think, fireball."

"Then we will work on it," I tell him. "We owe Tucker that much."

Gray nods his head. I use my thumbs to wipe away the black streaks on his cheeks. "Honestly, didn't your mother ever tell you to use waterproof eyeliner?"

Gray laughs and says, "I must have missed that lesson."

The darkness has passed and yet neither of us is ready to get up and face the house full of our friends. So we sit next to each other in the hallway, Gray's head resting on my shoulder, my head on his and we sit in silence. You can bury something deep inside yourself. You can keep it at bay. But once it's broken the surface, it's hard to push back into its box. Especially something so mean and ugly as grief and guilt. It fights to be known. It fights to be heard and felt. And once it's got its grip on you, it doesn't want to let go.

Once in a while a reprieve will come along and pull you away from guilt's clutches when you can't fight it on your own. Right now, that reprieve is my mom coming in to say dinner is ready.

"Casslyn, Gray, it's time to eat," she says, standing above us.

I'm not sure how long she's been there, but the look on her face says it's been long enough. I'm sorry she has to see me like this. I'm sorry I've brought her into this. One thing is for sure this go around, she is not going to end up like Tucker.

"We didn't get to play a board game," Gray says, standing up next to me.

"After we eat. I promise," I tell him.

Gray swings an arm around my shoulders, places his forehead against mine and says, "I'm glad you're in my life, fireball."

"Me too, Gray. Now let's eat. I'm starving."

He smiles and follows me into the kitchen where almost all of our house guests are seated at the table.

Gray and I take our seats. I make sure I sit next to Cohen so he feels more comfortable, though he looks like he's doing fine so far. My mom finishes putting the final dishes on the table then seats herself next to my dad. She holds her hand out to him. He clasps it and turns to Xander seated next to him. Everyone follows suit, clasping their hands together. My mom says, "Let's pray," and everyone bows their head to pray. When we're finished, everyone digs in. Silence falls over the table as everyone shovels food into their mouths. I can't even explain how good the food is. I pile my plate high with everything on the table. And once I've eaten it all, I pile it high again. I'm not the only one. Xander is familiar with my mom's cooking and isn't shy on taking extra helpings. Since Nash died I had to pick up a lot of the slack and do the cooking for myself, but my mom certainly hasn't lost her touch.

I watch Cohen as we eat. Mostly we all eat in silence, but between bites, some of my friends tell stories. Cohen tries to talk to some of my friends, and while they answer him, it's clipped and they don't add anything to the conversation. I feel bad for him, but I feel like it will just take time.

He did a big bad and it's going to take a lot of time for everyone to forgive him. I know he knows this, but I also know he still feels bad. The one thing we might actually have is time. If we are not killed, a phoenix will live forever. And griffins have a far longer lifespan than humans. So we have time.

I realize that what Cohen did was far worse than anything Xander has done, but it is still interesting to me that the phoenixes have practically welcomed Xander with open arms but are still standoffish to Cohen. I wonder if it is the difference in their personalities. I wonder if it is because Xander has spent more time with them than Cohen has. I wonder if it is because they see Cohen as more of a burden than an asset. Whatever it is, I am sure the phoenixes will come around to Cohen. I just have to be patient. And so does Cohen.

By the time we are finished eating, the serving dishes are empty and the pies are on the table, everyone has their hands over their swollen bellies and a pained look on their faces. But still we eat pie. I take an extra big slice of peach pie. It's rewarding to eat something I made. I notice a pleased look on Cohen's face when he takes a bit of the peach pie.

When we finish our pie and sit around the table in tired, full belly silence, my mom claps her hand and says, "Those of you who are new to our house, we have a small tradition after Thanksgiving dinner. And that is to go around the table and say what we are thankful for."

"Not exactly an original tradition, mom," I tell her.

"Nevertheless, it is our tradition," she says.

"Who would like to start?" my dad asks.

A heavy silence falls over the room. We are all, at least I know I am, wondering what we could possibly be thankful for.

"I'll go," Cohen says.

I didn't expect him to go at all, let alone be the first one to go.

"I am thankful that Casslyn gave me a second chance, and a third. I am thankful you have welcomed me into your home and fed me. I am thankful I don't have to lie awake at night wondering when my father is going to come and try to kill me."

Again, a heavy silence falls. No one is ever that honest when it comes to what they are thankful for. No one knows what to say. No one wants to follow that.

Cohen's glance circles the table then lands to stare at his plate. I'm not even sure he meant to be that open. I'm glad he was. I place my hand on his knee and squeeze, hoping it will convey to him that I am here for him.

Finally Nathan breaks the silence and says, "A little deep there, man."

Some of my friends chuckle. Others remain quiet. But at least the tension has lifted.

"I'll go," Nathan says. "I am thankful for the food in my belly. And I'm thankful my sister has found that stick up her ass and removed it."

That gets a resounding set of laughs out of everyone, even Cohen.

Taking the bait, Lydia says, "I am thankful my brother is so concerned with my ass." She smiles a wicked smile at him and continues on a more serious note. "I am thankful for the friends I have. And I'm thankful for a new one," she says and looks at me. She smirks at me then winks. I smile back at her.

We continue to go around the table. My parents are thankful for a house full of new friends and family. They are thankful they finally know the whole me. Thomas is thankful for the small vacation they are having. I'm not sure I'd call this a vacation. But to each his own. Thomas does have a certain sense of humor not all of us are up on. Aspen is thankful she has gotten to know the girl who made her brother fall in love. She is also thankful she got to spend as much time with him as she could before he died. Anna, likewise, is thankful for the time she got to spend with her dear friend Kristina. She's also thankful for her new friends. I can't help but notice she looks at Xander as she says this.

All this time I thought Xander was pining after the griffin girl he was dating. All the while Xander and Anna had started a thing. Right under my nose. All those times they chose each other as their guarding buddy at Cohen's. It's a surprise they haven't been attacked by now. Warmth flows in my cheeks. If there really is something going on between Anna and Xander, I couldn't be happier about it. Those two deserve a little happiness in their lives.

Xander, likewise looking at Anna as he says it, is thankful for his new friends. He is thankful he still has me in his life. And he is hopeful he can see his parents again soon. I can't imagine the toll it is taking on him being away from his parents for this long. Not even sure if Raphe is torturing them to get to him. Not sure if they even miss him. It's one thing I can't wait to fix. I owe that much to Xander.

There are three of us left. Gray, my father, and I.

Gray smiles and says, "I am thankful for Tucker. I may not have gotten to spend the lifetime I had planned for us with him, but I would never trade it for the time I did get with him. I love him with every fiber of my being and I will never forget him."

"Not sure how I'm going to follow that," my father says. "But I suppose I'll try my best. I am thankful for my people. For all of you who believed in me and Casslyn enough to stick around. I am thankful that you believe in me and my leadership. I am thankful that you fight for me and for each other. I am thankful for the bond you all have with each other. You are all a part of my family. And I hope you know how much each and every one of you means to me. I am thankful for our gracious hosts for welcoming me into your home. I am thankful that the two of you raised such a wonderful girl. I only wish I could have known Nash. From what Casslyn tells me, he was a great young man. I am thankful for my little girl. Casslyn, it has been a pleasure getting to know the person you are. You are bright and funny and you have the biggest heart of anyone I have ever known. You get angry but you care enough to forgive. You are open and honest and real. I am so thankful that you allow me to be a part of your life. Because you make mine better."

Holy shit. That's going to be hard to follow. I've seen my father give speeches on my behalf before. So I knew he was an eloquent speaker when he wanted to be. But damn. That was a lot. What do you do, how do you react when someone says you make their life better? How do you live up to that when you're not sure you can? You try. And that's what I've been doing.

But now it is my turn to say what I am thankful for. I am the last one. There is no way my mom is going to let me get away without saying something. Everyone is staring at me, waiting for me to speak. All that's left now, is to speak.

"I am thankful," I begin, though pause, trying to find the right words. "I am thankful for my parents. Mom, dad, thank you for loving me when things got tough. Thank you for accepting me as I am. Dad, thank you for coming here and being my father. You could have stayed away. You could have left well enough alone. Thank you for loving me, and teaching me, and bringing me into your world. I am thankful for all of my new friends. I have lost many friends recently, but gained many more. I have gained a whole other family. I am thankful for Logan. He changed my life. I was in a dark place when he met me. He helped to bring me out of it. He showed me I was strong enough to fight through to the light. He loved me as much as I loved him. He taught me so many things. And I am thankful for him every day. I am thankful for all of you. I love you all and I hope you all know that. There are many other things I am thankful for, but the dishes await and I am not doing them by myself."

Everyone around the table chuckles, but it doesn't exactly reach the surface. After literally everyone's heartfelt proclamations, there is not a dry eye around the table. After several moments of sniffling and hiccup sobbing, someone clears their throat and everyone disperses.

"I was serious about not doing the dishes on my own," I call out to them.

They all keep walking, as if I've said nothing, but as one they turn around and start clearing dishes from the table. In an assembly line, they stack dishes and carry them to the kitchen. One scrapes food of into the trash. One rinses the dishes, one washes, one dries, and one puts away. I end up not even having to wash a single dish. I do wash off the table just so no one can get on me about not doing anything.

When all the dishes are put away and everyone lies in various places in the living room, I feel the need to make my rounds. There are two people in particular I'd like to talk to.

But before I can go and find them, I run into my mom.

"Casslyn," she says, "What a lovely day. Your friends are all so nice and welcoming. We should have them over more often."

"Thank you for inviting them in the first place. The food was so good. And I think they all are having a really good time."

"I hope so," she says. "I'm just so glad you have more people in your life who care about you."

"Thanks, mom," I say, though I'm not entirely sure how

to take that.

"Go have fun, Casslyn. You know where the board games are. There is pop and snacks in the kitchen."

"Noted. Though I'm not sure any of us are going to be hungry any time soon."

"All the same," she says, then goes on the couch next to Aspen and Anna.

I spot Xander heading up the stairs. I'm not sure if he's going to use the bathroom or escape into his room, so I follow him and find him in his room.

I find him sitting on his bed flipping through the photos on his phone. Most of the ones he's looking at are of him and his parents.

"Are you hiding out?" I ask him.

"I just needed a minute," he says.

"Do you want me to leave?" I ask, because I know how important it is to be alone when you need to be alone.

"No, you can stay."

I sit on the bed next to him and lean against him. "I miss your parents too," I tell him.

"I wish it didn't have to be this way. I wish we could protect them like we do with Cohen. But I'm afraid that if we have any contact with them at all, Raphe will find out and use it against me."

"I know. I'm sorry. I wish I could tell you what to do. I wish that I knew what to do. But Cohen is trying to get inside. He knows some of the griffins who hate being under his father. We're going to meet with them. We're going to bring Raphe down and you can be with your parents again."

"I know," he says, a small smile playing on his lips. "I'm just impatient."

I feel the need to pull him out of this darkness, just like Gray. Just like Logan did for me. Everything is so bleak lately. Having hope is the hardest thing imaginable, especially when you are clinging to it for survival. But hope is all we have. Hope that our lives will be better. Hope that we didn't lose loved ones for nothing. Hope in a better world for ourselves and our loved ones.

"So I've been too afraid to talk to you about it," I start not exactly knowing what to say, "but before Tucker died, when you and I had no contact, Tucker told me about that girl you were seeing. Greer? Was that her name? What ever happened with her? I wanted to ask you before, but it always seemed like the wrong time."

"Well, she is a true believer in Raphe and everything he stands for. Even when we were together, she and Colt beat the shit out of me because they thought I was contacting you or had anything to do with helping you in anyway. When I left them, I kind of left her. End of story. I almost wished it had worked out. I really like her. She was tough and smart and pushed me to be better. Sometimes she pushed too hard, but I kind of liked that about her. She didn't let the fact that she was a girl stop her from proving she could kick my ass. Mine or anyone elses. She made me laugh. I had a lot of fun with her. But given the chance, she would have killed you. And I knew you meant more to me than she did. So here I am."

I crinkle my face at him and say, "I'm sorry."

"It's not your fault."

I tilt my head and raise an eyebrow at him.

"Ok, it kind of is. But I'm not sorry. It is what it is."

"Besides the fact that you and Anna have a bit of a thing going," I say, nudging his shoulder with mine.

"You noticed that, did you?" he asks.

"Noticed? You two were practically undressing each other at the table when we were all being thankful. I'm thankful you didn't leap over all of us and start making out on top of the pie. I would have been very upset if I didn't get any peach pie."

When Xander laughs I can feel it vibrate within him. It passes into me where we touch.

"Life is funny isn't it?" he asks.

"How so?"

"I've spent my entire life hating the phoenixes. I've wanted to kill any of them on sight. When I found out you were a phoenix, I hated you. I deeply hated you. And now, I hate my own leader. I've run away from my own people. I live with and spend time with the enemy. And now I'm dating one of them."

"Dating? It's that serious?"

"I really like her, Cass."

"I'm happy for you. I really am."

"Me too. I'm also really scared."

"Of what?"

"I'm afraid I'm going to care about her and then lose her. Seeing it happen to Gray and to you. It's nearly killed the both of you. And I am nowhere near as strong as either of you."

"Xander, if there is one thing I've learned over the past two years, it's that you don't know how strong you are until you have to find out."

"I don't want to have to find out."

"Then let's keep her safe. Let's keep everyone safe."

"Deal."

"Now," I tell him, digging my elbow into the top of his knee. He yelps and pushes me away. I shrug my shoulders at him. "Let's go downstairs and kick some ass at *Balderdash*. I promised Gray we would play some board games."

"Should one of us be crazy like Tucker used to be?"

"We can switch off."

"Let's go," he says and leads me from his room.

I wonder if he and Anna will be sneaking off later to come back to this very room, with the door closed. I'll have to keep an eye out for it. Not that I'm about to keep them from doing it. What I wouldn't give to sneak up to my room with Logan for a few moments of stolen kisses.

When we get to the bottom of the stairs I see my father leaning against the wall watching over the happenings of the living room. Xander and Gray head for the board game closet. I let them pick out the games and join the others around the coffee table. I decide to sit out the first few games. There is something that has been bugging me. Or at least that I've wondered about recently.

Something only my father can answer.

"You have time to talk?" I ask him.

"Any time," he tells me.

I lead him into the kitchen. He sits down at the table. I rummage through the cupboards, the fridge and the pantry until I find the makings for hot chocolate. We haven't had a father, daughter talk lately without hot chocolate. It might as well be one of our traditions.

When he sees what I'm doing he says, "Oh, you really wanted to talk."

"Is that okay?" I ask him.

"Of course. You can always come to me with anything. I hope you know that."

I nod then stare at him for a moment. The next seventeen years with him are going to be so strange and yet so thrilling. I'm going to get to see Nash grow older, even if it isn't Nash.

When I've got the hot chocolate made I set a mug down in front of my father then take a seat opposite him. I take a sip from my mug before speaking.

"This might be awkward, and you don't have to tell me if you don't want, but I've been wondering something."

"What's that?" he asks. There is no note of skepticism in his voice. No indication that he might not want to answer whatever it is I'm about to ask him.

"Do you have any other children?" I ask him.

"I do not," he says.

I pause before speaking next.

"May I ask why? I don't know how old you are, and I don't really know the workings of phoenix reproducing and anything like that. But I guess I thought, since you're the leader, you would have wanted to have children, someone to take over in case you were ever, you know."

"That's fair," he says.

"I just," I say, trying to find the right words. "You love me. I know you love me. And I know how much you wish you could have known Nash. I'm just wondering why you didn't have any other kids. Have you ever been married?"

"I have not ever been married. There have been a few women in the past that I have loved. But for various reasons, it never worked out. I loved your mother. But you know how that worked out. I've thought about having children. But I wanted them to grow up in a family and there was never the opportunity for that. The closest I came to having a family and children was when I took in Logan and Aspen. I want you to know that I would never give you up for the world."

"I know. I didn't mean it like that. I just want you to be happy. Do you think you will ever have any other kids?" I ask him.

I loved having Nash as my brother. I think I would love having other siblings. But at the same time, I'm not sure how I would feel about another sibling taking Nash's place in my heart.

"If the circumstances are right I think I could have other children. Would that be alright with you? Would you want brothers and sisters?"

"I think I could handle it. Besides, there is no way I would let you take what I wanted into account with something like that."

"Oh, but I would. I wouldn't have it any other way."

I stare at him, remembering how much I hated him when he first showed up in Cedars. How much I despised him for abandoning us. How much I loathed the fact that he was trying to be a drill sergeant and my friend at the same time. I think about how much we've both grown since the day we met.

"You're different than I expected," I tell him, taking a sip from my mug.

"In what way?"

"All of them. When Logan told me he was your best soldier I just expected an army leader. I expected someone tough. Your way or the highway. I didn't expect you to have any feelings. I even thought you'd come back and try to win my mom back. When I learned you were my father and that you had come to give blood to me at the hospital, I thought you were the reasons my parents split up. I'm really sorry I thought all that."

"All is forgiven. I admit, we could have started off better. I still feel bad about the part I played in Logan breaking up with you."

"All is forgiven," I parrot him.

"You're a good kid," he tells me.

I shrug my shoulders and smile like I'm up to something

but say, "I try."

I sip on my hot chocolate and bite down on another question I have for him. Invading someone's life, even if they tell you it's okay, is always just that, invasive. But, being my father, and a smart man, he can tell I'm itching at something.

"What is it?" he asks.

"Well, I was just wondering why you left all those years ago? Why didn't you ever come back?"

"Did Logan ever tell you that we all used to live here in Cedars?"

"No."

"I'm not surprised. Logan never actually lived here. But when I was a young leader, this was home base. There were few griffins in the area and it was a nice town to call home. And we did, for a long time. But then the griffins found it was a great place to settle too, besides the fact that there were plenty of phoenixes for them to kill. Once a full scale war started, I couldn't very well keep my people here while they were being slaughtered, so we moved on."

"But you came back," I say.

"I did. Once every ten to twenty years, I would come back to the area to see if I could find any traces of new phoenixes. This was our home base for so long, some stray phoenixes would come here looking for us. It was during one such return trip that I met your mother."

"Would you have come back again? Would you have come back if you hadn't learned about me and Nash?"

"I'm not sure. As you've found out, the place has become overrun by the griffins. It's not exactly a safe place for us any longer."

"Maybe we can change that," I tell him, thinking of liberating the town, my people, and the other griffins of Raphe and his horrible reign.

"Maybe. All we can do is try," my father says, smiling at me while placing his hand on my cheek.

I finish off my hot chocolate and sit with my father. I asked what I wanted to ask. And I don't have much else to say. But it is nice to sit in companionable silence once in a while. That is until someone yells at you.

"Cass," Xander yells at me. "Get your ass in here. I'm losing."

"Language," my mother yells at him.

"Sorry," Xander calls.

"Duty calls," I say to my father.

"Your people await you," he says to me.

I roll my eyes and move into the living room. Groups of my friends circle around different board games around the living room floor. Some playing *Balderdash* some shouting at each other in made up words playing *Mad Gab* while one group plays *Monopoly*. I join Xander, Gray, and Thomas around the *Balderdash* board and pick my playing piece. The room is loud and full of my friends having relaxing, care free fun for the first time in a long time. The scene around me melts my heart. This group of people is my heart and I'm thankful for each and every one of them.

Ten

Cohen has done his job. He has talked to some of the griffins he thinks want out as badly as he and Xander did. They have agreed to meet with us. To talk to us. To help us liberate themselves. I hope it works.

Tonight is the night. I can't wait any longer. I'm not sure Raphe will wait any longer to attack us. He could be gathering his forces, preparing for an attack. Waiting us out. We have to be ready for anything. We have to gather our own forces.

This was my plan so I will be going. Cohen set it up so he's in. Xander is as much a part of this as any of us, so he's on the team. My father insists he goes, just in case. To round out the team Lydia will be joining us.

There are only three of the griffins. We don't want to

overpower them with a large force. But we also don't want to be taken by surprise. And we don't want everyone in the same place in case the griffins attack. Beyond all that, I want someone to keep watch over my parents and I'm trusting Gray with that. He and Thomas will keep my parents company whilst pretending I'm not actually doing what I'm doing. Aspen and Nathan will stay at Logan's waiting for a signal should anyone need backup. Anna will be in position at Cohen's loft, to make it look like Cohen is there.

The plan is a go. We've been over it many times. The griffins didn't want to meet at Cohen's loft, which we suggested, because they felt it wasn't secure. We didn't want to meet them in any known griffin base in case Raphe were to get wind of the meeting. We needed a place that was neutral. A place no one would think of. A place secure and yet open enough should we need an escape. Xander was the genius who thought of meeting at the school. He and I knew the ins and outs of the building. We knew places to hide. We knew which doors were easily accessible, which were always locked and which were not always locked. It was the perfect place.

We're all at Logan's house. We sit around the kitchen table going over and over the plan. We're going to meet them in the gym. It's open. There aren't many access points so it will be easy to secure and guard. There aren't many places to hide so the griffins shouldn't be able to form a sneak attack.

Cohen, my father, and I will be speaking to the griffins. Xander and Lydia will be guarding the entrances. We've got pretyped messages on our phones should we need to alert any member of our group for any reason.

We know the plan. It should be easy. It should be safe. We are only talking to three griffins who want out of the prison Raphe has put them in. This meeting should be a secret. It should be safe. And yet I can't shake this nervous energy flowing in my veins.

My power senses my unease and aches to be let loose. I can't let it out. And I can't let my friends know I'm nervous. If I'm nervous they will call the whole thing off.

I look around me. My friends, my family, sit around me going over every detail. Though the more they talk about it, the easier they become. Not one of them seems nervous. Not one of them shows any visible ticks indicating any sort of discomfort with the meeting tonight. They sit around me casually talking, some even laughing. To my surprise, Cohen is even at ease. I think he's excited to have more people on his side, more people joining his cause.

When Cohen found the three of them he was ecstatic. The more time has passed, the more I can see the hunger inside of him grow for this. This rebellion, this freedom. He was a full-fledged part of the group while we planned our meeting. He wanted to be a part of it as much as he could. It was almost like he wanted to be leading the charge.

I've wondered what will become of the griffins if we do end up freeing them. Will they disband all together? Will they form their own new group? Will they replace Raphe with a new leader? Will Cohen take over for his father? Will he want to? What if not all of them want to be freed?

These are the things that worry me. These are the things that keep me up at night and make the black circles under my eyes more and more permanent.

But I have to believe it will all be over soon. I have to believe we will defeat Raphe and rid ourselves of the threat he's been to our lives for the last year.

And that is what tonight is about. Getting us one step closer to being free. Not just the griffins, but all of us.

When we have sufficiently gone over the plan and it is time to go, we say goodbye to Gray and Thomas who head towards my house. Then we say our goodbyes to Aspen and Nathan. Lydia and Nathan huddle together in the kitchen before we leave. My father, Xander, Cohen and I wait by the door.

"Can I talk to you?" Aspen asks me.

"Sure," I tell her and move away from the boys.

She stops once we are in the living room and turns to me.

"Please be careful," she tells me.

"It's going to be fine. We know what we are doing. Besides, we're just talking to them. Nothing to fear," I say, lying straight through my teeth. Apparently I wasn't the only one worried about tonight. I almost wish the rest of them were.

"Just promise me. I know we haven't known each other that long, but after losing Logan, it might kill me if I lose you too." Her arms are crossed and she grips her arms where they meet.

"I promise. I will be careful. We will all be careful."

"Ok. I'll see you later," Aspen says but she doesn't move away.

Without asking, I step toward her and wrap my arms around her shoulders. She sinks into my embrace and clutches me. I've only ever had a brother, and I loved having a brother, but holding onto Aspen now, I can imagine how it would be to have a sister. It's a nice image.

When I pull away from her I give her a reassuring smile and tell her I'll see her in a couple of hours.

When I get to the front door Lydia has joined the guys. We say goodbye to Aspen and Nathan and head out the door. When the car is started and we head down the lane, I breathe in deeply, hold it in, and release. I've never been the praying type, but I send up a little prayer to keep us all safe. I'm not sure why I'm so worked up about tonight. I'm sure we are going to be fine.

We are going to be fine, I tell myself. *We are going to be fine.*

Before I know it, we are at the school. We park over a block away. The school is on the highway and many people drive by. We don't want a passerby seeing the SUV and getting suspicious.

We walk to the school, scouting as we go. Everything looks quiet. Everything looks normal. We go in. The gym doors leading outside are padlocked but have never been secure. Nash, Xander, Tucker, and I broke into the gym our freshman year. Just to prove we could. And that's how we get in now.

We've come a bit early, so we have the drop on the griffins. If we need the drop on the griffins. Like I said, this should be easy. Go in, talk to the griffins, convince them they need to help us take down Raphe, then go home. Simple. Easy.

The gym is dark. There are several large sky lights in the ceiling, but they were recently covered. It's eerily dark. Good thing for supernaturally good eyesight. I can make out the bleachers, the stage, the other doors.

I nod to Xander and Lydia who make their way to the other doors. We haven't gotten far into the gym when I hear something off. The fact that I hear something at all, is off. My father, Cohen, and I exchange glances before moving towards the noise. I can't tell what the noise is. It's quiet and indistinct. But the closer we get to it the more I can make out. It sounds like raspy breathing. It sounds like clinking chains. It sounds like it's coming from the stage. The curtains are closed so I can't see anything but I swear there is something behind them.

My heart pounds in my chest. We haven't even met the griffins yet and already tonight has gone sideways. I should have known nothing could work out the way it is supposed to. My pulse quickens and I stop breathing when my father and Cohen go to open the curtain. I steel myself, preparing for anything we might find behind it. I hold my breath while the curtain parts listening for any indication we might be attacked.

The curtains are open. It's darker on the stage than the rest of the gym and harder to see, even with enhanced sight. But finally I make out shapes, just when Cohen sucks in a deep breath.

On the stage, hanging from chains hooked to the rafters, are the three griffins we are supposed to be talking to. I've never met them, but by the sound of Cohen's breathing and the fact that there are three of them in the place we were supposed to meet the griffins, they are one and the same. Cohen stands at the edge of the stage, in shock, while Aris and I move to the griffins. Their heads hang down to their chests. Blood wafts through the air and clings to their bodies. I reach for the griffin closest to me but when I touch him, he reels back. His breath hitches from the movement. It's an effort but he pulls up his head to face me. The griffin's face is black and bloody and beaten. From the smell in the air, I'd say they all are. And unless my friends escaped my attention at some point today, came to the gym, beat and strung up the people we were trying to get on our side, there is only one person responsible for the sight before me. And I've got a feeling he didn't just string them up and leave. Especially judging from the five other chains hanging from the rafters.

Cohen finally finds his legs, and his voice. "Who did this to you?" he asks the griffins.

The griffin in front of me looks pleadingly at Cohen. Pleading for mercy, or maybe forgiveness. Possibly help. The look in his eyes kills me. We have to get them out of this. If I wasn't sure before, I am now. If their own leader could do this to them, they need out. I purposely defied my father, our leader. I talked my friends into defying my father. And yet, my father didn't condemn us. As our leader, he didn't beat us or berate us. He took what we wanted into consideration and allowed us to do what we felt was right.

Raphe on the other hand, is his way or the highway. Xander and I have talked about how he led. How he treated his people. What he let them know and what he didn't. Everything Raphe ever did with his people was to benefit him. I hope I am never the leader of the phoenixes, merely because I don't want my father to die. But I hope if I ever became the leader of our people, I would be the type that has the good of my people at heart.

Cohen joins the hanging griffins, my father and I and tries to help us get them down. I take a look around us, trying to gauge how long we have before Raphe and his cronies attacks us. They may be hiding and waiting to strike. We have to get out of here quick. I see nothing. I don't even see Xander and Lydia guarding the doors. It's not something I can think of right now. They are tough. They can take care of themselves for the time it takes us to free the griffins of their bonds.

I grab at the chains attempting to find a way to release the griffins within. The metal clangs together and rattles against the rafters. The griffin in the chains winces as the metal pulls at their marred flesh. I try to be gentle, try not to harm them any further, but it's not easy.

Listening to my surroundings has gone out the window. I can't push my hearing out further around me without damaging my ears from the rattling chains in my hands. My father and Cohen work on their own set of chains next to us. I can't find a way of freeing the person in the chains. He looks scared. Worried I won't be able to free him. I'm worried too. There doesn't seem to be a lock to the shackles. There doesn't seem to be a clasp or opening. And I can't see how the chains connect to the rafters.

My breathing begins to quicken, but I try to even it out to keep the griffin calm. My pulse pounds in my fingers grasping the chains. Or is it the griffin's pulse pounding through the metal of the chains and into me?

I'm about to call out to Cohen or my father to see if they have had any more luck than I have when I hear footsteps.

"Cass. Run," I hear Xander call from behind me.

I turn around to see him and Lydia being manhandled by two griffins a piece.

There are only four of them, I think. *We can fight them off.*

I turn to the sound of a new struggle and see my father struck from behind. I charge for him as he goes down. But then the lights go out.

***

I wake to an intense throbbing at the back of my skull. My field of vision goes in and out as my head throbs. My fingers tingle from lack of blood. My wrists are chafed where the metal wraps around them. My shoulders feel ready to pop out of their sockets. My neck aches from my head hanging to my chest. Basically, my body hurts.

But I can't worry about that now. There are eight of us strung up by chains and we have to figure out a way to get out of this.

"Cass?" my father asks from three sets of chains down. "Are you okay?"

The griffins have us chained in a circle. Maybe so they can get to us easier, easy access. Or maybe so we have to face each other as they torture and kill us.

"I'm fine," I tell him.

"Everyone else okay?" he asks the rest of our group.

"I'm good," Xander and Lydia say.

"I'm okay," Cohen says.

The three griffins strung up next to us grunt out their replies. They look worse for wear, but there is still hope we can get them out of this. I just have to figure out how.

"How cute, a doting father," comes a voice from behind me. The voice that haunts my nightmares. Raphe.

Raphe, Ashley, and several other griffins enter the circle from between us. I recognize some of them from school, others from the attacks at mine and Logan's houses. Although I've never met her, I can spot Greer among the griffins. I saw her with Xander at the party Tucker and I went to, the party where I met Cohen and screwed up a lot in my life. Although I'd known the griffins were after me and the other phoenixes, that they'd already killed Nash and attempted to kill me several times, that party, meeting Cohen, is what really set me on the path of destruction. There are several times a day I wish I hadn't gone to that party. This is one of those times.

"I bet you're wondering how you got into this little mess," Raphe says to us all.

We remain silent, not giving in to his goading.

"It was simple really," he says. "When these three stopping reporting in I knew something was wrong. They were either dead, or about to betray me. All it took was a little prodding to find out about this little meeting. So betrayal it was. But after I'm through with them, they'll wish they were dead."

"Leave them alone," Cohen says. "This is my fault."

The shock of Cohen standing up to his father has to be written on my face. But in this moment, I couldn't be more proud of him.

"Oh, I'll get to you," Raphe says, contempt in his voice.

"Do let me," Ashley says, playing with a knife in her hands.

"Be my guest," Raphe says. "As for the three of you who thought you could betray me."

Greer steps up to one of the griffins strung from the rafters and punches them square in the gut. The griffin next to her follows suit. The one next to him, grips a knife in his hand as he steps up to the captured griffin.

Before he can plunge the knife into a person akin to him, I yell, "Stop."

Surprisingly he stops.

I stare at the griffin with the knife in his hand and turn to the rest of them, ending on Raphe. "You would kill your own people? You would kill your own people merely because they disagree with you?"

"You sound surprised," Raphe says.

"How could you be so heartless?" I ask.

"Don't ask dumb questions."

Greer moves on from the griffin she's tormenting to Xander. "Xander, my love, how nice it is to see you."

She grabs his face in her hand and squeezes. Xander doesn't even flinch. He stares her down, willing her to inflict her worst. I watch as his face shows nothing, but his body tells another story as his abs clench readying for impact. But instead of hitting him, Greer leans into him and kisses him, right on the mouth. Xander doesn't pull away, but he doesn't kiss her back.

When she pulls away, she says, "I missed you. Didn't you miss me?"

Xander leans into her. He gets right up to her face before he says, "Not for a second."

This is when she chooses to lay into him. She punches him in the stomach once, twice, again and again.

He just laughs. I know what he's doing. I only hope it works.

"Too good to hit me in the face?"

Again, Greer grabs Xander's face and squeezes.

"It's such a pretty face. I wouldn't want to mess it up," she says moving his head back and forth, playing with him.

For a mere second, a look passes over Xander's face. It's the look I gave Cohen right after he stabbed me all those months ago. The look that says, I was hoping there was something good in you. The look that says, you've let me down. I can tell by that look that Xander did care for Greer once, that he had hoped it would work between them. It makes me sad. There has been far too much heart ache and sadness for all of us in the past two years. It's about time at least one of us had some happiness in our lives. Maybe, if we get out of this in one piece, Xander and Anna can find true happiness together.

For good measure Greer punches Xander in the ribs and swing kicks at his knee. He cries out in pain and jerks in his chains. If he was standing on his own, he'd have gone down. When Greer steps away, Xander's knee is not sitting at a proper angle. If it's not broken, it's dislocated.

Before Greer can take another swing at him, Lydia says, "Get your hands off my boyfriend."

Greer looks between Xander and Lydia, almost as if she's trying to gauge whether or not Lydia might be telling the truth. She's not, but she is trying to take the heat off of Xander. The thankful look in his eyes says it all.

"Yeah right," Greer says. "Xander may have left me, but there's no way in Hell he would be shacking up with the likes of your kind."

"You're wrong," Xander says. Through the pain, Xander manages a playful glint in his eyes just to mess with Greer.

I can tell she doesn't believe either of them, but she strikes Lydia across the face with the back of her hand for good measure. Lydia spits in Greer's face and says, "Is that all you've got?"

Greer moves to strike her again but Raphe calls her off. "Enough. You can play with them later. I want to have a little chat with Aris."

My father looks at Raphe not with disdain, not with rage, but like he could care less. I wonder how long we can all get away with this. There is only so much torture we can all take. There is only so much the griffins can dole out before they get bored and decide to kill us.

While Raphe is distracted trying to rile up my father, I work on a way to get us out of this. I couldn't find a way to release the griffins when we first got here, but I'm hoping in their haste to get five of us chained up they might have made a mistake.

I want to try melting the chains, but if I couldn't melt the knife I used to kill the griffin, I don't see myself being able to melt these chains. At least not quickly enough to get me out of them without attracting the notice of a griffin or two.

"I have to tell you, Aris, I was quite disappointed when you took your phoenixes and fled all those years ago. We were having so much fun killing the lot of you."

"I'm so sorry to have ruined your fun," my father says. The smirk on his face is so like Nash's it's hard to remember that it's not actually Nash in chains beside me.

"Oh don't worry. I've had plenty of fun tormenting your

daughter. You know, I knew you were in town seventeen years ago. I just wasn't quick enough to kill you before you left. I didn't know you were so *busy* though. That is, until I attended a school event for Ashley two years ago and saw the face of your son. Your face." Raphe runs a finger down my father's face as he says this then slaps him across the cheek.

My father jerks back from the strike but doesn't otherwise react.

Inside, I'm reeling from what Raphe has just said. He knew my father was in town all those years ago. He had to have known he was with my mother. My mom could have been in danger this whole time. I have trouble believing Raphe would have left my mom alone knowing she meant something to my father. Maybe he didn't know about my mom. Maybe my father was careful enough with her. Maybe he kept his feelings for her concealed. Maybe they didn't go out in public together. Maybe he kept her hidden and that's the only reason Nash and I lived as long as we did.

If only Raphe was less of an involved parent, maybe Nash would still be with us today. If only my brother hadn't been a carbon copy of our father. But there is nothing I can do about that now. My father's genetics are strong. Raphe's hate runs deep. Change one thing, you change everything, but the outcome may remain the same.

I feel helpless locked in my chains, unable to fight off the griffins attacking my friends. I'm honestly not sure how we're all going to get out of this with our lives, but I still have hope. And sometimes hope is all you need in situations like these.

The griffins stand in the middle of the circle, some bouncing on the balls of their feet, some wringing the knives in their hands, all of them antsy to get the killing over with and be done with this. I can't say the same for Raphe. He seems keen on keeping the festivities going. Drawing out the torture, putting on a show. I'm okay with that, it gives me time to come up with a plan. I wonder how long we've been here. I wonder if by now Gray and Thomas and Nathan and the rest of my friends are worried about us, if they think something has gone wrong. I don't want them walking in on this, there could be other griffins waiting outside for them. But we could also use the help.

"Honestly, when I saw your son, I was hoping it was you," Raphe says. "But, beggars can't be choosers, am I right. And I have to say, killing your offspring was just the ticket I needed to get you back here. It has been fun killing your people these past several months."

"I think Cass has gotten a kick out of killing your people lately," my father spits back at Raphe.

"I will admit, she has been quite the thorn in my side," Raphe says. "But nothing I can't handle."

"Oh really? And what about your own people turning against you? Is that something you can handle?" Cohen butts in. "Oh wait, you're willing to kill them just to get them out of your way. Just like you wanted to kill me after I turned away from you."

Raphe turns away from my father and squares his attention on Cohen. Ashley is right on his heels, her knife at the ready. It isn't an ice knife, but rather a gleaming steel blade. She came prepared to kill her brother. I would have given my life if it meant Nash could live, and here Ashley is ready and willing to kill her brother. How different families can be.

"You," Raphe practically spits at Cohen. "What a disappointment you turned out to be. When you were born I was so excited. My heir had come to be. You were going to be everything I was and more. But then that bitch of a mother spoiled you. She wanted to turn you soft, lead you away from my way of doing things. When your sister came along your mother did the same thing with her. I knew I had to get rid of her. She would have ruined everything."

Cohen's jaw opens and falls.

"What do you mean get rid of her? Mom left because she hated you."

"You didn't really think she would leave me and not take you, did you?"

"You," Cohen starts, but can't find the words.

"Yes, I killed your mother," Raphe says.

I watch as every light in Cohen goes out. It's one thing for you to hate your father. It's another to know a parent left you and never came back for you. But to find out your father killed the one parent who ever treated you well, the one parent who ever loved you. I can't imagine how he must feel right now. But I see it. I see it in the fierce hatred growing behind his eyes. I see it in the tears leaking down his cheeks.

I see it in the forced flex of his jaw. I see it in the quiver of his chin. Cohen has taken hit after hit from his father. This latest blow might kill him. I only hope it will make him stronger.

And maybe it will.

"I'm going to murder you," Cohen tells his father.

"You're going to do that hanging from chains?" Raphe taunts him.

"I will find a way," Cohen says, struggling in his restraints.

"Not after I'm through with you," Ashley says.

"Idle threats, sister," Cohen says. "When have you ever gotten the best of me?"

Without warning Ashely steps forward and plunges her knife into Cohen's chest. My breath hitches inside my chest as Cohen's eyes go wide. He tries to suck in a breath but can't get it in.

"No," I yell and am joined by Lydia, Xander, and my father.

Ashley yanks her knife out from his chest. Cohen coughs and gags. His breaths become heavy, his face pales. Blood wells under his shirt and flows down, soaking the material. Cohen and I haven't had the best relationship since we met, but it hurts to see him in so much pain. As rocky as our past has been, Cohen is my friend and it tears me up to see him like this. As much blood as runs down his chest, I'm not sure how long he's got to survive this, or if he will at all. I could heal him, my father could heal him, we just need to get out of these fucking chains.

"A bit premature darling?" Raphe asks Ashley.

"He was getting on my nerves," she answers him.

I writhe in my chains and pull down hoping they might come loose from the rafters.

Ashley takes notice of me and moves my way. "Is it your turn?" she asks.

Fire flows through my veins and out through my skin without me giving it permission. The chains grow hot around my wrists. I might not be able to melt them through, but I could possibly weaken them.

She steps towards me and pulls her knife hand back to strike me. I scream in her face to throw her off and give my chains one last tug. By now she's in mid strike. I catch her off guard and grab at her face with my fiery hands. Her hair catches fire as I take hold of her chin and the back of her head.

Rage and hate fill my heart. Fear for our situation pulses in my veins. Need for this war to be over blinds my vision.

Raphe and his other griffins move towards me but they're not fast enough.

Ashley's eyes widen as fear grips her, right before I twist my hands and snap her neck. Her breath hitches in her throat and cuts off. I release my grip on her face and let her drop to the floor.

"No," Raphe bellows.

The griffins barrel down on me, but I've had enough.

Pulling at my fire I spray it at the approaching griffins. Alarm and surprise lights their faces as they try to escape my flaring flames. I move through them and head toward Raphe, but I'm too late.

He pulls an ice knife from his pocket and thrusts it into my father's chest.

"No," I scream and then my heart stops.

Fire spurts to life around the knife in his chest.

Nash stares up at me.

My father stares up at me.

They are one and the same.

Both of them dying in front of my eyes.

The pain of it killing me equally.

"Cass," he chokes out, fire spreading out from his wound.

Raphe steps away from him, satisfied knowing my father will die.

I rush to his side, where he still hangs from his chains. All of my friends do. I have to get them out of this. I turn in a circle, not knowing who to help first. But Lydia has taken a cue from me and melted her chains enough to break them apart. She's free and working on freeing Cohen. I know she will get to the rest of them.

Cohen.

My father.

Both of them dying.

Can I save them both?

I turn my attention back to my father, my eyes burning with tears, my heart slapping against my ribs. I can't breathe. I can't focus. Fire and smoke cloud my vision.

I try melting the metal of my father's chains. But it's taking too long and the fire is covering his body. My tears stream down my face and fall onto my father's body. They sizzle when they meet the flames. I cry freely, to heal him, but also because I've failed.

"Cass, I love you," my father says.

"Hold on, Dad," I tell him.

More tears meet the flames engulfing his body. They aren't enough.

I can hear a scuffle around me, but I can't tune into it. Lydia and Xander can handle it.

But then I'm grabbed from behind and whirled around.

I face off with Raphe who holds a new ice knife in his hand, ready to kill me with it. He says, "Your turn girlie."

My hands ignite on their own, my fire ready to be used.

"No," I scream at him, and lunge for him.

I hold my hands out before me and release a steady stream of flames at him. He ducks to avoid them, but I anticipate it and aim my fire accordingly. My fire strikes him and engulfs his clothes. He hollers and runs away from me.

I didn't expect it to be that easy. But I don't care. I have to heal my father.

When I turn around, my father's whole body is engulfed in flames and begins to disintegrate right in front of me. The flames burn out as ashes fall to the ground, the chains clinking free from the pressure of his body.

That's when my heart bursts into a million pieces.

That's when I lose all control.

That's when the flames consume me and explode outward like a bomb.

I fall to my knees in front of my father's ashes.

I can hear as the fire alarm rings out.

Water sprays down around me as the sprinklers kick in.

Strong hands grab at me and pull me away from my father's ashes, away from Ashley's body, away from the burning building.

Sirens wail from somewhere close by, getting closer.

Voices urgently chatter around me.

Someone lifts me up and throws me over their shoulder.

I don't care.

I can't feel anything but the broken shards of my heart scraping at my insides. Clawing their way through my body. Ripping at my lungs, shredding through my stomach.

It hurts.

I hurt.

A scream rings through my head and bounces around my brain like a pinball, jarring every time it touches an edge.

Cold, wet snow flakes touch my skin, melt, and run together. Lydia's footsteps crunch the snow beneath them. I wonder if someone will follow the tracks and lead them to us. But as we walk, it snows harder, which will no doubt cover our tracks and leave anyone none the wiser.

Eventually we make it to the car. I'm sure we took a roundabout route. I'm conscious enough to get myself in the car. I've still got the cuffs of the chains around my wrists. I'll have to see if I can get them off when we get home.

Lydia, Xander, and Cohen managed to get theirs off in the scuffle. And then I realize Cohen is still bleeding out. Sweat beads on his forehead and runs down his face. His cheeks are white, his lips blending into them.

"I couldn't heal him," Lydia says.

I understand what she means. And I know she doesn't want Xander or Cohen to know what she means. A phoenix can heal anyone whether they be phoenix, griffin, human, or otherwise. However, that phoenix has to want to heal that person. And while I know Lydia doesn't hate Cohen, that she has accepted him in our group, phoenixes and griffins have been enemies for centuries, and that's not something you can get over overnight. She can't heal him because though she wants to heal her friend, she doesn't want to heal the griffin inside of him.

Lydia and Xander sit in the front seats of the car. Lydia starts the engine and drives away.

Tears still flow from my eyes. I'm not sure I will stop crying any time soon. So I lean over Cohen in the backseat and let my tears spill onto his chest. I'm not even sure if I can heal him, if I want to. I couldn't heal my father. And there is no doubt I wanted to heal him. But I think I wouldn't have been able to heal him at all. Raphe wouldn't have made a mistake and not hit his heart.

Cohen's breath hitches in his throat as my tears touch his skin. His chest bounces up and down as he struggles to breathe.

I hold my breath and wait to see if my tears will work

their magic on him.

I watch as my tears and his blood mix and thin his blood making it run pink over his skin. It's moments before anything happens, but eventually the skin of Cohen's stab wound meets in the middle and melds itself back together.

I breathe out the breath I'd been holding, waiting to see if I could heal him. I'd avoided his gaze all along, not wanting to see his expression if I couldn't heal him, if he were to die. I'd seen that look once already tonight and I'm not sure I could survive two. But now I look up at him. Beyond anything, Cohen looks relieved. He nods his head at me, trying to even out his breathing.

Cohen moves his hands up to cup my cheeks. One of his hands is coated in blood and smears on my cheek, but I can't seem to find it in me to care.

"I'm so sorry," he says, his voice still weak.

He pulls me to him and kisses me on the forehead then lays my head on his chest.

He's sorry. Though I'm not sure what for. Does he mean he's sorry for the plan going south? Does he mean he's sorry for the trap his father set? Or is he sorry my father died? I don't want to think about it. If I did, I'd have to think about all the ways I'm sorry, a number that grows by the day.

I sit in the back seat of the SUV, my head on Cohen's chest, his resting against mine, and try to hold the pieces of myself together, just as long as it takes to get back to my house.

Eleven

When we get back to Logan's house I force myself to walk from the car to the house. It's a struggle, but I make it. Cohen walks alongside me, both our strides short and slow. Lydia and Xander don't make a show of wanting to go inside any more than we do. The four of us are quiet, still processing what happened tonight.

I'm not really sure what happened tonight. I can't figure out how it went so wrong. It was a sound plan. Now, the griffins may never trust us again, I may have burned down my school, and my father is dead. So much for a sound plan.

Eventually we all trudged into the house. Nathan and Aspen come from the kitchen and meet us by the door. One look from us, one count of our party, and they can see how the evening went.

Neither one of them wants to say it, that much is clear, but Aspen is the braver one and asks, "What happened?"

Xander and Lydia look at me for an answer. An answer that I don't have. So they tag team and tell Nathan and Aspen our story. Cohen jumps in once in a while, to add small but important details the two might have forgotten. I remain silent, using my power to heat and break the cuffs off my wrists, but listen, trying to root out where it all went wrong. I especially listen to the end, wanting to know how we got out of there with our lives when we were so outnumbered.

Xander is speaking when I hear him say, "And then Cass came out with her badass fire beams and freaked the griffins out and they ditched the place."

Lydia jumps in and says, "We were able to get the captured griffins out and to safety and came back for Casslyn and Cohen. We couldn't save Aris. Casslyn tried so hard."

"Are you doing okay?" Lydia asks Cohen.

I know the question isn't random. But there are many reasons she could ask this, many of which are not the actual reason she's asking. I just can't figure out what that reason it.

Until Cohen says, "My sister and I weren't close. But it's sad she couldn't pull herself out of my father's grip. I'm sad it had to end that way for her. Cass did tell me she was going to kill her, guess she wasn't lying. Though I don't blame her. She did what she had to. It was me or my sister. I'm glad Casslyn chose me."

"She has before," Xander tells him.

A contemplative silence falls over the room.

I killed Cohen's sister. Cohen is right, she would have killed him, tried to kill him. And I did kill her, another griffin to add to the list. A list I'm not actually proud is growing. I'm sure I'll acquire some new guilty tick over it. But I'm not sorry I did it. I'm especially not sorry I killed the only person Raphe had left after he took my father away from me.

My father is gone. It's my fault. I sound like a broken record, but everything bad that has fallen on my loved ones has been because they love me. Because they want to protect me. How can I not blame myself when I am the root of the problem?

I don't know where to go from here. I don't know what to do. I don't know how I'll recover from this most recent blow.

"What do we do now?" Nathan asks, echoing my thoughts.

"We regroup," Lydia says without missing a beat. "Casslyn is our leader now. We wait until she pulls herself together and then we follow her lead."

I can tell they don't think I'm listening to them. I'm not going to give them any indication I am.

"What if she can't survive this?" Aspen asks. "She's lost a lot of people in a short amount of time. What is she can't pull through this?"

"She's going to have to," Nathan says.

"She will," Xander says, determination powering his voice.

"She will," Cohen says, his voice filled with belief in

me.

I'm not sure I believe in myself.

As I sit there, listening to them, I feel myself crawling deeper inside the black hole where my heart once sat. It's safer there, quieter. I don't want to dig myself out.

I'm pulled to attention when silence fills the room. My partners have finished the story of our night. They all wait for me to tell them something, to lead them. I'm not ready. My father has been dead for no more than two hours, I am not ready to fill his shoes. I stare at every person in the room. They appear to understand how I feel without me telling them. I appreciate that.

I nearly jump out of my skin and my seat when Gray and Thomas burst through the front door. My heart hammers in my chest and refuses to calm down once I know I'm safe.

Without a word, without knowing how epically we failed tonight, Gray walks over to me and throws his arms around me, holding tight. I must have missed one of my friends calling or texting him while I was out of it. I sink into his arms and let him hold me up.

I'd stopped crying at some point while we sat here telling the story, but now, as Gray holds me in his arms, I become a blubbering mess.

I just watched my father die and fall apart in front of me. Not only was that destroying enough, but his face happened to be identical to my brothers. So for the second time I watched my brother die. I watched my father and my brother die at the same time.

Breathing becomes a challenge as my crying turns to sobbing. Gray squeezes me tighter and lets me cry. He doesn't say anything to calm me, doesn't use any words to comfort me. He holds me until I can pull myself together, until I can reign in my emotions and try and hide them like I have for the past several months.

When I pull away from him he holds me close and stares me down, trying to gauge my emotional status. I nod to him, indicating to him I won't break down again and return to my chair. Gray and Thomas join us around the table and begin to talk to the rest of our friends. This time, Lydia, Xander, and Cohen give a shortened version of the night. By the time they are finished it is really late and I am spent. It's clear by their faces, everyone else is too, even those who weren't fighting for their lives tonight.

We all stand up from the table and begin to head to rooms and to get ready for bed. Gray tells me to take Logan's room for the night, but I'd really rather sleep in my own bed for the night. He looks like he wants to argue, but he relents.

He relents, but only after telling me my house is empty. My dad left when my mom headed to the hospital for her shift. It's probably better this way. I would have to tell my mom what happened tonight. I would have to tell her I failed and my father died. I'm not currently up for that.

Gray offers to walk me home, but Xander interferes and tells Gray he's got it. I have gotten close to Gray in the past few months and I think it bothers Xander, like I'm replacing my old friends with new ones. I hope Xander has enough faith in me to know that could never happen.

Xander and I say goodnight to our friends and walk the mile back to my house in silence. A heavy snow falls around us. The snow melts under my feet and turns the dirty gravel to mud. My tracks looks dark and gross compared to Xander's snowy tracks. At the same time, Xander shivers as we walk while I can't gauge how cold it is. The night is dark and as quiet as we are. I'm not sure either of us knows what to say. Xander turns to me every once in a while. I'm sure he wants to tell me how sorry he is about my father. I know he is, he doesn't have to say it. Hearing him say it might actually make it real.

Xander and I both release a heavy sigh when we make it to the front door. Xander unlocks the door and we both head in. Without a word I walk towards the steps and head up. Xander follows.

"Do you want to shower first?" Xander asks me.

"No," I tell him. "I just want to curl up in my bed and pretend tonight never happened."

I expect him to tell me I'm covered in ash and blood, that I should shower and wash it all away. But he doesn't. Instead, Xander asks, "Do you want to me stay with you?"

"Wouldn't you rather go see Anna?" I ask him.

"Cass, right now you're my priority," he tells me.

"I want to be alone."

"Are you sure? I can stay."

I nod at him, telling him I'm sure, he can go.

He stares me down, trying to make me give in, but it

holds no sway over me. I'm done with tonight. I feel numb, hollowed out, and I just want to sleep so it will all be over.

"I'll leave," Xander says then takes a step closer to me, "but you can't cave in on yourself."

"What are you talking about?" I ask him.

"Ever since Logan and Tucker died you've hidden inside yourself. You put on a brave face and don't react to anything with any sort of emotion. Sure you cried on Gray's shoulders, but now you'll lie in your bed and shut down. You're hollow. You've tried to feel nothing because it's easier than the pain that holds your heart hostage. But your heart is still in there. I know you're hurting and you don't want to, but you just lost your father. You have to feel it. Let yourself feel it. If you don't, what good are you to us? If you don't feel it, why are you doing this?"

Xander steps into me and places his hands on my cheeks, not minding my blood coated cheek. He pulls me into him and kisses me on the forehead. I close my eyes and feel his lips on my skin.

When he pulls away he looks down on me and smiles a small smile.

"I love you, Cass," he tells me.

"I love you too, Xander," I tell him, swallowing around a lump in my throat.

"And you loved your father. Just like you loved Nash, and Tucker, and Logan. Feel it. Embrace it. Let it in, and let yourself grieve. And then come back to us. Lead us, like your father would have wanted."

Without allowing me to answer, Xander releases me and walks out of my room and out of the house.

I stand in my room staring at the doorway in Xander's wake. It occurs to me moments after he's gone that I might have wanted him to stay, but I know he wanted to be with Anna. I could have been selfish and asked him to stay, I've been selfish before, but I also do want to be alone.

Of course if I listen to Xander and open my heart to all the pain I've been displacing since Logan and Tucker died, it might kill me. I am seventeen years old and I currently feel like I've seventy. I have gone through more and lost more than any seventeen year old I know. What seventeen year old can go through all the trials I've been put through and come out okay on the other side? I'm not sure I will be okay, if I get to reach the other side. The war with Raphe isn't over and I'm not sure I'll survive it. Of course the way things have been going, I'll survive but no one I love will.

I can't think like that.

I promised myself I wouldn't lose another loved one, and while I failed myself of my own promise, I have to strive to keep it as best I can. My father will be the last one. I have to believe that.

After several minutes of Xander being gone, I turn around and face my room. I face something I haven't been able to look at since I placed it there after Logan's death. I stare at my desk and the silver urn sitting upon it holding Logan's ashes.

Hot tears burn the corners of my eyes and spill down

my face. I try swallowing but find that I can't, my throat obstructed by a mass of emotions. My breathing becomes ragged and I have to release breaths through my mouth in hard bursts as my chest fills with sorrow and anger and grief and anything I've been suppressing.

I have to sit on my bed to keep from collapsing to the floor.

My gaze moves to the picture of the four Musketeers Xander gave me for Christmas last year that sits above my dresser. I stare at it as memories of Tucker float through my head. Nights we spent together talking about boys and shopping. Days we spent laughing with Xander and Nash. Secrets we shared and advice we passed between each other. I think about how Tucker inadvertently brought Logan and I together. And how Tucker took my side when Xander and I began fighting. I think about how in love with Gray Tucker was and how happy I was because my best friend was so happy. Tucker was always there for me in thick and thin. He cared for me after I lost Nash, when I couldn't care for myself. He never once left my side, even when I wasn't being the best friend to him. The trip to the zoo Xander and Tucker took me on to cheer me up was a blast and everything I needed. The movie nights we had at his house cemented our friendship and will live on as some of my best memories. I will never have another friend like Tucker. He was one in a million. The best of them all.

Sobs threaten to overwhelm me as I think of the friend that I lost.

When I look back at Logan's urn sitting on my desk the base of my skull throbs and my vision darkens. I've suffered a lot of blows, but after Nash's death, losing Logan was the worst. It's been four months since he died. Four months I've felt nothing. Four months since my heart shattered.

I'm not sure if I believe in soul mates, but if I did, Logan was mine. Logan was my all and my everything. Logan made me stronger. He pushed me to be better. He believed in me and cared for me in a way no one else has.

I never would have believed we would end up where we did that first day he walked into class. He scared me for a long time after he moved to town. I wasn't sure about him. He was dark and mysterious and scary. But once I discovered that was a front he was using to scare off anyone who might be looking to hurt me, we got closer. Logan was tough, but sweet. He knew exactly when to push and exactly when to pull. He was the love of my life. I know that's dumb for a seventeen year old to say, but I truly believe it. I may fall in love again, I hope I fall in love again, but I know it will never be anything compared to what I had with Logan. Raw passion and desire. Trust built over time. And friendship.

When I woke up after Cohen stabbed me and realized Tucker and Logan had been killed, it nearly killed me. I haven't healed since, merely because I haven't allowed myself to feel their loss, haven't grieved.

As the grief hits me now, strike after strike, blow for blow, anger builds until I can't see through it. I can't feel my feet pushing off the floor until I'm standing. I can't see myself grasping Logan's urn in my hands and throwing it against the wall. The lid pops open as it crashes against the wall, ashes raining down in a dusty cloud around me.

My breath catches as I realize what I've done then a new wave of sorrow hits me.

A damn bursts inside me and I'm hit by a swell of emotion so big it knocks me back.

I move to pick up the urn and shovel the ashes with my hands back into it. When I pick up the urn off the floor I see a crack running from the lip to halfway down the metal. I look up to the wall and see a sizable whole in the plaster and a crack running up and down where the urn struck the wall. Small chunks of plaster lie on the floor, a cloud of it coating the air. I think about hiding it from my mom so she won't yell at me, but somehow I think she'll let this one slide.

Sobs wrack my body as I try to get the ashes back into the urn but I can't and soon my hands are caked in wet sticky mud, my tears mixed with the ashes of my dead boyfriend.

I pick up the urn and again throw it at the wall. I suck in big gulps of air but can't get a full breath. A weight sits on my chest preventing me from breathing properly. Nausea rolls my stomach and my cheeks fill with saliva. I'm going to puke if I can't keep it down. My vision is blurry and I can't make much out as I start throwing things at the wall in an attempt to quell the anger inside of me.

This whole feeling thing Xander wanted me to do is a bunch of bullshit.

I watched as my father died in front of my eyes. I

watched as his body turned to ash. And it wasn't enough that it was my father, no he had to look exactly like my brother so that I could feel the pain of two deaths. And then I killed a girl I've gone to school with since we were five. I felt her neck snap as I twisted her head. I watched the life go out, just like that. Like it was nothing. And maybe it was nothing. Maybe my life is nothing. Maybe no one means anything in this life. Maybe we're just here to take up space and the feelings we have, the hands we're given are nothing more than random deals. Or maybe we're just puppets with some sadistic person pulling the strings, seeing how far they can take it before we snap, before we can't take anymore.

Blood fills my mouth from biting my tongue to prevent myself from vomiting. My chest heaves in an attempt to get air in and out of my lungs. The ache from lack of oxygen. My chest hurts. My sides hurt. My stomach hurts. I hurt so completely emotionally and physically.

I grab the chair from my desk and hurl it at the door but I lose my balance and fall on my hands and knees to the floor. A burst of pain hits my knees and runs up and down my legs. My palms burn from the sudden friction. I roll onto my side and cry out, from the pain, from the sorrow. It hurts to breathe. It hurts to think. It hurts to feel.

I'm angry. And I'm sad. And I miss my friends and family so much. I miss spending every day with them. I miss hearing them laugh. I miss feeling Logan's touch. I miss talking to my father. I miss the twin bond Nash and I shared. I miss feeling whole and alive. I miss feeling like every day of my life isn't a battle of some kind.

I manage to pick myself up enough to lean my back against the side of my bed. I look around my room and see the damage I've wreaked. It's not pleasant. My lamp lies on its side on the floor, the lampshade askew and the bulb shattered. The drawers of my dresser are pulled out, one of them lies on my bed. The DVD of cartoons I gave to Logan on his birthday lies on the floor, the case smashed. There are several holes in my walls from various things I threw. My desk chair is in pieces near the door. Clothes lie strewn about the room. Chunks of plaster sit at the bottom of the walls and make a ring around the room. Plaster dust coats the air in a thick cloud. That's one thing about living in an old house, the walls were made with plaster, not sheet rock. I guess we'll have to do a little more renovating after tonight's episode.

While I feel a little better, because I can actually feel, nothing I did will bring them back. Destroying my room did nothing to bring them back, even if it made me relieve some of my pent up emotions. Ransacking my belongings did nothing to ease the pain of the losses I've been dealt. But at least maybe now I can move forward, maybe I can start to heal. Maybe now I can stop thinking about everything I've lost and start thinking about everything I still have.

But tonight is not the night for that. If it even is still night. Tonight I let my head fall into my hands as I sit against my bead and weep because that is all the courage I have.

***

I'm not sure when I pass out, but eventually the tears and exhaustion pull me into unconsciousness. It's a dreamless sleep. If sleep is what you can call it. It's more like a grief induced coma.

It's not long before I hear someone calling my name. Is it morning already? Is it time to go to school? Do I have to get up?

The voice calls to me, "Wake up, Casslyn."

The voice is a familiar one. I know it too well.

"Wake up, Casslyn."

My cheek tingles. Warmth spreads throughout my face. I know that feeling. I want to wake up but I'm so tired. Sleep threatens to pull me under again. But the voice is calling to me. My head throbs from a headache generated by everything that happened last night, but mostly from crying for hours on end. My eyes burn from weeping and when I open them, it's to blurred vision. Vision so blurred I can only make out an outline of a person kneeling in front of me.

"Wake up, love."

I know that voice.

I close my eyes tight and battle the pounding ache in my head.

When I open them again the person in front of me is still blurred, but no longer as much so. He kneels in front of me, keeping a distance but leaning in.

My heart slams into my rib cage as I continue to blink

and pull him into focus. My breath stops halfway up my throat.

"Logan?"

"I'm here, love," he says.

"Logan?" I ask, my ears ringing. My heart swells so much my chest aches and burns.

I thought I'd woken up, but I'm glad I didn't. This is the best dream I could imagine having. I haven't dreamt of Logan since he died. I've missed him. Even in my dreams.

"I've missed you so much," I tell him, watching his face grow clearer.

"You have no idea," he tells me, leaning in closer to me.

Fresh tears sting my eyes at the sight of him.

When I first started seeing Nash after he died I thought they were dreams. Turns out he was actually in my head because I hadn't let him go. Logan though, is not my twin, we did not share a soul, so I know this is a dream. And while I am so happy to see him in this dream, I know I'm going to wake up and be sad that it wasn't real.

I stare at Logan and he stares back, neither one of us willing to break the dream. Tears blur my eyes but Logan has never looked more beautiful.

"Why are you crying?" he asks me.

"I've missed you. And my life is so messed up right now. I've needed you here. You weren't here."

"I know, love. I know."

"You left me," I tell him, my voice quivering.

"I'm so sorry," he tells me, taking my face in his hands.

"I will never leave you again."

"But you will," I say, knowing that as soon as I wake up he will be gone. "You can't promise me that."

"I promise you, Casslyn. I will never leave you again. I promise."

My heart hammers in my chest driving its beat through my veins. I can feel Logan's pulse through his fingertips pressed against my cheeks, his heart beating as hard as mine.

I'm about to argue with him, to remind him this is only a dream, when he pulls my face to his and presses his lips to mine. Instantly I sink into him and into the kiss. His lips are soft and warm against mine and gentle, yet so demanding, like he's trying to make up for the months he's been gone. I kiss him back as urgently, trying to memorize the feeling, his lips, his taste, before I wake up and lose it all. Our bodies heat as we kiss, our fire reaching out for each other's.

My heart beats and swells and stutters and is completely overwhelmed by the emotions plaguing my body. Fire erupts from my fingertips where I grip his shoulders. I can feel Logan's fire against my face. We have never been able to control our power when we connect. I've wondered what would happen if we would ever have had sex, if we'd have burnt the house down. I guess we'll never know.

Logan and I sit on the floor of my bedroom encased in each other's arms. Butterflies erupt in my stomach. My lungs ache from the breath of life I haven't felt in a long time. I feel happy and content. Logan is my home and I've felt lost without him.

I pull away from him for a breath but he tugs me back to him and continues to kiss me. I feel light headed but I take hold of his shoulder and draw him closer to me. He can't get close enough. I can't get enough of him. When this dream ends it will destroy me. Tears fall from my eyes and stream between our touching faces.

Logan pulls away from me and asks again, "Why are you crying?"

I pull my lips into my mouth, bite down, and then say, "I wish you were real."

"Casslyn, I am real," he says, his hands still holding my face.

"You died. I saw your ashes. I cried on them. I spilled them on my floor."

"You did. You healed me and I came back."

I wrench away and look at him confused. "Logan, you died. Months ago. This is a dream."

"You are awake, love. I am here. In your room. Kissing you. Wake yourself up if you don't believe me."

I stare at him for moments. If this is a dream I don't want to wake myself up and disconnect from it. But if this is real. If Logan is alive. I can't bring myself to believe it. I can't let myself hope that there is a way that Logan is alive.

And yet.

Those kisses felt real. The fire that burned between us was real. And I certainly wouldn't have dreamt us together in the bedroom I destroyed tonight.

Logan waits for me to do something. Anything. I continue to stare at him. I should just do something. Pinch myself, slap myself, something to find out if this is real.

I take a deep breath, do a little sniff thing with my nose, and pinch my arm. Yep, I'm awake.

Holy shit.

Logan is alive.

No, this can't be real.

How can this be real?

Thoughts and emotions rush through my head.

"How is this possible?" I ask Logan, surprising myself by asking him a question and not attacking him.

"After I died, someone cried on my ashes, yes?"

"I did," I tell him.

Logan smiles, like he knew it was me that cried on his ashes and says, "You did. And I was going to regenerate. I don't know how it is even possible. No one that I have ever heard of has been able to bring back someone after they've turned to ash. But I was going to regenerate and then I couldn't."

"We put you in the urn," I say, as it clicks in my head.

"Yeah," he says.

We didn't give him enough time.

"And then tonight I wake up. I regenerate and I see you sitting against your bed passed out, tear stains down your face. It broke my heart, Casslyn."

My chin quivers as I look at Logan. Logan. He's alive. He's sitting right in front of me. This is real life and I can't process it.

Everything that has happened to me over the last two years, the last several months, last night. It all compounds and threatens to tear me apart at the seams. Emotions swell inside me and make every part of me hurt. All of the terrible things that have happened in my life. All the things that have broken me and then smashed the pieces. My twin dying. My father dying. Kristina, the other phoenixes, Tucker, Logan. Dying. Every death chipped away at me a little more, every betrayal and trap and back stab made it a little harder to put myself back together. I didn't realize until this moment, Logan siting before me, joy and happiness and love surging into me wave after wave, I didn't realize I'd been empty.

When Xander left, he told me to feel, to let in the pain. I didn't know what he meant. Until now. I hadn't let anything in since Logan and Tucker died. I haven't felt anything beyond anger and hate.

As I sit next to Logan, letting it all in, believing that the love of my life has once again entered it, I begin to weep. The sobs wracking my body until I can't breathe and need Logan to keep me upright. He wraps his arms around me and holds on tight lending me his strength until I can find my own. Until I can catch my breath and hold myself together.

Until I can appreciate the fact that my boyfriend is alive and sitting in front of me.

That's when I attack him.

Attack him with my hands, with my lips, with my body and my heart. He smiles at me right before I lunge at him. I kiss him and touch him and altogether cannot get enough of him.

Eventually he pulls back and tells me, “You stink.”

I’m almost offended and then I remember what happened to me what can’t be more than several hours ago.

I’m hit by a train of memory and sensory overload and I almost dissolve into tears again. But Logan is there to pull me back from the ledge.

“Tell me what happened,” he says to me.

I look into his eyes, knowing I’m about to break his heart along with mine, but I have to tell him.

“My father was killed tonight,” I say.

Logan sucks in a deep breath, his eyes burning that bright blue, his face contorts in pain.

“What happened?” he asks.

To tell him what happened would take all night and into tomorrow, maybe longer. A lot has happened in the months that he’s been gone. But he needs to know. Logan has known my father, has been a part of this world and this war for far longer than I have. He needs to know what has happened in his absence.

His long absence. The one that nearly killed me. The one that turned me into the person I’ve become. The person I wouldn’t recognize a year ago.

So I begin where he left off, his birthday. I tell him how Cohen betrayed me. How he stabbed me in the chest and nearly killed me. I tell him how while I was dying I saw Nash who told me to heal myself and let him go. I tell him how I came back and he and Tucker were dead. I tell him how I lost everything and gained a hatred so fierce it nearly burned me alive. How I decided to go after the griffins instead of playing the victim. How I decided to become the monster they think we are.

I tell him how the phoenixes got on board after that and we were able to take out a few of them. How I got my revenge on Tucker's killer and Nash's killer. I move on to most recently. I tell him about Cohen and Xander siding with us and trying to get their people on board to take out Raphe and end this war for good. I tell him how we were to meet with the griffins tonight, feel them out, make a plan. I tell him how wrong it went and how my father died before my eyes and how we had to get out of there, how we almost didn't.

When I end my story the both of us are in tears, sitting on the floor, clutching each other. We sit like that for a long time. Long minutes passed, the only sound is the sobs wracking our bodies. Logan loved my father. I loved my father. He's yet another person I have failed to keep safe. He was our leader. He was supposed to be the best of us. And he's gone.

"I'm sorry you had to go through all that. I'm sorry I wasn't here," Logan tells me as he pulls away from me, tears drying on his cheeks. I've never seen Logan cry before. I always thought he was too tough to cry. But watching him now, he's beautiful as he never has been before. Logan is always tough, which is damn sexy, but the rare times when he's vulnerable are the most beautiful and make me fall that much more in love with him.

"I'm sorry we didn't wait long enough for you to come back," I tell him.

"How could you have known? I've never known anyone come back from certain death before."

Tears sting my eyes and I start crying again. I can't believe Logan is back. I'm not sure how it's possible, but I have him back and I'm going to thank my lucky starts for it every night from now on.

"Casslyn," Logan says, still sitting beside me.

"Yeah?" I ask, expecting him to say something profound, for him to wipe away my tears and tell me everything is going to be okay.

But instead he says, "You still smell."

A weak laugh escapes from me. I probably do smell pretty rank.

I'm still coated in Cohen's blood and the smoke soaked clothes from before. I need to take a shower, to wash all the bad mojo from my body, because I can't wash it from my mind. But to take a shower, I'd need to leave Logan here, and I'm not about to ever leave him alone again.

Logan must sense my thoughts. He always has before. I don't know if I thought his death would have changed him, but so far he seems like the same Logan I fell in love with what feels like years ago.

"We could shower together," he says.

Logan has seen me naked a handful of times. I shouldn't feel embarrassed. I don't feel embarrassed. But we've never had sex before, and while I know this shower isn't about to turn into shower sex, it will be the most intimate thing we've ever done. I'm not even sure we are a couple. It was heading in that direction on his birthday before he died. But I'm not sure what he's feeling right now. We kissed when he came back. But for all he knows, I could have gotten back together with Cohen, or gotten together with anyone else. Who am I kidding, I love Logan, there is no one I could love besides him, and he's well aware of that. But with my father gone, he might not want to be with me. With everything that's happened and this person I've had to become, he might not want to be with me. And that scares me most of all.

"Casslyn, what's the matter?" Logan asks.

I'm not about to be the insecure girl who worries about her relationship when more important things are happening around her. I just lost my father. I just killed a girl I've known my entire life. I shouldn't be worrying about my love life right now.

So instead of answering him, I take his hand and lead him into the bathroom.

I don't think Xander is back. I'm sure he'd have wanted to spend as much time with Anna as he could. And with Cohen staying at Logan's for the time being, they will get plenty of alone time.

While we were in my room Logan covered himself with a blanket. He didn't exactly come back to life fully clothed. So he doesn't have much to take off to get in the shower. I've never seen Logan naked. I've never seen him any more than shirtless. I feel my cheeks redden as I stare at the naked man before me. He stands before me and lets me look. I've never seen so much muscle on a man before, not even in the movies. He's got more than a six pack. The muscles in his legs stand taut under his skin. He's got that happy little v that leads to happy places. I'm about to explode as I stare at the rest of him. My glance shifts when Logan clears his throat, though the sound of it is thick.

When I look back at him, his cheeks are just as red as mine. A side grin splits his face and he looks down. I'm glad I'm not the only one affected here. Logan steps into the shower and turns on the water, leaving me to undress without him looking.

I take off my clothes one item at a time, toss them into the sink and light them on fire. I hold my flaming hand to the clothes so they will burn more quickly. When they are reduced to ashes, I run water in the sink to wash them away. Only when I'm convinced all evidence of tonight is flowing down into the sewer do I step in the shower.

Logan is turned away from me, his face turned into the spray from the shower head. I step to him, lay my hands on his arms and rest my head against his back. He stills from the contact. I cling to him, trying to memorize the shape of him, the feel of his skin on mine, the heat of the flames that burn under his flesh. Logan is actually here. He is alive and standing before me. That realization alone is enough to bring me to my knees. How could something so amazing happen on a night when something so horrible went down? How could I possibly be allowed to be happy right now, when I should be grieving for my father?

After several moments of standing like we are, Logan finally turns around to face me. He takes me in his arms and pulls me to him. His lips find mine and claim them as his. Heat burns through me as our passion for each other ignites. Logan moves us under the spray of the water. Steam rolls off us in waves and wafts to the ceiling.

I feel lighter as the ash and smoke and blood run off of me and down the drain. I will never be able to wash away the events of tonight, but at least I don't have to carry the guilt of it on my skin. For weeks after Kristina died, I always felt the coating of her ashes on my skin. I can only hope tonight won't carry the same weight.

Logan finds a wash cloth, lathers it up, and begins to wash me. I shiver as his hands roam over my body. He is gentle and pays close attention to areas that might need a little something extra. He massages my aching muscles as he goes and lays kisses down on spots he's washed. My body hums and tingles. Every nerve ending comes alive at Logan's touch. Parts of me ache with want.

Logan spins me around so my back is facing his front. He pulls me flush against him and holds me to him with an arm under my chest. He's never taken my bra off to feel my chest. He's never put his hand between my legs. Logan has never touched me beyond anything I was ready for. But now, as his arm grazed the underside of my boobs, I want him to touch every part of me. I want every inch of my body to be discovered by him. And if I had to guess, the hard length of him pressed against my butt would indicate he wants the same.

Logan and I have been through too much together, and apart, to hold back now. Loving him and losing him, more than once, if in different ways, proves tomorrow isn't a given, that I could lose him at any moment, again. I need to make the most of the time we have together. And that's what I plan to do.

I inhale sharply as Logan's hand and the washcloth run over my lower stomach. Logan's body tightens against me. His hand stops where it is. Fire ignites between his hand and my stomach. I watch as it spreads over my body and passes to his. My chest rises and falls rapidly in anticipation, lust, desire, need. Call it what you want, but my body vibrates in Logan's embrace.

I turn around to face Logan. The blue flames in his eyes smolder and dance. His ragged breaths match mine. Still watching him, I take one of his hands in mine and bring it up to cup my boob. When I pull my hand away Logan's remains. I have to close my eyes as a shockwave of pleasure ripples through me when he gently squeezes my breast. He uses his other hand to pull me closer to him. His hard on pokes my belly and turns my knees to jelly. Logan catches me before I can slip through his hands. In one swift motion he hoists me up and swings my legs around him. He nearly collapses as I'm positioned right on top of his erection. The feeling of it against me has me squeezing my legs together. This, again, makes him loose his grip on me. Instead of dropping me, he rests me against the wall of the shower and leans into me.

The water of the shower now runs cold but the fire surrounding us heats it before it touches our skin. We are pressed together as tightly as can be and yet it's not enough. I want more of him, I want all of him.

I grab for his face and thread my hands through his wet hair, pulling him to me. Our lips seal and move together. Flames ignite as our tongues do, filling our mouths with heat. Up until now, the water put out the fire dancing on our skin, but the passion burning between us has the flames growing and overpowering the spray from the shower head. Every time Logan's body touches my sensitive spot I squeeze me thighs together and his body quakes. We're on the verge of combusting and we can't get enough.

Logan shuts the water off but doesn't release his grip on me. He steps out of the shower, still holding me, our lips still locked. Picking up the towel, he drapes it over me and walks to my room. Dripping wet he places me on my bed and leans over me. My legs are still wrapped around his waist, still pressed against his erection. I can't imagine the pressure he feels, knowing how tightly wound I am.

We don't have a condom, but I desperately want to have sex with him. I'm ready. I know he's ready. I need a little good in my life right now. But if I'm going to have sex with him just to mask the hurt I'm feeling right now, it isn't right. My first time with Logan should be something special between the both of us, not something I use to block out something else. And that is why we won't be having sex tonight.

Logan slows our kiss, sensing how I feel. I know Logan wouldn't have slept with me without a condom. It's not something we've really talked about at length, but I'm hoping that box of condoms I found in his drawer next to my picture was for me. As Logan lies next to me, holding me, and gently kissing, I can sense he knew we weren't going to have sex. But we got caught up in the moment, him being back from the dead, us being back together.

I can't keep my hands off of him. Part of me still can't believe he is here, alive. Another part of me is afraid I'm going to lose him again as soon as I've gotten him back.

At some point, after the frenzied make out session has come to a gradual slowdown, the both of us exhausted, we find clothes, Logan borrowing a t-shirt and shorts from Xander's room. We lay together on my bed, under the drying comforter, and cling to each other as sleep consumes us.

***

I wake up, sore, tired, and sad. Last night should have gone off without a hitch. Instead, we walked right into a trap. A trap the ended in the death of Ashley and my father. Ashley I'm not so sad about. But I was just getting to know my father, our relationship growing stronger. I was finally happy to have him in my life. I was ready to spend the rest of my long life getting to know him, and loving him more as my father.

Now I won't get that chance. The lives of too many

people I love have ended too quickly. I lost Nash, Kristina, Tucker, Logan, and now my father. I don't see the appeal in living forever if I can't live with them. I don't want to live without them.

I lie in my bed with my eyes closed contemplating existence. I think about how my parents feel without Nash in their lives. I don't think it's true that time heals all wounds, because I certainly feel the same ache now that I felt when I lost Nash. But time makes it easier to bear those losses.

I'm not sure what time it is, but it can't be very early. Fighting our way out of last night left me exhausted. I vaguely remember coming home and destroying my room. I'll have to clean all that up at some point.

I know I will need to go to Logan's and talk with the rest of the phoenixes. I am their new leader. But I'm not ready for that. I'm not ready to face my friends as their leader, being the reason their former one is dead. I don't know where to go from here. I am going to kill Raphe and end this once and for all. I'm just not sure how I'm going to pull it off. He always seems to be a few steps ahead of us.

Facing them would be so much easier with someone by my side. I know Gray will stick by me, and Xander, but it's not quite the same as if I had Logan with me. I wish Logan was with me. I had the greatest dream last night that he came back from the dead. That crying on his ashes had actually worked and he regenerated. If only dreams could come true.

I take a deep breath, realizing I will have to face the world at some point, I can't just hide in my bed forever, something I am willing to do.

I open my eyes, turn to the side, and scream.

There is a body lying next to me.

I try to scream again but it is cut off by a hand covering my mouth.

I watch as the body rises up above me. Watch as I realize dreams can come true.

Logan pulls his hand away from my mouth and smiles at me.

"Good morning, love," he says to me as my bedroom door bursts open.

Xander rushes in, Anna behind him, both of them ready to murder someone.

Anna screams as she sees Logan lying next to me.

Xander stares at Logan like he's seeing a ghost.

I fall back onto my pillow, an exasperated sigh escaping my chest.

"Surprise," Logan says.

Twelve

The next few days are a huge adjustment. Logan is back, my father is gone, I am the new leader, I'm sure there are some things I'm forgetting.

I tried to step down as leader of the phoenixes. I tried to get someone else to take the position, Gray, Logan, anyone but me. I'm not ready for this. I haven't been a part of them for long enough. I have no idea what I am doing. But Gray and Logan both refused. And the rest of them reminded me that my father had faith in me, he knew I could do this. So it stuck. I am the leader of the phoenixes. Not sure the rest of them will be as excited about it as my few friends here are.

I'm glad I don't have school to contend with right now. The administration called off school this week, extending the Christmas break. They are doing repairs to the gym. I didn't hear the extent of the damage to it, but I hope it's not major. I would hate to have that on my conscience. When we watched the news report about it, they didn't say anything about the chains hanging from the rafters or any dead bodies found on the stage. I'm guessing Raphe was able to get Ashley out in time before the fire trucks came. He must have had his lackeys go in and clear out the chains and anything else they might have left lying around.

I'm surprised he had the presence of mind after losing his daughter to get all that done. If I were in his shoes and I would have been lost in my grief and wouldn't have cared about the consequences.

But I'm glad I get another week before school starts again to sort this all out.

My friends are being patient with me as their new leader and not pushing me for decisions and leading. I'll get there. I'll have to get there. Just one step at a time.

The fact that Logan is back and alive has everyone in the house a bit on edge. Not only because no phoenix they have ever known has come back from an actual death. Our friends stare at Logan like he is a ghost. It's almost like they are afraid of him, like he's a zombie or something. Logan's sister, Aspen can't stop crying. Every time she sees him she bursts into tears. I know they are happy tears but seeing her react in such a way makes Logan and the rest of us uncomfortable. I still wake up convinced that he is still ashes on my desk, that is until I roll over and see I'm lying next to him. I stopped screaming after the second morning.

The other reason we are a little unsure of having Logan back is the fact that we were not going after the griffins when he died. We were on the defense only. Now we are on the offense. And yes we got my father's approval, but my father is no longer here to convince Logan of that. And while I stand by what I've done, I'm not sure how Logan feels about it.

I haven't told my parents yet about the death of my father. For one, they will worry that I am in too much danger. Plus they will worry about my emotional state. I also haven't told them about Logan's resurrection. I'm not sure they will be able to grasp that one. If he comes to my house we are careful to sneak him in and hide him, but otherwise we hang out at his house.

The mood around his house is dark and gloomy. My friends lost their leader, their friend. They feel like we've failed. I haven't stepped up yet. They try to hide it as best they can. But I don't want them to. I want to see them hurting, not because it brings me joy, but because I want it to bring us closer. I want us to grieve together and then to grow stronger together.

I have been trying to spend time alone with each of them. Especially Lydia, Xander, and Cohen, those who were there that night. I want everyone to feel like I care about them individually as well as a whole. I want them to be able to feel like they can come to me with anything. And most importantly I want them to feel like they can trust me. I want to believe I'm emulating my father, but really I'm just pulling this out of my ass as I go along. Logan helps. He guides me in the right directions without every telling me what to do. And he helps me to know when I'm doing something wrong.

We haven't talked about the direction in which I have lead the phoenixes. It started out as my own personal vengeance. I never expected the others to join in with me, never expected that my father would give his blessing and also join in. I know we will have to talk about it. I'm ready to talk about it. But with everything else going on, it hasn't come up. Nor has the fact that Cohen isn't among the dead griffins after betraying me. Logan almost killed Cohen the first time he saw him after regenerating. It took everyone in the house to stop him.

When they pull Logan away and Cohen is able to escape, Logan trembles at my side. Gray and Thomas haul him onto the couch, make sure I've got him under control, and walk away. I've never seen him this agitated as long as I've known him. I've seen him angry, I've even seen him vulnerable, but I've never seen him like this. Like someone is torturing him. Like he is dying from the inside out. I watch him shake, his face crumpled and haunted. I'm afraid to touch him. Logan pulls his legs up, resting his feet on the cushion of the couch. It would look comical, Logan being so big and burly and pulling his knees to his chest, if he wasn't so upset. I know he has every right to be angry with Cohen, to hate him, but as many times as I've interacted with Cohen in the past, Logan has never reacted to him like that.

Cautiously I place my hand on Logan's back. When he doesn't flinch away from me I move closer to him, curling my arms around his back and chest, and rest my chin on his shoulder.

I make sure to keep my voice soft and low as I call to him, "Logan."

He doesn't react, keeps trembling.

I try again. "Logan?"

He turns his head to me, resting his chin on my arm. He doesn't say anything, just stares deep into my eyes. His are a darker blue than they've been before. Like his eyes have lost their light, their life.

"What's eating at you?" I ask him.

"I saw him," Logan says.

He doesn't finish the sentiment. He saw Cohen what? He saw him with me? He saw him kiss me? What did Logan see Cohen do that would affect such hatred?

I'm not about to ask him what he means. He knows the question is implied. And I know he'll tell me eventually.

"That night," he says, closing his eyes and swallowing hard. "The night the griffins attacked. The night I died. I saw Cohen kiss you. I saw him stab you."

Oh.

Oh man.

I get it.

Waking up to the news Logan had died nearly killed me. Watching Kristina and my father die nearly killed me. If I had to watch Logan die, it would have killed me.

Logan and I haven't gotten the chance to talk about what happened that night. The fact that Logan saw Cohen stab me, he thought I'd died, and then he died. It's very Romeo and Juliet, though I don't think I can be proud of that.

I could never deal with the fact that Logan had died. I didn't want to let it set in and have to deal with the fact that I would never again have him in my life. And even though I didn't want to face his death, the people around me did. Aspen dealt with it. Gray dealt with it. So did my father.

And while I tried not to be around when they were talking about him, I couldn't always escape it. At one point, when Gray and I were talking about the night he died, he told me how Logan reacted to seeing me stabbed by Cohen. He told me how Logan didn't react well. How he lost his mind and started going after the griffins without any regard to his life. He keened like a broken beast and entered the fight with reckless abandon. He was so broken he let himself be overtaken by the griffins and stabbed until he died. Gray wasn't convinced Logan fought hard enough to save himself. It made me sad. It made me upset to think that Logan wasn't strong enough to hold himself together. I wouldn't have been strong enough to hold myself together in the event of his death. I wasn't. But the fighting was over when I woke up. And in the case of my father's death, I had to be dragged away from the fray. I can't hold myself in check when grief hits me. I don't know why I would hold Logan in a higher regard, but the fact that he didn't handle himself well, unsettles me.

I don't know what to say to Logan. I don't know how to settle his sorrow. We are both alive and together, but he saw me die, and I woke up to him dead. Even though we are both here now, neither of us will be able to get over living through the loss we both suffered. Logan didn't know I was coming back. I didn't know he could regenerate. In the moment we both had to deal with losing each other. As awful as it sounds it was like we were Romeo and Juliet. And while a lot of people love Romeo and Juliet, I find them melodramatic and pathetic. I don't like it that Logan and I resembled them.

"He stabbed you, Casslyn. He betrayed you. You died because of him. And then I come back to find that you've not only not killed him, but you're friends with him. You've let him into the group. You've let him into your heart. I just, I can't wrap my head around that."

"Logan, I," I start, but I'm still not sure what to say to him.

I try again, "A lot happened when you weren't here. I know that's not your fault. I know you can't understand a lot of it. But you have to trust me. I am trying to save us from the griffins. Yeah, I don't know what I'm doing a lot of the time. But I am doing my best. I just need you to be on my side."

Logan continues to rest his chin on my arm and stares at me for several moments before he says anything. But he finally says, "I am always on your side. But that image is planted in my mind. Every time I close my eyes I see him stab you, over and over again. I can't get over it and I can't forgive him. You might have, but I can't."

"I understand," I tell him. Honestly I never thought I'd

be able to forgive Cohen. Things change. People change their minds.

It's only been a few days, but Logan hasn't tried to kill Cohen since. And they've seen each other a number of times. I feel bad for the both of them. Logan because he hates Cohen so much. And Cohen, because no one wants to be hated as vehemently as Logan hates Cohen, and so up close.

Once I'd gotten Logan calmed down and let a little time pass, I had to make sure Cohen was okay. Logan literally would have killed Cohen if we hadn't stopped him. It isn't anything unusual to fear for your life in this world, but when it comes from your own side, then it's an issue. Plus I hadn't been able to give Cohen any heads up that Logan was alive. The fact that he was alive took over my brain and made it slightly difficult to function properly.

So I went in search of Cohen. As I had assumed I found him in his loft licking his wounds. Really he was sitting on his couch staring at the TV but it was turned off and he was clearly sulking. I couldn't blame him.

"Are you okay?" I asked him before I sat down next to him.

"Fine," he says and though it's a short word the way he says it is clipped.

"I'm really sorry he did that to you."

"It's my own fault," Cohen says. "I had it coming. I did try to kill the love of his life and he watched me do it."

"I'm still sorry," I say then lapse into silence. I'm not sure what else to say. I still need Cohen on my side. I still need him to help me take down his father. And despite the fact that he tried to kill me, Cohen is my friend and I need him in my life. Logan is going to have to get past that.

Cohen sits next to me, quiet, sullen, his arms crossed over his chest.

His eyes are closed and for half a second I think he's fallen asleep on me when he opens them and says, "So Logan's alive."

"He is."

"Xander told me he was. I guess I didn't believe him."

"I can't really believe it myself."

"How do you feel about that?" Cohen asks me, still not looking at me.

I turn my body towards him in hopes he'll at least look at me and show me he's invested in the conversation.

"Happy. Obviously. I love him. I know that's not exactly what you want to hear and I'm sorry. How are you doing with it?"

"Pretty shitty," he says still not looking towards me. He returns to silence. I want to chastise him. I made it clear to him that I loved Logan and that I didn't want to be with anyone else. But I let him remain quiet. I don't give him shit about it because I wouldn't want that if I was in this situation. Finally Cohen turns to me and looks me in the eye. "But I care about you, Casslyn. I told you once before that if you only wanted to be friends I could handle that because I just wanted to get to spend time with you. And though I may have been in the process of betraying you, I still meant every word I said. I want to be in your life, and if that means only being your friend, then that's what I'll be."

I lean forward and wrap my arms around Cohen's neck. I was prepared for him to say he no longer wanted to come around, to be my friend, especially if Logan was going to try killing him every time he does. But I'm so glad he wants to be my friend. I feel selfish though, like I'm asking too much of him. Like I'll be putting him in pain if I can only give him friendship and he wants more.

Cohen hugs me back and I close my eyes and thank anyone listening.

When I pull back I smile at him and say, "You are an amazing friend, Cohen. You've had your rough patches, you know, stabbing me and all that, but I am really glad you're my friend. I really am."

"Me too, Casslyn."

I left his loft feeling better about the situation. I'd defused Logan's tension and comforted him from the pain of reliving Cohen's betrayal. I made sure Cohen was okay after Logan tried to kill him and got to keep him as a friend. Successful mission.

Besides the Cohen ordeal, Logan has come around to most of the changes we've made to our group in the last several months. He wasn't pleased the rest of the phoenixes left after the attack at my house. He was very happy with those who decided to stay.

Once we got used to the fact that Logan was back and my father was gone, Logan got in contact with the phoenixes who had left and told them of my father's death and the funeral we plan to have for him. He told them to spread the word. It's only been a handful of days, but we've heard nothing back. I can't say that I'm surprised, but Logan hasn't taken it rather well. Nor have any of our friends. Gray called a few of them to chew them out but his calls went to voicemail, and you can't properly chew someone out through a voicemail. It's just not as satisfying. But, we did our part, we extended an olive branch. They decided not to accept it.

Because we plan to have a funeral, and because I can't exactly hide it from them for too long, I'm going to have to tell my parents. They deserve the right to know. And they, or at least my mom, deserve the right to say goodbye to him. He is part of the reason they had two children. And at one point in time my mom really did love him.

The funeral is tomorrow. It's a Sunday. And while we don't have a body to bury, we plan to go to the gym, my father's final resting place, and pay our last respects. I have been to far too many funerals in the last few years and am not looking forward to another one. I am just hoping this will be the last one I attend for a long time.

I'll tell my parents about my father today, but first Logan and I are taking a break. We sit on the couch, cuddled into each other, watching Saturday morning cartoons. They aren't quite as good as Sunday morning cartoons, but we will take whatever mind numbing animation we can get right now.

I'm seated on Logan's lap with his arms wrapped around

me. His thumbs trace circles where they meet my flesh. The heat that flows from his skin and into mine nearly puts me to sleep. He rests his chin on my shoulder and about every two minutes kisses my shoulder. I'm not sure if he's aware he's doing it or if he's just reassuring himself that I'm here, that I'm real, that I'm in his arms. Whatever the reason, I'm not going to complain. Every time his lips caress my skin, little shoots of pleasure zip from my shoulder into my chest. And every time he kisses me, a hum escapes the back of my throat.

But, just like Logan touching me, reminding himself I'm real, I have to do the same. Every time he walks in a room I hold my breath and wait for him to disappear like he's a figment of my imagination. Every time he calls my name or smiles at me I have to pinch myself to make sure I'm not dreaming.

Because how can this be real? How could I have lost my father but gotten Logan back? Is someone playing a joke on me? Am I involved in some evil hoax? Because real life doesn't work this way. You don't get someone back who you've lost. But then again, being a phoenix isn't really like real life. Not the one I used to live.

So I take it in. I relish in the fact that I have Logan back. And I try not to dwell on the thoughts that plague me. The thoughts that remind me I've lost him once. I could lose him again. I try not to dwell on it and sit and watch cartoons with him.

If our lives weren't so chaotic at the moment. If we

weren't facing such dire problems. If we didn't have so much awful crap to focus on, I could really get used to this. Spending my mornings curled up on the couch with Logan watching cartoons and getting lost in each other's touch. If I can defeat Raphe, I can see that dream becoming a reality.

I just need to figure out how.

It always seems as though he is one step ahead of us. I'm not sure how. But I'm bound and determined to beat him at his own game. I might actually be able to do that now. We have killed a number of his people, though I know he has more. We've corrupted a number of them into joining our side, or at least we're working on it. But most importantly, we've taken away his children. And while he didn't think much of Cohen, the fact that his own son has sided against him has got to wound him. But the thing that might be his undoing, is the loss of his daughter. I saw pure devastation in Raphe's eyes after I snapped Ashley's neck. It was time he lost something, instead of taking everything away from me.

It was also time I told my parents of what I'd lost.

I sit up away from Logan. He grabs on to my arms and tries to pull me back to him. I would love to let him. I would love to sit back nestled into him and do nothing all day. But if I don't buck up and tell my parents today, then I won't have time to do it tomorrow, and they will miss their chance to say goodbye to him.

I turn to Logan and say, "I can't stay."

A frown settles on his face and he says, "I know. I know what you have to do. Do you want me to come with you?"

"No," I tell him. "I haven't even told them about you yet. Seeing you, after seeing my father look exactly like Nash, might just give them both heart attacks. I will tell them about Aris, and about you, and then they can see you at the funeral tomorrow."

"I just want to be there for you," he tells me, planting a kiss to my forehead.

"I know you do. But you are, Logan. You are always there for me, even if you're not actually there. Do you know how many times I've gotten out of a situation because I've got your voice playing in my head, telling me what to do?"

"I love you, Casslyn."

"I love you too, Logan."

I lean forward and place my lips on his. He moves his hands to my face and pulls me further into him, opening up to the kiss. I missed Logan in several ways when I thought he was dead, but this, these hot kisses, our bodies melded together, might be the thing I missed most.

I have to be the one to pull away, remove his hands from me, and walk out of the house. If I didn't, neither of us would have moved from that couch.

I walk to my house with trepidation. This is what it must have been like for them to tell me that Nash had died. It's a little different situation, but I imagine the feeling is the same. This gnawing feeling in the pit of your stomach. This deep ache in your heart. The pull at your tear ducts. I've never, in my life, had to tell another person that someone in their lives had died. The guilt eats away at me with every closer step I take to my house.

I enter silently, listening around the house for my parents. My dad has been spending most of his nights, and mornings, and days here, so I know he'll be here. I don't have to search far. My parents sit on the couch, my dad's arm strung over my mom's shoulders, the two of them watching some morning talk show, but not really paying attention to it.

I watch them, curled into each other in a similar fashion Logan and I were in minutes ago. I know they know about me, and Xander, and our friends, and our world, but they are removed from it in a way I will never be. And that is freeing. Sure, they have to worry about whether or not I will come home every night, but they don't have to worry about fighting in a battle, or watching their friends die. I envy them of that. But I am also so happy they don't have to bear that weight. Because it is a burden I'm not so sure I can handle.

I watch them for a moment longer before I step around into the living room and shut the TV off.

My parents sit up from the couch and stare at me, concern in their eyes. They may be free of the fighting and the full frontal carnage of this war, but they have to face the instant fear of situations like these. Any normal teenager shutting off the TV their parents were watching would be to get them out of the room or to argue with them. Not to tell them that someone has died.

I can tell they both want to jump in, to ask what is wrong, to know what happened. But they don't. I came to them, they know I will open up.

They know something is wrong, I can see it on their faces, and they can see it on mine. I don't need any preamble, so I jump right into the story.

"A few nights ago Xander, Cohen, Lydia, Aris and I went to talk with some of the griffins."

My mother jumps in her seat but remains on the couch.

I continue, "Cohen has wanted out of the griffins for as long as he can remember. We thought there might be others who wanted out. Turns out, there is. So we went to talk to them in hopes they would join us in taking down their leader."

I haven't told my parents who the leader of the griffins is, or who any specific members of their race are. I don't need them getting into it with those people and risking their lives.

"We were just going to talk to them. But, we walked into a trap."

This time my dad jumps in his seat. My parents turn to each other and clutch their hands together. Neither of them says a word, but the looks on their faces speaks volumes.

"They knocked us out and strung us up. The griffins we were meeting too. They betrayed their leader, so why shouldn't they share the same fate. They started torturing us," I say, then stop. I've done all I can to keep my parents almost completely out of this. I'm not about to share the gory details with them.

"One of them was coming for me, but I was able to get out of my chains and defend myself. I killed the griffin coming after me. But their leader retaliated," I say, my throat thickening until I can't speak.

Tears spring to my eyes but remain on my lids, refusing to fall. I try to blink them away but it only results in blurring my eyes.

"What happened, baby?" my dad asks.

Emotions well in my chest and weigh it down. I want to sit down, I want to curl up in my bed and not go on with the story. I didn't know it would be this hard. My breathing is heavy and I can't seem to get a full breath.

"He," I start. "He-."

I choke on a sob and it catches in my throat. I try to swallow around it but nearly dry heave.

"He killed my father," I say just before collapsing.

My dad jumps up from the couch and catches me before I hit the ground. He pulls me into him and I bury my head in his chest, the tears released from their cage. I cry into his chest as he pulls me onto the couch between he and my mom. I can feel my mom crying as she holds onto me.

I didn't want my parents to say they were sorry. I didn't want them to say anything. Because what could they say to comfort me? What could they say to take away the guilt crushing me from the inside?

So they hold me until I've run out of tears and my breathing returns to normal. They hold me until it doesn't hurt so much to be broken. They hold me until I can coherently speak to them.

And then we talk about the funeral. They ask me if it

was at the gym. They aren't stupid, I'm sure they'd had it figured out. They ask me about Xander and Cohen and Lydia and how they are doing. They ask me if I'd sent Gray and Thomas over here to watch over them. Again, they aren't stupid. We talk about the fact that I am now the leader of the phoenixes. This, they aren't too happy about.

"But you're still in high school. Can't someone else do it? How can you possibly handle all this?" my mom asks me.

It's a question I've asked myself. How am I supposed to finish and win a war, finish my last year of high school, and then go on to college, all the while leading a whole race of people. I can't say that I've got it all figured out, or any of it.

And then for the finale, I tell them that Logan is alive.

This one they can't believe.

I have to tell them that if we'd just waited a little longer, he would have regenerated a long time ago and I wouldn't have had to live months without him.

They don't quite understand. And when I try to explain it to them, I can't say I totally understand. But Logan is alive and I need to stop questioning it.

After all that has happened and all that I have told them, my parents are extremely reluctant to let me out of their sight. I agree to spend the rest of the day with them. It's not like it takes much convincing. I've lost one parent, I'd like to spend as much time with my remaining parents as I can. Especially since I don't know if I'll be able to defeat Raphe and make it out alive. I know my parents would love to lock me in my room and wait out this war, but it's not like they could stop me from leaving. I can't say I blame them. If I was in their situation I would be out of my mind with worry for my child. Not simply for the fact that I am their child, but I am, still a child. I am a seventeen year old who is supposed to lead a people, win a war, finish high school and have some semblance of a life. I'm not sure I'm up for this. Whoever decided it was a good idea to set me in this particular life has a wicked sense of humor, or an evil streak.

After cooking dinner together, the menu entirely chosen by me, we do the dishes as a family. We play board games as a family. I beat both of my parents, several times, in Battleship. They then beat me in Clue.

In the middle of our second game of Life, my parents have me invite Logan over. In all the time that I've known Logan, as a couple or otherwise, my parents haven't spent that much time with him. When they mention inviting him over, to spend time with him, to get to know him, my heart leaps and does a little happy dance in my chest. My relationship with Logan has been a little rocky here and there, but we are together now, and I think it's the for-good kind, and I want him to be included in every part of my life and my parents are a big part of that. It's not like I've been trying to keep him away from them, or that he doesn't want to be around them, or that they don't want to be around him, it just has never worked out, or never been the right time. And I like that it finally is the right time.

When Logan walks through the door I can sense apprehension coming off of him in waves. I've never really seen

Logan nervous before. Or, nervous in the way of hanging out with his girlfriend's parents.

I was worried it would be a little awkward to start out, and honestly, it was a little more than a little awkward. But as we started playing games and talking and laughing we became comfortable with each other and a new dynamic was formed. My parents ask Logan questions about himself and his interests and his past. They bring him in on their own conversations and ask his opinions. They don't balk when Logan touches me or I kiss him right in front of them. By the time we started to make supper I was having so much fun I forgot that the outside world still existed. And only this, my family and my boyfriend, mattered. But bubbles always burst.

***

It's a Sunday, during Christmas break, so no one is at the school, more specifically the gym, even more specifically, the final resting place of my father.

Gray and Nathan came early to scope the place out, make sure we'd have peace and privacy for the funeral.

I have to say, it's a bit odd to have a funeral at my school, but not totally weird. Once, when we were freshmen, a couple of seniors had died in a car accident the first week of school. They held a wake service at the school where nearly the whole town attended. It wouldn't be the first time the gym has been used for something more somber than basketball games, pep rallies, or school dances.

There are twelve of us here and not one of us has spoken a word, not since we left the house. While I wasn't sure if the other phoenixes would be comfortable with Cohen and Xander attending, they welcomed them with open arms. My father was kind to them and welcoming when they needed shelter. I thought it only right that they be allowed to give their goodbyes. I'm beyond glad my friends agreed.

I was a little worried bringing my parents here. I wanted them to have a chance to say goodbye to my father, but that nagging feeling in the back of my head telling me we could be walking into another trap wouldn't leave me alone. But every one of my friends assured me we would be fine, and if we weren't that they would do everything in their powers to keep my parents safe.

We walk into the gym using the busted door we are the cause of. I haven't been here since the night of the attack and I didn't know how extensive the damage was. But as we walk in, the smell of smoke and char and ash assaults my nose. I want to shut down my sense of smell, to keep it from reminding me of that night. But I don't. The results of that night are my fault and I will not remove the guilt from myself so easily.

I stand in the doorway as my friends crowd around me and survey the gym. The fire must have gotten a lot worse before the fire department could get to it. Light shines in from holes in the ceiling, snow covering those parts of the floor. The stage is all but a black ruined mess. Flashes of being up there, dangling from chains, surrounded by my people, those I promised to keep safe, my enemies, Ashley, Raphe, they attack my mind and would have me collapsing to the floor. But I take a deep breath, release the images, and step forward. I am the leader of the phoenixes now, I need to put on a brave face and lead by example.

As one, we make our way to the ashes of my father, step by step. I remember the exact spot Raphe stabbed my father. The exact place he stared at me as his body burned alive and reduced to ash. It would be like something from a movie if there was a hole in that spot of the ceiling and light shone down on that exact spot. But this is not a movie. This is my life, and light doesn't tend to shine down on it.

I've never been to a phoenix funeral before. I'm not sure if they are any different from a normal funeral or if they do some crazy shit like the ceremony they performed when they welcomed me into their group. I have to admit that was extremely cool, so I wouldn't mind something like that. Something a little happier than Tucker's funeral.

One by one, the twelve of us walk onto the stage, gingerly, as to not fall through the floor. We stand in a circle around the spot where my father died. It's so still and silent you could hear a pin drop. It's like we are all holding our breath, waiting for my father to regenerate like Logan did. When nothing happens someone in the circle clears their throat.

I look from Logan to Gray, to everyone else in the circle. I have no idea what to say. I may be his daughter, but am I really the best one to speak at his funeral? Logan was practically his son, and for far longer than I knew him. Shouldn't Logan say something? What about Thomas? What about Anna? Gray? Nathan? Lydia for goodness sake.

But, instead of any one of them stepping forward to say something, my mom steps up.

"I didn't know Aris for long, but I did love him for the short amount of time I did. Aris was an extraordinary man, and yet he was just like the rest of us. But the greatest gift he gave me was my children. Our children. Aris didn't know Casslyn and Nash, and that is my fault. I can't tell you how bad I feel that he didn't get to know Nash. But in the time he got to spend with Casslyn, he loved her. She was everything to him, as she is to me. I never got the chance to thank him. So thank you, Aris. Thank you for our children. I wish you could have seen them grow up. I will forever regret it, but be ever thankful for the part of them that was all you."

My mom falls quiet. Because my heart and eyes are defective, I've got tears leaking out the corners of my eyes and down my cheeks. But I'm glad to see I'm not the only one.

I take courage from my mom and step forward. Move closer to my father's ashes, or where they should be. Gray and Logan came to recover them after that night but were unable to. The ashes of the stage curtains, the ashes from the wood floor, the ashes from my father, all mingled together and blew around the gym from the holes in the ceiling and the open door. My father will forever be a part of this gym. It may not be the most glamorous resting place, but it is his.

But the closer I get to where he took his last breath, I can almost feel like he is with me. And whether he is, or it was a gust of wind I felt, I want to believe he is here with me in this moment.

"There are many of us who regret many things, whether it be their relationship with my father, or any number of things. I've got too many regrets to count. I regret not being able to warn Nash in time. I regret not being able to get to Kristina in time. I regret not being conscious when Logan was killed. I regret a lot more than that. But I regret, maybe the most, how I treated my father. When he came into my life I was bitter and angry and didn't want anything to do with him. I regret being mean to him and speaking badly to him and not letting him into my life. Because once I did it was like the flood gates opened and I had this new, incredible man in my life who loved me, and supported me, and was there for me, and only wanted what was best for me. My father was kind and caring and everything you could possibly want in a leader, a friend, but mostly a father. And I let him down. I only knew him for a short time, but I loved him. I will never forget you, dad. I love you. And I'm sorry."

When I step back into the ring of the circle Logan takes my hand in his and squeezes, not unlike Xander did at Tucker's funeral. And then, on the other side of me, Xander takes my hand. A tear slips out of each of my eyes and trails after the others down my cheeks.

Around the circle we go, each of my friends and family members saying their peace about my father, how much they loved him, how much he did for them, what he meant to them. There is not a dry eye in the room when we are finished.

Before we can finish we all turn towards the door, our ears trained to a disturbance there. When I turn and my eyes focus on the door, my breath catches in my throat. Every one of the phoenixes who left, has returned, and brought friends.

They huddle in the doorway as if waiting for something. It slowly dawns on me that they are all staring at me. Waiting for me to do something. I nod my head at them, allowing them entrance. It didn't really dawn on me, until this very moment, that I am the leader of the phoenixes. It was one thing when it was just my group of friends. But from that entrance, all those phoenixes waiting on my command, it is clear to me now, that I really am their leader, they have all accepted me as their leader, or can't find any other way around it. Either way, it is humbling, and nearly crippling.

As a group they all move towards us. It is a force to be reckoned with and they aren't even trying to be menacing. Before they can all get to us, Gray and Logan step forward and in front of me. I roll my eyes at them, and am ready to tell them to step down, but this is not the time to pull my weight or get mad over them trying to protect me. It's not the time for an I-can-take-care-of-myself tantrum.

"What are you doing here?" Gray asks, not to anyone specifically, but addressing the collective.

The person in the front, one of the phoenixes that left months ago steps forward and says, "We came to pay our respects." Then she moves her glance until she's looking directly at me and says, "And we came here to fight."

A pressure settles on my chest. Not one altogether uncomfortable. Feelings of anger and spite shoot through me. But that's how the old Casslyn would feel. The old Casslyn would lash out and say she could do it on her own, that she didn't need these people who left her. But the new Casslyn, the leader of an entire race, feels powerful, and grateful, because she now has an army to end this forsaken war.

Thirteen

The funeral lasted a lot longer once the other phoenixes showed up. They all paid their respects to my father. Which took a while. A lot of people had a lot of things to say. It was nice though, to see how much my father meant to so many people. Then, like with my welcoming ceremony, we all came together, joined hands, and ignited them with fire. Unlike my welcoming ceremony, we kept the fire to our hands. None of us brought extra clothes. But our ignited hands were meant to show that we are still joined as one even in the midst of tragedy.

After the funeral we all gathered at Logan's house. It was packed and tight and you couldn't really move around a lot, but it was nice to have everyone there. If not a little awkward. I can tell that my friends are angry with the other phoenixes who left. They feel betrayed and abandoned. I can't blame them. Then there is the fact that the new phoenixes are not happy that Xander and Cohen are here and not in an early grave. When someone raises the questions, Lydia is quick to shoot them down and remind them they weren't here for everything that went down.

Only, reminding them of that leads to a lot of excess story telling. Rehashing the events of the last several months is not the most fun thing in the world. And hearing it all at once doesn't cast the greatest light on me. Some of the choices I made were questionable. Some of my actions were dangerous to myself and others. I got a lot of side glances and outright glares from some of the phoenixes. But I stand by what I've done, and what I've had to do. I wouldn't take anything back, unless my father could come back.

Once everyone was nearly settled, my friends staying at Logan's, Xander at my house, Cohen at his apartment, and the new phoenixes in hotels in surrounding cities, Logan and I decided to head back to my house. It's nice to have a house full of your friends, but sometimes we need a little privacy, or at least as much privacy as we can get with my parents and Xander at my house.

The closer we get to the final showdown with Raphe, or at least what I'm hoping is the last showdown with him, the more things Logan and I have to talk about. Every time Lydia or Xander or Gray brought up me going after the griffins Logan visibly winced. When he regenerated I had to tell him what he had missed while he was gone. I'm not sure if he didn't hear me tell him the parts about me killing the griffins or if his mind glossed over them but he didn't react as badly then as he did tonight. I thought he was okay with me killing the griffins, I didn't think he looked down on me for what I had to do, but I guess I was wrong.

When we get to my house Logan and I sit down on the couch and put a DVD into the player. As soon as it starts I know neither of us is going to get anything out of it.

Logan stares at the TV like he's watching it but I can tell he's zoned out. I want to bring him into the moment, I want him to be here with me, but I don't know what's bothering him. If he hates me for killing those griffins, that's not something I can take back. We will have to work through it, Logan will have to get over it, or I'm not sure we can get past it. I'm not sure I can be with someone who hates me and I'm not sure Logan can be with someone he holds in contempt.

And there's no time like the present to start working through something. Especially if tomorrow is not promised. And it's really not in the life we live.

"Logan, we need to talk," I say to him, pulling on his arm, trying to pull him from wherever he is in his mind.

It takes him a moment but he finally focuses on me. "What is it, love?"

"I was hoping you could tell me," I say. The urge to rest my chin on his shoulder and stare deep into his eyes is strong, but I hold myself in check and keep a good six inches between us.

Logan's eyebrows pull together like he's confused, like

he missed himself flinching only hours ago in his own house.

"When we were at the house. Talking with the newcomers. About everything that's happened these last months," I say, each thought a complete sentence, giving Logan a chance to jump in. When he doesn't, I continue, "You didn't seem to be taking it well. Everything we said I've told you before. You've heard it all before. And yet when we were talking about me and Xander and Gray taking out some of the griffins, you looked like you were hurt or like you were going to be sick. Tell me I imagined that."

Logan inhales deeply and holds the breath in his chest for several seconds. When he exhales it's heavy and filled with a lot of emotion.

Logan takes my hand in his, looks me in the eye and says, "I know you've told me everything before. It's not like I thought you were hiding things from me. That's not it." Again, Logan takes a deep breath and holds it.

I know he didn't think I was lying to him or withholding information. I know that. But I'm not going to confirm it. He knows, I know. We all know. I just need him to get to what is really bothering him so I stay silent, waiting for him to unload.

I can tell when he's ready to tell me the root of his pain when he looks away from me. I've only seen Logan cry once, maybe twice, in the time I've known him, but as he looks away from me I can smell salt wafting in the air. I watch as a tear drops from the side of Logan's face and splashes on his jean covered knee.

"I don't like that you went after the griffins," he says.

I'm half tempted to yell at him. If this is some macho I-must-protect-you thing or a you're-a-girl-and-shouldn't-be-fighting thing then we have no business having this conversation, but the fact that there are tears in his eyes tells me it's far more serious than that.

"When my father was killed, my mom lost the love of her life. The grief consumed her. She went after the griffins without a single look back. She still had Aspen and I. But without my father, it was like she wanted to go out and take as many griffins with her as she could. It finally caught up to her. She was killed going after the griffins on her own because she'd lost my father."

Before I can say that is essentially how the griffins killed him, Logan beats me to it.

He finally turns to me and says, "I know I did the same thing. When I saw Cohen stab you, when you lit up like a torch and I thought I'd lost you, I lost my mind. And they were able to kill me. That's part of the reason your father was so against us being together, why I was so adamant in the beginning that we shouldn't be together. I didn't want either of us to lose our lives because the other perished."

I find myself inhaling deeply at the same moment as Logan. We stare at each other acknowledging the moment. We might smile or even laugh if the conversation wasn't so heated.

I had no idea that is what was troubling him. He'd told me once before how he lost his parents. I didn't see the parallels when I was going after the griffins. I'd just lost Tucker and Logan, all I was thinking about was getting my revenge. But the way Logan tells it, his mom was looking to lose her life beyond getting her revenge. That's not what I was doing but I can see why he would see it that way.

"When I found out you had been going after and killing the griffins it nearly killed me. It was like all those years ago, all over again. It was like you were my mother and I was about to lose you. I could still lose you at any moment and that fear has a death grip on my heart. You have no idea. I can't lose you, Casslyn. Not again."

"I would love to promise you that you won't lose me. But I can't do that. It would be a false promise and I'm not going to do that to you. I don't want to lose you again, but we both know nothing is certain. We have to do what we can to keep ourselves, each other, and our friends and family safe. But we can't go further than doing everything we can. Anything beyond that isn't up to us."

I place my hands on either side of Logan's face. The tears have stopped falling from the corners of his eyes but they are red rimmed. He doesn't say anything but he nods his head in my hands as though he understands. It's good enough for now.

"I'm sorry I scared you. I'm sorry I reminded you of your mother. I was doing what I had to do at that time. I needed my revenge. I got it. I can't say that it felt good. I had convulsions and the shakes. But I got my revenge. And then I needed to do something bigger. And that's what I'm doing now. Are you on board with that? Are you on board with who I am now? Are you on board with our new mission? Because if you're not," I stop midsentence, not sure how to finish it. "I need you on board with this. I need you by my side."

The look in Logan's eyes says he's on my side, that he always will be, but he says it anyway, "You are the most important person in my life. I will always be on your side. Always."

"I love you, Logan," I tell him, pulling his face towards me with my hands on his cheeks.

"I love you," Logan says before he lays his lips on mine.

When he pulls away from the kiss Logan sits back on the couch and pulls me into him. I fold myself into the crook between his arm and side. He kisses me on the top of the head then turns his focus on the movie. I watch the screen but can't keep my attention on the story.

Logan bringing up his parents makes me think of my father and how I failed him. I'm not only plagued by the guilt of getting him killed, but the onslaught of how much I miss him could bring a grown man to his knees. My relationship with my father had grown so strong. I was finally in a place where I felt I could trust that he wouldn't leave me and that I could fully love him.

The sorrow that grips my heart from losing him is unbearable. It's almost always hard to breathe anymore. I've lost too many people far too quickly and I'm not sure how I'm still standing. Every day is a battle to wake up, to drag myself out of bed, to put on a brave face for my parents and my friends. It's a battle I'm not sure I'm winning. Every day I feel myself fall a little further into the pit of despair. If it weren't for Logan and Xander and all my other friends, I'd already be consumed by the pain.

But tomorrow is another day. Another day to pull myself inch by inch from the bottom of the pit. And that's all I can do. I lost my father merely a week ago. There is no way I'm going to get through his death quickly, especially since it's compounded on Nash and Tucker and what I thought was Logan's death. But tomorrow is another day.

So I curl up into my boyfriend's warmth and find comfort in him, in his touch, in his nearness.

I didn't have a plan as far as leading the phoenixes and ending this war with the griffins, but if my losses have taught me anything, it's that I'm not about to lose another person in my life. I've said this before, and I failed, but I'm not going to fail again.

I appreciate the fact that the phoenixes that left have returned. I appreciate that they want to fight in this war and take down the griffins once and for all. I appreciate that my friends want to fight by my side, to live and die with me as their leader. But that's not how it's going to happen. I finally have a plan.

I'm going after Raphe alone.

***

"Like Hell you are," Gray practically shouts at me from

across the island.

"Absolutely not," Cohen says next to Xander who looks at me like he could wring my neck.

"Are you insane?" Anna asks.

"Are you on drugs?" Lydia chimes in.

Logan quietly shakes next to me. I hadn't told him my plan. Not since I'd made up my mind last night. Unlike the rest of them, who stare at me as though I've lost my mind, Logan won't even look at me.

I can't say I imagined this going over well, but I figured as their leader they would eventually go along with my plan, if they didn't at least agree to it.

I was wrong.

"You can't do this," Cohen says slamming his hand down on the table.

Almost all of the phoenixes and the two griffins stand huddled in the kitchen of Logan's house. The stragglers who came late hover in the living room, listening at the kitchen door.

"We came to help you, and this is how you would treat us?" one of the new phoenixes says. I feel slightly bad about it, but I haven't learned all their names yet. It's awful of me, but I can't say I've put much effort into it. They always hated me, and then they left us. And they just thought I'd welcome them back with open arms? My father would. But I'm not my father.

"You would dare insult us in such a way?" another asks.

"I'm not trying to insult you. And I appreciate your

help," I tell them, finally getting a word in.

I am their leader, the be all and end all, but I feel so small standing in front of the kitchen sink, a large group of imposing people looming before me. I'm their leader, and yet I still feel incredibly like a child.

I reach for Logan's hand, for a little strength, but he pulls away from me. My heart breaks a little, but how could I not see this coming, after what we'd talked about just last night. I couldn't honestly have believed that my friends would let me go through with this, but why can't they see that I'm trying to protect them. And isn't that what their leader is supposed to be doing.

"You show your appreciation so well," one of the phoenixes says, haughtily crossing her arms over her chest.

"I am trying to protect you," I tell them. "If I go after Raphe alone. If I can kill him, the rest of them will stand down. I can't lose another one of you. Not any of you."

"It will never work," Xander says.

"My father is never alone. He has people guarding him at all times. His house is never empty. And even if he didn't have guards, he is more powerful than you, Cass," Cohen says, his shoulders tight. "And even if you kill him, there are those who are so completely loyal to him they would pick up right where he left off. Cutting the head off the snake, in this scenario, will not kill the rest of the body. I'm sorry, but it won't work."

"When they attacked us here, and you had to face Raphe, you froze. I saw it," Gray says, his eyes filled with sadness.

I instantly feel betrayed by him, but I know he's right.

But he doesn't stop there, "You froze and he would have killed you if your father hadn't stepped in. When he killed your father, you broke down and Lydia had to drag you out of there."

I turn to Lydia, again feeling betrayed by those closest to me. I know they had to have known. Those who weren't there when my father was killed, saw me directly afterwards. Saw how broken I was. Even if Lydia didn't tell them what happened, it was written on my face.

"What happens when you have to face him alone?" Gray asks. "What happens when he reminds you of your father's death, of Nash's death, Kristina's, the others'? What happens when you freeze, when you lose it? Instead of protecting yourself from losing us, we will lose you."

When he finishes, Gray has tears in his eyes.

Lydia looks at me and says, "You want to protect us, and that's noble, but did you ever think that in protecting us, you need to protect yourself?"

I take my time and look at each individual in the room. Most of them I don't know too well and can't read their expressions very well. But those I know, those I know too well, cut through me like an ice knife. Logan still refuses to look at me. Gray looks as though I've betrayed him. Lydia looks like she wants to kill me. Nathan and Thomas look angry if not slightly amused at my public chastisement. Cohen and Xander look disappointed in me. And that hurts. I'm trying to save their people and mine. If Raphe is taken out of the equation, the griffins can be free of their oppressor. Don't they see that?

My throat thickens until it's difficult to swallow. Tears sting my eyes but I refuse to cry. This is not a time for crying. The vice on my heart cinches tighter every moment I look upon my friends, my people. Their love for me is evident, more evident than I'd ever realized. They love me as much as I love them. For some reason I didn't think that was the case. It simultaneously humbles me and shames me. How could I have not known they loved me? Yeah we are friends, but I never realized how much I meant to them and I feel so ashamed.

"Okay," I say, my voice hoarse. "We will come up with a different plan."

Someone takes my hand and squeezes it. I know that hand. I know that heat. I look down at our joined hands and look up to Logan who still refuses to look at me, but his posture is less tight, more relaxed.

A collective release of breath sounds around the room. Bodies move and exit the kitchen to find something better to do. I said we'd come up with a new plan, but I didn't say we'd do it now, I don't even think I could come up with a better plan now.

And that's when it dawns on me. Why am I the one coming up with the plan? This war affects us all, we should be making a plan together. When it's time to make that plan, I will be including them all in the decisions.

I lean against the counter and watch the people filter through the room. Those closest to me remain. I'm not sure if they're waiting to be dismissed or if they want to yell at me apart from the rest of the phoenixes. The rest of the phoenixes may have returned, but the time away from them changed us all. We now have our crew and they will always be a part of the fringes. I feel bad about that, and yet I don't.

I look down at my feet and wait for the yelling to begin, but it never does. Suddenly a pair of boots stand before my feet. I look up to see Gray standing before me, his white mohawk standing tall, his slightly red tinged eyes ringed in black.

Before I can say I'm sorry for causing him pain, Gray wraps his arms around me and holds me tight. It takes my brain a moment to catch up, but when it does, I hug him back just as fiercely. I could never have imagined that when my father said the phoenixes would be coming to town that I would have made such an amazing friend as I have in Gray. I'm sure there is someone out there, maybe someone in our group, who thinks I've replaced my gay friend with another. But I know for a fact that if Tucker were still here, I would love Gray the same as I do now. He is my newest best friend. And it's not because he's gay. It's because of who he is. And I wouldn't trade him for the world.

When he pulls away from the hug, a tear falls from each eye. He says, "I love you, fireball, but you're crazy."

"Damn right you are," Thomas says.

"You guys get why I was doing this," I say to them, as a

statement and a question.

"We get it," Nathan says, "We just don't agree with it."

"So no more stupid plans. Got it?" Xander says.

I nod my head at all of them and say, "Got it."

"Where do we go from here?" Anna asks.

"I don't know yet," I tell them. Because isn't honesty the best policy? "I'm kind of hoping something just sort of falls into our laps."

A laugh rings around the kitchen. Every one of my friends is laughing at me. It's okay though. I'd laugh at myself too.

I'm not sure what we're going to do from here. I can't wait for this war to be over, until I can relax. I feel in this constant state of alertness, of fear, of anxiety. I'm so ready to let it all go and live one day where I can do nothing, worry about nothing.

We're all laughing together when we hear a knock at the door. We are all here so it's odd someone would be at the door, much less knocking.

It's Logan's house so he moves to open the door. On the other side, standing on the porch, a hesitant smile on her face, stands my mom.

I walk through the kitchen, into the living room, worry setting in.

Logan has invited her in as I step before her.

"Mom, what's wrong?" I ask, thinking of possible reasons she's here. None of which are good. The griffins have kidnapped my father. They've lit the house on fire. Someone knows I'm the one who burned the gym down.

"Oh, ah, well," she stammers, hearing the concern in my voice. "I know you all have a lot going on and I figured you might have forgotten what time of the year it is. So I came to see if any of you might need to do a little Christmas shopping."

A stream of relief soaked air rushes from my chest.

Nothing is wrong.

Nothing is wrong. Everything is ok, Casslyn. Nothing is wrong.

"Christmas shopping," I say, no inflection to my voice.

"Is this a bad time?" my mom asks. "I can come back. Um. I didn't mean to intrude."

I pull myself from my funk and say, "No, Mom. It's fine. Sorry. Come in. I'm sure there are many of us who need to do some Christmas shopping. Are you sure you can handle all of us?"

"I would love to spend the afternoon with your group," she says.

"Thanks, Mom."

I go back into the kitchen where all my friends have remained. They sit around the table and wait to see who was at the door. They already know, and they already know why she's here. Perks of having superhuman hearing.

"Who wants to go?" I ask, instead of pretending like they don't know who was at the door.

Hands go in the air faster than I've ever seen.

"I'll get my coat," Gray says jumping from his chair.

"Right behind you," Aspen says.

Anna, and Thomas race for the front door saying hi to my mom as they pass her. Nathan and Lydia remain seated at the table.

"You two coming?" I ask.

"Um, we're fine," Nathan says.

I turn my attention to Lydia and cock my head at her.

"Now, we'll have to take two vehicles," my mom says.

"I'll drive," Gray says rushing past Logan and my mom, out the door, until I hear the door to the SUV close.

"Lydia, Nathan, let's go. What's the deal?"

Lydia gets up from the table and walks towards me. She doesn't stop until she's about an inch from my face. She leans in close and speaks into my ear.

"We don't really celebrate Christmas anymore," she tells me. "Our mom was a human. Christmas was her favorite time of the year. She went all out every year. Food, decorations, the biggest tree she could find. And the presents. We got everything we ever wanted."

I feel like this story is about to take a sharp turn into the sad territory.

"She got old and we had to put her in a nursing home. It was so sad. We tried to make Christmas just as special for her there as it was at home. Her third Christmas in the nursing home, we went in, we had everything ready, we were so excited to see her. We found her in her rocker, facing the tree all lit up. Her heart gave out just before we got there. We haven't really celebrated Christmas since. It wasn't ever about how much we loved the holiday but about how much our mom loved it and how much we loved her."

Lydia pulls away from me and shrugs her shoulders, a sad smile on her face.

"I'm so sorry," I tell her.

"It's okay," she says.

"Maybe we could help you find love for it. I don't want you two to be sad on Christmas. Please come shopping with us. And you can join us at my house on Christmas morning."

Lydia looks from me to Nathan, getting his feelings on the matter. He shrugs but I swear I can see on his face that he really wants to go. Not just to go shopping but to start loving Christmas again with all his friends and his sister.

"Okay. We'll go," Lydia says, turning back to me.

"Good. Let's go," I say, waiting for her and Nathan to get into one of the cars before I leave the house.

Logan waits by the door for me. When I walk up to him he holds out his hand for me.

I take it but don't immediately walk with him out the door.

"I'm sorry," I tell him, knowing he's got to be mad at me for my plan of going after Raphe alone. He hasn't spoken a word to me since I told everyone.

"I'm just glad you told us your plan instead of actually doing it," he says, hurt in his eyes.

"You know why I wanted to do it."

"I do," he says, pulling me to him and kissing me of the forehead.

Just like that he's forgiven me.

We walk hand in hand and hop in my mom's car, already piled with people. When we get in my mom pulls away from the house, followed by Gray and the rest of our friends in the SUV. We head for the city and some well needed frivolous money spending.

I can't honestly believe I forgot Christmas was in two weeks. I don't have any idea what gifts I'm going to get for anyone. And I've got a lot more people to shop for now than I did last year. This time last year was a mess in and of itself. Just as messed up as this year, but in a different way. Xander and I practically hated each other. Tucker was trying to bring us back together. Logan and I weren't together but we both wanted to be.

I'm glad we have a little over half an hour to think of what I'm going to get everyone. I need more time than that, but I'll try to think fast. I know for sure that Logan's gift will be the hardest. I can always get the others gift cards. Gray and Lydia like clothes so gift cards for clothing stores is an easy gift that they will like. Thomas likes movies and TV shows. DVDs of his favorite shows, or shows and movies I think he'll like will be easy. Some of the others, like Anna and Nathan and Xander might be a little more difficult, but I have no idea what I'm going to get Logan.

When we get to the mall we disperse, but in groups of two or three. All claiming they need to buy gifts for people not in their group. Logan, being the ever present guardian, makes sure to tell everyone to be careful, to watch out for their surroundings, to never be in a confined space alone, to be on their guard. Like most teenagers, though most of them aren't teens, roll their eyes, tell him they will be safe and walk away. Xander and Anna walk off together, though not before asking if anyone wants to join them. No one wants to join a brand new couple as a third wheel. Aspen, Gray, and Thomas head in a different direction. I don't want Lydia and Nathan to be alone since I practically forced them to come so they join Logan, my mom and I as we make our way through the mall.

Every once in a while Logan breaks from the group because he needs to buy something alone, aka without me. I smile every time he darts off. My mom comes out of stores with several bags on her arms. Lydia and Nathan seem to be enjoying themselves and that fills my heart. We run across others from their different groups, talk for a bit, and dart off in other directions.

By the end of the day we all meet back near the entrance, nearly all of us loaded down with bags, tired and ready to go home. Before we leave the city we stop at Famous Daves to eat. When we walk in my dad stands next to the hostess podium waiting for us.

The hostess leads us to an upper level of the restaurant and has to move tables together to fit us all together. Watching the hostess and waiter move the tables, my friends and family waiting for a seat, with some of us helping to move the tables and chairs, something so powerful dawns on me.

I may be having the worst two years of my entire life, I

may have lost so many things and so many important people in my life, but I have also gotten so much out of it. I gained a parent I loved so much. I found the love of my life. I have gained so many new friends I can't imagine my life without. And I've discovered more about myself. A new strength. New depths. New understandings.

The new people in my life are some of the best people I've ever known. They help me. They make me smile. They hold me accountable. They love me. And I love them back. I love each and every one of them for different reasons and in different ways. I would give everything I have to keep them safe. I am thankful for every single one of them and I hope once this war is over we can have more days like today. Because today is one of the best days I've had in a while.

***

My mom, Logan, and I waddle into our house after a long day of shopping. I'm tired and ready for a shower, then bed. Logan takes my bags from me and heads up the stairs for my room.

I'm right behind him when my mom says, "Casslyn, can I talk to you?"

"Sure, Mom," I say, backing into the kitchen where my mom sets down her bags. I'm tired and don't have a lot of energy to talk, but she's given me one of the greatest days I've had in a long time so I'll give her my time.

My mom walks up to me, places her hands on my shoulders, which only slightly weirds me out, and says, "How are you holding up, honey? I know you've had a rough couple of weeks. I know losing your father is hard. I just wanted to check in."

Her question catches me off guard. Not that it's unexpected, but no one has asked me that since my father died. My friends have given me side glances and silently wondered if I'm going to lose it, but none of them has asked me. And to be honest, I have no idea how I'm doing. I'm making it through every day, and trying to process everything, but at the end of the day, I can't really remember everything that took place that day. It frightens me. I feel like an outsider looking in but at the same time being in the moment and not having a clue what's going on. My father's death haunts me and there's nothing I can do about it. I walk around with a vice strangling my heart making it hard to breathe.

Does my mom want to know that? Or does she want to know that I'm doing okay? That yes, I'm having a hard time, but I'm pushing through it. Because what is she really going to be able to do about my situation? I'm doing everything I can to keep her out of this, to keep her safe. The more I pull her into my world, the more danger she is faced with.

"I'm doing okay, Mom. About as good as can be expected," I tell her.

She pulls me in for a hug and says to me, "I'm here for you, baby. Always."

When she tugs me back I smile at her, glad she's my mom and she's here for me, and say, "I know. I love you,"

"I love you."

We join together for another hug, this time both of us holding on longer than we need to until we part. I smile at her again and move away, towards the stairs.

Before I can get too far she says, "Casslyn, one more thing."

"What's up?" I ask.

"I wanted to talk about Logan," she says, sort of backing away from me like I might freak out.

"What about Logan?" I ask, knowing better than to jump down her throat.

"I am so unbelievably happy he is alive and here with you."

She pauses.

"Go on," I say.

"I know he helps you through hard times and I know how much he means to you."

I raise an eyebrow at her when she pauses again.

"I also know that he's been spending the night in your room."

And like a faucet turned all the way on, she can't stop the flow of words that come out next.

"I just wanted to know if he treats you right. I know you are more mature than a lot of people your age, what with everything you're dealing with, so I'm not going to forbid you. But I also know how teens in love are and I wanted to make sure you are using protection. I don't know how STDs work with your kind, but I don't think you would like to have a child at seventeen."

"Mom, stop!" I nearly scream at her.

"Cass, you need to-," she says.

"No, mom, stop," I say, then mumble through my teeth. "We're not having sex."

"Oh good," my mom says, clasping her hand over her heart. "Not that I would forbid it, like I said. Though I don't really condone a seventeen year old having sex. But of course you're going to do what you're going to do, I can't stop you."

"Mom!" I say to cut off the rambling.

I can only imagine Logan up in my bedroom laughing his ass off.

My cheeks are so heated I'm surprised they're not aflame. I knew my mom would give me the sex talk eventually, though I can't say that's really what this is, and I knew it would be awkward, but I didn't know it would be so embarrassing, especially when your boyfriend can hear every word of it.

"I just want you to be safe," she finally tells me.

"I know you do. And I appreciate that. I do," I say, though I'm so embarrassed right now I can't separate the appreciation from the humiliation. "Don't you have to go to work or something?"

"Oh shoot," she says, her eyes darting to the clock on the stove. "I do have to go to work. But smooth move on the topic change. We will talk more about this. This wasn't exactly how I had planned this talk."

"Can't imagine that," I say under my breath but loud enough she can hear.

"I heard that young lady. Now go to bed, you've had a long day."

"Yes, ma'am," I say, mocking her.

I watch as my mom heads to her room to change for work. I don't even make an attempt to go to my room and face Logan. At least I'm not going to until my cheeks are not so hot. And not until I think I can face him, with a straight face, without laughing, and when I'm not so mortified.

My mom fills her coffee mug, kisses me on the cheek, says, "Good night, baby," then heads out the door for work. I listen to her drive down the road before I finally head up to my room. I think about making a pit stop in the bathroom before I see Logan, but eventually I will have to face the music, and his laughter.

I pause at my doorway with my eyes closed, take a deep breath, and step through.

But I don't hear any laughter. I open my eyes to see Logan sitting on my bed, his eyes closed, a wry smile on him face. So at some point he was laughing at me, but now he's only amused.

I know Logan heard the conversation I had with my mom. And I know he listened. If he thought it was something more private he would have tuned us out. Not that that conversation wasn't private, because I wish he hadn't heard it. But I'm not about to be mad at him. If I had the opportunity to listen to someone give him the sex talk, I would have.

But Logan and I haven't really talked about sex. Every time we get close to talking about it or doing it, I can't go through with it. I'm not sure what that says about me other than that I'm not ready.

I love Logan. I want to be with him. I am finally ready. I hope he is on the same page.

I've been thinking about it. A lot. It's kind of unfortunate that my mom had to have the talk with me now, when I planned on moving forward with Logan tonight. But when you want something, you can't let something like an embarrassing conversation with your mom get in your way.

Logan and I have been through a lot. We haven't been together that long, haven't even known each other longer than two years, but I know in my heart that there is no one else for me, that I want to spend the rest of my life with him. And with our lives, tomorrow is never guaranteed. The rest of my life could be a million years or two days. I want to spend it with Logan knowing what it is like to be with him in every way.

There is something I want to talk to him about first, before we go any further. Something I need to know.

Before Gray and Aspen and Lydia and all the other phoenixes showed up to town, before Logan died, I didn't think he and I were even close to having sex. At least I didn't think so. I don't know how Logan felt. He never pushes me into anything like that, never pressures me.

And then Logan breaks up with me and the phoenixes show up and it looks as though Logan and Lydia are chummy. And then I find a box of condoms in his bedside table. At the time I thought he'd gotten them for Lydia. Now that I know he was never going to get together with her I know they weren't for her, but I need to talk to Logan about them. About where he thinks our relationship is and where he wants it to be.

Logan is far more experienced than I am, and the fact that he has been this patient with me for this long blows me away, but what scares me is that I won't be enough for him. I know that's the stupidest thing I could think. I know that Logan loves me. I know he does. I just need to get out of my own head.

Before I can talk myself out of going any further and running out of the room, I push myself further into it. Logan's eyes snap open and hold me in his gaze.

He smiles at me and says, "Did you have a nice talk with your mom?"

I give him an evil glare and say, "Shut up. You know exactly how it went."

He straightens up from resting against the back of my bed and opens his arms gesturing for me to come to him. I walk over to him and sit on the side of the bed next to him, but not directly into his arms.

"Do you want to talk about it?" he asks me.

I'm not sure if he's referring to the conversation with my mom or about sex.

"I think we need to talk about it," I tell him.

"You know I'd never pressure you. I love you. I don't

need anything more from you than spending time with you and getting to kiss you."

"That's a nice gesture. But we both know it's not true."

Logan's eyebrows pull together when I say this, like I've offended him.

"Casslyn."

"You're a guy, Logan. You have needs. I wouldn't expect anything less. And I'm not trying to be mean. There's nothing wrong with that."

"Casslyn," Logan says, again trying to defend himself.

"I have to ask you something?"

"Shoot," he says.

"When the phoenixes came earlier this year and I thought you'd gotten back together with Lydia," I say and stop. That fact that I truly believed Logan had left me for Lydia makes me feel ashamed.

"Go on," Logan says, raising a single eyebrow at me.

"I was in your room taking a phone call and I found a box of condoms in your bedside table. At the time I thought you'd gotten them for her."

"And now."

My cheeks must be on fire because I've never been more embarrassed in my life. Well except for minutes ago when I was talking to my mom. Wow. What a night for my reddened cheeks and my self-esteem.

"I was wondering. . .,"

Without missing a beat Logan finishes my sentence, "If I'd gotten them for you?"

I turn my head away from him and very quietly say, "Yes."

Logan waits to answer. He waits for me to look back to him. But what if they were never for Lydia, or for me? What if I'm just an idiot. In any manner. Logan continues to wait. I should be braver than this. I should be able to face him. I've heard the saying if you can't talk about it then you shouldn't be doing it. I am talking about it, so I should get some points there, I'm just a little wary on some of the topics.

Finally, when I still haven't turned back to him, Logan says, "Are you going to look at me, love?"

I'm not about to be one of those girls who needs the guy to cup her chin and coax her to look at him. I am a big girl who can talk about sex with her boyfriend, especially if she wants to be having sex with her boyfriend.

So I look at my boyfriend. I look him in the eye and wait for him to tell me who he bought a box of condoms for.

Logan stares at me with a complicated look in his eyes. There's love and adoration there, but a little bit of pain too.

Before he says a word, he leans forward and kisses me on the nose. Again, it's one of those moments where he's reminding himself he's alive, I'm alive, and we're together.

I wrinkle my nose at him to ease some of his tension.

He starts his story. "That day you were taken by the griffins, before you went to the grocery store, we had a very intense make out on the couch. Our relationship was growing stronger and deeper. I thought it could go further. When you went to the grocery store I made my own trip. Before Xander came to me and said you'd been taken, I'd gone to the drug store and gotten the condoms. For you. Because I love you. I want to be with you. I bought the condoms to be prepared for when you were ready. But I am also patient enough to wait, until you are ready."

A heavy breath escapes Logan. Who knew a box of condoms could carry such weight. I had no idea Logan had bought them the day I was captured by the griffins. What hurts so much is that he broke up with me only days after he bought something to take our relationship in the next direction.

"What if I said I was ready?"

"I would hope it is because you are ready, and not because of my manly urges," Logan says, his statement starting somber and turning comedic.

I laugh with him for a moment and then slowly stop because of the wild look in his eyes.

"I've wanted this for a long time," I tell him. "I was just scared."

"Of what?"

"I was afraid that I wouldn't be good enough. That you'd get tired of being with me. I was afraid that you'd find someone you wanted more than me."

"Casslyn, my love, I will never get tired of being with you. Every day with you is an adventure, whether you love or hate me that day. And I will never want anyone more than I want you. Never. Do you understand me?"

I nod my head, knowing he's telling the truth, because I

can't find the words to reciprocate.

So instead I lean into him and kiss him. He waits a full heartbeat before kissing me back. Our kisses are slow, measured, deliberate. I lean further into him, pushing him back onto the bed.

I kiss Logan harder and run a hand under the hem of his shirt, feeling his skin burn as my hand moves upward.

He pulls back from the kiss and says, "You have to be sure."

"Do you have one of those condoms with you?" I ask.

Logan watches me for a reaction, for some hidden agenda, like I'm testing his manly urges, but when he finds nothing he nods and says, "Yes."

"I'm sure."

He brings his hands up to my face and pulls me into him, kissing me deep and hard. I open up to him when he runs his tongue along the seam of my mouth. Fire and ice run through my body at the taste of him. Flames ignite from my hands as they roam over Logan's chest. He sucks in a breath from the contact causing his stomach to cave in. I pull at Logan's shirt, needing it to be off and out of the way. Logan obliges, pushing us into a sitting position. It causes me to straddle his lap and sit right on his erection. An aroused moan forms in my throat and bubbles up until I groan right into his mouth. His hips jump under me, pressing him further into me. I've never been this turned on before and we've barely begun.

I withdraw from him to take a breath and pull his shirt

over his head. Mine is soon to follow before we reconnect. Flames dance between and over our joined skin. We're bound to set the house on fire and I'm not sure I care. Logan runs his hands down my sides, extinguishing the flames.

The tension in my lower belly is tight and uncomfortable and yet feels so good. I sway my hips over Logan. He jerks under me and pulls us back until we're lying on the bed. His lips leave my mouth and move lower, trailing kisses from my jaw to my chest. He hovers over my breasts, only kissing where my bra doesn't cover. And that's not enough for me. I reach around myself, unlatch my bra, and pull it off my arms. Logan looks up at me as if asking permission. I would have thought taking off my bra in front of him would have been permission enough. I nod preparing myself for his mouth on me.

But nothing could have prepared me for the heat of his tongue on my boob. Absolutely nothing. A deep moan escapes without my permission. Logan shifts under me. He's so hard now as he presses into me, the layers of fabric doing little to hide how either of us feels.

The pressure has become too full I'm afraid I'll combust before we actually have sex.

I push up from Logan, making sure he staying lying on the bed. He watches me, the flames in his bright blue eyes dancing with pleasure and want and need. I reach down between us and unbutton his jeans. I pull down the zipper, the strain from Logan pushing against it. He raises his hips so I can pull them off. My heart starts to pound harder, nervousness setting in. I'm about to see him naked. I have before, but not with the knowledge that I am about to have him inside me. I'm nervous, and yet thrilled.

I pull his jeans and take his boxers at the same time. My breath catches in my throat as I look at him. When my gaze moves to his face he's got that sexy smirk going on. I smirk back at him. I'm thankful though. That little move, that smirk, did a lot to ease the tension building in my chest.

I'm about to unbutton my jeans and join Logan in the fully naked spectrum when he leans up and says, "Come here."

I release my grip on my jeans, not realizing my fingers were trembling.

I crawl into bed next to Logan and curl up next to him.

"We can stop if you want," he says.

I shake my head, knowing I want to keep going.

"Are you nervous?" he asks.

"Only a little," I lie. "But I'm excited. That's not the right word. But I want this Logan. Right now. With you."

"It's all you, love," Logan says. "I'll follow your lead."

I lie next to him and remove my jeans and panties as quickly as I can. Logan fishes in the back pocket of his jeans for his wallet. Then he fishes inside his wallet for the condom. I stare at him waiting for him to do something. He raises an eyebrow at me then tears open the wrapper and folds the condom over himself. I lie down next to him. I expect Logan to crawl on top of me, as I've seen in every movie ever, but he watches me, smiles, and shakes his head.

Taking that as my cue, I maneuver on top of him, sitting in front of his erection.

Logan's eyes are hooded, his breathing heavy. I can't breathe. I want to feel everything.

"Casslyn," Logan says, grabbing my attention. "I love you."

I push myself up from him, my hands on his chest. I move over him until I can feel the tip of him in my middle. I lower myself down, millimeter by millimeter, every touch of him sending sparks through my already sensitive body. I stop, hovering over him, the pressure building. I look at Logan near panic settling over me.

I can't move and he knows it.

"Are you okay?" he asks me.

I nod, my eyes wide on him.

"Are you hurt?" he asks, leaning up.

I shake my head, breathing heavy.

"Are you ready?" he asks, bracing himself on his elbows.

I nod, ready for him.

Logan gently but forcefully thrusts up into me.

The movement hurts and I try to adjust to ease it. Logan catches me and stills me in his arms.

"Wait."

He holds me in his arms for several moments, waiting for me to adjust around him. When I do he tells me to lift myself up and ease back down. When I do, it aches but not as badly. I do it again until the ache subsides and pleasure blooms. And then we move together. And then we shower together. And eventually we lie on my bed together, exhausted and close to sleep.

"So how do STDs work with us?" I ask him.

Logan bursts out laughing, his chest bouncing up and down hard, the laugh coming from deep in his core. I haven't heard him laugh so intensely in a long time. I missed it.

Eventually he settles down and kisses me on the forehead.

"Answer the question."

"We don't get them. But we're still using protection."

"Good to know."

I lie curled into his side, almost asleep. Logan's hand moves up and down my arm, his fingers drawing lazy circles over my skin. I listen to the hum of his breathing as I lie on his chest. As shitty as my life has been in the last two years, I am fully and completely happy right this moment and I wouldn't trade it for the world.

"I love you," Logan says, his voice deep with sleep.

"I love you," I tell him and close my eyes welcoming the pull of sleep.

***

It's pitch black out when I'm woken by pounding on my bedroom door. Logan jumps up from the bed ready for a fight. I sit up in my bed, hoping it won't come to that.

Logan opens the door, light from the hallway spilling

into my room. I have to shield my eyes until they adjust. When they do I see Gray and Nathan standing on the other side of Logan. He looks back at me to make sure I'm not exposed then steps aside to let them in.

"It's nice to know you two finally got it on," Gray says.

"That took long enough. I thought Logan was going to kill one of us."

Logan growls at them both. They just laugh at him. I can't say I'm thrilled my friends are talking about my love life, but as close as we are, it was bound to happen. Tucker told me about the first time he and Gray had sex. Xander spilled the beans once I finally knew about he and Anna.

"What's going on?" I ask them, trying to steer the conversation in any direction besides me and Logan.

Nathan looks to Logan and says, "Cohen is at your house."

Gray turns to me and says, "And he's brought two griffins with him."

Fourteen

Logan and I dress as quickly as we can. Nerves wrack my brain.

I'm too afraid of what's going on to ask questions.

The four of us make our way to Logan's house. I stop by Xander's room to tell him what's going on but I find it empty. We walk the mile in silence. Thousands of possibilities run through my head, none of them good.

What could the griffins want? Why are they here? Have they come to help us? Have they come to warn us of something?

After what can only be minutes, but what seems like hours, we get to Logan's house. The lights are on, every one of us is up, voices ring out from several rooms. Because it seems to be the central meeting room, we find mostly everyone in the kitchen, Xander included. When we get into the kitchen, everyone goes silent. The air surrounding us is hostile. The griffins are nervous and afraid to be so outnumbered by those who would be their enemies. I can't blame them. I'm awed by their bravery at coming here. My friends, Lydia, Thomas, Aspen, Anna, the rest of them aren't as wary as the others. The others though, cast cold stares at the newcomers. They are frightened of them, but also, hatred fills their eyes. I can't blame them. In the week or so they've been back to town, they haven't exactly come to grips with the fact that Cohen and Xander are now a part of our family, part of our group. They accept the fact that my word is final but they don't interact with Cohen or Xander, they do whatever they can to avoid them. I don't like it, but I'm not about to force them into anything. I won't force them into anything they aren't comfortable with. I just hope one day they can see beyond race and hatred and see that we are all just people.

In that moment of silence, as I stare at everyone staring at me, I forget that I'm the leader. Once I remember that, time continues and I kick myself into gear. I find Cohen and the two griffins huddled in front of the sink. I've never seen these griffins before. I would have suspected they would have been members of the group we were to meet at the gym that night, but I was wrong. I really hope nothing serious happened to those griffins. That if Raphe were to make an example out of them we would have heard about it.

"Cohen?" I say, as a way of starting whatever this is.

Cohen nods towards the two griffins and says, "They have information I thought you might find interesting."

I glance toward the griffins. They, in turn, glance around the room, clearly afraid to speak to so many phoenixes.

"This is a safe space," I tell them. "No one will harm you. You have my word."

As I say this I look around the room, at every single phoenix in it, sending the message around. I have no doubt I can trust every one of them, but I will make myself clear as their leader.

The two griffins, a man and a woman, look at each other, then back at me.

"What are your names?" I ask them.

"I'm Derek," the man says, and turns to the woman, "and this is my wife, Sydney."

"Welcome," I tell them. Logan stands off to my side, close to me so he can protect me, but far enough away so as not to be crowding. "If you do not feel comfortable in here, we can move to the living room and sit down. But please tell me why you have come."

I'd like them to know they are welcome, but I also want them to get to the damn point. I'm not a patient person when tensions are high and they are about as sky rocketing as they could be.

"We want this war to end," Derek says.

"As do we all," Gray says from the other side of me.

I'm not sure Gray's role when my father was alive. I know he was important, but I also know Logan was my father's next in line. But, things being what they are, Logan and I's relationship as it is, we thought it best to make Gray my second in command. It made sense as a tactical move, and Gray has become one of my best friends, I want him at my side.

"We know you've taken in Cohen and Xander," Sydney says. "Raphe tried to spin it as you were holding them hostage and torturing them. But then Cohen came to us, telling us of how you were treating them and how you just wanted to survive, how you weren't ever killing innocent humans or even the griffins."

"Oh, because Cohen told you, you were convinced?" Lydia says.

I turn my gaze on her, not pleased with her outburst, but she has a point. When the griffins held me captive and Xander was hitting me up for information, he thought I had been burning families alive, that Logan was too. He'd known me all my life and yet took the word of Raphe, the psychopath who had actually been the one murdering innocent people and framing us.

"We apologize," Derek says. "When something is ingrained in you your whole life, you tend to believe it, even without proof. We have been waging this war with the phoenixes for as long as anyone can remember. We forgot what we were actually fighting for."

"And that should be excused?" Thomas says.

But Derek and Sydney flinch at his words.

"Thomas," I say, though again, I don't disagree with

him.

He looks at me apologetically for his transgression. I nod my head at him to indicate I'm not mad but that I won't tolerate it again.

"The past is the past," I tell them, even though every phoenix in the room groans at me.

"We know you have been killing griffins, and we know it was in revenge, but we also know the griffins you killed were directly involved in the deaths of your loved ones. As hard as it was to admit to ourselves, to know we've been wrong for generations, we also know your group of phoenixes has never attacked us unprovoked."

I want to snipe at them and say that they can't say the same thing. I'm sure everyone in this room would like to. But after Lydia and Thomas's lapse, everyone remains quiet. Apart from some unwelcomed snorts.

"May I ask why you are here?" I ask them, again, trying to steer them to the point.

"There are more of us," Derek says. "More of us who would fight on your side to end this war."

"We thought it best to come alone, seeing as how the last meeting went," Sydney says. It's not meant to be snide, just the fact, but it still stings.

I wish my father were here right now. He would be doing a way better job of this than I am. He would know what to say. He would know what to do. Me? I'm just acting like I know what I'm doing. Hopefully I'm good at it.

Sydney goes on, "Raphe is having a meeting at his

house two nights from now. He is gathering every griffin in the area to plan an attack on you. You could attack the meeting and kill Raphe. Half of the people in that house would back you."

"How do we know you aren't lying?" Gray asks. "How do we know this isn't a trap?"

He has a valid point. It's not like we haven't walked into traps before.

"Cohen betrayed us not that long ago. He brought you here tonight. How do we know this isn't some elaborate trap we've all been falling into?" Aspen asks, she looks at Cohen as if to apologize for even bringing it up.

Cohen keeps eye contact with her for several seconds and then looks to his feet.

My mind would have gone in the same direction had I not seen how broken Cohen was after he betrayed me. I have forgiven him, as I know my friends have, but it is something that has to be asked.

"There is no way to prove it, other than to trust us," Derek says. "I know that is difficult. I can't tell you how difficult it was to come here tonight. We have children. We don't want them to grow up in this war. We want peace."

"We want out from under Raphe's rule," Sydney says. "He watches our every move. He controls how we raise our children. What they learn. What they know about the war and how they feel about you. All of you. He uses our children, us, all of us, as weapons, as pawns. He doesn't care what happens to us as long as we are killing phoenixes. We want our children to be children, not soldiers."

I let their words sink in. I let them dance around my head and settle in before I speak. There are a lot of things to consider. A lot of ways all of this could go wrong. I know I can't wait forever to speak, that I can't think on everything for too long. I even know that I'm bound so say the wrong thing, but there are a room full of my people to correct me, to back me up.

So I start in, as best as I can. "I want to thank you for coming here. It took bravery I cannot fathom. If what you are saying is true, that we have a chance to kill Raphe, that is truly a gift. But, there are so many things to consider. Even if half of the griffins in that house are on our side, that means half of them aren't. We would need numbers. We would need a guarantee that the half on our side would fight with us, or get out of our way. I'm not looking to incite civil war amongst your people, but I have to have the best interest of my people ahead of yours. I'm sorry but that is the way it is."

"We understand," Derek says.

"Do you?" Gray asks. "You say you want out from under Raphe, but you have to consider every possible outcome of this. What if he finds out you met with us? You're putting your children at risk. You're putting yourselves at risk. He had no problem attempting murder of his own people when Casslyn, Cohen, and my other friends tried to meet with them. You realize this?"

"Of course we realize it," Sydney says. "He did kill one of them. My best friend. The other two barely escaped with their lives. They went on the run. We haven't seen or heard from them since. We know exactly the cost of this. And yet we are still here. We may not have the best track record with your people, but we are willing to put aside everything for a chance to be rid of him."

"And what happens when someone worse takes his place?"

"That won't happen," Derek says. "We already have a new leader picked once Raphe is out of the way."

"And who is that?" Xander says, giving his first words to the conversation. Tonight is significantly important to him. The griffins are his people, his parents are still under Raphes rule, plus he is a part of my family, and thus a part of the phoenixes, not to mention he's fallen in love with one of them.

"We will have a duel leadership," Derek says. "One of them will be you, Xander. And the other will be Cohen."

"No way," Cohen says, too loudly for how close he stands to us.

"We left," Xander says. "Why would you want us to lead?"

"Cohen, we all loved your mother. We know she was raising you and Ashley to be better than your father. And then your father killed her. You may have wanted out, but it was from a hatred of your father, not for your race. And Xander, you left because of loyalty and love for your best friend. We never hated you for it. We worshiped you."

Cohen stands beside the griffins laughing darkly. "There

is no way this is happening," he says.

"We must first focus on defeating Raphe," Logan says. "You will have no chance of having new leaders if we do not first get rid of your current one."

"That is why we are here," Sydney says. "We want him dead as much as you do. It is time for a change. And we're here to help."

"I am seriously considering what you have told us, but I must first discuss this with my people," I tell the two griffins.

"We understand," Derek says.

"Please do not go anywhere. But please do not listen in," I tell them.

They both incline their heads at me in acceptance.

We move from the kitchen to the front yard. This way we will be able to somewhat monitor the griffins in the house, we will also be able to keep them there, as well as be privy to an attack, should that happen. I'm the last one out of the house, but not before I see Cohen and Xander still in the kitchen.

"Are you two coming?" I ask them.

They give me quizzical looks, curious as to why I'm inviting them to a meeting of the phoenixes.

"If you two really don't think I'd want you in on this, then you have no business being here," I tell them.

They nearly run for the door, afraid I'll uninvited them from the meeting, and possibly from my life. It would never happen, but sometimes you need to lay down the law.

I break through the circle of people, voices buzzing

around me. When I enter the middle, everyone goes quiet. Being the leader is an oddly satisfying power when people go silent for you. No wonder people go power hungry. Maybe that's what turned Raphe into such a terrible person.

Nope.

He's just a psychopath.

"Please don't all speak at once. But I would like your opinions."

They remain quiet, like they are waiting to be called on. I search their faces, gauging which one is bursting to speak.

"Lydia," I say.

"This could be our shot," she says. "We could finally be free of him."

"Nathan."

"This could be dangerous. It could be a trap."

"Xander."

"Everyone in town knows him. We don't know how many people will be at his house. Them attacking us, your house is in the middle of nowhere, concealed. If we attack his house, in the middle of town, everyone is going to know. There will be police, we'll have to leave town. We won't be able to hide this."

"What other way would we have?" I ask. "This is a solid chance to bring him down. No, there are no guarantees it will work. There are no guarantees we will all survive. I think we should consider it."

"So that's it? Because you think it's a good idea, we should do it?"

"No," I tell them. "I said I want your opinions and I do. I also want to take a vote. I will not ask any of you to put yourselves in danger if this isn't what we all want. But I want you to consider that it is not just our people in danger from Raphe. Yes, he tries to slaughter us. But he also kills innocent humans to frame us. And he's not afraid to torture and kill his own people. We are the beacons of hope, of change, if we can't kill this man merely for ourselves, we should be doing it for every single person who's ever been in danger because of him."

"I'm in," Gray says beside me.

"Me too," Cohen and Xander say.

"I'm in," come the other voices of my friends.

Some of the other phoenixes chime in their acceptance.

"Thank you, all of you. But before we all just blindly agree to an attack on Raphe and his people, I think we need to talk tactic and strategy. If we do this, we only have two days to plan it. We have to account for anything that could happen. And if the griffins will actually fight with us, we have to plan it with them, in secret, so Raphe doesn't find out about it."

"This is going to take a lot of work," Logan says. "Are you all up for it?"

Everyone around me thrusts their fist into the air and shouts. It's not discernable, and it's not something I've seen them do before, but it has got to be some kind of battle tradition the way they all do it and all know it. I'm going to have to learn it if I'm going to be their leader for the foreseeable future.

We all start to march back into the house, but I stay back, and pull Cohen and Xander with me.

"How do you both feel about this?" I ask them.

"I want him gone," Cohen says.

"Me too," Xander agrees.

"I think we all do. But what I meant was, we will be fighting your people. There may be some of them close to you who get in the way."

"My parents," Xander says, knowing who I meant.

"Yeah."

"I want them safe," Xander says. "They have followed Raphe all their lives, but they've done it with fear in their eyes. I don't think they are loyal to him. Please don't kill them."

"You know I would never do that. But is there any way you could get a message to them? Do you think they would fight on your side?"

"I can do it," Cohen says. "Raphe killed my mother. I won't let him take your parents away from you."

"Thank you," Xander says.

"What about you two being their new leaders once this is all over?" I ask them.

"That was one hell of a shock, wasn't it," Xander says. "I don't think I'm leader material."

"And I am?" I ask him.

"One hundred percent," Cohen says, a fierceness in his eyes I haven't seen in a while.

I can't say it hasn't been slightly awkward to have Cohen so close to me recently. We discussed how we were before he betrayed me. He also told me how he feels about me, and we've both done what we can to put it behind us, especially since Logan is back. Logan has always been it for me, and I told Cohen that, but I can't help but feel bad that I can't share his feelings. It was the same when Xander told me he loved me. I know there is someone else out there for Cohen, someone better than me, I just hope he can get past how he feels for me and find her. He's become a very close friend, a friend I need in my life. I don't want how he feels for me to get in the way of that. Besides, this war with his father is far more important than our emotions right now.

"But seriously, will you guys do it?" I ask.

"I don't know. It's a lot," Xander says.

"We could make them better than they are. If we lead the griffins we could teach them about friendship, and loyalty, and love, get rid of the hatred in their hearts."

"Would they accept us?" Xander asks. "We've been chumming it with the enemy for a long time. No offense."

"None taken," I tell him. "But I think they have already accepted you. They chose you are their future leaders."

"Then I guess we, or at least, I will give it the best shot I can," Xander says.

"Right there with you," Cohen says, "If you'll have me."

"You have more right to it than I do," Xander says.

I didn't know the two of them were friendly, beyond being with us, but it warms my heart to see them joining forces like this. I think they will be great leaders, and that's not just because of their relationships to me, though it may have something to do with it.

I truly believe if Cohen had succeeded in killing me, it would have killed him. His father would have never let him go. He would have killed him or forced him to follow him. But I was able to get him out of his situation, able to turn him into the guy I know he can be. A friend. Someone who will fight for what he believes in. After he got away from his father, he wanted to help others get free of his father, and that's what we've been working for. Freeing my people from the constant threat of death, but also liberating his people from a tyrannical leader.

And Xander. The fact that he chose his friend over what he's know his entire life shows character and leadership. It showed he could choose a new path, one that was different but not necessarily wrong.

I think they will both be great leaders. Plus, when your two best friends are the leaders of your enemies, it sure takes away from the whole enemy factor. And the constant threat of being attacked.

"Ok boys, let's go plan to kill Raphe."

When we're inside, Gray and Logan have already begun talking to the griffins about how many of them will be at Raphe's house. How many we can count on being on our side. How many will just have to leave or get out of the way. How many we will have to fight through to get to Raphe. And so on.

Cohen finds a piece of paper and draws the layout of his father's home. He, Xander, and the griffins discuss how many of them will be positioned outside, guarding the house. We talk about possibly switching the guards to those who would be sympathetic to our cause, and thus get us into the house easier.

The planning goes on into the morning. When the sun rises we've all already consumed about a pot of coffee each. I'm exhausted, but wired from the caffeine. My leg bounces up and down as I stand around the island looking over papers and discussing plans.

We've decided it best to take turns sleeping on the off chance that this could still be a trap and we would need fresh fighters.

"You should get some sleep," Logan says from behind me as he wraps his arms around my waist and pulls me back into him.

I sigh heavily when his hot breath caresses my skin before his lips kiss my neck.

"I can't. There's still too much to do. Too much to work out," I say to him.

He rests his chin on my shoulder and says, "We can do this without you. And we can update you when you wake up."

"Logan," I start but am cut off.

"Casslyn," Logan says, turning me so I'm facing him. "Your father would have slept. He would have known we needed him at his best."

"Fine," I tell him, conceding fairly quickly because as stubborn as we both are we could be at this for hours. "But you will wake me up if you need me."

"Of course," Logan says, leaning in to kiss me before he prods me in the direction of his bedroom.

I immediately lay down on Logan's bed to sleep because trying to stay awake would be pointless. Thoughts of the upcoming days ram my brain so I'm afraid I won't actually be able to fall asleep, but as I lie there, my brain heavy, exhaustion weighs more and sleep takes me, allowing me to shut my brain off and relax, if only for a few hours.

***

It's the day of the attack. The plan is ready. The phoenixes are set. The griffins have been let in on the plan and are geared up for their part in the battle. There is only one thing to do before we begin the fight and end the war.

I have to say goodbye to my parents.

There is no guarantee I'm coming out of this alive. And a goodbye is not something they got when Nash died. It's not something they would have gotten if I'd have died when Cohen stabbed me.

It is something they are going to get now. I understand why someone wouldn't want to warn their parents they could die that night. I understand that the parents would try to talk them out of it, or lock them up to keep them safe. And while my parents don't exactly know what's going on and they don't completely understand this war. And they know nothing about Raphe and his crusade against us. But they do know that I am now the leader of the phoenixes. They know about casualties, they know about sacrifices of war, they know they could lose me.

They need to know what is happening. Even if the outcome might kill them. Even if the outcome is as good as it can be and I come back to them unscathed.

They need a goodbye.

I need a goodbye.

Logan offered to come with me.

Gray offered to come with me.

All of my friends offered to come with me.

I think they wanted to lend their support.

I also think they wanted their own goodbyes with my parents.

But in the end, I needed to do this on my own.

I'm waiting for my parents to wake up to talk to them. I've got breakfast going in hopes they will smell the food cooking, the coffee brewing and wake up. It's not exactly the conversation you want to have when you first wake up in the morning. But, I want to spend some time with them before I have to leave and set up the attack.

I'm plating the food when they walk down the stairs.

"Who died this time?" my dad asks when he hits the last step.

"No one." I tell him. "Yet."

"Casslyn," my mom says, cautiously. "What's going

on?"

"Eat. Then we'll talk."

"You're frightening me," my mom says.

"Nothing you have told us lately has been good," my dad says.

"And that's not about to change," I tell them. "Please, sit down."

We eat in near silence. I wish it wouldn't be so, but now that my parents know I'm about to tell them something they don't want to hear, they are quietly waiting it out on baited breath. They finish their meals before I'm halfway through mine. I really wanted to enjoy my food, especially the bacon, if it's going to be my last. I really don't want to be morbid, but I also want to be realistic.

I continue to eat, with my parents watching me, even though I know they are dying to know what is happening, or about to happen. I'm not trying to torture them, but I'm not about to just rip off the Band-Aid. They are patient enough with me to allow it.

But then their patience runs out.

"Please tell us what's going on," my mom says.

What prelude do I give them for what is happening tonight? There is none. So I do what I didn't want to do. I rip of the Band-Aid. "We're attacking the griffins tonight," I tell them.

Both my mom and my dad gasp and reel back in their chairs.

They stare at me, their mouths closed, but their eyes

wide. They don't say a word. They don't utter a sound. Their faces contort from shock to fear. I knew this would hurt them, but I knew we all needed it to be done.

"Is there any other way?" my mom asks me.

"No," I tell her. Because even if there was, this is what we have to do. If we don't attack Raphe and the griffins tonight, we could lose the upper hand and Raphe could kill more of my friends and family. Plus, he could decide to use my parents against me. He could kill them or kidnap them to lure me into a trap. No. We must attack the griffins tonight. We must take down Raphe and end this war with the griffins. One day they will understand. I'm doing this for them, and for my people.

"Will you be safe?" my dad asks.

"No," I answer. I'm not going to give them false hope.

"So there's a chance you won't come back to us."

"There is. We have to do this. We need to end this. And this is our chance. I wanted the chance to say goodbye to you. It's not something you or I got with Nash. It's not something I got with my father. I needed to say goodbye to you in case I didn't get the chance."

Tears well in the corners of my mom's eyes, spill over, and fall down her cheeks. Both my parents get up from the chairs and move to me, wrapping me in their arms. My dad's ragged breath echoes in his chest. He's not much of a crier, but facing the potential death of your last child would make anyone cry.

I have become a crier in the last two years and am not

surprised to find my cheeks suddenly wet.

"How do we deal with this, Cass? How do we just let you go?" my mom asks me.

"You have to. I'm doing this for you. We'll be saving a lot of people."

"Logan will keep you safe. Won't he," my dad says, though not as a question.

"He'll give his life doing it," I tell him.

They continue to hold me, not letting go, just talking around my head and theirs.

I pull out of their grasp because I need them to understand why I'm doing this. Why I'm hurting them now. "I know you're going to be worried about me all night. I know there's nothing I can do about that. But would you have wanted me to keep it a secret and possibly never come back to you? Never get a chance to tell you how much I love you. How much the both of you have meant to me my entire life. How much you mean to me now? You are the best parents a girl could ever ask for. You loved Nash and I more than we could have hoped. I love you both more than you could know. I'm trying to keep you safe."

"We know, sweetheart," my mom says, taking hold of my hands in hers. "We're just scared. We want you to be safe. Isn't it our job as parents?" asks my mom.

"You can't keep me safe from this," I say.

"We love you, kid. You and your brother are the best things to ever happen to us. I promise you. We love you so much."

"When do you leave?" my dad asks.

"We've got a couple hours."

"Let's make them count," he says.

My parents and I spend the next couple of hours talking. Just talking. Not about anything special. No one brings up the future. But we do spend a lot of time on the past. We talk about things Nash and I did as kids. We reminisce about memories we love and some we wish we could forget. About every three sentences one of us reminds one of the others how much we love and cherish the others.

We don't do anything important. My dad makes me a cup of hot chocolate with extra cocoa powder and marshmallows.

We talk about movies and books we love. We play board games. We laugh and cry and smile and enjoy each other's company.

When it's time for me to go my parents don't want to let me go. I don't want to let them go. My dad holds me tight, nearly squeezing the breath from my lungs. "You will always be my little girl, you know that right."

I nod, unable to speak, tears spilling from my eyes.

"I love you, baby girl. Be safe," my dad says to me before pulling away. Just before he lets me go, before he passes me off to my mom, he kisses me on the forehead, his lips wet from his tears.

"I love you, dad."

I move to my mom. She holds me in her arms, one hand on my head. She weeps and tells me how much she loves me.

I think back to the last seventeen years of my life. I think back to how I was always closer to my dad, how Nash was always my mom's favorite. I think about how much I wish we were closer then, but how close we've gotten in the last year. I skip right past the year after Nash died, when both my parents had somewhat abandoned me. That's not something I need to rehash while I'm saying goodbye to them.

I hope this isn't a real goodbye. I pray I will return to them after tonight. But I can't make any guarantees. I'm not about to promise them I will come back. I don't make false promises, promises I can't keep.

"I love you, Cass. Come back to me," my mom says, with one last squeeze, one last pass of her hand down my hair, one last kiss to my cheek.

"I love you, mom."

Before either of them can pull me back, before I can chicken out, I open the door and slam it closed behind me.

I hear both of my parents weeping as I run all the way to Logan's house.

Tears sting my eyes and run into my hair as I run away from my home and my parents. My chest aches from the pain of letting them go. My legs beg me to turn around and go back to them. But I can't. I need to move forward.

I run all the way to Logan's and keep running until I run through the door, until Logan catches me in his arms before I collapse on the floor.

"It's time to get ready," he says, without giving me a moment to catch my breath.

It's for the best. If he gave me a moment, I would end up curled in a ball on his bed crying until my tears ducts are dry. I need to get down to business. I have two races to liberate. There is no time to dwell on things you can't control.

The house is bustling. Everyone is in action. Derek and Sydney aren't here but they are prepared for the night. As well as the griffins they have brought to our cause. Cohen and Xander are here running through the finer details of the plan as it coincides with the layout of Raphe's house. Logan and I run through more tactical plans with Gray, Aspen, Lydia, and the rest of the phoenixes. I have asked two of the phoenixes, any two, if they would be willing to stay behind and guard my parents. Gray and Thomas had that responsibility last time we tried any sort of plan. Tonight, Lydia and Nathan have agreed to it. I would love to have them with us tonight, but I also could not ask for two better people to watch over my parents.

It is strange to think about how much Lydia and I hated each other when we first met to how close we are now.

When darkness has crept in and we've gone over every plan and every possibility, when it is time to make our move, when we can no longer stand to stay in the house without attacking the griffins, we move out.

The bulk of us travel in the SUVs, each group having a different part of the plan. The rest of the groups travel on foot. Running for them would be just as fast as travelling in a vehicle, plus they have their own set of steps to the plan to take care of. And should the cops, fire department, or any other groups of people become privy to tonight's activity, some of us will be able to make it out and away from the action without notice.

In any other situation like this my knees would be bouncing up and down, my stomach would be twisting into a dozen knots. I'd get tunnel vision, a pulsing at the back of my skull. My heart would be racing. But not tonight. Not right now. I sit in my seat with clear vision, a steady beating in my chest and crisp focus on taking down my enemy.

We park blocks away from Raphe's house and blocks away from each other, but encircle his house. A few phoenixes will stay with each vehicle in case any of the enemy griffins decide to make an escape from the party.

I get out of our car holding my breath. I want to feel the air on my skin, feel my heart pumping in my chest. I want to hear every sound around me, the crunch of the snow under my feet, the wind as it passes through the ice covered trees, my people moving into position.

We move towards Raphe's house. It's past midnight so most houses on every block are dark, their occupants asleep for the night, no one privy to the fact that a secret mythical race is having a meeting, no one privy to the fact that another secret mythical race is about to attack and kill them.

Raphe's house comes into view. We get into position.

I take a deep breath and let it out.

Logan squeezes my hand and let's go. We agreed not to let our love for each other get in the way of our jobs tonight. We agreed not to say I love you. We agreed not to kiss or otherwise be sentimental. We can do all that when this is over.

We said our own goodbyes this morning in my bedroom before anyone else in the house was up.

I squeeze back and move forward.

There are griffins guarding all the entrances into Raphe's house. But if Derek and Sydney got to the right people, we will have allies guarding the door, meaning we will be able to get into the house no problem.

Logan, Gray, Xander, Cohen, Anna, Aspen, and I wait in the cover of another house on the block, waiting for the signal that the rest of the groups are in position, waiting for the signal to attack. I'm ready for this. I've never been so ready for anything. I'm going to end this. We, me and my people, are going to end this.

Whether we win or lose, tonight will be the end.

Whistles sound around the house.

It's a go. We're ready.

If the attacks on the griffins I planned and followed through on taught me anything, it's that variety is best, and that everything I did was effective in some way, and to implement all methods of destruction at the same time. Inflict chaos, but controlled chaos.

I whistle back, telling everyone to move in.

We move in.

My group and I run up to the door and the two griffins guarding it. We ambush them, two on one. Logan and I point our knives at the griffins while Gray, Xander, Cohen and Aspen hold them down. Anna looks around to make sure we haven't alerted anyone else to our presence.

It's an intense few seconds before we realize our captive griffins are Derek and Sydney.

They are quickly released and we apologize. But we didn't know exactly who would be placed where and it's best not to take chances.

"They are all in the living room. There are forty of them. We got to ten. There are ten people in there who will not oppose you. The other thirty will. For sure," Derek says.

"We've got this," I tell him.

"Thank you," Sydney says to me, then to the rest of my group.

"Don't thank us yet," I say to her.

"Will you be fighting with us?" Gray asks.

"We will be right behind you," Sydney says.

"Let's go," Logan says.

With that we burst through the door and rush into the house, moving through rooms until we find Raphe and the forty griffins seated in the living room.

"What a lovely party," I tell Raphe when he whips around to us. "I seem to have misplaced my invitation."

In an instant chaos erupts. The griffins search for any weapons they can use. Raphe pulls a knife from his back and rushes for me. Windows break, wood splinters, doors are thrown off their hinges, chairs are flung.

The sound is deafening. Bodies collide, fists are thrown, fire erupts.

Raphe is after me and then he's not. One second I see

him charging for me, a knife in his hand, the next he's nowhere to be seen.

I look to Logan who is headed into another room. Like his father, Cohen is nowhere to be seen. For a second I think he's betraying me again. But no. He wouldn't. I know Cohen. I know what his father has put him through. I know that his sister tried to kill him. He would go through all that just to betray me. Falling in love with me is one thing, nearly dying is an entirely different thing.

I'm hit from behind and nearly lose my balance before I can catch myself.

I turn around to face my attacker. It's a girl I've only seen a few times before, though none of those times were pleasant. Xander's ex-girlfriend, Greer stands in front of me waving a knife in front of herself. How did they all get knives all of a sudden? I'm sure Raphe has at least three knives in every room of his house, under pillows, behind the TV, under couch cushions, hidden under floor boards, taped to the bottom of chairs. At least they aren't ice knives.

Greer lunges at me moving for my left side. I spin fully around and punch her in the face. She manages to swing the knife and slice open the top of my arm. It heals instantly and I'm back to attacking her. I've got a knife of my own and it's about time I used it.

But, before I can get to that, Xander comes in from the side and tackles Greer.

More bodies crowd into the living room. I move into a different room and try to garner the attention of fighting enemy griffins to follow me and give my people a little more room to fight.

I look around me to see furniture and various other parts of Raphe's house on fire. There is a Christmas tree in the corner of his living room ablaze in flames. If the house burns down with the griffins inside it, I hope the fire department will rule it an accidental fire from the Christmas tree. Those kinds of fires happen all the time. Though if they find bodies anywhere besides a bed, they might think it suspicious the occupants couldn't get out in time. We'll cross that bridge when we come to it. First we have to actually kill Raphe, and right now I don't even know where he's at.

I know groups of the phoenixes are busy sealing off the exits of the house besides the front door. I know other phoenixes are making sure no one escapes. I have to focus on what's going on in the house and make sure we win this battle. I know I need to focus on fighting, but as the leader of the phoenixes, it's hard not to try and spot every one of my people and make sure they are ok. It would be dangerous to do so, but the urge is so apparent I can't let it go.

I search the living room, my eyes roving over bodies and faces rapidly. I find Logan first. He's in a fight with another griffin about his size but he's holding his own. Then I find Xander and Anna taking on three griffins at the same time. But they don't look to be in any certain harm. I can't find Gray in my initial search. I have to find Gray. I can't lose him, too. When I leave the living room I run into him coming back into it. I can't help myself, I throw my arms around him in a quick hug then go back to finding the rest of my people safe. Or relatively. As safe as they can be in this situation.

After I spot my last person, Thomas, fighting a griffin in front of the blazing Christmas tree, I'm about to return my focus to my own fight, looking for my own griffin when I'm side swiped.

My attacker hits me from the side, their shoulder laying into my ribs. I try to suck in a breath but the impact causes all the air in my lungs to rush out as I'm breathing in. I lose my breath entirely and my vision blurs. My attacker and I fall to the ground, my shoulder slamming into the hard wood floor. The griffin on top of me pushes into me to get her footing to stand back up. I grab her wrist and let the flame under my skin burn hers. She screams but doesn't let it deter her from using her other hand to punch me in the face.

She's able to use my distraction to get off the floor. I roll over and follow her. I hold my knife in front of myself and aim it at her.

"Stop. It doesn't have to be this way," I tell her. "Stop fighting and I won't kill you."

"Never," she says and launches herself at me.

I lunge forward, meeting her in the air, my knife impaling her chest as she lands on me. I not only hear but feel as she inhales a deep shocked breath. The girl's blood runs from her chest and flows over my knife and around my hand. Her body weight pushes into me as she begins to die. My heart clenches in my chest as she stares at me, her head cock-ing to the side like she's confused, like she wonders how this could have happened to her.

Moments ago she was fierce and determined to fight me, like a tiger on the hunt. Now she looks like an animal with its foot caught in a snare the arrow of a hunter aimed and fired.

I feel bad. I can't help but hurt for her. I literally hold this girl's life in my hands, on the tip of my knife. This is my fault. Partly hers, mostly Raphes, but also mine.

I look into her eyes, silently apologizing for this war, for what I've done, and see something in them, some new determination. A second later I feel the bite of metal on my skin in the middle of my belly. I pull back and push her away from me simultaneously before she can inflict too much damage. Her body hits the floor with a dull thud, the light gone from her eyes. She's dead before her body hits the ground.

I was sorry. I felt pity for her. I underestimated her. I keep doing that. I keep thinking these people aren't as bad as they are.

The skin of my belly lights on fire, the broken flesh from the piercing of her knife knitting back together.

I turn around, looking for my next target. I'm going to kill any of the griffins here who oppose us. As I spin around a guy rushes me. I let him get close. I let him take a swing at me. Then I lay into him, my fist hitting his jaw, connecting with his ribs, his side. I even get a fist into his throat. He coughs and clutches his throat. I push him into the wall and light my hands on fire, pressing them into his chest. He bats at my hands trying to get me off of him. I use his focus against him and kick his legs out from under him. He falls to his knees. I grab my knife and plunge it into his chest. He reaches up and uses his hand to grab hold of my neck, squeezing tight.

I'm losing my breath, his grip tight despite the knife in his chest. I press it in deeper, twisting as I do. He coughs, blood splattering onto my shirt. He tries to clasp harder onto my neck but is losing his grasp. I'm winning this fight. He will be dead soon and I'll move onto the next fight.

His grip on my neck loosens and I'm about to pull the knife out of his chest when a sharp and intense pain enters me back. My breath leaves my body. Fire erupts around the knife in my back. I scream out in pain as the wielder twists the blade in my back.

The griffin in front of me is dead. He's slumped against the wall, his chest still, his eyes blank. I pull my knife out of his chest, lean forward then buck backward. The move catches the griffin at my back off guard. I slam my head back and catch them in the nose. They back away from me enough for me to whip around and catch their arms in my flaming hands. My attacker, the griffin, is a teenager. Just like me. I'm caught up for a moment in the craziness that we are teenagers caught up in a war that's been going on for centuries. But then the moment is gone and we are fighting for our lives.

The guy's knife juts out of my back but I make no move to remove it. I keep my hands around his arms and continue to burn him. He's strong, so strong as he wrestles around with me trying to get me to loosen my grip on him.

The knife in my back throws pain out in every direction. My arms begin to tingle the longer it remains there. I'm afraid I'm going to lose my hold on the griffin the longer we fight. I'm going to have to burn his arms off soon or find an alternative way to take him down. My knife is lost on the floor somewhere. I let it go in order to grab the griffin by both hands.

Just when I'm about to lose my grip on the griffin, when I'm about to let him go, despite his burning arms, the knife is ripped out of my back. I can't help but release the griffin the pain so intense I can't see for several seconds. I fall to my knees as my healing fire seals the wound in my back. Those seconds on my knees are going to be the death of me. I'm going to open my eyes to the knife plunged into my heart.

But when I open my eyes the griffin I was fighting with has his own knife imbedded in his chest and Gray stands before me holding his hand out to me.

"Thanks," I tell him through ragged breaths.

"Don't mention it," Gray says, pulling me to my feet.

"How are we doing?"

"Good."

"Where's Raphe?"

"Don't know. Lost him in the fray."

"We need to find him."

"Yeah," Gray says as he rushes forward to attack another griffin.

I follow another griffin into the kitchen and stop short

when I see Greer fighting Xander. I can't believe they are still fighting. They have got to be exhausted. I know I am.

Blood runs out of various wounds on both fighters. Each of them favors their weakest sides, their dominant sides taken out by the other. They dance around the island doing the classic dart and weave everyone did as kids with their friends or siblings. Only this time it's for their lives.

In one corner of the kitchen, Anna fights with a griffin who looks to be in his fifties. He's a big guy with tattoos and a wicked scar running the length of his face. The mammoth griffin swings his arm at Anna who bobs her head quick enough to avoid it but moves right in the line of his other swinging fist. She takes the hit hard, hard enough to collapse onto the floor.

Xander hears her go down and whips his head to her. It's the second of distraction Greer needs to thrust her knife into his chest. Xander drops to a knee, blood pouring out of his chest. I scream. Anna screams. Xander's mom screams as she and his dad burst through the kitchen door.

Greer sneers down at Xander, knowing she's won. Knowing she's killed him and that his new love is her next target.

Xander's chest rises heavily and it's all I can do not to rush to him. But then another griffin enters the kitchen and it's too crowded and I can't get to Xander. This griffin has an ice knife in his hand.

I need to destroy that knife.

But I can't lose my best friend. I can't lose the last remaining musketeer.

Instead of coming after me with the ice knife, the griffin charges Xander's parents with a steel blade.

Figuring they can handle themselves I move for Greer and Xander. Greer twists the blade in Xanders chest.

Xander yells at me to save his parents. Then he drops his head as though he's lost. As though he's given up.

My heart stops.

I don't move for a solid second.

Then I move for the griffin. If I've lost Xander I will fulfill his last wish. I will save his parents. Xander's parents are looking at their son. Their only son. The son they lost several months ago because he no longer believed in what they did. Tears stream down his mom's face. His dad's face has turned pale. The griffin charges them, two knives in hand. He swings down to stab Xander's mom when Anna and I take him out football style, one of us hitting his chest and the other his legs.

We each take a knife and stab him in the chest with his own blades. Not caring whether he dies quickly or not we rise off the griffin's body.

We look to Xander and Greer. Greer is drawing it out. Relishing in the sight of Xander's blood flowing out of his chest. Xander's head rests on his chest. Like he is already dead.

My heart breaks in my chest. I've lost my last best friend. I've truly lost this war. I couldn't keep any of my loved ones safe.

Xander reaches out, grabs Greer's arm, pulls her forward. She's caught off guard. We're all caught off guard. Greer loses her balance. Xander puts a hand on each side of Greer's face and twists with all his strength. Greer's neck snaps loudly, her body slumping in Xander's grasp. He stares at her for a long time then releases her. Greer's dead body falls to the floor.

Xander follows her.

Anna and Xander's parents rush to him.

I follow.

Anna weeps over Xander's body. His eyes are glassy and glazed over, unseeing. Anna's tears flow over Xander's chest. I know Xander and Anna have been seeing each other. I know they care for each other. And I know I was able to heal Cohen, but I'm not sure if she will be able to heal him. You have to desperately want to heal another person for the healing tears to work. You have to have a deeper connection than dating. Lydia wanted to heal Cohen when he was stabbed, I know she did, but her hatred for the griffins was stronger than her desire to heal him.

If Anna's tears don't work I'm jumping in and saving my best friend. I'm not losing him.

But Anna's tears work.

Xander gasps for breath and clutches at his chest trying to find the hole.

Then he and Anna are desperately kissing and grasping at each other telling the other I love you. It's sweet and emotional and beautiful. It mends my broken heart.

I fall to my knees in front of them, overwhelmed by tonight.

Xander's parents join the emotional love fest, clinging to their son and his girlfriend.

I can't linger on the floor. I have to get back to the fight. I have to find Raphe and end this. Cut the head off the snake and all that.

I leave Anna, Xander, and his parents in the kitchen and return to the living room. I stop short when I see Raphe sitting in a chair, his hands bound behind him. His body bound to the chair by ropes. Cohen stands in front of him. Logan next to Cohen and Gray on the other side of him.

The remaining griffins are either dead or cowering in a corner guarded by their own people, those loyal to our cause.

I look around the house, taking in what we've done here tonight. There are so many bodies on the floor. So much blood everywhere. There is no way we're going to be able to cover this up. Not unless we burn the house to the ground.

Fires blaze all around every room. Flames from the burning Christmas tree have spread to the wall and lick at the ceiling burning their way across it.

I can't believe no one has called the fire department yet. There is no way we haven't gotten caught yet. And yet, here we are, no police, no firefighters.

I turn back to the group of my friends, my people, surrounding my worst enemy.

It seems too easy. How could this man, someone who looks so weak right now, have inflicted so much pain and anguish to me in the past two years? How could I have feared this man for so long, and now here he sits, tied to a chair, waiting his execution. It seems too easy.

How can it be this easy?

I'm not this lucky.

This is exactly what we've been working for and it's finally here. After so many deaths. After so many months of pain. After so many lost nights of sleep. We're finally here. We're going to get exactly what we came here for.

And yet, it seems too easy.

"Casslyn," Logan says, grasping my attention from my wondering thoughts.

I move towards them, joining the circle around our enemy.

Logan hands me a knife.

I take it and stare at it. If this is the last time I hold a knife it will be too soon. I have done far too much killing with a blade just like this one. I've done enough killing to last me a lifetime. All of my lifetimes.

I asked Logan once how it felt to kill. He died before he could answer me. I had to learn the answer for myself. I didn't like the answer I found. Tonight will haunt me for a long time. Years. If the deaths I caused months ago are any indication, I'm not going to sleep. I'll get body shakes and hand quakes. My mind will be plagued by the images of the lives I took. Guilt will riddle my heart and fill my veins. It will be worth it to save the people I love, to liberate the griffins from their tyrannical ruler. But it still means so many had to die in order to achieve that. And while it had to be, I'm not okay with it. I may never be.

"So you caught me. Congratulations," Raphe says, a catch in his voice. He's bloody and looks tired.

I turn to Cohen who's covered head to toe in blood, whether it's his or someone else's I'm not sure. Maybe both.

"Are you okay?" I ask him.

"What a weak question my dear," Raphe says to me. "He's alive. He's okay. You're either alive or your dead. There's no room for emotions."

"And that's how you wound up here," Cohen says to his father.

I feel bad for Cohen. I got to have two dads in my life. Two dads who loved me. Two dads who cared for me. Cohen didn't even have one dad who loved him. Raphe treated Cohen like a soldier, and when he refused to be a soldier, Raphe treated him like a pawn, moving him around and using him without a care as to what happened to him.

If I'd ever have found out Cohen was going to betray me he would have been killed, either by me, Logan, my father, or any other phoenix who cared for me. And Raphe didn't care. As long as Cohen was doing what his father told him to.

My heart is heavy watching Cohen and his father stare each other down. Raphe is caught. He's not about to get out of this. He knows it. I know it. We all know it. And yet he can't help but play mind games with his only son. Only remaining child.

The last thing my father said to me was that he loved me. I can't see that happening between these two.

"How does it feel to be just like me, son?" Raphe asks Cohen.

"I'm nothing like you," Cohen says to his father.

I reach beside me for Cohen's hand and take hold of it.

"You want to know why I'm nothing like you? Because I've got friends. I've got people I care about and who love me back. People like me. They fear you. Love is a far stronger emotion than fear. And that is why I will never be like you. You beat people down until they will do anything you ask as long as you don't hurt them or the ones they love. I would never do that to someone. And that is why I will never be like you."

I don't feel comfortable delaying this. I don't like the useless banter going on. I want Raphe gone. I don't want some random griffin we might have missed to come in and try to save Raphe and kill one of my friends in the process.

"Do you have anything to say for yourself?" I ask him, calling back to a time when he had me chained to the ceiling in front of his people, ready to kill me.

Raphe sits in his chair and stares me down, not saying a word.

"So be it," I tell him.

We never discussed who would get the final killing blow. There is more than one person in this room with right to end this man. Most recently I come to mind. He killed my father only weeks ago. I'd say Cohen has a bit longer of a claim than the rest of us. Though I'm not sure anyone could come back from killing their father.

But I don't care if I am the one to kill him. As long as he dies.

I turn to Cohen and see he's looking back at me. I nod to him. Telling him, without telling him, it's time. He can kill his father. He can end this war.

He shakes his head. I'm not sure why. If it's because he doesn't want to. Or because he can't. Or because he doesn't think he has the right.

"One of you just do it," Raphe says. "Don't be pathetic."

Without warning Cohen and I both lunge forward, thrusting our knives into Raphes chest. His breath hitches in his throat, partly from shock, partly from pain. He stares us down as blood flows from the two holes in his chest. His mouth contorts into a sneer. Blood bubbles at the corners of his mouth and his nostrils.

Cohen and I stand back linking hands with Logan and Gray. Hands connect all around the circle. At some point Xander, his parents, and Anna join the group. The room is packed, all of us watching the death of a man who has tormented, harassed, tortured us, made our lives a living Hell.

My heart beats in time with Raphe's. Rapid at first, then more slowly until it stops.

And then mine starts up again.

As do the tears.

I cry for every one I've lost. I cry for everything I've lost. I cry for everything I've gained. I weep, the sobs wracking my body. I wish I could be stronger. I wish I could stare at my tormenter and feel nothing at his death. But it has nothing to do with him and everything to do with how my life has changed, how I have changed because of him, because of this war, because of who I am.

I'm not sure if I'm a better person. I'm not sure if I'm worse. But I know I'm not the same. I will never be the same person I was two years ago when I had a twin brother and two best friends. When we were the four musketeers and the only thing we worried about was what we were getting for our birthdays and whether or not we'd passed our biology test that week.

Now I've fought battles. I've been killed and brought back to life. The love of my life has been killed and brought back to life. My twin, my best friend, a new friend, my father, have all died and will never return to me. I was a human, I became a phoenix, I inherited a people and a leadership. I made friends and enemies. Some of those friends became enemies and enemies friends.

My friends and loved ones hold my hands as I weep. They hold my hands as my enemy's house burns around us.

Then they let go.

I let go.

I point my hands, palms out, in the direction of my dead enemy and let loose. Flames shoot in a stream from my palms into the body of who was once my nightmare. His body combusts the longer my flames barrage his body, until he's ashes on the ground. Then I move on. To other bodies.

To other parts of the house. The phoenixes do their parts. They can't shoot flames from their hands like I can, but they can ignite their hands and burn the bodies.

So far no firetrucks. We move through the house, doing what we can to remove any evidence we were ever here. Then we back ourselves out of the house while I shoot streams of flame into every room of the house, the walls, the ceilings, the carpet, everything. When we close the front door the entire house is engulfed and the sirens blaze.

We make a break for it. All of us breaking off into our groups and heading off in different directions.

My core group, Logan, Gray, Xander, Cohen, Anna, Aspen, and I hide behind a neighboring house and watch as our enemy's house burns to the ground. I hold Cohen's hand as we watch. He hated his father and his sister. He hated growing up in that house. But his mom lived in that house. He has good memories of her in that house and now they are gone.

The firefighters do what they can to put out the flames but there is no use. They cannot stop them. Those flames are a part of me and they will not stop until every remnant of my enemy is gone.

When Cohen's childhood home is nothing but cinders caved into the basement, and before the sun comes up, we all retreat to Logan's house.

Everyone takes turns showering. Some of the phoenixes celebrate. Some sit in silence. Some make out on the couches.

I need to see my parents.

They collapse the moment I walk through the door. I hug them both, never wanting to let go. They squeeze the breath from my lungs. We all cry. I hug Lydia and Nathan and thank them before they head over to Logan's.

I collapse in the shower, too tired to do anything. I'm not sure I've ever been this tired before. Never been this worn out before. Never this wary.

The war is over.

We defeated the griffins.

We killed Raphe.

Was it too easy?

Was his end worthy of everything he's done to us?

I can't answer that.

But the war is over.

The griffins are free.

The phoenixes are free.

I am free.

Fifteen

It's been three days since the attack. Three days since we killed Raphe and ended the war with him.

The phoenixes who came back only a couple weeks ago have left again. They did their part. And while they left, they no longer hold any animosity towards me. We are going to keep in touch and stay friendly. I am their leader now but I don't want to hold that over them. My father wouldn't have and I'm not about to.

There is an investigation going on into the fire and the deaths of so many people, but as of yet there has not been any backlash towards us. I'm not sure why anyone would suspect me or any of my friends, but there is always that paranoia.

Yesterday was Christmas. I'd actually forgotten about

Christmas in all the chaos. We were all happy to celebrate it, all of us free of our troubles, of our oppressors. We had a lot of fun. My parents and Xander's parents made food. We played games and talked and laughed. We exchanged gifts, though Logan and I waited until we got to my room to do so. I didn't have a lot of time to shop for him and I didn't really know what to get him. He's extremely hard to shop for. My gift to Logan was a cookbook with off the wall recipes I thought we could try cooking together. He got me a DVD set of Sunday morning cartoons. He saw that I'd broken his the night my father died. I laughed when I opened it. But I cried too. The day was enjoyable but I was glad when it was over. I love my friends and family more than I could imagine, but sometimes I need a break from them. I was thrust into this world without so much as a warning and I didn't realize it came with at least ten other people around you at all times. Sometimes I need to be alone, to be alone in my own space, alone with my own thoughts. So when everyone left after the party it was nice to have the house to myself and Logan. My parents decided to go out and have the night to themselves. They too love my friends but also need some time to themselves.

My parents are finally able to relax and not worry about the safety of their only remaining child. We spent almost the entire day after the battle together. My mom even took the day off of work. It was a bittersweet day. Now that my parents are back together, for good this time, my dad is going to move in with us. They had discussed moving back into our house in town, but they decided that we would stay here. My mom and I are finally all the way moved in and the old house holds all the memories of Nash and while most of them are good memories, neither of them have reentered his bedroom since he died.

The day after the attack, the day after I killed the person responsible for Nash's death, we finally entered his room. I'd always wanted to. I wanted something of his. But my parents refused to go in there themselves and forbade me from going in.

My heart beat so hard in my chest before I opened the door to his bedroom I thought it might burst from my chest. My hands clam up and my throat goes dry.

Then the door is opened and it's as though I'm thrown back in time to two years ago. Nash's room is exactly the same as it was. Aside from about an inch of dust coating every surface. I spent so much time in here with Nash, or with Nash, Tucker, and Xander. Memories of the four of us playing in here flash through my mind and bring a smile to my face. Those were the days. We were the best of friends. I wouldn't trade those memories for anything.

My fingers leave trails in the dust as I touch Nash's things. On his desk sits his math book, open to the page we had homework on the night he died. His bed is still unmade from the last time he slept in it. Dirty clothes are piled and lay strewn on the floor just in front of his hamper, like he took them off in a hurry and threw them in the direction of the hamper and didn't look to see if they'd made it in.

Nash hasn't been in my head for months now. Not since I died and healed myself. I've missed him. Not only in my head, but just overall. I've missed having my twin in my life. Being back here, it's like I have to say goodbye all over again. I said goodbye to him when I healed myself, when his half of our soul moved on. But standing in his room, about to pack up his stuff, it's like I'm saying goodbye again. But also like I'm finally getting closure. He's gone, and I miss him, I always will, but I can finally come to terms with the fact that he is gone and will never be returning. I will live the rest of my life, my long life, without him. That's daunting, but not as overwhelming as it once was.

My parents bring in boxes and cleaning supplies to pack up his stuff and clear the dust. They hand me a box and tell me I can have whatever I want. By the time we leave the box is overflowing. Keeping his stuff will never bring my brother back, but it will keep the memory of him alive in my heart and my memory.

Before we leave our old house, I make a venture into my old room. Like with Nash's room, I haven't been in there since the accident. While I was in the hospital one of my parents came in and packed up everything they thought I would need in the new house. I didn't argue with them and I have lived with everything they packed me, but there are a few things I want to grab before we leave.

Some of my favorite clothes make the list. Some books and stuffed animals are thrown into a box on top of the clothes. But the most important thing in my room is my birthday gift for Nash. The one I never got to give him. It sits, still wrapped, on my dresser. I unwrap the box and pull out the watch I planned on giving him. The battery is dead but I unfasten the strap and clasp it to my wrist. It's a little big, but it'll do. It looks good next to the bracelet Nash gave me for our birthday. I'd thought I'd lost the bracelet. For all the times I'd lit my hands on fire I thought I'd burned the cord off my wrist and lost the pendant. But then I found it the other day sitting under the cabinet under the sink in the bathroom. The cord was crusted in dried blood but once I washed it in the sink it was as good as new.

Going back to my old house, getting to enter Nash's room, clearing out the rest of my stuff from my room, was a good day. I got closure, I turned the page on a chapter in my life, I was finally able to feel good about leaving my old house and my old life.

Now I can truly move on with my life, to move forward.

Some of my friends have spent the last few days relaxing. Gray, Aspen, Anna, Thomas, Lydia and Nathan lounge around Logan's house watching TV, movies, playing video games, board games. They go out to eat, they do nothing. But they do it without fear. They are relaxed and happy.

I can't exactly say that about two of my friends.

Cohen and Xander have spent the last few days trying to pick up the pieces of what is left of the griffins. A lot of the griffins were loyal to Raphe. A lot of them. Some refuse to follow Xander and Cohen and have since moved out of town. Those loyal to Raphe but unwilling to move have been reluctant but pliable to what their new leaders have in store for them. Those who fought with us three nights ago are completely willing to embrace the leadership of Cohen and Xander. I wish them all the best. I really do. They are two of my very best friends in a new and scary role. They will do fine. They have each other and their people. Plus I will be here to guide them. As though I know what I'm doing. But we're going to learn together and be here to lean on each other when we need it. I have the complete backing of my people and Xander and Cohen have my complete faith. We will all be okay.

It hasn't all been fun and games in the few days since the battle.

I have had to have a serious talk with my people. All of my friends who have stayed in town with me are far older than me. They may look like teens and young adults, but I am the only true teen among us. They have all graduated high school and college and do not wish to repeat those times. I, on the other hand, would like to graduate from high school and then maybe from college. Maybe I'll take up a degree in leadership skills. We all know I could use those.

I wasn't sure if my friends would want to stick around my small town while I finished high school and move on from there. I've only got five months before I graduate, but what would they do while they wait? They could get jobs, but when you're mythological creatures who've fought a war with another race of mythological creature, flipping burgers or working an office job doesn't seem too appealing.

I did learn that some of them have actual degrees in actual interests. Anna got her doctorate in medicine and has been talking to my mom about maybe getting a job at the hospital. Lydia has a degree in cosmetology and wants to open her own salon. Gray would obviously partner with her. Thomas got his degree in education with an emphasis in History.

I had no clue. It's hard to focus on what your passion is when you're fighting for your life every day of your life. Nathan never did go to college. He didn't see the point when he was involved in a never ending war.

I made sure to sit down and talk with everyone who was involved in the attack that night. Just to get a feel for their emotional state. A lot of lives were taken that night. My friends are more practiced in the art of battle and taking lives, but I wanted to make sure they were all processing that night well. Most of them were handling themselves quite well. Lydia and Nathan were fine because they were with my parents. They are sad they missed Raphe's death, but glad it is all over. Anna was still shaken over Xander nearly dying but is happier than ever with him.

When I talked to Thomas he was completely okay with the battle, the lives he took, the outcome of the night. Thomas is someone who doesn't hide his true feelings. I can always count on him to tell me the world as he sees it. He had one bit of wisdom he left with me before we finished our conversation.

His exact words were, "You realize that Raphe was just

one crazy griffin leader in one small town in one country of the entire world?"

I have to admit, it felt like he was trying to rain on my parade, but he would have been raining on his own parade as well. He wasn't trying to be mean. He was trying to be real. And I appreciate that.

I did have an answer for him.

"I know," I told him. "But that's tomorrow's problem."

"Atta girl," he said to me. He patted my arm and went to his room to watch some fantasy movie.

When I talked to Gray it was less about the battle and more about each other. Gray has become one of my very best friends. We are similar people. We find comfort in each other. Plus, he's a little like my brother and a little like Tucker and a whole lot like Gray. I love spending time with him. He can read my moods, but of course so can literally everyone else so I think that has more to do with me and less to do with him. But depending on how we feel Gray and I can be crazy and goofy and hysterical, or we can be quiet and just enjoy each other's company in silence.

Instead of talking to him in the house, Gray and I went to the cemetery to visit Nash and Tucker. We filled them in on the end of the war. We told them how much we love them and how much we miss them.

On the way back to the house I asked Gray if he thought he'd ever find love again.

I could see him saying that Tucker was it for him, like I'd said with Logan, which was true. Gray and Tucker were only together for a short time before Tucker was taken from him, but in that short time they fell so deeply in love I could have seen Gray never wanting to fall in love again.

And this is what he told me, "I don't know. I think Tucker would want me to. I'm not sure I want to. I truly loved him. I might. I don't know. If I do, it won't be for a while."

"I hope you do," I told him. "You deserve to be happy."

"You too, fireball."

When we got back to the house Logan was waiting for me. I've been so worried about saying goodbye to the other phoenixes, getting my friends settled in town, making sure the griffins weren't giving Xander and Cohen too much trouble, making sure my parents were okay, and making sure I'm doing okay and not about to lose it, that I haven't gotten to check in with Logan.

He's the toughest guy I know so I knew he'd be okay. But I should have checked in on him. When Logan died and regenerated months later, it did something. He didn't come back exactly the same person he was. He's still the same tough guy I fell in love with. But he's got a softer edge to him. I'm not too worried about him, if anything I've fallen more in love with him.

I smile at him as I walk in the door and walk directly into his arms. Gray makes a gagging sound in the back of his throat at us. Logan punches him in the shoulder as he walks by but makes sure to kiss me extra showy to get to Gray. Gray laughs and joins some of our friends in the living room watching a girly TV show.

Logan and I walk out of the house and back to my house. My parents are at our old house, going through everything, bringing back what they want to keep and pitching the rest, getting the house ready to sell.

Xander has since moved out of my house. I miss him more than I thought I would. I loved having him live with me. But he and his parents made up. They begged his forgiveness. He forgave them and has since moved back into his old room. Xander's parents didn't even balk at him falling in love with a griffin. I suspect it has something to do with her saving his life. But that's just a guess.

So Logan and I have the house to ourselves. We haven't had anything to ourselves since my father came to town and the rest of the griffins followed him. The quiet is nice, if not weird.

Logan and I go straight to my room.

We fall back onto my bed our lips and bodies locked onto each other. Heat spreads between us but no flames ignite. I've since learned how to control that little trick.

"I've missed you," he says to me.

I'm tempted to tease him and say I've been here the whole time but I don't.

"You too," I tell him.

Between kisses Logan says, "I love you so much."

"I love you, too."

We make out for a while longer, relishing in the feel of each other, the taste of each other, the love between us.

Then Logan pulls away from me and stares at me. I

smile at him, knowing he's not trying to be creepy. Since we lost each other, or at least we thought we lost each other, we've spent a lot more time checking in, finding each other across a room just to make sure the other is still there, touching each other to make sure the other is real and alive and here. This is one of those times.

I let him stare because he needs to, and because it allows me to stare back at him.

After a while Logan says, "Is this real? Do I really get to keep you? Are you mine forever?"

"It's real," I tell him with a kiss to his perfect lips.

He leans over me and says, "Be gentle with me."

I push him onto his back, swing myself over until I'm straddling his lap. I lean in close so I can whisper into his ear and say, "Never."

Laci Maskell grew up in Northeast Nebraska. Her love of reading began when her sister handed her the Harry Potter books. Laci spent her childhood telling hour long stories on half hour TV shows. She began writing not long after. Laci attended Wayne State College where she earned a degree in English Writing and Literature as well as Editing and Publishing. Laci has worked as a secretary for a physical therapy department, a tax firm, and a computer repair company. She currently works as a Subway sandwich artist and for a daycare when she is not writing her books. In what little spare time she has, Laci enjoys spending time with her family, listening to music, watching movies, and reading.

Follow Me:

Twitter:
Laci Maskell

Facebook:
Laci Maskell

My Blog:
Laci Kay With Words To Say

Snapchat:
lacikay7

Made in the USA
Columbia, SC
28 November 2017